Dauntless Transgressions:

NEW JERSEY

Dauntless Transgressions: NEW JERSEY

Dex Marick

DauntLess Transgressions: New Jersey

Published by
Nuclear Fallout Family Publishing House

All characters and events depicted in this book are entirely fictional. Any similarity to actual events or persons, living or dead, is purely coincidental.

ISBN: 979-8-218-23951-0

Cover designed by: Vinnie Valenzvela

To Pumpkin,
None of this would be possible without you, my eternal and effervescent sparkle

1

Is it at all possible that there are other individuals who've found themselves toying with the thought of execution by firing squad every so often? Or does that deranged thought solely marinate inside of my dreary loaf? There's a chance that such a question might come off as a touch unsettling, yes, but there's a just reason for me to ponder it. See, while the thought of such a dramatic, excessive departure appears as a headliner in my cauldron on an infrequent basis, it's still certainly more than desired. Usually, as the thought strikes the match my sensical awareness melts away. And in this defenceless state, my mental facilities become enveloped by the *charm* of these maddening daydreams. However, despite the grisly nature of these visions, it would be utterly inane to claim that they aren't aggressively fascinating in their brutality.

It's been a handful of months since these visions decided that it'd be so riveting to storm my brain with a vengeance. And the full workprint of this trashy film reel remains unchanged after repeated viewings. Even down to the most insignificant features within the images, from the scuffs on my suit to the location of my demise, they're as true to consistency as taxes or a snuff film. The mental movie commences with me, alone, in a dingy room crafted by tan bricks. Each individual brick is cracked, chipped, and stained with plum-tinted splotches. As displayed by their weathered appearance, it's evident that the building this room resides in has been here for eons. These *blissfully* despairing sights are convincing enough for me to accept my fate without deliberating otherwise.

Hanging above me from the ceiling is a single lightbulb that flickers with the same unmanageable ecstasy as an overdosing drug addict. It's unlikely that its radiance will withstand time much longer, though neither will the loose cord struggling to remain joined to the ceiling. I stand in front of the back wall, as the room is devoid of seats. Before me is a hefty yet battered steel door that sports a filthy rectangular window. The coats of grime are dense enough to entirely obscure the outside of this crummy room. However, the decision to retain such a grotty surface works in its favour as it leaves me unaware as to when my captors will arrive. The prospect of waiting about is utterly tedious but what else is there to do? There's always the thought of counting the bricks, but I'd rather preserve the final remnants of my sanity before the impending slaughter.

Ridiculous as it may sound, I startle a bit and stand to attention when the door handle is abruptly and forcefully shoved down. The resulting echo of the creaking steel swarms my ears, its shrill wail lingering on a tad longer than ideal. As the door pushes open, this is where my thoughts decide to meld realism with personal desire. See, most circumstances that involve firing squads normally include soldiers as the marvellous performers of the grand deed. Sometimes, however, the executors are members of delirious militias or they're pseudo-revolutionaries. None of those options are what I would choose for my execution if the decision rested in my hands. They're all much too humdrum compared to what could be. And though my preference is not necessarily remarkable, they're certainly less conventional in this day and age.

Barrelling through the door are interchangeable figures of similar heights and builds. Each of these beings are clad in identical forest green outfits that consist of bulky, sweater-like tops and equally shapeless trousers. They also sport leather gloves and shiny laced up boots that are as white as pearls. Completing their unsightly garbs are archaic executioner hoods of the same green hue as their uniform. The hoods mask all but their bloodshot and bloodthirsty eyes, which stare me down as though *I'm* the maniac. Every item of clothing has been tarnished by the blood of those who met the same fate that I ultimately will. Such is far from satisfying as my blood is considerably less worthy of being a mere badge compared to those anonymous victims.

It's uncertain as to why I'd select these figures to perform my execution. They're merely the product of my visions conjuring an impeccable specimen for the episode. On top of that, these films reels were constructed by my brain with insignificant input from logic or purpose. I've never taken adequate time to carefully deconstruct these daydreams as they'll only engulf me in duvets of agony for hours. Besides, they're the least of my concerns in comparison to all the other mental woes that wield a reprehensible dominion over me.

My executioners, nine in all, stand at least four feet away from one another and carry submachine guns, namely the Heckler and Koch MP5. To be fair, they're not precisely the arms I'd expect to be dispatched by if such a scenario was to arise. Personally, I'm of the belief that the weapons would be RPKs, but only because it'd be immensely entertaining if Soviet arms were my downfall. That'd be bloody hysterical, if also wholly humiliating as the Soviets are a bunch of pitiful nits. But such would be my good fortune. At this point, however, the mental film reel has shifted more toward the sombre side of delight.

In spectacular unison, my executioners convert their standing positions to a general combat stance, their weapons hungrily pointed at me. None of them speak, nor do they offer the common decency of asking me if I'd wish to share any final words. To be fair, that's precisely how such a grim occasion should play out. Why the bloody hell should I be permitted any closing statements or an opportunity to plead my case? Considering my situation, I apparently ventured to the depths of misery and tangoed with a disastrous dilemma. The fault of my irresponsible behaviour rests solely on my forsaken soul. Besides, even if the suggestion of final words were offered by my captors they'd be declined without hesitation. Words are meaningless to swine who ask you to speak out of callousness. Therefore, these bastards are the least deserving to hear any vexed drivel spew from my mouth.

Few murky memories flash in my bonce, but they dissipate swiftly without having the chance to truly bid me farewell. It's distressing that I cannot decisively embrace these fleeting fragments of joy. Unfortunately, it's dreadfully strenuous to concentrate when there are nine submachine guns eyeing me down like malnourished beasts.

I haven't shifted from my position, yet there's a fuming determination to continue exchanging eye contact with these fiends. Some of the damned are forced to turn away and stare blankly at the wall before they're slain. Others are given the initial pleasure of facing their captors, but it's ultimately futile because they're blindfolded. Executioners probably believe it to be more harrowing if their victims are oblivious as to when their departure will come to pass. I disagree with that notion. Matching the harsh glares of these assailants, while somewhat courageous, is far more unnerving. Watching them intently. Fully recognizing the inevitable but not having the slightest inkling as to *when* they'll initiate their assault. Appreciating the fact that the impact of the first few bullets might torture me momentarily, but that I'll be numb to the barrage in a matter of milliseconds. The expiration of my life, of course, will be messier than the padlocked room of a demented painter. But it will be painless, which makes up for the carnage.

A flurry of bullets dart through the air and my ruined body, coated with thick sheets of crimson and only somewhat recognizable, collapses to the ground with sloppy might. The ordeal, as anticipated, is grisly and overblown in its presentation. The executioners are static as they observe their hideous masterpiece in its full glory. They finally walk out of the room in sluggish fashion, gently pulling the door shut behind them. And this batty mental movie ends with a still image of my mangled face, various components of my features marred or non-existent. That single frame of the movie has a vile tendency to burst through my thoughts at random, which startles me over and again. Despite my disdain for that bloody ambush, the sheer vibrancy of the image is, without question, the most fascinating aspect of this despicable film.

Aside from the final frame, the whole haunting visualisation only rears up every few weeks. However, for the past month, I've chosen to hold constant viewings when alone and in control of my facilities. Reliving those visions has become somewhat of an exercise for me as of late, a burdensome attempt to scrub the reels out of existence. It's rather daft, and I believe the reasoning behind the strategy was based off my constantly associating visions to actual movies. In a way, re-watching the vile images could potentially erode these imaginary video tapes. And unless I settle on talking to someone about this lunacy, which is doubtful, revisiting and analysing the anguish seems to be my sole option.

Blinking harshly, I snapped out of my reflections so to return to reality. The raging blizzard that had apprehended my head vanished and my living room slowly emerged from the blurred commotion. There's a stark contrast between the dim, shabby execution room and my residence. It's nothing too brill or breath-taking. Despite residing in an ordinary three-bedroom terraced house, what one would expect to be inviting and pleasant is rather dull. My homestead is fit to be the lowly sibling of a hotel, with decorations ranging from cheap paintings to dingy plastic plants. The sole highlight of my abode is the fully stocked bar that inhabits the kitchen. Though I treasure the imposing yet nearly vacant mahogany entertainment centre in front of me, it along with every other appliance in this house is utterly unremarkable. There's not even a scuff parading about on any of the basic beige walls. Yet, even with my criticisms, I haven't a desire to alter anything. As boring as it may be, the house does do a satisfactory job in providing me solitude.

My weary eyes meandered to the plastic clock that rested atop the entertainment centre. It was seven thirty-three and, with all hints of that drab imagery erased for now, I could allocate my attention to upcoming affairs. See, right upon awaking I made a phone call and shaped together some plans for a *mischievous* evening with a spellbinding moon-kissed mistress. She's due to arrive around eight sharp and, yes, that's rather specific, but promptness is among her many admirable traits. Fortunately, there's plenty of time to prepare dinner and rinse any remnants of despair from my caustic bonce.

Rising from the comfortable charcoal wool couch, the first course of action is to get dressed. I had showered over an hour ago but neglected to don anything more than a bath towel afterward as my subconscious pleaded with me to immediately dissect the firing squad film again. Raking the mental coals seemed like a poor choice, considering my approaching date, but it's somewhat vindicated because the frenzy has mostly subsided.

In my closet, a dozen suits of varying dark and cool colours craft the entirety of my daily wardrobe. No matter the trivial occasion or harsh weather, a suit will always be my sole selection. T-shirts, polos, jeans, not only do they do damn all for me but they're *too* casual and barren. Ambling about in those clothes generates sluggishness, as though they're informing me that the entire day will be spent being sedentary and rotting away. If only that could ever be the case. Mental rot, well, such is life. But physically? Absolutely not, as that's a sin. There's never a shortage of physical pleasure to bask in.

Anyhow, wearing a suit demonstrates an aura of refinement, a trait that's sorely lacking in my department, but one can still *try* to bestow courteousness toward absent behaviours. And these suits of mine are particularly sophisticated in their demeanour. Each of them are professionally tailored by a respected colleague of mine who can produce any style of clothing you so desire. The meticulousness of his ability allows every suit he's ever crafted to exude more flair than anything tossed together by some arrogant, overly exorbitant designer.

My preferred style has morphed throughout the decades and, at this point, the bulky power suits that those in the business community sport are the most affable. Even though they present an untidy presence, very similar to a garbage bag, they're what's in vogue now. So be it. Conformity can be necessary, as much as it may be utterly agonizing. Fashion is among the few areas of life where conformity truly is key in my ridiculous opinion.

Taking into consideration tonight's objective, a navy-blue dress shirt and light grey suit make for a sterling option. Placing the clothing on my tidy, queen-sized bed, I crouched down to sift through the footwear in my closest. All of them are dress shoes, black and nearly identical despite differing brands. Unlike suits, shoes are of meagre value to me. The main requirement is that they complement the outfit, and that they don't go to pieces in less than a month. Retrieving a laced pair of dress shoes, I returned to my bed and got dressed.

The rickety chest of drawers in front of my bed stores all my personal items. I'm incredibly cautious when it pertains to pulling the cabinets out too swiftly. Otherwise, they'll burst out and toss everything about like a vindictive earthquake. Tightening these loose cabinets have been on my fix-it list since I moved into this residence five years ago. It's a shame that the problematic issue has yet to be resolved, but life and madness have continuously impeded less significant matters.

Opening the top left cabinet with a degree of patience, I located my Stork Sultan watch next to my car keys and wallet. Relatively inexpensive Stork watches are my fancied brand. Sure, they sell for around five hundred, but they're a high-quality English brand that flies under the radar. This watch, which was a gift from my ex-wife, has a wooden dial, contains silver stick indices, and has a brown leather strap that bodes well with the overall air. On the back of the watch is an engraved quote that states "to my all-seeing sun," which stemmed from my ex-wife's penchant for classical literature. Unfortunately, it's not my favourite sight to ruminate on being that it's obsolete in my eyes. However, I don't have much of an urge to purchase a new watch or even a different back. So be it.

I exited my bedroom and briskly ventured to the nearby bathroom for additional enhancements, so to speak. There's a bottle of cologne that resides next to the sink. It's Ruggine, an Italian brand that's celebrated for this one fragrance which also happens to be the only product it sells: Ruggine 8. Lifting my chin up, I sprayed a dash of the sharp, clean, and woodsy scent that also possesses a distinct hit of citrus. Ruggine 8 also doesn't linger in the atmosphere too long, which works in its favour. I buttoned the top half of my shirt after setting the cologne back on the sink. The top button is left unfastened as ties aren't among my wardrobe. They tend to intrude quite a bit.

Up next on the preparation list is dinner. Now, one privilege my job bestows unto its chief personnel is the inclusion of a personal chef who would stay most of the day to prepare meals before returning home for the night. However, rejecting this privilege was an easy decision. Not only is it rather pointless for a chef to come by every day solely to cook tirelessly for hours on end, but it's also a bit too upper crust for my liking. Yes, sporting suits daily might discharge a frightening cloud of affluence, but that's where the ticket ceases. Lavish meals aren't a priority for me, unlike most of my co-workers who happily indulge in this benefit.

Before noon, I picked up dinner from a café a couple blocks from my residence. It's operated exclusively by a couple, both of whom are well into their seventies. I've gotten meals from them enough to be considered a regular, though the two weren't initially pleased with my tendency to request meals on the go. They'd expressed to me, quite often actually, that it would be much preferred if customers enjoyed their food at the café. That's fair and granted it's a quaint establishment. Sits around fifteen and possesses an atmosphere so quiet that you almost question whether the people around you are real or not. Somehow, thankfully, the couple grew fond enough of me to cease the grief they'd give me in regard to staying and eating. Granted, I did have to dine at the café for almost a year before securing the sanction to take meals home, but it was worth it.

Dinner resides in the refrigerator. It's cottage pie, a rather unremarkable dish that's far too filling and transforms my body into a piece of lead. Though the husband of the couple prepares the meals brilliantly, including this cottage pie, it's safe to admit that I can do without it ever rummaging about in my life. However, it's my date's favourite meal and if she relishes something then anything in this mad world will be accomplished to meet her wishes. Even with my reservation about the meal, I checked inside the fridge for no reason other than to confirm everything is arranged for later.

The pie rests on the bottom next to a bottle of orange juice. Eggs, a quart of milk, lime juice, and a peach reside above those items on the middle rack. There's some hot sauce as well, as my date thoroughly enjoys it on her pie, so it's necessary to have a bottle around whenever she's over. And that comprises my entire fridge. Isn't it lovely? Such a lack of food would alarm most, and several of my dates have pointed it out when they're here. Instead of placing the blame on grave truth, that being my abominable eating habits, their concerns are waved away by my explanation of being habitually away from home due to my job. That's also the reason why I haven't much drive to do up the house any. It's more of a crash pad than a home. My necessities live here more than I.

With dinner as prepared as it can be, considering it's just to be warmed up, I glanced down at my watch. Seven forty-six. My date's arrival was closing in, but thankfully almost everything was fulfilled. There was one final check to mark off my internal to-do list. This, without any shadow of a doubt, was crucial though it'd surely seem peculiar to others. Returning to my bedroom closet, I knelt and unearthed a brown leather briefcase near my shoes. To unlock it, the briefcase requires a four-digit numeric code. Scanning the code currently in place, it's nowhere close to the correct number. Just had to be certain that the possibility of the briefcase being unlocked was at zero.

This briefcase is the only element of my job that *always* goes everywhere with me. As such, it's kept tucked away in the depths of the closet if guests are due to be over. What dwells inside isn't explicitly shocking or upsetting, at least not to me, but the confidential items shouldn't be left out in the open. My date has been here countless times and, while there's no doubt that she's probably noticed it on accident, it remains unclear if she's ever poked around at night while I'm dead to the world. Or if she's tried unlocking it. Same applies to the others who've been here through the night. Though my trust in my date is sturdy, you never know who could try disfiguring that confidence. Fortunately, she's never made any mention of it, so that's certainly comforting. Whenever guests are about, there should never be a sliver of menace lurking in the gloom. Safety takes precedence over all else.

***

Never has "Rule, Britannia!" rung as blissfully in my ears as it does during my date's rendition of it. Every time she arrives, she'll gently knock the first several notes of the ageless song. Now, several other dates of mine have performed the knock as well, but there's a certain serenity that sails through the winds of June when she's knocking. However, while it's certainly her at the door, I have a stringent habit of opening any door in a deliberate, calm manner. There isn't a peephole, and you never know when an uninvited guest might rear their despicable heads up from the netherworld. In the past, such events occurred almost regularly while on assignment, so you learn to better train yourself, abate any unnecessary haste, and augment awareness.

Thankfully, as expected, my date is the sole person standing at the door. Her name is June, twenty-six, and, upon first glance, she's not someone you'd imagine knocking "Rule, Britannia!" in the slightest. To be fair, if one was to judge everything off the basis of exteriors then the two of us appear as incompatible as knives in an ice cream shop. June has tremendous sapphire eyes, mesmerizing enough that they could undoubtedly resurrect a fresh corpse if she so dared. Wavy and clearly unnatural electric blue hair falls messily to the end of her neck, the top teased with shedloads of holding spray. She's part of the UK punk sub-culture, a trend that I'm scarcely familiar with. All my knowledge of it derives from her, and June's certainly taught me quite a good bit about it. This includes the music, as she's played me various cassettes of groups whose songs are far too aggressive and disordered for me to admit I relish.

The outfit she picked out for tonight personified the general appearance of a female "punk," at least from what she's shown and told me. Almost everything June wore was black. A leather jacket adorned with actual spikes atop her shoulders that could honestly be utilized as a weapon if she dared pleased. It's immensely worn out, to the point several patches of leather are, or already have, chipped off. There's a massive burgundy button on the jacket, directly over her heart, with the words *The Queen is a Cunt* printed oh so clearly on it. A point of contention between us, but not one that paints June in a poor light. The top of her right sleeve has torn from the seams, but it doesn't seem as though she's given much thought to it.

Decorating June's bottom half are a pair of jean shorts that squeezed her groin to the point I couldn't help but ponder how she's able to move about in them. Or how she's able to slip into them in the first place, being that her waist curved into her hips with a certain fleetness. Transparent fishnets with mosaic star patterns and a pair of worn-out sneakers complete her getup, though with her jacket fully zipped up what resides underneath is currently up in the air.

"Will I be staying for breakfast this time?" Her Yorkshire accent, a pleasing blend of dainty and poised, rallied around my ears. "Or do I have to leave by sunrise?"

"You'll be waking up to fried eggs in the morning. Just a tad runny," I said.

"Exactly how I love them."

June embraced me, her arms latching onto my neck so that she could draw me closer to her modest five-five frame. Relief vigorously travelled around me as the spikes on June's jacket just barely wasted the opportunity to puncture my face. Mercifully each of those slender, inch-and-a-half weapons pointed straight up and could not inflict any damage unless she unnaturally angled herself. As June rested her head on my chest, she displayed a firmness on par with a child clutching a stuffed toy tiger. It was as though she was conveying my belonging to her.

"You treat me too well, Mark," she said.

I matched her hearty grip and kissed the top of her head, inhaling a trillion trails of pleasurable cinnamon fragrance. June stepped inside after we separated and, as she walked before me, I took note of the words *Do What Thou Wilt* messily scribbled on the back of her jacket in white paint. Its meaning most likely lodges in the punk underground or something. I'd ask her about it, but no doubt her explanation would still be utterly confusing.

June began to unzip her jacket, and I carefully helped her slip out of it. Her top, formerly concealed, now seduced my fixed gaze. A lace bustier, complete with a front zipper, so tight it stuck to her torso and enriched her fit bust. Her curvaceous body was mightily dangerous as it was racy. And though I'd the great fortune of viewing June in her natural state before, there is a mystifying quality that she wields like a crescent mistress in the stars. Between her garb and her tempting scent, it brewed a euphoric potion of lust. Purely potent. As June took a seat on the couch, I went to the bedroom and placed her jacket neatly on the bed.

"You really ought to tart up this place," June called out from the living area.

Leaving the bedroom, I said, "there's no need. You know I'm rarely here" before sitting next to June and placing an arm up as she cozied up to me.

"That's no reason to leave your house looking like one of those boring models." She pointed at the walls near the entertainment centre. "You could add some posters here. Maybe a few statues in the cubbies by the tv. You have this quiet, egghead quality to you. How about a globe?"

"Egghead?" I chuckled softly. "That's a first."

"It's not a bad thing. It's the way you come off."

"Reminiscent of a teacher, perhaps?"

"Exactly. You could command a classroom just by stepping through the door."

"While I disagree, that's very kind. If only I actually possessed enough knowledge of subjects to teach them."

"You could teach business and management since you're in that field."

Business and management…not particularly a conversation route that we should continue down. Primarily because I'm *not* in that field, despite what June believes. See, my true occupation has damn all in common with business and management. And the difference between the two isn't merely drastic. It's also harrowing, which is why there's adequate reason for my unapologetic deception.

Rotating the door back to our first date, June's intrigue with my profession began after an undesirable dinner of rather pedestrian bangers and mash. While I was washing the dishes, she asked me about my career. Fair enough, especially because it enabled us to discover more about one another as a sound date provides. However, she didn't stop at one question. June happened to be persistent in her line of questioning. Whether it pertained to my job title, my various co-workers, or what exactly my daily routine consisted of, every meaningless detail had an iota of significance to her.

At the time, I figured the bombardment of questions stemmed from rampant nerves prickling about upon chatting with a stranger. Understandable. You'd aim to garner as much information as you can, especially if you're eager to continue seeing the person. Build trust while lessening anxiety. So, to appease June, I told her all that she wished to *learn*. My answers, however, had to be satisfactory without being utterly immersive. Contain enough information so that she trusted my word enough to *never* question whether I was being deceitful or not. Thankfully, she believed all the incessant drivel, kindly wrapped in layers of slop, that I gifted her. But…the concept of *sincerity* backfired dramatically as June revels in bringing up my fictional occupation because she's interested in it. And though I'm pleased that she finds something stimulating about me, why must it be the sole lie?

Regardless, all that truly matter is that she continues to buy and follow my unending falsehoods. Selecting business as the occupational mask works fittingly because of how often I'm away from Vrycastle. And the whole "routine business trip" excuse does a decent job at dwindling some questions, much to my surprise. But I can only labour away with these fictious rambles about my position for so long before the dam bursts.

Revealing the truth to June is not an option. Seven years ago, upon taking my oath of allegiance, I swore to my superior that any conversations regarding my assignments would be executed with a restricted group of individuals. Namely my colleagues…and contacts though they're all but useless. Those in my personal life would have to be forever duped into believing tall tales about my supposed business dealings. In a way, the me that is accessible to them is a bloody fraud. Those like June know slivers of me, but anything that pertains to the most indispensable aspects of my life is a sham. That shreds my heart to the point it's been splatted across the room in piles of tissue and blood for years without the possibility of repair.

From the start, my superior warned me that this double life might impair my mental state. I brazenly brushed off those warnings, deeming them to hold true only to the weak-minded unable to abide by their oath. Then, the turbulent conditions of my job enveloped me. They feasted on me from the inside, in a manner that stirred up all the tormenting and unstable fantasies that continue to rummage in the depths of my gnarled enclosure.

Some days I can't even bear to observe myself in a mirror because my face is warped and gluey from the extent of my anguish. A sight once recognizable now too severe to have confidence in. Some days I cannot even accurately identify myself. It's to the point where I haven't a clue if these images of my corrupted face are faults of my tainted imagination or if that's truly what appears in a mirror. Like those extreme desires of facing an execution squad, these visions vacation in my head like frequent travellers. However, a certain peace bathes my accelerated heart whenever I'm greeted by those silent green figures. Such never occurs when the twisted human in the mirror glares at me, as though it's filled with wrath over my resistance to acknowledge we're one and the same.

Resting a hand on June's cheek, I watched as her eyes journeyed up to meet mine. Foggy lilac eyeshadow and unmistakably impressive fake eyelashes aid in maximizing her enthralling symmetry. June put her hand on mine, the placement of her fingers allowing me to notice a common characteristic she's exhibited since we've met. Black nail polish that appeared to be applied in a hurry, with freshly painted streaks settled on the tips of nearly every finger.

"If we're going to talk about teaching, I'm in no mood to talk about my ventures. Instead, I think it's about time I give you another lesson," I said, accentuating the rigidity of my voice to draw her toward a more riveting subject.

Walking her hand to my jaw, a finger purposefully brushing against my chin, June's body language spoke as teasingly as her words. "Well, whatcha got, teach?"

While I could've responded to her mischievous question with either a suggestive remark or a mere command, actions tend to be far more appropriate in times like these. Guiding her fingers to my lips and brushing them across, I kissed them tenderly before rising from my seat. Without hesitation, June's athletic body became one with the air as she practically levitated like an intoxicated tarot card reader upon following my lead.

2

Usually, I'd assume, it's a tad worrisome if one finds a stocked bar lounging in someone's residence. A trumpet of alarms might set off, along with warning signs that display an emergence of out-of-control flashes as the whole lot gets rowdy. Surely most people who have bottles and bottles of liquor presented to their guests like precious art are alcoholics. Perhaps there are also alcohol collectors who proudly showcase their collection of liquor in the same manner as foolish college-aged nits. But who's to say they aren't alcoholics as well? In my case, I'm not one though with all the malignant spirits scrabbling at me from the inside such would be an easy out. It's haunting to admit such a truth as distressing as that one. But, no, while all the liquor that stands stately on the shelves in my kitchen might give off a wary air, they were all gifts from generous associates over the course of a few years. They're symbolic, in a way, as they celebrate the successful completion of an assignment. My colleagues all chip in and bestow a bottle unto me, and I reciprocate the gesture when one of them is also successful. It's a hallmark of our comradery.

For all of June's claims that my house is barely more than a model home, or that the decorations are lacking, I'd have to respectfully disagree. Although it consists of more rooms and space than necessary for a single person, there's insufficient use for posters or ornaments that have the potential to spruce up the place. They do as much for me as having collections such as records or tapes. Inessential items for your eyes to waste away on.

Hordes of whiskey and scotch, totalling about thirty, now that's worthy of attention. Bottles produced in distinct shapes, all from diverse countries. Truly eye-catching the second it enters your view. What makes this lot the model collection is that only the finest liquor is allowed to join the ranks. Rum will be greeted with disinterest, but still accepted. Vodka, however, is expressly barred from ever coming through my front door. It's vile poison raging with a standoffish taste. Inhale the odour of a decades old airplane, convert it to a liquid, and there you have vodka.

As my intake of liquor is uncommon, a sporadic pastime of mine, most of the collection has sat untouched and exists as an altar of worship. While I'd prefer that the alcohol remains in that capacity, a well-mannered host should extend the consideration of offering their guests a drink. But I go a step further. Among my modest book selection is a guide to crafting cocktails. This bulky, brown, matte-finished guide does not host very many recipes, though age might play a part in that. Being that it's nearly twenty years old, cocktails have become more sensational and garish compared to the more relaxed quality of times past. On top of that, this guide is more of a gag book than one an actual bartender would utilize. Even on the cover, it calls itself a "guide for making impure cocktails." So, whenever June or another date is over, I retrieve this book and give them a ridiculous lesson in drink mixing.

During these lessons, however, I obey a very specific rule. Only one person is allowed to touch my date's drink, and that is the woman herself. She pours it and adds any additional requirements to it. If she needs something, I'll tell her where she can locate it. Aside from that, all I do is observe and instruct her along the way. Even though we've been relishing these lessons for quite a while, and it's clear as all mercy June trusts me, the practice of a man never handling a woman's drink is one that's steadfastly adhered to in my residence.

Since dark liquor makes up the entirety of the bar, every lesson is a variation of the true recipe. Substitutions may be considered unholy to cocktail enthusiasts, but thankfully they're not here to snivel about at these potent creations. Tonight's concoction involves two ounces of whiskey, half an ounce of scotch, a pinch of lime juice, and a peach slice. Utterly divine, isn't it? Granted, the book instructed us to use one and a half ounces of whiskey but June thought that was a fool's choice.

On the bar's simple, fatigued grey counter sits a tall foghorn styled jigger. Distressed stainless steel betrays its longevity. June stood before it, vigilantly holding a robust, square glass bottle of Munster Caisleán, an Irish whiskey. This brand specializes in pure pot still whiskeys, which tend to be unsympathetically pungent compared to a single malt variety. However, Munster Caisleán is known to add a sweet hit of butterscotch syrup to their whiskey, providing a counterbalance between the two flavours. As I believe adding sweetness to a pot still whiskey is improper, considering it's the pure kick that makes the selection so beloved, using this liquor is not an issue to me. Besides, it's certainly perfect for the revolting concoction that will be produced soon.

Facing June on the opposite side of the bar, I closed the cocktail guide and placed it near the jigger. The sight of her attempting the pour the whiskey like a barman is endearing as it is amusing. Her legs are, for some reason, stretched out and create an upside down "V" while the bottle is raised high and just before her sapphires. I've questioned her decision to pour drinks in such a pose and her response was that it "adds to the intensity."

"Now, you have to make sure you pour it as gently as a languid breeze," I said.

June's concentrated stare shot up at me for a glimmer of a moment before darting back toward the bottle. No doubt my words displeased her dogged concentration.

"I should've made a bet with you," June said.

"Regarding?"

"What you just said about pouring it slowly." June's voice produced a cute and cartoony air when she uttered the last part of her sentence. Her focus did not budge from the whiskey, which closed in on the bottle's rim. "I could've won heaps of money because I knew you'd say that."

"Which is precisely why I would've rebuffed your bet."

At long last, the dark amber liquid grazed the bottle's rim. The first few drops dived with delicate grace into the jigger. An Olympic swimming coach would've shed some tears without question. However, this delicacy abruptly ended the moment June's hand made the slightest tremble. Whiskey sloshed into the jigger with enough velocity to rush it entirely, causing it to overflow. June yelped and nearly vaulted as the downpour commenced, but I caught both her hand and the bottle in time to prevent any more whiskey from sailing about my kitchen.

"I could've won some money myself, as I saw that coming," I said.

June crafted a frown, though naughty tinges in those glittering sapphires exhibited the presence of a ruse. Sure enough, a cunning smile formed as she said, "you arse."

Reciprocating June's smile, I snatched some kitchen paper that stood nearby and at the ready for a moment like this. Normally it's closer to the sink, but it was relocated to the bar counter earlier this morning. June is keen on practicing her mixing skills as though she's an expert barman, and such an outcome is rather uniform. Having the kitchen paper on standby prohibits the mess from worsening, as there's been times in the past where more formidable downpours of liquor accidentally raged atop this counter. Grabbing a few more sheets, I handed some to June.

"Wet these," I said.

June nodded. She moved to the sink and ran them under the water to dampen them a tad.

Being that this whiskey is expendable, not to mention sinful, seeing it squandered like this is of no major concern. Flicking through June's recent reactions compared to those from last year, the contrast is noticeably substantial. What once comprised of multiple apologies and utter humiliation has morphed into pure merriment. Rightfully so. I have never, and would never, scold her or flip my lid over such miniscule accidents. What good would that do either of us? Reacting like a child would not only push June away, and cause her to take on so no less, but it'd also demonstrate a feeble-minded attitude. If someone gets into a whole whirl over such utterly trivial matters as accidentally spilling a drink, they're imbeciles.

Once June returned to her spot at the bar, I rounded the area with a leisure stride, travelling to her side. While gliding an arm around her waist, I began to dab up the spilled whiskey. Prompt manoeuvres forbade the liquid from reaching the edge of the counter, but the impact of the splashes caused it to settle about on various sections. After I wiped down all the spots where the liquor landed, June began to coat the counter with the wet kitchen paper. I used one more sheet to give the counter a final touch up, eliminating any last traces of water streaks.

Now that the kitchen had reverted to its standard form, all my interest diverted back to the wondrous June. Firmly pressing myself closer to her, I gently brushed the ends of her electric blue hair to the right of her neck. In doing so, this brought about the perfect view of June's most distinctive feature. A scorpion tattoo, about four inches in size, that resides on the back left section of her neck and curves just slightly toward the innermost area of her clavicle. The scorpion, along with the crescent moon its pincers clutch, is quite detailed for line art. Each plate, or *tergite* as is the scientific wording, on the scorpion's back is defined, as are the ridges of its legs. Comprising almost entirely of black ink, the sole dash of colour comes from the two hits of red that drip from the scorpion's stinger.

"Remember when you first saw it?" June asked. "And you thought the blood drops were *actual* scrapes?"

"I'd never seen blood in the guise of a tattoo until I met you," I replied.

"You were so concerned. It was startling, to be honest, but cute."

June gently swirled around, with as much grace as a novice ballerina, to face me. Throughout her swirl, my hand remained latched to her waist. The gleam of her sapphires bustled as they surrounded intensifying pupils. June planted a hand over my heart, the other dozing on my shoulder. Though our faces had practically been united the entire evening, only now did I spot her facial piercings. A silver nose ring on her left nostril and two symmetrical, barely discernible silver bits below her bottom lip on the outermost part. She's had these piercings since our first meeting, but I tend to forget their existence time and time again. Making matters more intricate is that her porcelain skin causes the jewellery to blend in to her general appearance. Of course, the nymph-like splendour of her face was enough to overshadow all else.

"Why wouldn't I be?" I asked.

"We'd only just met. Usually when I meet with someone, they pay no attention— "

"June…don't."

Judging by her immediate reaction, widened gems and slightly ajar lips, it seemed as though June had identified her lapse. She drew the hand that slept on my heart up to my chin and muttered "I know. I'm sorry."

"No apologies necessary, my dear. Just disregard all else. You're here with me tonight. All other affairs mean damn all."

A cumulonimbus cloud billowing with apprehension entered from the air conditioning unit and drifted among the room. It must be acknowledged I have a tinge of displeasure toward myself for shutting June off in such a terse manner. From the moment I told her not to continue speaking, recognizable waves of rough severity overtook my voice. Warmth receded while detachment surfaced. However, while I resent the grim shift in tone to an extent, there's no remorse intertwined with it. For all that June loves to pester me about my occupation, I don't need to be reminded of what she does on the nights we're not together.

See, I don't walk out with June. We're not in a relationship, at least not in that "honey and roses" sense. At this moment, even with the merriment we've been sharing, she's currently at work and I'm merely a client of hers. It strains me to admit this truth…and I haven't an ounce of a clue as to why it's so bloody excruciating.

When Darla, my ex-wife, left fourteen years ago, whatever strewn about passion I held for romance was lost to the graveyard of forbidden urges. Considering I spent almost the entirety of my twenties, close to a full decade, with one person, it was horribly trying to be with someone else in a romantic sense. I'd never been serious with or about anyone but Darla. The women before her played about as just a game. And, when my marriage ceased to exist, everyone after Darla ended up as a game too.

As the restless nature of my profession hauls me away from my house with such persistency, uncovering a long-term relationship would be fruitless even it was desired. When the topic settles on love, only one has ever entered my life and it's bloody doubtful that it'll reappear. After all, most women could do better. Those who take pity on miserable souls with shedloads of baggage…they're more likely to take a gamble on me.

Regardless of those titbits, I've found it easier to avoid being alone with the help of certain attractions with a lurid nature. After all, seeking out companions in England is a rather effortless task if you know where to investigate. Magazines and newspapers, for example, have an assortment of ads to enable your vices. Unfortunately, my motives for jumping into this smutty pool are…disturbing and cruel. Would I have decided on engaging in these lustful means without tyrannical motives? Certainly. But these motives have accelerated most of my tribulations.

No one is aware of this plague, and I'll be damned if anyone ever unearths it. The raving fact is one that will never be expressly disclosed by me. One that I'll merrily heave into the grave with me someday. So…almost every day for the past six and a half years…several voices will emerge from the shadows and disrupt my thoughts. They'll mangle my loaf by chattering away in my ears, speaking in distinctive voices that've at the very least enabled me to recognize who's talking. Most are shy and have admitted they're deathly fearful of ever showing their faces, but one will occasionally peek into my surroundings just to stir drama. This sounds utterly insane, yes, and that's precisely why such information will stay buried within me forever. How else is one to ever disclose that madness to their loved ones, let alone live with it? I'm barely able to accomplish the latter.

There are two specific voices that follow me. They're the main conspirators in demanding I submit to my vices. The first one has a feminine tone, and I named her Edith the Tempest, after the actress Edith von Romoff. She was best known as the leading lady in one of Egil Priesy's movies, *Prison Boat Hawk*, until an on-set malfunction involving an axe and a rope led to her untimely demise in 1956. Von Romoff was only twenty-three and the news devastated me because mercy I was infatuated with her. Despite that, my rationale for naming this voice after a long-deceased and relatively obscure actress wasn't because of my adolescent ardour toward her. No, it's because Edith the Tempest has such a similar tone in her voice. Professional yet youthful. She was the initial voice I'd hear, and she typically arises when sexual pleasures have been absent for over two days. This narks her, so she'll demand I give into my obsessive itches for eroticism.

The other *voices* that goad me are newer, probably three years old. In a hysterical change, they didn't originate as mere voices. On one murky day, I awoke to two figures sitting on the edge of my bed. Upon my first glances, shrouded by haze, the two appeared to be standard humans. They were of shorter statures, just under five feet if a guess was required. But, as the residual post-sleep stupor dissipated, their features sharpened. Their craggy skin was bluish grey, a hue that drifted like dust when they'd reposition themselves. Shadowy rings encompassed impassive, bloodshot eyes that whirled around at a sluggish pace. Androgynous faces left their genders incalculable, though it's possible that these humanoids are genderless altogether. It's also immensely possible that the two are transparent, as there'd be the occasional instance where I'm able to briefly make out the objects they're blocking. However, they've never ventured closer than five feet to me, so that's all speculation.

I refer to these figures, who have crackled and warped voices, as "the Phantasms." They're the ones who've accelerated the gruelling stress that's caused the constant destruction in my bonce. Sly and hostile, they're able to drive my mental faculties to unbearable limits whenever they please, producing a deranged monstrosity that satiates in the unhinged madness. The Phantasms are clever bastards too, solely barging into my sanctuaries if they're certain I'm alone. I could be basking in a serene stroll out in a garden when an onslaught of gruesome, inhumane visualizations suddenly swells in my thoughts. Visions too toxic for even the netherworld to process, let alone me. Too graphic to play a role in an X-rated film. Yes, even more graphic than the firing squad dilemma. It's uncommon for them to terrorize me to such an extent, but it's still occurred sparingly and that's more than enough.

Warding off the voices is an exhausting, daily chore that's as damaging as allowing them to mistreat me. Once they've identified even the slightest mental fissure during our routine struggle for supremacy, they've succeeded in their conquest. They'll proceed to dangle me like a miserable marionette and cast a barrage of demented visions into those fissures. However, to be quite honest, it's also unfair to accuse the voices of manufacturing every mental defect of mine. Astounding to admit such, considering my utter revulsion for them is vigorous. No, despite how eager those bastards are to devastate the surviving tatters of my sanity, blaming them for *everything* is an act of cowardice.

Regardless, there was one disturbing day when the voices were so unspeakably malicious that I desperately demanded a refuge at once. Though in a grim state, I left my residence to obtain some reading from a paper shop down near the old couple's café. Matter of fact, the man who operates that paper shop happens to be the elderly woman's brother. Quite an uninteresting factoid. Nevertheless, the man had a very personable nature, which boded well with me as I struggled with my inner torment.

I bought a few insipid magazines and a single newspaper. Unless I have company, reading is one of the few saving graces when it comes to successfully combatting the voices. Reading anything at all enables my thoughts to concentrate on other words, sort of similar to how one has to focus while listening to someone speak. The voices very well might believe that I'm not alone during these instances because of my engagement with words.

Upon returning from the paper stand, however, Edith the Tempest stressed that I should flick through the paper first. Relaxing on my bed, I explored the various stories before coming across a meagre rectangle in the ads section that was cramped with words and numbers. It was for a company by the name of Your Sweet Cherry Treats, and it listed nothing more than a phone number and fifteen feminine names. The contents spoke for itself. Before this shoddy day, I'd never had a modicum of interest in such an ad. Then again, I suppose I never investigated the matter thoroughly. However, the discreet mystique drew me into its fairly tempting grasp. So much so that I impulsively drifted over to the phone in my kitchen. Upon ringing the number, a clearly uninterested male exasperatedly listed off the names on the ad, followed by set prices. I dug a bit, mentioning a couple of names and inquiring about their descriptions. The man's annoyance became more obvious as he gave me their hair and eye colours, but nothing more than the vaguest details possible.

Now, this entire conversation seeped of seediness. I could sense the scents of cigar smoke and worn books that swarmed the room this man inhabited. Sometimes you just know. But being that I'd plunged too deep into my inquisitiveness to back out, I was compelled to select a woman during this call. Also, out of politeness, I didn't want this miserable man to believe his time was wasted. My final question dealt with permissible and prohibited activities. I discovered anything goes. Excellent. And from there on, Your Sweet Cherry Treats became a grand acquaintance of mine.

There were two women before June, both immensely polite and lively. But neither brought about the glimmer June possesses. Her playfulness was exhilarating, and the enamour of her raucous yet erotic attire could cure all my ailments if she were a drug. And I became better educated in her generation's energy than I ever would've been otherwise. It's safe to say June successfully resurrects me whenever my will starts decaying.

To my chagrin, though not remotely unexpected, June isn't always available. Although frustrating, I'll end up requesting someone else. It does, however, depend on how potent my fix is that day. Unfortunately, such tends to be almost intolerably potent. On the days where I'm able to keep it at arm's length, I'll scour for some other pursuit to dive into. It's quite obviously a treacherous dilemma when these ads are among the least sordid of my pursuits. But between satiating my fix or being massacred by manic voices, what else am I do?

***

All tension between June and I dispersed with the draw of a new hand. She has a knack for understanding where I'm coming from when it pertains to separating reality from our overnight fantasy romp. I also recognize that she's *at work* right now. So, with a couple soft kisses, we let this topic dissipate like wafted dust. The likelihood of it coming up again is above average, as she's accidentally brought it up a handful of times in the past, but it's not lingering anymore. For now, we'll do whatever's possible to forbid it from disturbing our evening. It doesn't matter that we know one another through lurid means, not a romantic fashion. At least, I try not to admit it matters.

Our evening continued as it had been before June spilled the whiskey. Although her barman-like conduct caused the botch, she resumed the position to try at it once more. This time around, however, June asked if I could guide her as she poured just in case her hand trembled again. Settled behind her with our arms stretched to the ceiling, I mildly led her through the tipping of the bottle. As the whiskey surged into the jigger, I deliberately withdrew my grasp, allowing June to handle the brunt of the pour. Once the liquid rose to the two-ounce notch, June set the bottle onto the counter. A successful job.

The remainder of the lesson transpired smoothly, and June transported the whiskey into a cocktail shaker. It's a relic of times passed, as I'd gotten it as a wedding present. The date of the ceremony is engraved in the middle, though I positioned a piece of duct tape over it sometime after the divorce. Duct tape causes everything it's on to have a shabby appearance, and the shaker is no different here. So be it.

As June finished filling the jigger up with half an ounce of scotch, I stood before the sink, slicing up the peach. The scotch, some ice, and a dot of lime juice sprung into the shaker, greeting the whiskey inside. Shaking up the concoction is June's favourite portion of the lesson. She grinned brilliantly as she mixed the drink around, the ice creating its signature rattle. Once she'd shaken it up to perfection, our monstrous cocktail creation finally came alive like the beautiful undead. Speaking of the undead, they'd be the sole beings aside from June and I who'd even risk tasting this eccentric fusion. The finishing touch came in the form of a peach slice added to each of our glasses. With our drinks prepared and *presentable*, we clinked our glasses.

"Scale of one to ten, how drab do you think it'll be?" June asked.

"A three," I said.

"You have *so much* faith in me." June scrunched her mouth into a defiant smile.

Gulping down the drink, I gazed at the empty glass with a frown. As anticipated, the taste of pure pot still whiskey with butterscotch syrup proved utterly unsatisfactory. The sweetness thumped the spice more than I would've preferred. What's more, the addition of the lime juice was reprehensible and caused the cocktail to have a taste not dissimilar from what I believe the flavour of window cleaner is.

"Make it a zero," I said.

Seeing that June wore a grimace, I could tell she found the drink soared well below her expectations as well.

"Why did we use that liquor again?" She asked as she examined the whiskey bottle.

"Expendability. It's a cheap brand. Did you really expect me to use something first-rate?"

"No." June smiled. "But we *have* used better tasting alcohol before."

To sweep away the unspectacular taste of our cocktails, we moved on to our cottage pie dinner. It outshined the drink by a stone's throw, though it still did next to nothing for me. This piece of pie possessed appetizing mashed potatoes, I will say, but it failed to convert me to its cult. I just don't find much contentment with the dish. It's a palate game perhaps. What mattered more to me was that June cherished every bite of her portion. The size of her slice pummelled mine into the soil, and I've never seen someone submerge a piece of food in hot sauce the way she does. Had a priest been here, the cottage pie could've been baptized. But if the priest stayed through the baptism, both June and I would have been dosed in holy water that undoubtedly would've contained consecrated tears too.

After dinner, I voraciously finished off the dishes. Since childhood, this abhorrent task has been my utter bane, but my mother held firm to the chore chart she created for my siblings and I. Dishes were my responsibility and it's not as though they're a pain, but the chore is the most tedious of them all. Laundry can be quite soothing and the same applies to mopping, dusting, and vacuuming. But with dishes you're in one place and lacking much movement. And if the dishes stack up due to negligence, it worsens the mood. Due to this, I will routinely wash them at the end of the day to avoid a mountain of plates and cutlery. Quite juvenile of me, I confess, as well as bloody ridiculous. But with all the dinnerware clean and back in their usual cabinets, the night can continue.

I retired to the couch and exhaled deeply, spreading my arms to rest them on the back pillows. June's head found comfort on my lap as she perched her legs on the couch's arm. To her credit, she asked me if she could be of any assistance with the dishes, but her inquiry was rejected. She's my guest and guests don't do chores. They aren't her responsibility, but the fact that June even asked said more than most any other guest who's ever stepped foot into my abode.

June grasped my hand and began to hike her index and middle fingers up and down mine. There's an undeniable leisure in these moments of calm. Words appreciate that they're not mandatory, so they cede their spotlight to the stillness of the atmosphere. When alone, I dread silence's requirement of meticulous internal torment. Company renders such discomfort non-existent. Especially when I'm with June. We bask in each other's mellow serenity, which ceaselessly evolves into zealous yearning for each other's allure. June rose from my lap and draped her hands on my jaw. My hands fell to her lower back, and I pressed my lips onto her scorpion, trailing my lips upward to reunite with her mouth, wet from her slithering tongue. We kissed, until the sudden ringing of the phone interrupted us.

"One moment," I said.

Although a tad sore at the disturbance, I mustered myself from June and the couch. Perched on the wall by the refrigerator rests the phone, which I retrieved.

Calls to my house are quite sporadic, and I've come to expect them from four different categories. The most often is *entertainment*, which consists of a group of colleagues inviting me to a nearby pub if most are in town. If not occupied with vices, I'll take them up on their offer. These outings are more for the purpose of our sturdy comradery than drinking. Unfortunately, it's rare for more than one of us to be in town at the same time as another.

Then there's *familial* calls, which speaks for itself. Usually, it's one of my elder sisters checking in to see how I'm doing. These calls are amiable yet brief, and I tend to question if they're ringing solely to confirm their younger brother is still alive. Each of them comes off a dot too merry when I answer, and there's been the occasional relieved sigh on more than a few occasions. My parents will also ring me, as does Darla. I also toss Tawny Schnall-Glynnis, my oldest friend, into this category. Alas, my irregular availability has caused their calls to lessen in recent years.

Now and then, there'd be women on the other line who confess they fancy a rendezvous. Honestly, with many of them I'll have the vaguest recollection of who they are while we're chatting. It's not out of disrespect, but because eons have soared by since we last spoke or saw one another. Odds are that I met these women while out on the town and slipped them my number. Or it's equally possible that they're previous liaisons anxious for a reprise. No matter the case, once I survey their face again my memories will *always* recall our previous encounter, sexual or not. For me, it's impossible to forget a woman's face. As such, these calls are sorted into the *intimate* category.

Finally, I might get a ring from work. The most unpredictable of the lot, these calls will typically come around a handful of times a year. Of all the probable parties on the other line, this is the one I'm dreading most. It's not out of the fear that my double life will accidentally bare itself in front of June. Discretion reigns throughout these conversations, as they rightly should. If June has any questions after I've hung up, sneaking around that maze is child's play. I've done it before. My dilemma doesn't pertain to anything involving June.

No, nothing feeds more into the Phantasms' furore than being on the job. Understandably, most would scoff and relentlessly ridicule me for such a remark. They'd claim I'm being far too overdramatic. Millions confront utter displeasure when they toil about at work. But, like a busted brawler aching for war, they still scrap it out with a resolute will. I can comprehend it. If employed by *almost any* other institution, I'd wholeheartedly concur with those who'd have a go at me. However, there's nothing remotely identical between my position and that of the masses. Even in related occupations, scant as they are, those employees could never fathom my sombre anguish. This unquestionable awareness of your sanity being forcibly extracted from your core, then watching its gelatinous ruins smoulder.

Sluggishly placing the handset to my ear, wary as a wildebeest, no jots of optimism assembled to assistance me. "Yes?" I asked.

"From sympathy's turquoise commotion," said the all too familiar Mancunian voice of a young woman.

Warm, hypnotic, swirling pastel colours engulf me when she speaks. Whenever I hear her, the word *floral* summons about. Yes, *floral* refers to flowers, obviously, but her tone transmits a lush tinge which matches it brilliantly. Such an identifiable voice belongs to Francine Hitchencamp, the personal secretary of my superior.

Though Francine's remark may seem unclear, it's all part of the protocol. Upon securing a position within this organization, each employee is asked to respond to a meaningless, abstract phrase with one of their own. Such an answer does not require an ounce of deliberation. It can be pulled out of thin air and fulfil the task without issue. This is done so that the organization can contact its employees without the trepidation of security breaches. And it's of vital importance that personnel remember the sayings they created.

"Emerges February's bouquet," I replied.

"Lovely to 'ear from you, Mark," Francine said, "please come to HQ tomorrow at eight o'clock in the morning. Lord President Trailsby has an assignment for you."

Without having the chance to conjure up a response, the line disconnected. That's commonplace with this organization. When they contact me, I'll receive my directives and that's it. Nevertheless, I routinely find myself prepared to respond out of sheer inclination to converse. At the very least, I'm not in the minority. My colleagues have mentioned that the abrupt manner of these conversations tend to throw them off too. But such is how work-related calls proceed. Straight to the point.

One aspect of the call started to repeat itself in jest as I hung the phone back onto its base. Eight o'clock in the morning. Damn. Out of all the hours I could be summoned, it had to be at the most mediocre. Unfortunately, directives aren't to be altered. Therefore, my personal plans must be. I could be attending a family member's birthday party and, if a work call gets through to me, it takes precedence even over that.

June was sitting upright with her legs on the couch throughout the entire call. With her arms draped on a bent knee, disappointment clearly vanquished a once tantalizing demeanour. Between a locked frown and her grand eyes having washed away their glimmer, she must've seen the pained defeat my face held.

"We'll have to do breakfast at another time," I said.

3

Mechanical lovemaking is a phrase that most, I'd assume, would deem unpleasurable. Negative connotations mingle particularly with the term *mechanical.* Hearing such produces shoddy imagery crammed with severe, unemotional aloofness. Some might instead think of rusted machinery complete with the shrill, grating noises of components wearily attempting to rotate. Who could possibly believe the act of *mechanical lovemaking* contains a hint of affection? Honestly, I'm all in to bet on zilch. And I would include myself in such a bet. Absolutely nothing revolving around the concept of *mechanical lovemaking* is remotely appealing. It's almost as affectionate as insect repellent. Yet this is precisely how I would describe my actions with *select* partners.

Without shame, my approach to lovemaking can be horribly conventional when cavorting with women who've seized my devotion for them. Those who've ascended far above the bar of mere lust. Women who've revealed their vulnerabilities and exhibited raw honesty in how they present themselves. Oftentimes I can discern these charming women from those who suffer from the putrid disease known as vanity. They're quite easy to spot, as they'll waste everyone's precious brain cells by nattering on about their "humility" and "righteousness" without an ounce of care for another's aspirations. Occasionally they're a pleasure to spare with, but their selfish desires don't dwindle during intimacy. Therefore, they're not ones I'd be willing to invite back for a second round.

Rummaging through copious positions is a thirst that'll never cease. And by copious, that includes even the most bizarrely unusual that some sexual lunatic correctly guessed would be pleasurable. This is especially fulfilling when a partner possesses the uncanny ability to be bent into numerous shapes due to flexibility, a skill that only fools take for granted. Despite my itch for browsing through an assortment of positions while intimate, I'm void of kinks when a potent connection has developed between myself and a partner. Whereas a brief tryst will unleash additional equipment, such as whips, from the barbaric trove that resides under my bed, these items are forbidden from encounters with someone I've fallen for. Though the prospect of utilizing these devices have made numerous appeals, aiming to convince me otherwise, they strike me as dehumanizing. Whips and paddles succeed only if carnal desire trounces affection in the room, not to mention if and only if she's nothing more than a name.

June may be an escort, and someone who I'd never walk out with for a multitude of reasons, but in a bizarre respect she's still become somewhat of a *girlfriend*. Childish phrase. Regardless, she's my routine request and has been to my house shedloads more than any of the other escorts, let alone any other sexual partner. Due to this, June's revealed pieces of her background to me over time and has talked at length about many of her interests. Some of these interests are surprisingly compatible with mine, such as a mutual affinity for bats, spiders, and researching Satanism. To some degree, this enabled her to shed the "sinful" nature of her occupation and sprout into much more than a rendezvous to me.

Sex demands both parties be wholly submitting to the fiery intertwinement of sweaty bodies. A one-night stand boisterously invites these sleazy pursuits and there's no halting the almost untamed craze that'll arise in the bedroom. Seeing that she provides the verbal green light, nearly every section of her body will be painted by bite marks, scratches, and welts. Salty sweat creates a carnal blend with saliva that sticks to our bodies. Her messy lipstick will brand my flesh along with throbbing, sublime bruises. On the other hand, the conventionality that arises between myself and someone like June plays a major factor in my sexual activities converting to a mechanical nature. And the contrast between me and any of these partners is stark as it is colossal.

Whether it's June or someone else, they'll be absorbed in the moment. Writhing on the sheets, moaning, ruthlessly scratching at my back, the world outside of a bedroom seems to have evaporated while they're engaged in lovemaking. And though a semblance of amorous verve dwells within me, I can't help but notice my lacking any external warmth. I'm merely sailing simultaneously with her body in an apathetic current. My atrociously aloof conduct does not go unnoticed, as I recognize how bloody flawed and dreadful it sounds. A shred of optimism tells me that partners who experience this are unable to detect the machinelike quality of my movements, but there's never been an explicit answer. This assumption is judged by the sheer number of repeat requests I've gotten from partners.

Despite the differing behaviours my ardour displays while savouring a fervent one-night stand versus a romantic get-together, there is a vital similarity the two share, as outlandish as that might be. It's a justifiable enough similarity that might allow the aloofness aspect to not convey such negative connotations. Well, there's a glaring chance it might only be justifiable to me, but regardless it's worth explaining.

Plainly stated, my sexual intentions embrace a single purpose, which is to serve *her*. Whether that *her* is June or some other partner, I have zero qualms if she designates me as her sex object. Positions, commands, and general rule settle in my grasp, but I am still the servant seeking to satisfy, searching to uncover her buried pleasures, and working like a wolf to conquer them. If she has a sly aspiration to make love in a public setting, it'll be granted without hesitation. A bizarre request to play big band music while we're intimate? Sure. Pretend she's a virginal saint struggling to resist temptation from me, an evil spirit? I don't see why not. Her pleasure is vastly paramount compared to mine.

Yes, pleasure is a splendour that I relish as well but I'm also trying to placate a bloody fix. An addiction too vicious, complete with an appetite so mighty it diminishes passion if any sexual designs present fair sunflowers instead of immoral thorns. Contending with the vexed voice of Edith the Tempest, who expresses her exasperation if my addiction goes unconsumed for too many days. How I long for the days when my ravenous passion for lustful gratification existed as a modest vice.

Vices, naturally, are filthy behaviours. Inevitably, infernal turmoil will devour you without an inkling of guilt. Urges overtake your conscience. Your mindset will billow with the notion that these unforgiving actions are beneficial, guarding you from the suffering that waits for any resistance from its clutches. What initially may have been considered a mere vice has swiftly progressed into an addiction. And because you're utterly indebted to the corrupt rule these addictions boast, you, like me, might be free of guilt too.

Despite the immeasurable adoration that's regularly exhibited for June, all of which stems from pure fondness, I acknowledge the blatant fact that she fuels my addiction. Admitting this is challenging because she also contributes to much of the elation in my life. Our time spent together is soaked in liveliness, whether we're conversing, partaking in jovial activities, or in the bedroom. But I only ever invite her to my residence if I'm requesting her services. And since these services involve the tending of sordid habits, June supplements my fix.

To be clear, allocating June to my list of enablers is not me blaming her. The blame also doesn't hover over those who come around to finance the fix when June's not available. All responsibility for habitually engaging in a vice rest at my feet. Addictions are toxic and perhaps there shouldn't be a twinge a guilt for my overindulgence because it's an uncontrollable predicament. But continuously conceding to its cruel demands doesn't cleanse my soul. It only soils it more. On top of that, June may not be the sole stimulant but she's undoubtedly the most formidable. Refusing an opportunity to spend the night with her would, admittingly, deconstruct my heart because I *need* her.

Situated underneath me, June's hands navigated my back and shoulders with a meticulously leisure slither, reminiscent of a lethal serpent. The crevice of my neck enshrouded her face as she adorned me with a considerable array of kisses. My ears revelled in the exquisite allure of her feathery gasps, uttered concurrently with each kiss. However, they had the misfortune of blending with the bed's unmelodious croak, courtesy of weathered box springs and *excessive* overuse.

***

Wild cackles that emit from the alarm clock are forever and inanely eager to commence a new morning. Restrained by an invisible mass, it was a struggle to spin myself toward the wooden stand where the clock was perched. The cackles increased in volume, so much so that it sounded like there were more chortling people swarming into my ears. Unable to bear the hysteria anymore, I seized a sudden burst born of frustration and hurled myself at the clock. Snatching the twin-bell device, I switched off the alarm as the burst simmered. The clock slipped from my hand as the fatigue returned, accusing me of a failure to bid it farewell. Lounging on the bed, the fact my mattress is devoid of another body doesn't startle me.

If we don't have breakfast together, then it's routine for the escorts or general partners to slip out of my house around the crack of dawn. It makes sense, being that it's undoubtedly the most fitting opportunity to sneak off without garnering unneeded attention. Like the rest of them, June will materialise at the front door and then vanish by daybreak. I haven't an inkling if someone gives her a lift, or if she just up and walks. Pertaining to escorts, even if they leave after we enjoy a meal and a bedroom joust, they'll say it's *against practice* for me to walk them out the door. And although curiosity has reared from the depths, urging me to check the blinds, it's a lost cause. That's a touch eerie in my eyes. Instead, the belief is that the escorts will disappear without a trace, only to reappear when I request them again. Somewhat like apparitions, but smuttier. Turning to the pillow June once rested on, I discovered a standard remnant of her having been here. A handwritten note that read as follows:

Can't wait for next time

xx
Your Favourite

June's left these mischievous notes only recently, I believe for the past handful of meetings. While I'm already longing for her presence to inhabit my residence again, now is not the time for images of her to clutter my vision. Out of the numerous stipulations my job is not tolerant of, running late to a meeting with the Lord President is in the top three. The organization I work for deems respect to be among the divinest traits a human can wield. That respect extends to the decency of promptness.

Placing the sweet note on the stand, I stretched and rose from the mattress before briskly making the bed. I seized the clock that lazily tumbled from my hands and set it by the note. Next, I collected my clothes that splashed throughout the bedroom. That was June's doing, being that she has a propensity for ripping and flinging off my garbs before intimacy. Socks and y-fronts sat in a heap at the end of the bed, while the slacks drooped from my chest of drawers. My shirt had been lobbed toward the closet, and near the door sat the jacket. Realizing that I wouldn't be back here following the meeting, all my clothes were arranged on the bed neatly to the dealt with at a later date.

A sweltering shower rinsed away the swarming aura of sweat, saliva, and cherry blossom perfume that coated my body. While drying off my hair, I had no choice but to wipe off some steam from the mirror so check if my face required a shave before leaving. A cleaner, smooth-faced appearance better suits me compared to wearing a beard and, thankfully, the lack of scruff meant I could abstain from shaving for a few more days. Facial hair ages me poorly as patches of grey have recently begun to infiltrate the area.

Unfortunately, gazing into the mirror caused my face to gradually distort into that of a faulty, cartoonish caricature. This was an indication that my reflection had grown tired of being incessantly stared at. Coiled lines of pale pinks and greens etched my face as a vile, elastic mouth stretched down to the sink's faucet. Sclerae consumed my hazel irises, which sank like an embattled ship. You know what would terminate this horrid psychosis? Brutishly ramming my head straight into the glass. No, don't you fret, I'm not *that* senseless. Instead, I managed to wrench myself from the terror that had materialised in the glass, though it took quite a bit of determination to fully obtain freedom from its callous control. I hurriedly seized the bottle of Ruggine and left the bathroom while rubbing my eyes with fierce pressure.

Those bloody mirrors harbour a distaste for me, and it's fully mutual. That might've been among the most appalling deconstructions of my appearance in recent memory, and no doubt returning to work will increase the severity of these demented plagues of disgust. There's nothing that can dimmish the thoughts in the slightest. Medication…maybe, but that's too grave a treatment for now. More hours of sleep would be a more appropriate route, perhaps, but it's doubtful that it'd wholly sway those images. Guaranteed it won't reduce the voices, who've been relatively quiet for the most part since June left, let alone conquer them. My vision is devoid of distortion now, so preparations for work can continue.

Today's outfit is a classic yet basic black power suit with a cream dress shirt, complete with another pair of black dress shoes. Though owning a decent selection of Stork watches, I chose to wear the same one from last night again. Checking the watch to discover the hands stood at six forty-four, time is firmly an ally for now. Collecting my keys and brown leather wallet, I added a hit of cologne before tossing the bottle on the clothes. The final order of business was to claim my briefcase from the closet floor. Before leaving, I thoroughly confirmed it remained untampered with. The numeric code still flaunted the same incorrect combination it did yesterday, which is nothing short of a relief.

***

If weather had the ability to settle on one unbothered option for the rest of eternity, these overcast skies and moderately cool temperatures have my vote. Hot weather is nothing more than a burden, especially when you're outside for mere moments before becoming drenched in sweat. Worse is when your hair gets pillaged by the intensity of the heat. My hair is healthy, though it's begun to recede a tad in the past couple of years, which has generated a slight vampiric quality. Normally to combat that style, I'll comb and part it to the right. Thankfully my hair is still thick enough to not be considered a comb-over, overwise it'd be shaved off. Anyhow, the heat causes my hair to lose its shaped form, in turn allowing my receding hairline to become more obvious than I'd wish.

Clouds, and cooler air, tend to be far more amicable than the sun. Their only downside, in my eyes, is when they're itching for a skirmish. Rain is lovely, but I could get along just fine without enduring a storm. Surprisingly, Vrycastle's skies are being rather courteous today as they're composed and at ease. The modest town typically obscures the blue skies behind cushions of soft grey, which isn't an issue. It's pleasing, however, that the two are co-existing up above for now.

Encompassing me are the terraced houses of my neighbours. Our residences all follow a similar mould in terms of exterior. Composed entirely of rich coral bricks, with charcoal roofs reminiscent of imposing pyramids, they also boast a few too many windows for my liking. However, all the blinds are lowered, as they should be. The one major disparity between the houses are the door colours. Mine is similar in hue to the roof, while others present green and burgundy doors. It is barren of any greenery, which is a tad unfortunate, but so red the rose.

There is a quietude that swirls in this general vicinity, even if the environment is somewhat shoddy. After all, unless an industrial atmosphere is something you fancy, bricks don't provide any kind of inviting magnetism. Nevertheless, everyone who lives in this section happen to be quite affable. Upon leaving my residence, I briefly greeted an older gentleman who lives a few houses to the right of mine. Though his nose was burrowed into the paper he held, the man wished me well as he continued his stroll. Interactions between myself and *most* other residents are rare, not only because I'm seldom here, but because everyone is rather unobtrusive. Yet they'll take time out of their day to express kindness. Could one ask for more considerate neighbours?

Parking facilities don't exist in this neighbourhood, so everyone is required to park on the street in spaces located before each house. Spaces are not permitted to be reserved, so occasionally I'll have to leave my car down the road some because another person secured the spot in front of my house. This time around, it is my car that occupies the heralded space just outside my front door.

Though the relationship I have with my job can be contentious due to…personal matters, it'd be inconsiderate to say the organization doesn't accommodate their employees with some superb amenities. First off, their chief employees are provided with a roof over their head. Yes, my profession allows me to live in this terraced house without paying a cent out of my pocket, which is staggering. Being afforded such an exceptional amenity is a perquisite that I'm unimaginably grateful for.

Secondly, upon being sworn into the profession, those same employees who are gifted a residence are also given a personal vehicle. Lord President Trailsby explained, before presenting me with my car, that the vehicle is supposed to represent the type of employee we're destined to shape into over the years. With that being said, I'm deeply unsure as to what he expected from me as he gave me a Triumph TR7.

Sporting a stately emerald coat and a sharp, gold trim, owing to a custom paint job, the TR7 is certainly more distinctive than the other vehicles that roam the streets around Vrycastle. Frontal glances display a sleek bonnet with an obtuse angled beak jutting out. Believing it to include all the components of a gallant, high-end sports car isn't a stretch, that is, until you take a gander at its sideview.

The rear of the Triumph TR7 is bulkier and more elevated than the bonnet, giving the car an irregular build like that of a swan's back. Such a form isn't unattractive, but it's challenging to see what exactly the designers were aiming for. Much worse, in comparison, have been the oil leaks but I'd prefer not to re-examine those issues. Thankfully, the car is used sparingly, usually just to work and back.

Upon getting settled in my car, earthy hints of Autumn leaves help me unwind. The scent emanates from an orange, octagonal disposable air freshener. It's supposed to be hanging from the rear-view mirror, but I have it situated on the passenger window crank. Disposable air fresheners are considered safety hazards for allegedly obscuring your view, and you can be rewarded with a paltry fine. Such a miserable issue is not worth spending pounds over, so it's best to avoid dealing with it.

Decorating the seats and door panel are matching plaid fabrics of emerald and black. Custom-made to coordinate with the paint job, its dated demeanour is cornier than the orderly exterior. Though the manufacturers *could've* chosen to redesign the interiors out-of-date appearance, there's still a buoyant appeal surrounding the design. Bearing in mind the era of the car's production, it's "family couch" composition is merely a sign of times past. It's amusingly reminiscent of the couch that resides in my parent's living room.

On an average day, the trek to work is an uncomplicated matter. Normally it'll take around fifty minutes, primarily because the main road I'm travelling on generates some daily congestion. Typical predicaments. Fortunately, such traffic is workable and even if there's a slight jam on the roads, there's no doubt I'll arrive at HQ well before the meeting. Extensive drives can be euphoric, though it's largely dependent on the scenery. The route I take to get to work, unfortunately, is dismal. Surrounding me are mundane brick flats, dormant and well along in years. They're horribly indifferent to the people walking the streets. Stone-faced men and women slug along the pavement, hauling an invisible mound of tribulations on both their sagged shoulders and depleted faces. Their distraught images are relatable, which might be why viewing them on the way to work is so troublesome.

Instead of inviting the dejected atmosphere of the outside world into my psyche as is the repetitive choice, I decided to reflect on warmer scenes from a somewhat less muddled time in my life. Long ago, while married to Darla, I resided in Augusta, Georgia. Her genealogical tree spanned generations within the Peach State, and she had no desire to ever move away from her family or friends. Struggling with a major deficiency in ambition during this period, I concurred her decision and truly believed living in Augusta would resolve this dilemma. This concluded with blinding failure, as did my marriage, but that's beside the point.

Of all the cities or towns that I've ever called home, Augusta remains the nicest and most invigorating of the lot. While downtown bursts with a stream of creative zest, full of vigorous musicians and animated artists, there's still a robust homey sense that comforts the city. Broad, adventurous hills jovially sail for miles, adding exhilaration to rides and exercise. Aged houses, factories, and restaurants have endured countless years of unremitting development, proving they're here to stay.

If someone is well acquainted with Augusta, then they're aware of the U.S. Masters, quite possibly the most prestigious tournament in professional golf. While I've never attended any tournament at the Augusta National Golf Club, I used to drive past the prestigious area frequently while traveling down Washington Road. Beyond the gated entrance is a regal line of enormous magnolia trees that are truly breath-taking. If I had a bucket list, being allowed entrance into Augusta National would certainly be at the top of it.

Suddenly, the pure sedative beauty of Georgia dissolved as I became hampered by an irate avalanche bustling in my stomach. I haven't eaten much as of late, which I blame on my warped headspace routinely interfering with proper nourishment. Hours will be exhausted while battling the rioting voices, which will impede essential basics such as eating and exercise. Unfortunately, I'll have to hold off on snapping up a meal until all work-related procedures have concluded at the headquarters of Her Majesty's Dauntless Church of Secret Intelligence. Quite a mouthful, isn't it? I'll never be able to utter that theatrical name without chuckling, so I refer to it as *the organization* or *Her Majesty's Church* for a logical reason.

I'm sure it makes more sense now, as to why I'm required to deceive those in my personal life. Breaking my oath is one issue that'd be catastrophic for all involved, but the notion of being candid about what I'm assigned to do would be drastically unwise. Masquerading as a businessman is my only choice if I wish to come off as *normal*, which is bloody laughable in of itself. Is it *normal* to be harassed by aggressive voices and visions? And what of facing a tainted reflection in the mirror every day?

Working as a field operative, how I detest that title, for an organization that has far less prestige than MI6 has permanently mutated me into a different being. It has exacerbated all the mental impairments I've been reeling with. On the bright side, my colleagues seem to be content with what they do in comparison to me, and they should be fortunate. Although I have nothing but respect for them and the missions they're given, they'd be in ruins if they handled my assignments.

Eventually, I arrived at the intelligence headquarters. Located on the south bank of the River Tyr, which flows through southern England, Gothic architecture deeply influenced the design of the seven-story structure. With pointed arches, interspersing columns and piers, and rose windows, you'd be forgiven if you mistook the stone building for an ancient cathedral. Lord President Trailsby educated me on the building's history during a tour shortly after my swearing in. Her Majesty's Church has always comprised fifteen intelligence operatives, and the original members were wholly enthralled by the threatening construction of cathedrals. They envisioned their headquarters to be so foreboding that it'd stir apprehension from those who gaze upon it. I'd say they succeeded in that aspect, especially when observing the building in the present day. Between contemporary structures turning up nearby and the lack of external renovations HQ has undergone, its archaic presence is massively uninviting. Not to me, though, as I find such architecture to be among the most extraordinary ever designed.

Behind the building is a car park for employees, positioned between a man-made pond and a pocket-sized cemetery. Reaching the frontside without clearing this section is impossible, as the river and overwhelming steel fences rightly enclose it. So, to enter this area, you must continue down the road and stop at a guarded gate. Pulling up to the guard, a bearded man possibly in his fifties, I handed him my blue identification card. Aside from the colour, the card is barren of any information – just a magnetic stripe on one side.

The guard used a handheld scanner to illuminate the stripe, after which a soft beep emitted from the portable device. He handed back my card and tipped his cap as he opened the gate for me. I drove inside the half-empty car park, admiring the hazel trees that neatly garnished the surrounding range, and settled in a reserved spot that had my personal identification number, 109, written on the parking chock.

Grasping the door handle, a low hiss like that of white noise disturbed my ears. It's nothing of alarm, as I've been coping with these aural bothers since the start of this year. There's reason to believe it's mild tinnitus, but I haven't spoken to a doctor about it, so nothing has been confirmed. I'm horribly unqualified to go about diagnosing anyone, even myself, so for now it's best to just continue with my business.

Stepping out of the car, faint calls from the river glided through the air and overwhelmed the hisses, which gradually waned. I turned and took a moment to the survey the surreptitious car park's dormancy. Or, in all honesty, maybe I was just taking a minute to bid farewell to additional slivers of my sanity. Either way, trifling whispers from the breeze were telling me to scutter. Retrieving my briefcase, I shut the TR7's door and made my way to HQ's entrance.

4

While the general public is certainly aware that Her Majesty's Dauntless Church of Secret Intelligence exists, the organization tends to be far more guarded with their history than MI6. Same applies to its inner workings and the identities of the administrators who direct it. The only individuals who could possibly possess a dot of familiarity with either are all members, past and present, of the organization as well as the highest-ranking officials in the British government. Even those affiliated with the British Armed Forces, who are the primary recruiters for Her Majesty's Church, are told impressively vague information by the organization. In a multitude of ways, Her Majesty's Church functions like a one of those rum secret societies…complete with similar amounts of malice and bone-chillingly wicked activities. The one major disparity between the two is that Her Majesty's Church partakes in these deeds with a knowingness that it's for the safety of England, as well as the numerous countries who've gotten into bed with them. Recognizing such permits us to feel somewhat less toffee-nosed compared to those daft secret fraternities.

Roger V, the former king, had requested the formation of a secondary intelligence agency *only a year* after the implementation of MI6. Although the Government of the United Kingdom was initially perplexed by the concept, they still went through with its establishment without argument. Upon being assembled by former prime minister Hardy Lemsquit, the initial structure of what was formerly *His* Majesty's Church was very much unlike our current institution. In that form, the original fifteen members of the organization adhered to direct orders provided by the commanders of the British Armed Forces. In that guise, they were perceived as a special forces unit for the United Kingdom's military during their first five years. Although their unit would be dismantled after that brief timespan, it would later be resurrected and utilized in an effective approach.

In time, Prime Minister Lemsquit and Roger V mutually decided to break *His* Majesty's Church apart from the military and craft the organization as more of an untraditional, standalone intelligence agency. This was because Lemsquit believed the original fifteen members were better suited as an MI6 replica considering the amount of specialized training they had during their time as a special forces unit. He claimed that MI6 was better equipped to conduct the more professional espionage assignments within intelligence gathering, but that there was a dire need for a similar team that was willing to do *dirtier* work.

Once *His* Majesty's Church acquired this new figure, six new high-level positions were created by Roger V so to continue order and guidance for the fifteen field operatives. The most important position that was established by the organization under these changes was that of the lord president. Whoever holds this position is the head of operations of the organization. They oversee and authorize all potential assignments, correspond with the heads of other intelligence agencies, and report all assignment outcomes back to the Prime Minister among numerous other responsibilities.

Second in line after the lord president is the deputy lord president. This position doesn't possess many significant purposes as it's more of a preparation role being that whoever ascends to this position inevitably becomes lord president. Therefore, the lord president takes their deputy under their wing and entrenches every last facet of necessary information into their head so that they're beyond qualified to assume the top responsibilities once the time comes.

By order of both Roger V and Lemsquit, the lord president was also presented the opportunity to develop and head their own *government*, which consists of four positions that operate like a modified administration's ministry or cabinet. These positions, the minister of state affairs, the minister of combat, the minister of the assets, and the minister of justice, are more subdued and mostly invisible compared to the lord president. Aside from the minister of combat, operatives might see the other ministers once a year or less. Even I, personally, have never formally met the current minister of state affairs or the minister of the assets. The only instance where they have ever made their attendance known to me was during my swearing in. It's been said by other members with longer tenure that the ministers simply have a preference to do their dealings in the shadows instead of corresponding directly with operatives.

The minister of state affairs works with the lord president in cooperating with the heads of other intelligence agencies. They're the ones who stockpile information on possible assignments and parlay the information to the lord president. The person who holds this position is also a key voice in deciding which member of Her Majesty's Church has the best chance of completing an assignment. Though the final choice, of course, is decided by the lord president, this minister tends to be held accountable for most decisions that have ended with the loss of an operative.

The minister of combat has more direct involvement with the operatives in that they're the ones who guide us throughout the entirety of our first year. During that stretch of time, new operatives do not interact with anyone from Her Majesty's Church aside from the minister of combat and the lord president. Our time is spent being trained by this minister in diverse fields of martial arts, as well as the handling of weaponry, whether it be arms or blades. Aside from their direction over us, this minister also selects the weapons that compose the arsenal of Her Majesty's Church. They'll commission the head of the Weapons Department, their deputy, to produce practical gadgets or even bespoke weapons for the operatives to use during a mission.

The minister of the assets is the most "ghoulish" when it pertains to interactions or appearances. They rarely make their presence known, preferring to do their work away from the whirl of HQ. The minister of the assets handles the finances of Her Majesty's Church. For example, after the minister of combat has chosen weapons for the arsenal, this minister will manage all transactions. They're also the ones who've purchased residences for the operatives, along with our vehicles. This minister also funds any other expenses that we might rack up, which certainly appals them considering some of the purchases we make. But, on a less raucous page, these purchases do include any vacations that we wish to embark on.

There is, however, an alleged sinister side to this position that has been expressed to me by other members of the organization. I've heard claims that some of the weapons purchased by the minister of the assets derive from hostile countries, such as the Soviet Union. These arms have never been seen by those who contend they exist within HQ, but they scurry around that charge by explaining the weapons at hand are stored in a secret compartment within the building. While that in of itself, if true, is already immensely immoral, it gets even grimmer. It's also claimed that while the Government of the United Kingdom has knowledge of these purchases, many allied countries, such as the United States, are oblivious. And they'd be bloody livid if they were to find out. Among the perks of being a part of this "saintly" organization, right?

Finally, the minister of justice supervises the "clean-up" business that arises upon the completion of an assignment. They scale the walls to make sure all necessary intelligence agencies, as well as law enforcement, are fully mindful of the events that ensued between our organization and the targets we were assigned. And, most importantly, that everything was justly handled. That, even if some assignments had to follow a darkened path, they were authorized by whichever country we were in. As shady as it is to admit, the minister of justice assists us in evading arrest. While we're gearing up to embark back to England, they'll be making phone calls to clear everything up as swiftly as possible.

Unlike the positions of both lord president and deputy lord president, who can serve until whenever they keel over or retire, there are age limits in place for ministers. They are able to serve until they're sixty-five, standard and unsurprising, at which point their "term" has concluded. The lord president will then select another individual to succeed the outgoing minister. Field operatives are never eligible for these positions unless they decide to continue with the organization in other roles following the conclusion of their active service. See, aside from the upper-level roles and the field operatives, there are several hundreds of other obscure employees who complete the hierarchy of Her Majesty's Church by comprising the bottom-level. These positions are wide-ranging and include data gatherers, secretaries, assignment coordinators, electronics technicians, and forgery experts. So, whenever an upper-level role is vacant, those titles are up for grabs among these so-called *obscured employees*.

Although field operatives are only eligible to be considered for an upper-level role if they continue in a "lesser" position following the end of their initial tenure, they do have an unfair advantage when it comes to the selection of new officials. Their inner familiarity with the organization and its structure, plus an understanding of how assignments are to be followed, give them shedloads more experience than a random employee who was hired through other means. Due to this, most individuals who've held the highest positions were, indeed, former field operatives.

In the decades since the organization was transferred out from the military's clutches, most rules and guidelines have not been altered. During the subsequent reigns of King Roger VI and, our current monarch, Queen Matilda, the two preferred to keep the organization as is. But Roger VI was a tad indifferent to *His* Majesty's Church in that he was less involved with the inner workings of the organization. He preferred to let prime ministers conduct meetings with the lord presidents, and rarely wished to receive updates. Her Majesty the Queen, on the other hand, was much like her grandfather in regard to the extent of her cooperation.

A staunch supporter of Her Majesty's Church, the Queen has been more in tune with the details of our undertakings and successes than her father was. She's also been more willing to meet the operatives, to learn more about them, than her father was as well. Granted, the Queen normally meets with operatives for the first time when their tenth year on the job arrives. That is, unless you've been an otherworldly force who stands out among your peers. Then she and her husband, the Duke of Loutshire, are even more keen on learning about you. Though I'm surprisingly eager for our eventual conference several years from now, hopefully she doesn't have incredibly in-depth material about my *wretched* assignments.

The circumstances surrounding my recruitment to Her Majesty's Church, or my descent into the bedlam of the Church as I refer to it, were not out of the ordinary upon first glance. They were right along the lines of just about every other person who got involved in its ranks, past and present. It's not as though I was some extraordinary individual with implausible qualifications. No, that's not the case. Besides, that's also not how the recruitment process works. That was something I had to learn upon my initial selection.

At thirty-five years old, I'd been divorced for six years, hadn't seen my children in five, and dwelled in the Royal Special Forces Unit for five. When I'd joined the Royal Special Forces Unit, I was aware that the branch had been instilled during the Korean War as the fifth warfare force. However, it appeared that everyone was entirely oblivious to the fact that it was the resurrection of the original incarnation of Her Majesty's Church. But even if that information was more notorious, I wouldn't have given a damn.

The Royal Special Forces Unit was a last resort option for someone with no bloody future. Why lie and claim otherwise? After my divorce, everything else crumbled around me and made me ponder the purpose of life. A mid-life crisis at thirty-five, isn't that wonderful? That is something I'll be honest about. The four years that followed my divorce saw me bouncing around meaningless jobs and with an assortment of interchangeable women. Throughout this apathetic yet lust-fuelled period, my former father-in-law was doing all he could to aid me in securing long-term stability. But, when you're someone who's devoid of any true career passions, it's rather shoddy working your arse off when you're just bloody miserable.

There was one job I desired, though it paid next to nothing. It might be preposterous, but it was to be a park ranger in Georgia. Parks, and nature in general, bring me a mist of peace that's rare and lustrous. It seemed like a reasonable enough career. Though my history degree from the University of Georgia provided me next to nothing in terms of proper educational experience, my former father-in-law, again, had the right connections. He could've gotten me that position with relative ease. However, the poor pay, and the lack of decent credentials made me reconsider that option. On top of that, knowing that the job would've been gifted instead of earned, just like every other one I'd held, made me think of myself as a fraud. So, much to my displeasure, there was no choice but to decline it.

My father, who served as secretary of the interior under former United States president Bert Ambossmauer, was eager to secure me a job in politics. To his disappointment, I rejected the idea because that was a treacherous field to enter as a divorced father of three with a flawed background. Ultimately, my father ended up being the one who convinced me to move back to Wales and join the British Armed Forces. He claimed it that while it wasn't a particularly lucrative choice, it would allow me to get away from the United States for a while to find myself while staying active. That it would keep my mind sharp and on a brighter path.

Before leaving for Wales, I stopped by Darla's house to say goodbye to her and the children. She was confused by the decision, but ultimately came to accept it...after quite some time. I assured her that my family would help raise the children, which she appreciated. Most importantly, I told her, as well as everyone important to me, that this excursion would require me to be gone for a few years at most. At least...that's what we all predicted.

Enlisting in the Royal Special Forces Unit was easier than expected, though upon gathering the circumstances behind the relative simplicity, everything made more sense. Far less people applied to serve in the Royal Special Forces Unit compared to the major branches of service, so my entry was based off a need for more servicepeople than possessing ideal qualifications. However, my time in the Royal Special Forces Unit was a mundane beast. There was a distinct lack of joy, which was communicated by a murky grey raincloud that materialised each morning in the barracks without shame. Yes, the position kept me fed, showered, durable, and occasionally rested - so there was that at the very least. But, otherwise, it was a bloody drag. Maybe it was because the future progressively shrank into a stodgy ball of yarn with each passing day? Perhaps I missed my children and wallowed over the fact that I'd failed them as a father by running off after Darla cast me aside. No matter what the case happened to be, there was no bigger waste of time for me than rotting away in the hallowed halls of the Royal Special Forces Unit.

During my fifth year, specifically in December of 1978, one of the sergeants who supervised my unit summoned me to the field where we did our daily miles. It was dusk and, frankly, I yearned to be put out of my misery like a rabid hound. Had that happened, I knew that the sergeant would cover it up by claiming my demise was self-inflicted. But upon arriving at the field, the sergeant was not the only person anticipating my arrival. Standing with him was a modest-sized man who had thick, dyed brown hair neatly parted to his left. He wore a dark suit with a blue tie that was splattered with decorations of red polka dots. In his left hand was a black leather briefcase.

The modest-sized man immediately shook my hand. "Mark McGarriff?"

"Yes," I said.

"Pleased to meet you. Now, I'll make this as brief as possible. Sergeant Bosley here has been scouting you for as long as you've been part of Her Majesty's Royal Special Forces Unit. Says your work ethic is uncanny and unlike any he's ever witnessed in his years of service. He's recommended you be part of a select group of individuals who work for Her Majesty's government. A secret intelligence organization…but *not* MI6. Do you wish to proceed?"

As I was about to open my mouth, this man waved out his sleeve to reveal a watch that he began staring at.

"You have ten seconds to answer yes…or no," he said.

Usually, I'm less abrupt when it comes to answering questions. Sifting through the positives and negatives are required and haphazard decisions normally end in dire circumstances. But the peculiar nature of this ordeal had me enraptured. It also helped that joining this man meant removing myself from the mind-numbing clutches of the Royal Special Forces Unit. So, I blurted out "yes." Little did I know, at the time, that this man happened to be Nigel Esprine, the minister of combat for Her Majesty's Church.

Soon thereafter, I embarked on an unaccompanied two-hour flight to a base in…who bloody knows where. The location, to this day, remains undisclosed and classified. Upon arriving at the base, I convened with two females and two males in a warship grey meeting room. The females were new sprogs in the Royal Army, while one of the males had recently enlisted in the Royal Marine Force. The other was a recruit from the Royal Naval Force. It should be noted that Her Majesty's Church follows a specific procedure as they scout for prospects. See, you're qualified to serve immediately upon completion of basic training for the Royal Special Forces Unit. As it pertains to all other branches of the Royal Armed Forces, however, only new recruits amidst their training are eligible for shadow scouting.

Once in this room for around five minutes, Minister Esprine, still anonymous to us, entered and explained the circumstances regarding our being at this base. He restated that, in my case, my superior had clocked me for the past several years without my realization. As for the other hapless individuals, their scouting took mere weeks. Then, he went on to reveal that our information had been passed on to senior-ranking officers who'd never even met us. These officers were also impressed by what we'd shown while we'd been enlisted in the British Armed Forces, so they were proud to sign off on our being potentially recruited by this mysterious organization.

Minister Esprine said that we were the only five individuals selected for this class, but that we'd be undergoing a severe, non-stop training session for the next three days. He made it clear that only one of us would make it to the end of the training, and that the sole individual who stood tall would be the one sworn into the heralded halls of this secret intelligence group. Of course, questions flew at the minister regarding what was to be expected with this training ordeal. But he merely wagged a finger at us and said that it'd be a "fool's game" to disclose any of that information. He then said that we had ten minutes to collect ourselves before the training began. And, with that, he left the room.

What transpired immediately after those ten minutes dragged by was…the literal embodiment of the netherworld embedding itself into the world. What some random bloke might constitute as *torture*, what with all the waterboarding and white room shit, doesn't come anywhere close to what we five unfortunate ghouls had to endure. Thinking back to the ordeal, several thoughts jockey for the position of worst offender. How was this bloody legal? How did none of us meet our demise? Did I deserve to be *rewarded* a victory when the experience was far from *rewarding*?

Nevertheless, the proceeding three days following my arrival at this undisclosed base were loaded with all methods of mistreatment one could scrounge up. These punishments were conducted by hooded individuals whose identities are unknown. Others who were involved, whose faces I did observe, are also shrouded in mystery. Everyone ran their routines under the supervision of the Minister of Combat, who didn't reappear until the trials had concluded.

First was the physical torture. This included having to escape mazes of razor-sharp barbed wire in under a minute. That diabolical jumble all but shredded my flesh. If that wasn't cruel enough, we were then subjected to don some of this barbed wire around our necks for a few hours. A mocking gift to remind us of our brutal accomplishment. Another method of physical torture that we were forced to endure was that of sparing contests. We were to challenge trained brawlers who were seemingly impervious to pain and possessed an assortment of combat styles. To sweeten the horror of these bouts, some of the brawlers were also equipped with brutish accessories. Some wore gloves with either spikes or studs attached to the knuckles. Others had gauze wrapped around their hands, but the gauze had been rubbed about in glass before the brawl.

Sure, I was a touch adept at some methods of hand-to-hand combat, but neither me nor the other *victims* could equal the skill level of these brutes, most of whom appeared to be your average, run of the mill lads. As such, successive bouts ended up leaving us battered, bloodied, and shamed. Our wounds would then be mended by the same fiends who'd just beaten the living mercy out of us. However, that doesn't mean they had a sliver of humanity. No, because they certainly revelled in repeatedly striking those stitched and patched up sections come the next scuffle. Sickening.

We also suffered from starvation and dehydration due to a withholding of nutrients. And there were worse trials too…scenarios far too vile to reminiscence on. So much so that the naval recuit and one of the female privates were eliminated after the first day. Neither could take any more suffering, so they both shouted out the safe word *cargo* and scurried out as swift as their damaged legs could take them. The other female private and the marine were as physically and mentally broken as I was, but they were fighters who weren't willing to give up after the first day. Why did we all wish to continue with two more days of this crap? I like to believe it's because we refused to be perceived as quitters like the other two. *Dauntless*, right?

When the psychological aspect was mixed in with the predominant physical struggles during the second day, the tables began to turn in my favour and pushed me onto the turnip of triumph. My thoughts were already dangerously bleak, so these methods did next to nothing in its efforts to shatter my will. Sleep deprivation was attempted, but my miserable sleep schedule provided uncountable sleepless nights.

Next was being tossed, literally, into a room with loud noises, mostly those of projectile barrages and screaming. To my chagrin, among other sentiments, the floor in that room was littered with jagged thumbtacks that dug into my anguished body once it collapsed to the ground. Being locked in that room took dire toil, as ruthless anxiety made me my temperature rise, causing me to wither into a profusely sweaty bag of rocks. But somehow…it was unable to fracture my psyche any more than it already was.

Finally, there was no other choice for the hooded tyrants but to drag me to a chipped wooden door that had the phrase "*einzelhaft*" scrappily etched into it. Solitary confinement. That nearly did me in. Suffering alone with my murky and antagonistic thoughts, as well as the voices that were by now beginning to emerge in my ears…I frantically rifled through the dingy confinement room. Not for a way out of the room, but for a way to wrench my soul from my body because all my emotions, anxieties, mania, it had swelled up to the point I was questioning my purpose. Why I was existing in this infernal world when these barbaric struggles should've killed me instead of bringing me to end myself.

As I was readying to ram my head into one of the walls, a frustrating but essential end for a weakened bloke, the door unlocked, and the still anonymous Combat Minister entered. If it wasn't for the marine giving in and uttering "cargo" when he did, I would've been done for.

"You've succeeded, Mark. You've won," he said. "Where others toiled, scrapped, and failed, you trawled to the finish line. Congratulations."

When one is rewarded a worthy victory, it should result in that person experiencing a torrent of warm sensations that'll sweep them off their feet. Instead, I plunged to my knees and barely managed to sputter out "p-put me out of my misery."

Then the world silenced and spun out into black.

Waking up in a hospital bed, the Combat Minister explained that I'd passed out from the punishing exhaustion. Could've fooled me. He then told me that there were now two options to choose from. Either I could formally accept the invitation into this secret intelligence group, or I could be sent to another classified location to wither away. Too fatigued to ask any more questions or relive the haunting and sadistic events, I muttered "option one."

"Brill," he said. "Welcome, Mark, to Her Majesty's Dauntless Church of Secret Intelligence. I'm Nigel Esprine, the organization's Minister of Combat."

He later told me that he was merely cracking wise with the *classified location* remark, and that it was another way of saying I'd be sent back to the Royal Special Forces Unit. To this day, it's ambiguous as to whether that's true or not. After all, if Her Majesty's Church is willing to torture potential operatives, then who's to say they won't dump failed prospects somewhere to let them rot? There's plenty of reason to believe the latter, especially due to the fact they'd most definitely prefer to keep those distressing methods under wraps.

After my wounds had been healed and a doctor deemed me fit for travel, Minister Esprine had me whisked to England so that I could take the governmental oath of allegiance to Her Majesty's Church. This event was attended by shedloads of people, many of whom I now call my chums. Fellow operatives, all four ministers, various bottom-level personnel. It's odd, recalling the swearing in and being surrounded by current allies who were all once strangers. How they, too, were exposed to these bouts with literal demons. How they, like me, are reminded of those dismal memories every time a new operative is sworn into Her Majesty's Church.

The ceremony was held at HQ, in the lobby of the first floor. Everyone was lined up in rows, like parting waves, watching as I mustered up enough strength to trudge before them. Despite being mostly healed at this point, my ability to walk was still hampered by the various damages that had been inflicted upon me. So, I had to limp my way to the Lord President himself, who swore me into Her Majesty's Church. Like most oaths of allegiance, he had me repeat the words after him. The oath I took went as follows:

I, Mark McGarriff, do swear to uphold true allegiance to the United Kingdom. To Her Majesty Queen Matilda, her heirs, and successors. To Prime Minister Harbold and the Government of the United Kingdom. To Lord President Trailsby, and to my fellow associates within Her Majesty's Church. I will serve in my capacity as Operative

Number One Hundred and Nine with good faith, with a determined moral compass, and will revere all protocol without hesitation.

Before officially settling into my role, Minister Esprine trained me for three hundred and sixty-five days, from six in the morning until nine in the evening. It's a tad embarrassing to recall how humorous it was when he attempted to engage in a sparring contest with me at random. At five-foot eight, with a wrinkled eagle like-face and a clear voice that sounded a touch older than he was, I found it to be an awful joke. But he convinced me that it was part of training, so if he told me to spar with him then I had no other choice. Though it seemed discourteous and immoral to spar with a much older lad, I threw the first strike.

The then-fifty-six-year-old man astounded me by owning the reflexes of a tabby, evading my strike with unbelievable ease. He then proceeded to place me in an armbar that would've ripped my limb from its socket had this not been a friendly joust. Admittingly, even with undertaking the deranged episode that was the three-day torture display, it was at this moment that I truly comprehended the bewildering, madcap, and menacing amazement that was this job.

Minister Esprine taught me how to correctly engage in hand-to-hand combat, instilling in me styles ranging from taekwondo and hapkido to kickboxing and street brawling. Though the sessions were friendly yet gruelling, he demanded the rule of *no restraint* if I happened to secure the advantage. He also aided me in developing a proficiency with all sorts of martial arts, such as tai chi, hapkido, and judo. I firmly believed the old bastard was a loon, but a tough one at that.

Whenever I summon the circumstances behind my occupation, the prevalence of anguishing memories provokes the disdain for my occupation. Working for an organization that dehumanizes and distresses its recruits, that recommends we use sinful methods if we must. One that stimulates the most sullen and wrathful sections of my head without remorse. How Her Majesty's Church has demanded I spout untruths to my family and others about my true profession. How they've assisted in tearing me away from my family, most importantly my children, though most of that fault does indeed rest with me.

And yet, they've afforded me with every possible necessity to allow an easy lifestyle. My residence, my car, my expenses, none of that would be imaginable without Her Majesty's Church. Though it occasionally seems like I've just been gifted these privileges in the same guise my former father-in-law would organise, the two are truly poles apart. In this case, I did earn the right to these privileges, no matter the unease. I decimated myself to work for Her Majesty's Church, so while I may never cease my loathing of this job…to express my gratitude toward it takes more than words or actions ever could elicit.

5

Rounding the front of HQ, the steady amplification of ripples from the River Tyr signified my crossing into a realm unlike the one I inhabit. A pathway made of rich, English violet marble directed me to curved, discoloured sea green doors. Complete with an arch at the top, they're staggering and utterly durable. These doors are the building's sole entryway, though no guards are posted here. However, my ID is warranted for me to gain access. There's a scanner on the door that's nearly eye-level, and I hover the back of my ID directly before the red laser. Unlike the guard's handheld scanner, this one emitted three harsh beeps in rapid succession. Simultaneously, a thunderous clunking bellowed within the doors as they unlocked.

"Welcome, one hundred and nine," spoke a synthetic voice from a miniscule speaker installed on top of the right pull handle.

Programmed with a feminine French accent, there's a rather affectionate reason behind such a selection. If I remember correctly, one of the organization's original members modelled this accented voice as a tribute to his wife. Though some colleagues have complained about it diluting the ominous intrigue of HQ, I believe otherwise. When activated, a storm of crackles spew out to the point it nearly warps the speaker's already indifferent vocal pattern.

Once inside, I walked down the spacious lobby and to the front desk. Shunning the exterior's Gothic approach, the lobby is conservative and cultured. Fierce gusts of hurried, smoky currents, similar in scent to a timeworn library, rushed me. Goldenrod walls with patterns of shadowy, elongated shapes gave the intended impression of ancient maps. Dark wood floors were covered by a distressed Oriental rug, which included a daffodil-hued medallion encompassed by warmer yet murkier colours. Neatly arranged on both sides were two wingback chairs and one cabriole sofa, all cherry-hued, as well as a rectangular, wooden coffee table. The tables were placed precisely in the middle of both setups, so that each seated individual could set their drinks on them with ease.

Hanging on the wall before me rests an imposing black and white portrait of the original fifteen members. I'm sure by now that you can recognize just how much the organization values them. The portrait is between two bookshelves, one considerably wider than the other, and behind a lengthy, sizable, curved desk.

Standing directly in sight is Marjorie Beacy, forty-seven, the front desk officer. Her neck length hair is chestnut brown, greying at the roots, and marginally parted to her right without intruding her forehead. The style reminds me of a church bell. Apple red lipstick adorns Marjorie's thin lips, and a touch of rouge compliments her cheekbones. Her contemporary business attire consists of a powder blue button-down and a loose-fitting white jacket. The base of the desk Marjorie stands behind is made of glass, which revealed a white knee length skirt to make up the bottom half of her outfit. Capping off her appearance were a diamond pendant necklace and matching stud earrings that I've never seen her without.

Marjorie has been employed by Her Majesty's Dauntless Church of Secret Intelligence for around fifteen years. This happens to be one of the few slivers of information regarding her past that have been disclosed. Within the organization, Marjorie is known for being immensely private, never permitting conversations to go further than the topic at hand. And, if you dare attempt to ask her anything remotely personal, she'll form a tense smile and inquire whether you have somewhere to be or not.

It's vastly important to respect someone else's privacy, but Marjorie's aversion to revelations has caused me to question Lord President Trailsby some so to unearth additional data. Granted, this occurred early on in my tenure, so you can't fault my inquisitiveness. Trailsby informed me that the only information I could be given pertained to Marjorie's prior career. For twelve years she served in the Woman's Royal Naval Service, where she attained the rank of first officer. The Lord President did break protocol by revealing that information, as Her Majesty's Church considers military service to be classified and off-limits to everyone except the Lord President himself. He most likely divulged that aspect of Marjorie's background to me out of fear that I'd pester him. It's not as though Marjorie's military service assists me in supplementary knowledge. Besides, anything revolving around her subsequent move to the organization is still an utter mystery.

"It's a pleasure to see you this morning, Marjorie," I said. "Is the world treating you well?"

"Good morning, one hundred and nine," Marjorie said. She sidestepped my question by handing me a clipboard with both a sheet of paper and a pen attached. "You know what to do. Please sign in and you can go on your way up."

I signed my name in the first box of the otherwise barren sign-in sheet. It's eerie to witness my cursive become increasingly more illegible with each successive year. Some letters are still easy to make out, but for the most part my handwriting's downward spiral continues to heckle me. Anyways, checking my watch, it was nice to see that the time stood at ten minutes to eight. I handed the clipboard back to Marjorie upon jotting down the time and my identification number of 109 in their required boxes.

"Thank you," Marjorie said.

"How did you spend your weekend?" I asked in a knowingly audacious tone. "Anything particularly entertaining?"

Marjorie eyed me for a second before her ever-expected taut smile developed.

"It's best you're not late to your meeting, one hundred and nine," she said.

See what I mean? Now you get it. Returning her smile, I journeyed down a nearby corridor to the right of the front desk where the lifts were. They're next to the smoking room, which follows the same refined ambiance of the lobby. Upon entering the lift, which was done out in faux wooden panels and flooring, I ascended to the fourth floor where the Lord President's office is located.

Pure beige walls appeared as the lift's doors retracted, but they're hardly my favourite sight on this floor. Immediately upon stepping forward, I encountered Francine Hitchencamp, twenty-five, Lord President Trailsby's personal secretary. She was seated behind an aluminium desk with a walnut surface, filling out paperwork though my entrance caused her to glance up and glow infinitely.

Francine's cobalt blue irises exuded overwhelming enchantment, a hypnotic rush of celestial charm. Her slightly wavy, tawny hair was parted to her right, and the ends rolled directly above her chest. The eyeliner she wore was gentle and barely apparent, as was her warm, taupe eyeshadow. Francine also preferred sleek lip-gloss over lipstick, and it dazzles like a brilliant Acapulco beach escape whenever that wondrous smile of hers emanates. Exactly as it's doing now. Mercy her beam was as splendid as a maiden's calico dress.

"Your entrance…it plays out almost exactly like my dreams, Marky honey," Francine said. Her cobalt blues were zipping up and down as she stared at me. "Except you're usually holding a giant sunflower."

"One of these days," I said.

When we converse, Francine has a propensity to disregard the organization's mandatory formality regarding the proper way to address personnel. She should refer to me as "one hundred and nine," as Marjorie did, but it's not as though I take offense to this indifference toward primness. Our personal identification numbers are a vital part of this organization's history, but the fact that a considerable amount of the staff here only calls us by number and never by name is a dot dehumanizing.

On the opposite end, Francine should be referred to as "Miss Hitchencamp," but I only ever call her by her first name unless Lord President Trailsby is around. Unlike Marjorie, who I refer to by first name primarily to get a reaction out of her, Francine's utterly enchanting name is always spoken as such because it's…*right.* It should also be made clear that Francine is the sole person on this planet with permission to call me "Marky."

Considering her age, Francine is among the youngest staff members currently employed by the organization. While she did acquire her position as Lord President Trailsby's secretary with the aid of her MP father's successful persuasion, that or our interaction shouldn't diminish one's impression of her. She's a reliable planner and a proficient, one-hundred wpm typist who's never made an error. Not only that, but Francine's position also designates her as the Lord President's de facto bodyguard. This is because her workstation leads to his private office, which means she is tasked with protecting him at all costs. Lord President Trailsby puts a significant amount of trust in Francine, and he's told me that she relates to him better than anyone else in his life ever has. This, in addition to her sheer aptitude and loyalty, demonstrates why she's been a valued employee for three years.

Rising from her seat in a gentle manner, Francine motioned for me to approach her. I did so, taking in the splendour of her pastel salmon belted blazer dress that's complete with short sleeves, shoulder pads, a white undershirt, and a black, three-point handkerchief in the breast pocket. Pastel salmon outfits are Francine's favourite, and I've never seen her wear something of a different colour. Her adoration of this hue derives from the fact her greatest influence, Queen Matilda, adores it as well.

It's fascinating to think that, among the people I've become acquainted with throughout my life, it's doubtful there's anyone as staunchly monarchist as Francine. She's routinely repeated her belief that there's a certain elegance with the word *kingdom*, and that the poise of the Queen is the personification of how an Englishwoman should conduct herself. Surely that's a severely bold statement to make.

Then there's the commemorative mug on her desk that celebrated the Queen's Silver Jubilee from six years ago. Francine's stated time and again that this mug is her most cherished possession, and its presence on her desk is for display and not for drinking. Sitting near the mug are a miniature stand bearing the Union Jack flag, and a black leather handbag. Francine seized the latter and began rummaging around in it.

"Since I knew you'd be 'ere today, I stopped at the supermarket earlier to grab you a little something," Francine said.

From her handbag, she secured a red carton of cigarettes and handed it to me. They're Capsize, an English brand that'd been my favourite since I initially picked up the ridiculous habit. Note how I said *been*, which isn't a reference to my brand preferences changing over time. No, instead I'm currently attempting to curtail my use of cigarettes, which at one point reached two cartons a day. No matter how long it's been since then, I'm gravely dissatisfied with myself for allowing it to intensify to that level.

Thankfully, Francine is aware of my efforts to end these habits. See, instead of smoking regular cigarettes, I've taken up herbal cigarettes to satisfy my compulsive behaviours and the carton of

Capsize she bought me has the word *herbal* printed on the top right corner. Though they're just as toxic as an actual cigarette, smoking these have lessened my nicotine affliction at the very least. Withdrawal punished me, but at this point what troubles aren't mercilessly punishing me?

"These ones have rose petals in 'em," Francine said. "Can you believe that?"

"Strangely romantic," I said, putting the carton into my inner jacket pocket.

"Romantic? Maybe in a ghoulish way. They're still harmful."

"Romance is—"

"Romance is *harmful*," Francine said, shaking her head. "Sometimes you show up sweet as marmalade, Marky honey. Or you're all brooding. Romance isn't as horrible as you like to believe it is. It's what beautifies our lives."

Perhaps she has a point, in an innocent sense. But Francine's never been married before. She's young and continues to live in a world of roses and honey, blissfully unaware of how the wrong circumstances make you rather jaded in your outlook. Maybe I'm a tad harsh in calling romance *harmful*, and yes, she did correctly finish my sentence, but would it have been wiser to admit my preference for games over romance?

"That's fair," I said, opting to agree with her to deviate from the subject. "And thank you for the cigarettes."

Francine smiled. "Of course. Now, before I let you into Trailsby's office, are you in the mood for a solid or a pattern?"

"Let's go with a pattern today."

Remember earlier on how I mentioned my disdain for neckties? Well, I'm obligated by protocol to wear one while within the confines of this building. It's one of the first rules Lord President Trailsby informed me of. But being that there are no ties in my possession, Francine keeps a collection of them in her bottom desk drawer.

"Personally, I'm thinking this one." Francine presented a burgundy tie with small, embossed diamonds on it. "What do you think?"

"I'm inclined to agree."

Years ago, before Francine worked here, I'd neglect to buy neckties despite my awareness of protocol. I wouldn't say it derived from disrespecting procedure, but instead from habitual forgetfulness. Also, they'd be wasted in my possession as they'd only be utilized for meetings and nothing more. Nevertheless, my constant lack of neckties would spur Lord President Trailsby's scorn on numerous occasions. He's a strict old bastard with this rule, which is rich, considering how *he* spurns neckties for cravats.

When Francine joined the organization, however, she was quick to recognize this mediocre pattern of mine. So, she began stocking up on ties to keep me from troubling the Lord President any further. It's very kind of her to go out of her way in this regard, as the previous secretary couldn't have been bothered with such acts of decency. She'd dully remark "you forgot a tie again" before hounding me to no end as to why this bloody practice persisted.

As for Francine, she did have a condition when it came to the arrangement of this custom, however. *She* had to be the one who fastened my necktie, claiming it's because she wishes to improve her abilities for future reference. *Right.* Anyhow I, of course, obliged as there's no issue at all with such a condition.

Watching her careful fingers delicately slither the necktie under the collar of my shirt, I will say that Francine's improved significantly. My preferred tie knot is the Balthus, as it's the one knot my father taught back in the day due to his personal penchant for that style. Initially, Francine would accidentally blunder the knot, shaping it more in the vein of a classic knot than the more robust Balthus.

Now, though, her loops are applied with the pristine grace of a seasoned professional.

As the tip of the necktie ventured down the central loop, Francine tightened it with such an abrupt jerk that the resulting jolt caused me to drop my briefcase. The jolt also propelled me even closer to her. Our bodies had been virtually clasped together while she'd applied the tie, so my face and hers now had barely an inch between us. Francine's lips stirred ever so slightly as my hands instinctively latched themselves onto her curvaceous waist.

Unquestionably unprofessional, yes, I am thoroughly aware of this. Even though I know for absolute fact that I'm not the sole person in this profession who flirtatiously dallies with a secretary, there's this menacing nag in my brain demanding that I terminate this pleasure. Francine is a colleague, and I've recently made it a point to never get involved with a colleague. It's a dangerous sin, in my opinion, as it can seriously maim the morals of one's occupation.

Brains and the heart never see eye to eye, though, as my hands drew Francine's body as close to mine as it could possibly be. Her candied watermelon scent, firmly intoxicating, asked me to dance with it. And I dreadfully want to. Francine's lips twitched, causing a reciprocation of mine as they're maddeningly anxious to finally touch. Then, as though life had the knowing jovialness of a cartoon, the phone's intercom buzzed.

"Miss Hitchencamp," spoke the Lord President, his Lancastrian voice clearly irked, "has one hundred and nine arrived? Or are you holding him up?"

Francine pushed a button on the phone's dial pad. "Looks like 'e's just arrived, sir."

"Hmm." I chuckled once Francine had removed her finger from the button. My hands were still firmly latched on her waist. "Do I have your permission to carry on with my business?"

Sighing with a faint smile, Francine nodded as she released her grip on my tie.

The meeting couldn't be held off, despite my desires to have been with Francine just a *touch* longer. As I motioned toward the aluminium door to my supervisor's personal office, my hands slipped away from Francine's waist. Her hands brushed against mine, as her fingers made a vain attempt to latch onto my ring finger and pinkie. It's strange, I must say. Had Trailsby not interrupted that moment between myself and Francine, I'm truly unsure as to what might've occurred. Would I have kissed her? No, I don't think I would've disregarded my respect for the rules I placed unto myself while at work. But I'll be damned if I said it's not something I'll continuously regret.

***

When first starting out at Her Majesty's Dauntless Church of Secret Intelligence, I found Lord President Trailsby's office gave off a strangely dismal impression. Its interior consisted of dark mahogany floors and obsidian black walls with embossed drawings of medieval warriors battling winged demons. Impressively tacky, in a way, though the black-on-black style kind of brought about an aura of vigour to the design. However, Trailsby's original desk might've been the most intriguing component within that previous office décor: a monolithic piece of furniture made of hickory and brilliantly carved to feature grizzly bear pillars. The theme of grizzly bears made its way to the front and centre of the desk's front panel too, in the form of a deep carving of the bear's growling face.

That dreary office had damn all in common with the one I walked inside of. Rich emerald green carpets replaced the mahogany, while the old obsidian wallpaper had been swapped with plain cream paint. And the robust desk that had the effortless ability to overawe most the second it came into view no longer inhabited this office either. Instead, one of a more contemporary variety filled the spot.

Made of teak and sporting a beige granite top, this desk appeared more fit for a business executive than a lord president. Though this updated interior has been in place for over a year now, anyone who witnessed the dramatic swap between designs would tell you they're not accustomed to it.

Closing the aluminium doors behind me, I found Lord President Wallace Trailsby, seventy-one, sitting behind the desk with his fingers clasped. Deputy Lord President Pierce Laughton, fifty-four, stood near him.

"One hundred and nine," Trailsby said.

Judging by the stern manner of Trailsby's wrinkled face, I'd clearly squandered his precious time. Immediately my body morphed into that of a statue, stiff and immovable. When greeting the Lord President, each employee of Her Majesty's Church must stand at attention in a certain pose to convey respect. This pose has all of us position our arms behind our backs with our hands clasped lightly, and our chins raised in the air as though we're a bunch of arrogant arses. It's horribly demeaning, but it's part of the job.

"Lord President," I said, "Deputy Lord President. My sincerest apologies."

Trailsby made an almost inaudible grunt as he extended his hand to one of the chairs before his desk. "Please have a seat."

Despite my severe disdain for the whole *standing at attention* bit, to say I held twelve oceans of respect for Wallace Trailsby would be an understatement. The man has given most of his life to serve in this profession and, no matter how I may personally scorn this job, what he had accomplished throughout his tenure was utterly respectable.

At the age of twenty-eight, Trailsby took Her Majesty's oath to serve as number 70, and he exerted himself in this capacity for seventeen years. Retiring from active duty at forty-five, he took a position within the organization as a strategist. This job involves working with operatives of other intelligence communities, both nationally and internationally, to compile files on various high-profile criminals for the purpose of tracking and capturing. Immersing yourself into this investigative work must be decidedly demanding, as a strategist must have indisputable proof that the subject they're tracing is known to roam the areas listed within the paperwork. In doing so, that enables my colleagues and I to have the necessary data that'll permit us to infiltrate their base.

Any former employee who vows to remain on board with Her Majesty's Church once active duty has ceased holds one coveted goal: becoming lord president. By the age of fifty-nine, Trailsby achieved that treasured position. To attain this position, one is first selected by the current lord president to be their deputy lord president. One is considered for that job by means of possessing a work ethic that is almost impossible to match and for demonstrating a brill knack for whichever field they've chosen to dedicate their lives to. Yes, by remaining a member of Her Majesty's Church, one is dedicating the remainder of their lives to this organization. So much so that the initiation involves slashing your hand with a blade and stamping a bloody handprint onto your original membership forms. Loyalty is routinely tested by the Lord President, both to the organization and to the Queen. If one's loyalty has faltered in any way, I've heard that the punishment is unquestionably more inhumane than the trials potential operatives faced before attaining membership. What more can be said there?

Deputy lord presidents are usually selected once the current lord president is contemplating retirement. Most of the employees believe it to be astoundingly risky to forgo having a deputy for such a lengthy period, as there are no rules in place revolving around the appointment of a lord president if the current one is suddenly unable to do their job. This is because the founders stood by a virtue of the lord president being invincible in their primes, not having to fret about the prospect of a second in command because nothing would ever impair them. Respectable, I suppose, if not highly irresponsible. Last I heard, Trailsby said he'd consider making changes to this rule so to lessen the worry surrounding this issue. We're all thankful, however, that Trailsby's made it this far to have a deputy anyhow.

Pierce Laughton, formerly number 87, made history in the organization by becoming the first Australian to be named deputy lord president. Until now, only men and women who hailed from England managed to reach the top positions within Her Majesty's Church. That says quite a lot, being that our organization has been accepting members from Australia, Canada, the Republic of Ireland, Jamaica, New Zealand, Scotland, and Wales since its inception. It's important, however, to regrettably mention that both countries in the Oceania region rescinded their allegiance to our organization upon the conclusions of their most recent elections. So, with people from his homeland now barred from joining our ranks, Pierce wears the honour of deputy lord president with spirited bravadoes and a determination to prove himself.

The son of a judge and a homemaker, Pierce was raised in a household like mine in that it was deluged with chatter of law and politics. While my family was able to supress such conversations, if need be, Pierce's father was a judicial zealot. The man would badger his family with his personal beliefs, determined to ensure they'd agree no matter the issue. He'd dominate conversation at the dinner table, restating his rigid views on honour and justice to the exasperation of Pierce and the others.

Though his father was adamant on his eldest child ascending the judicial ladder in his tenacious footsteps, that was far from what Pierce coveted. By thirteen, he'd already established his professional ambitions: to be an architect. He chalked up these aspirations to an immeasurable fascination for cathedrals. How they could distil such dramatic majesty while being simultaneously intimidating due to their titanic physiques. Pierce's father, begrudgingly, yielded to his son's goals by allowing him to study architecture in place of law.

Pierce deems his architectural era as bursting with unexploited vision. Receiving his architect's licence at the age of twenty-five, he lacked the general experience to even be considered for cathedral designs. It would take several decades to attain adequate expertise, so he instead had to settle on planning mundane residential dwellings. Employed by a housing construction company in Brisbane, Pierce swiftly discovered that the droning banality of sketching the same windows, walls, and doors for two hundred plus cookie-cutter town homes was not how he'd envisioned his dream to play out. To further complicate matters, most of his imaginative concepts, such as the addition of skylights to roofs, were outright rejected in favour of customary designs.

His ambitions decisively eradicated by unstimulating endeavours and undeviating superiors, Pierce moved on from the once enthralling world of architecture after two years. He left his job a jaded bloke, disillusioned by what he referred to as a *hapless debacle.* So, faced with the prospect of a glum but fresh start, Pierce instead did what many overwrought, knackered individuals do. He, much like myself, chose to enlist in the military in lieu of ambling about crumbled dreams.

Although Pierce's recruit training in the Australian Army, of course, led him to the frosty embrace of Her Majesty's Church, it was far from his sole life-altering trial during that chapter. On his sixtieth day at the training establishment in New South Wales, Pierce's parents notified him that his wife of four years, Gail, had gone into labour. Permitted to take a momentary leave of absence, he was personally flown back to Brisbane so to be with her for the birth of their triplet daughters.

He's told me, in confidence, that he will be forever grateful for that flight. Not only because it led him straight to the three girls, now women, who made him a father. But, also, because it was so brief in length that it ushered him into the hospital room just as Gail drew her last breath. He was able to cradle his wife and tell her what an exceptional job she'd done with the births before he had to watch the rainbow leave her eyes, the doctors voices rumbling in the background about post-partem bleeding while initiating CPR. Pierce gained so much, and lost so bloody much, because of that flight. He returned to New South Wales a new man. One might ask why he elected to resume his training, and the answer is quite simple: it diverted him from the unspeakable grief that would've otherwise scuppered him.

For as much as Pierce believes that he owes everything to Her Majesty's Church for all its gifted him, his most substantial regret is enlisting in the Australian Army and leaving Gail behind. He aimed to afford them stability, even though it required him to be swept away by the confines of recruit training. Pierce has since likened it to a form of abandonment, as it forbade him from spending adequate nights being a doting husband to a pregnant wife. And, though he's thankful that both sets of their parents bore the responsibility of raising the triplets, enlisting meant he couldn't be the ideal father as the girls aged.

Today, Pierce is a rather amiable fellow who's prone to warmer exchanges in comparison to the grimmer Trailsby. He's also one of those blokes who won't refrain from stating exactly what's running through his bonce, though he'll often speak before his thoughts have uncluttered. That's gotten him reprimanded quite a bit, which surely has exasperated Trailsby. One of the key instances of this came about two years ago, upon the last Australian federal election. Maxwell Croxnur, the then-incumbent prime minister who Pierce strongly admired, lost in a landslide to former car salesman turned politician Reid Maucke. We were all in a meeting when Pierce learned of the results and he, ever so bluntly, uttered in his broad as a wall accent "how the fuck is the second coming of a Nazi supposed to lead Australia?"

Despite that incident, the two of us get on well partly because, once he retired, it happened to be I who assumed his membership slot. This led to Pierce becoming somewhat of a mentor to me, keeping a vigilant eye on my handling of tasks and providing key advice for the riskier assignments that have come around. As the ratio of former operatives continuing within the organization is in the minority, I'm quite thankful to have had Pierce as a personal counsellor.

"Welcome, one hundred and nine," Pierce said, taking a seat next to me. "Your late arrival is of no issue."

6

Within most organizations, I could say with certainty that it's quite easy to deduce the atmosphere of a meeting the instance you've taken your seat. It doesn't even matter if you're a sub-zero level employee or the head of the board. The demeanour of those surrounding you, whether they're colleagues or superiors, will inform you of either impending jubilation or utter dread. Well before joining Her Majesty's Church, I stumbled about as a history teacher at Ed Endingwell Junior High in Augusta for almost ten years. The administrators at Endingwell seemed to radiate joyous sunshine when they welcomed me into their *nurturing* arms. Then they began summoning me for innumerable meetings, where their vacant stares would let me know that I must've kicked someone's gerbil *again*. Failure to wait at my door for students to arrive, taking the kids to the playground after a strenuous test. Even teaching with the lights off even though it was for the sake of a child whose eyes were severely sensitive to the brilliance of the ceiling lights. Could I have been a better educator? Without a shadow of a doubt. But to be dragged to meetings for these trivial matters? Ridiculous. I believe the administrators retained my shackled soul because my students were decently educated. However, it wouldn't be shocking if it were also because they were bloody sadists who delighted in picking their employees apart like vultures.

At Her Majesty's Church, however, most of us are privy to the normal flow of a meeting. Lord President Trailsby will be flat yet forceful as he's speaking, his words almost verbatim from a script though undoubtedly serious about the topics at hand. Pierce is keener to lessen the gravity of the issues by the means of wisecracks, usually at Trailsby's expense. The wisecracks are never disrespectful, but oftentimes they pertain to an open secret around the organization. One that Trailsby has honestly tried his damndest to conceal. Sure enough, Pierce grabbed one of the three framed photographs sitting on Trailsby's desk.

"You haven't seen this one yet, have you?" Pierce asked.

I only recalled the other photos that were still residing on the desk. One had been there since I'd started: a portrait of Trailsby with his only child, Charles. They stood proudly at Charles' college graduation in the photo, embracing each other with a movement evidenced only in the graduation cap's tassel. Trailsby had every reason to be proud of his son it seems. However, it must sting to look at him and see the face of his second wife, Rosalind, staring back. The boy does share most of his features with his mother, whose picture I'd seen once. Pierce once told me that photographs of Rosalind are locked away in a file cabinet underneath the desk, along with ones of wife number three and wife number four. But now, understandably, Charles was the sole family member on display.

The other portrait is of Trailsby with our current prime minister, Maud Harbold. This one found its home here shortly after her election in 1979, which also happened to be a year I spent training with Minister Esprine. The image featured the two of them at some sort of gala, brilliantly dressed in formal attire. However, Trailsby has staunchly refused to go into detail about the circumstances surrounding the picture.

Pierce handed me the photograph he had. "Make sure you read the note too."

"Mister Laughton," Trailsby said, his face hardening.

This image happened to be the official portrait of Prime Minister Harbold, following her re-election two years ago. It's true that if you take one glance into her steel blue eyes, you can definitively see why Harbold exudes command. She's confident and striking. Endlessly picture ready too, between her neatly brushed golden brown hair that falls to the beginning of her shoulders and her winning smile complete with pearly teeth on display.

Cursive lettering adorned the top right corner of this portrait, the contents of which immediately caused the slightest smile to crawl about my face. Usually, you must take all the clues that make up the open secret that sails around HQ with a pinch of salt. But this message just makes our theories that much more apparent.

Can't wait for next time

Love always,
Maudlyn

"I actually woke up this morning to a note with these exact words," I said.

This revelation caused Pierce to summon a devious grin, like that of a madcap tabby. Trailsby, however, appeared to be in no mood for amusements. Nothing out of the ordinary there. He rose from his chair, slowly with a reaper-like wrath, and eyed us sharply.

"Enough," Trailsby said, his sole word spoken calmly but swathed with severity like barbed wire around a bat.

Lord President Trailsby is not one to raise his voice and yell to rouse up decorum. His approach is firm yet composed, and though he's mildly irked he never grows incensed by this kind of behaviour. However, he has a strong aversion to humour during these serious meetings. And if it pertains to his primrose the Prime Minister, he's even less entertained. It's understandable, and I'm normally respectful of such when interacting with Trailsby one on one. But, at the same time, I'm highly appreciative of the humour Pierce invokes during these meetings because rarely does it come about elsewhere while at HQ. And, while on assignment, I'm horribly moody and stuck in my rabid thoughts so often that instances like these bring a modicum of kick to my otherwise dreary days.

Trailsby returned to his seat and went on to say, "it's unwise of you to amplify such behaviour, Mister Laughton, especially when one hundred and nine is the most, dare I say, sensible of our members."

Sensible? It's a horrendous challenge trying to hold in even the most meagre chuckle at such a remark. If Trailsby honestly believes *I'm* the most sensible member of our organization then that's utterly pitiful. While the others can be rather jovially loony, it's clear as ice that their sanity is at the very least more intact than mine ever has been. There's not much basis behind that claim aside from personally knowing damn well just how much rot dwells deep in my skull, but it's adequate for me to stand by it.

"It is not a secret that you wish you get on with this meeting, one hundred and nine," Trailsby said. "Let's discuss the matter at hand, shall we?"

Atop Trailsby's desk sat two manila folders with both my identification number and the word *confidential* stamped on them. He handed them to me, his other hand peevishly reaching out for the portrait of the Prime Minister. We swapped items and I opened the first envelope to find it contained the standard five pages of authorised paperwork, as well as a passport booklet.

"You'll be going to the United States for this assignment, one hundred and nine," Trailsby said. "Specifically, to Howslip Township, New Jersey."

"It's been some time since I've rummaged about the New England area," I said, listening to Trailsby while scanning the papers.

"Your target is Abraham Scobretti. We have thoroughly investigated him for the past year and a half and, with the great help of the CIA, have concluded that he is the head of an illegal wildlife trade operation."

"Any specific type of wildlife?"

"Exotic sea animals."

The first page encompassed all of Abraham Scobretti's personal information, with a decent sized black and white image of the man in top right corner. Although the photo derived from his driver's licence, as is the common pattern with the image included on this page, Scobretti's features bore malice. His bleak eyes sported bags under them, and the strident manner of their locking with the camera caused them to burn into mine. Then there's the modest scowl dragged on his stubbled face. Is he that much of a bloody thorn or does he just relentlessly loathe getting his licence renewed?

Anyhow, I took careful notice of Scobretti's most prominent feature: a crooked nose that points to his left. Whenever there's a defining characteristic on my target, I'll sear that image into my brain with such vicious force that it never abandons me. This cautious study avoids any humiliating occurrences. Imagine how bloody dreadful it'd be to corner the wrong person?

As we moved on to the next page, Pierce took over from Trailsby as per the typical sequence during these meetings. I believe it's to prepare the Deputy Lord President for future briefings once they hold the top job, but the abrupt shift between the two as they're providing me with information is nothing short of clunky.

"While Scobretti has a small group of minions, they're not of much concern and are easy to pick out while scoping out his hideouts. All are men in their thirties and forties, usually armed with pistols. From everything we've gathered, they're not trained in any forms of hand-to-hand combat, nor are they particularly skilled with their weapons."

"Are they planted outside his base?" I asked.

"No," Pierce said, "they're always indoors. From what we know, Scobretti employs these men in case *competitors* attempt to infiltrate his base."

"Seems as though he's not particularly worried about the law."

"That's what our contacts have told us. Now, although his minions are of little worry, you must be wary of his two closest associates: his brother, Sergio Scobretti, and Rocco Abruzzoli.

The page containing Sergio's and Abruzzoli's write ups had a similar structure to Abraham's. However, everything had been condensed to take up separate halves of the paper. Sergio Scobretti's information comprised the top half. At twenty-seven, he's eight years younger than Abraham and appeared nowhere near as foreboding as his brother. Instead, his picture held a calm, if not exceedingly confident, demeanour that I attributed to his lopsided smile.

One aspect of this job that you must get used to is facing off with the *muscle* of a faction. Don't let anyone try jumping your jester because there is *always* one. In this case, it's Rocco Abruzzoli. Oftentimes you can tell by their picture, which has the six-foot three and stone jawed Abruzzoli tilting his head to his right while sporting a face devoid of any emotion. There's the off chance that I'm mistaken here, but I'm willing to guarantee my accuracy.

"Be aware. Sergio Scobretti is always armed with a Beretta Eighty-Four. Just because he appears harmless *doesn't* mean you can try the intimidation tactic," Pierce said. "As for Abruzzoli, he is also a member of the Scobretti family, but not by blood. He's their brother-in-law. Also, with regard to Abruzzoli, it's crucial that you know he's—"

"Armed with a shotgun, correct? The top *henchman* always carries some sort of shotgun," I said.

Pierce shook his head as he said, "no, no, no, that's not quite what I was intending to say."

"My apologies."

Pierce told me that it was all right and proceeded to continue with what he was trying to explain. As he'd already told me that Abruzzoli was a brother-in-law to these scumbags, I figured Pierce would tell me more about this bloke's personal life. Being that he's a target of mine, and not even the grail of the assignment, whatever Pierce said went in one ear and skipped off a cliff. To be moderately successful this profession, you must dehumanize your targets. For me, it's a relatively uncomplicated demand. The reprehensible nature of their offences is enough to induce a bitterness within me that causes me to scorn them. On top of that, the circumstances surrounding my entrance into Her Majesty's Church dehumanized *me* for such an extensive period. It's to the point that I doubt my familiarity with myself will ever manage to surpass seventy-five percent. And then there's the voices who have made a valiant effort to continue that distress by routinely mocking my mental health and infatuation with vices. It's nothing out of the ordinary.

"Understood?" Pierce asked.

"Yes," I responded in a mostly polite yet somewhat nonchalant tone.

The third page listed names of all the bases as well as important addresses that were essential to the assignment. This page fluctuates the most, as it all depends on how mobile a target might be. Long ago there was a target who sprung around eight different places as he apparently had an inkling that the law was following him. Normally, however, this page lists between two to four addresses, and I'll typically utilize any extra space for note taking. I found there to be four addresses listed on this page, which Trailsby began to explain.

"Abraham Scobretti's main base is a fishing tackle shop called Hooking Up."

What a horribly unfortunate yet hysterical name. It's clever, not because of it actually being a first-rate pun, but because it's inconspicuous. The average person who'd explore the shop absolutely would not have any reason to believe such a shabby individual ran a business with such a *youthful, cheery* name. Now, a more predictable and reticent name would've been Fish Depot. Scobretti, however, *must* recognize the importance of running his operations under a jovial guise.

Trailsby continued to say, "he is there every Tuesday through Sunday between ten o'clock in the morning and six o'clock in the evening. These hours are listed in your address log, correct?"

"Correct," I said.

"Good. Now, Sergio Scobretti tends to meet clients at the Nesmith Docks, where he completes all his illicit transactions. Abruzzoli has been with him during each dealing. When the CIA tracked the two here a few times, they always arrived at eleven o'clock in the morning. That hour is listed in your address log, correct?"

"Correct."

"The third address is the most vital, one hundred and nine. It is for Sepia Harvest, a notable ballroom in the area. We've confirmed that an invite-only gala hosted by the Grand Howslip Aquarium is taking place there tonight between seven and eleven o'clock. The Scobretti brothers and Abruzzoli are expected to attend as they're friendly with some of the people who are hosting the event. You will be attending this gala too, so that you can scrounge for details. If the brothers pull off any deals, you must be aware of such to continue tracking them. Is that understood?"

"Not quite."

Trailsby reclined in his seat a tad while shifting his jaw. "Might I ask why that is?"

"I don't attend galas, nor do I engage in the extensive monitoring of my targets. That's already been accomplished by Her

Majesty's Church and the CIA. With all due respect, sir, this isn't how I go about my assignments, and you know that."

"I do know that, one hundred and nine," Trailsby said. He sighed, clasped his fingers together and leaned in close to me. "This assignment is out of the ordinary for you, but with reason. While Abraham Scobretti is known to take part in these illegal endeavours, we don't know how he's able to acquire these animals."

"And you believe there's the possibility of another person's involvement in these dealings? From this aquarium no less?"

"It's unconfirmed, but yes it's highly possible. See, this gala is a crucial puzzle piece because last year, after the same event, our personnel discovered a spike in illegal sea animal trade."

"Scobretti runs a fishing shop," Pierce said, pointing to the shop's address on the paper. "Some ordinary fishing shop bloke wouldn't be able to attend a gala like this unless they were well acquainted with someone from within. Someone who can help them organize deals."

"If I figure out who this fourth person is, *if* there is a fourth, then I have permission to continue the assignment how I see fit?" I asked.

"Absolutely," Trailsby said.

How I revel in hearing such confirmation from my superiors. Normally my assignments are rather straightforward, and the execution is almost always effortless. There's no continued pursuits or asinine functions to attend. Instead, my usual routine while on the job is just about as utterly plain as my daily life is. Well, unless I'm bathing in a river of dalliances that day. The work routine goes as follows: retrieving my orders, flying to whichever country I'm required to, confirming addresses, maybe enjoying a nice dinner somewhere, and then apprehending the target. On average it takes two days, maybe three. So, while this ordeal won't be as undemanding as I'm used to, I'll just have to deal with it.

Trailsby continued to say, "the final address on your paper belongs to a warehouse that has been rented out to Sergio Scobretti for about four years. While we have evidence that Abraham Scobretti will have some smaller sea animals transported to his fishing shop, they are usually brought to this warehouse. Scobretti will house them here until they are purchased and sent off."

It can be rather unnerving that, with all the evidence presented before me, Her Majesty's Church and the CIA couldn't simply do a pinch and apprehend these arses. A multitude of animals could then meet a less unfortunate end. But that's not how these situations tend to play out. Not only must the evidence supporting these assignments be as precise as possible, but none of the organizations involved in these ordeals tend to revere prison sentences over other means.

"This warehouse also happens to be where Scobretti's minions are situated, so be very careful once you've made it this far," Trailsby said.

"Understood," I said.

The fourth page in the folder included all my false identification paperwork. Upon becoming an operative of Her Majesty's Church, you're given five fake names chosen at random by the lord president. You're strictly not allowed to change any of them, and a name is only retired if dire circumstances plague you while operating under that guise. Having these names is a matter of safety, though I honestly loathe all the ones that've been afforded to me. For this assignment, I'll be Basil Courtauld. If I had to be quite honest, this might be my favourite of the pseudonyms.

Opening the passport, a driver licence fell into my lap. It's made especially for this mission, as it features the Basil Courtauld name as well as other assorted information printed pristinely on a New Jersey licence. Of considerable importance to both pieces of identification was the picture. My colleagues and I are required to have a new picture taken every year, not only for these purposes but also to update the personal files Her Majesty's Church possesses of their personnel. My disinterested picture, which had been taken earlier this year, doesn't look much more affable than Abraham's.

Photographs of the bases taken by the intelligence officers fill the other manilla folder. These I can examine while on my flight to New Jersey. And, as for the fifth page in the first folder, it's irrelevant. Enough said. My colleagues utilize the material on this page every assignment, whereas I temporarily did only to discover it was dreadfully impractical. Trailsby and Pierce have come to recognize my disdain for page five, so we'll skip over it.

As it appeared the meeting had concluded, I said, "thank you, gentleman," while rising from my chair, putting the papers and other documents back into the folder.

"Wait just a minute," Trailsby said as he pointed at the folders in my hands. "You think you're sly, one hundred and nine, trying to bypass discussions pertaining to the contact page. Now I know how adverse you are to working with CIA contacts, not to mention contacts from all over the world. However, you must promise me that you'll work with the contact listed for this assignment. You're going to need assistance; I can assure you of that."

"And to be quite honest, from here on out you're going to have to utilize your contacts more often, one hundred and nine," Pierce said. "Now is probably the right time to inform you of the boatload of grievances we've been receiving from the CIA. All of it relates to your leaving their people high and dry recently."

All of it? All their grievances have to do with me? Surely, a good lot of my colleagues have done their fair share in rousing the ire of the CIA, certainly piles more than I have. Needless to say, the sheer fact that I'm the sole source of their misery is something that raids at my heart with joy. It's not on me that I'm able to fulfil the obligations of these assignments alone. Accomplishing assignments calls for means of celebration, as we do here in Her Majesty's Church, instead of mourning like the CIA apparently does. However, while I see no reason whatsoever to work with some incompetent contact, maybe in this case it would be beneficial. For what reason I'm not quite sure but still. Besides, not once have both Trailsby and Pierce so adamantly requested this of me so perhaps this is the appropriate option. Mercy do I loathe it, but it's what must be done.

"That's fair. I'll do as you both ask," I said.

"Thank you," Trailsby said.

"We wish you well on this assignment, one hundred and nine," Pierce said. "We'll be in touch."

Shaking hands with both men, this signified the *official* conclusion of our meeting. I leisurely left Trailsby's office, closing the doors behind me out of both decency and a twinge of roguishness. After all, I'm away from my superiors and back with Francine again. She was sitting at her desk and searching for who knows what in one of her drawers, but the sound of the doors shutting promptly caused her to eye me with a smile.

"Don't you sneak away without saying goodbye," she said.

"Now what good would that do me?"

Upon strolling toward Francine, she took my hand and caressed it soothingly before placing it on her soft as silk cheek.

"Whenever you're on an assignment I worry. Isn't that daft? We barely know each other, Marky. Everything I know about you comes from your personal files and that's because I'm required to memorize everything in those documents. And yet I can't stomach seeing you leave because I'll just be wondering if it's the last time I'll see you. It's bloody daft."

Mercy on rye. I…wasn't expecting Francine to start spilling her heart all over me like this. With her words, however, it is interesting to note the lack of actual woe in her voice. It's more along the lines of confusion over our relationship, which is reasonable. I don't bloody know what we have aside from an office flirtation. I respect Francine as much as I do anyone else who works for Her Majesty's Church. Her work ethic and steadfast allegiance to this organization is lightyears more than anyone who's not either the Lord President or DLP. And yet I don't know what else to consider her as aside from being Trailsby's personal secretary. She's not a friend, nor a romantic partner. And deeming her an object of lust is downright disrespectful.

Does Francine frolic about in my daydreams when I'm not on active duty? Certainly, but I can also undoubtfully say it's in the same vein as June or any other escort I've had the pleasure of spending time with. Darla, my ex-wife, will be there every now and then too. If my head isn't morphing into paste from the usual ominous affairs I deal with, various women will just materialise and—

Go on and kiss her, Mark. You both clearly desire one another.

The thudding pressure of Edith's words assembled in my head. Oh joy. If my fix isn't satisfied soon, she'll throw a fit. But Edith, surely, realizes this twisted plot of hers. She's aware that my kissing Francine would make for a grave error, regardless of how muddled my fervour for her is. But no, it will not happen. The wishes of a rogue cannot, in this case, persuade me to enter treacherous territory. With most any other woman, Edith has control of my untamed libido. But here, I must dispel the urge…unless it's too challenging. Is it? Mercy I loathe my being with such an unyielding fury.

Aware that it's crucial to move along with my matters before my sacred oath with regards to colleagues is irreversibly broken, I hastily weaved a plan. Keeping my hand within Francine's grasp, I kneeled before her. I let my folders slip of my grasp and they landed gracefully on the floor beside us. This freed my other hand from obligation, and so I placed it on her opposite cheek, cupping her perfect, sweet face as gently as it deserved.

"It's not daft, Francine. We'll talk about all of this when I return. And I promise you that I *will* return."

Francine frowned and said damn all in return, so I found myself unable to tell if she believed any of my words. Personally, as much as it pains me to realize it, the likelihood of my return is far greater than my discussing these emotions with her. And even if we did continue these chats, the logical answer Francine deserves if that we just cannot be together. We've got zilch in common. She's idealistic and sincere whereas I'm anguished and aloof. Francine Hitchencamp is a woman who deserves to be with someone who can offer her all the unrevealed planets out in the depths of the galaxy. That's not me. She and her blissful world view would all but wither away if she were to irresponsibly splash out her love on a damaged nutter.

But…damn it…at the same time I admit, selfishly, that our flirtatious banter satisfies a raunchy craving. It leaves me anxious for our subsequent engagements, and the mutual arousal that circulates in our blood every moment our mouths itch to touch. Self-centred arse I am. Perhaps all her worries will dwindle until the next time we're together.

The way Francine proceeded to gently grip each of my fingertips did alleviate some of the tension that attempted to make itself at home in this room. In moments like these, her age makes itself more apparent in my eyes. She's playful though still sombre about her sentiments. Her toying about like this was probably an attempt at reeling in what she truly wished to express.

With regret, however, this interaction had to cease so that the assignment may commence. There's no telling whether Trailsby would lean his head out his door and catch me chatting about with his secretary while on the clock. He'd be utterly displeased at such behaviour, even if I tried to explain that comforting Francine was equally as important as work. It was a struggle, surely, as an invisible jostle urged me to continue consoling Francine but, alas, there was no more time for that. There was an undertaking, however, that I needed to complete before entering the lifts, so maybe that would ease her a tad.

"Francine, would you be so good as to do me a favour before I leave?" I asked.

"Anything."

"Place the rubbish bin on your desk for me."

Francine must sincerely delight in me and my company because she immediately brought the bin onto the desk without hesitation. Not a curious eyebrow, not a perplexed expression, none of that. Just a genuine willingness to put up with my dreadful antics.

Returning to my feet, I retrieved the folders from the floor and sifted through the one containing paperwork. Snatching the contact's page, a beautiful scene emerged that saw the paper morph into a crumpled makeshift ball. At no point did I waste a single second to memorize this person's name or face. It wasn't necessary. Turning toward the lifts, I attempted to revisit to my youth by tossing the paper ball into the bin without looking.

"Was it a success?" I asked upon hearing the ball land.

"No," Francine said with the slightest giggle, "it hit the Lord President's door."

One would think I'd be relieved Trailsby wasn't on his way out of his office when I threw the paper ball, but he'd merely give a stern demand that I proceed to where I must go. That's one of the perks that comes with staying on his good side. Some of my colleagues try mightily to ruffle his feathers, so their tarrying about might cause them to be chased out of the building. Even though I made it an effort to continue about my way to escape Trailsby's scorn, I'm just trying to be respectful of protocol.

Right, what a lie that must sound like when I just went about and disobeyed orders regarding the contact. No, I'm respectful of all protocol this organization implements unless it deals with a contact. In my opinion, nothing decent spurs about when working with a contact, at least not in how I manage my assignments. Contacts dramatically decelerate the entire assignment because they want to waste time with all of that tracking rot Trailsby and Pierce went on about. If I must identify this mystery third associate of Abraham Scobretti, I'll do it alone.

"Do not let the Lord President find that paper. He's not to know I discarded it," I said.

"Your secret's safe with me," Francine said.

Watching as her striking face restored a smile, we exchanged waves as I grabbed my nearly forgotten briefcase and finally continued to the lifts. As satisfyingly glorious a sight Francine Hitchencamp might be, all aspects of leisure had to terminate for the time being. From here on out, until this undertaking has been officially accomplished, several vital personal rules must be obeyed. Well…almost all as my fix was revelling in the havoc it was causing within my head. Medicine wouldn't protect me from this headache that's billowing, though food might assist a tad. In due time. Just have to finalize all matters at HQ before flying to New Jersey. Then, if time decides to take some money and politely turn its back away for half an hour, we'll be golden.

7

I've never been too fond of the wallpaper that consumed the third floor. Unlike the antiquated but sophisticated style that the lobby commands, these walls are an ecstatic pale green with blue, pink, and golden watercolour flower petals. Even the plain paintjobs in both Trailsby's office and Francine's workspace have more of a purpose to exist within the confines of this building. There's even an argument for Trailsby's original warrior wallpaper being superior to these exceedingly cheery designs, though that'll no doubt cause tense disagreements between myself some of my colleagues. Everyone at Her Majesty's Church seems to have their own extraordinarily intense stances concerning just about every facet of the building. Some love this watercolour wallpaper, for example, and I think they're bloody ridiculous for it.

This clearly outdated wallpaper had tainted the third floor since before I became a member, and it did everything possible to showcase such an unfortunate feature. There were areas where the wallpaper was beginning to show its age by means of chipping and sections where it's come undone, though a touch-up is all but futile. Rumours echoed by various colleagues claimed that this nauseating print was obsolete now and impossible to find. Not remotely hard to believe.

Despite all the displeasure that this wallpaper brought me, I, unfortunately, had no authority to request a change in design. All interior and exterior revamps are implemented solely by the Lord

President, and he has a firm adoration for these unfashionable patterns. Why is that? Well, I have Pierce to thank for giving me all the sensational details.

Several years ago, Prime Minister Harbold toured the building with Trailsby as per proper practice for a new PM. This is for them to understand the purpose of our organization, and how vastly it differs compared to MI6. Anyhow, the Prime Minister apparently held a fondness for these watercolours and told Trailsby of how they brought some sort of life into this otherwise dreary building. Now Trailsby is completely averse to changing up these dreadful walls, but at the very least I'm *somewhat* hopeful he'll patch them up.

This hallway also includes a row of seven doors to my left and eight on the right. These doors lead to the private offices that are allocated to me and my colleagues. Our respective ID numbers are engraved on black granite plaques that reside on the otherwise dull cream doors. Mine is the third on the side of seven, nearer to the lifts.

Having a private office is a nice perk, sure, but it's also a touch ludicrous because I hardly ever utilize the space. To be quite honest none of us operatives really do. My colleagues tend to inhabit theirs a touch more, but that's because they'll chat with contacts over the implementation of plans or do a bag of research before embarking on their assignment. I, on the other hand, merely acquire whatever is needed at HQ and embark on my obligations.

The other operatives must all either be on an assignment or basking in the several privileges their free time allows them. When they're in this building, they roam around like a pack of harmlessly eccentric fraternity and sorority siblings. Their boisterous voices reverberate throughout a floor, full of guffaws and jokes a plenty. Most of them are stirred up by pouches of excess adrenaline, rarely decreasing their vigour even in the face of grimness. They're a wacky bunch, but their presence is missed.

Around October, for whatever reason, there's a three-week period where a good deal of us operatives are free to convene and dine together. Those present at these dinners are the colleagues I'm closest to, including my closest lads Bart O'Cloigeann and Oswald Ospreington, which makes these occasions especially pleasant. We tend to gather in the late afternoon, dining, chatting, and cracking wise well into the night until the establishment closes. Normally when I talk about my goings, I lie and act as though I'm not dealing with mental torture and mad voices daily. However, if the conversation becomes a tad raunchy, I'm not shy in recounting my many rendezvous with escorts.

Everyone is incredibly candid with their moments of leisure. The ones living the single life, like Bart, natter on about their numerous vacations and how heavily they'll indulge in their vices. They basically do just about everything that's along the lines of what a stereotypical English intelligence operative would. Those who are in relationships, like Oswald, or married are vastly more modest in their behaviours. However, they'll still take full advantage of the posh privileges this job affords, such as using the services of private chefs.

When the topic of conversations inevitably turns to our most recent assignments, it's consistently astounding to hear the others go on about their exploits. How someone as zany as Bart will literally save the world from some demented radical while guzzling bottles of exorbitant champagne. It's impressive, though also nonsensical how humble they are in recounting these tales. Well, almost everyone is humble in this regard. But still, they each wear these buoyant smiles while reliving their exploits, especially when they explain how they apprehended their rogues. Then they go on to describe the enormous satisfaction they experienced upon completing their job. Each of their smiles are genuine, and I know they are because these glistering orbs sprinkle along their irises as they're talking. How greatly I yearn to share those experiences.

Sure, I'll be the first to admit how much I envy my colleagues. It's not this destructive envy, instead more of a craving to comprehend that sort of pride in my own work. Such is non-existent for me because my assignments are rather unique compared to theirs. Don't get me wrong, it's sort of an honour to serve Her Majesty's Church in a manner unlike my colleagues, but the only emotions I haul home from my work are hatred and distress. I'll never admit this to anyone, however, because there's this aching piece of me that requires this position to keep myself whole. Revealing this to a soul would spell disaster and it's not worth all the commotion.

***

Directly at the end of the hall is a triple-panel dark oak door. This door leads to an office too, but it has damn all in common with all the others. I took my ID and scanned it over a black square panel that sits where a handle should be. It beeped before the locks slowly twisted themselves open, the concurrent sound giving the synthetic impression of a howling wolf. Upon entering, I'm greeted by walls featuring red and black paint, their mixture and design reminiscent of lava. But, more significantly, there are vases containing various bouquets of flowers, all of them purple hydrangeas, encompassing the entire room on shelves.

Javis Macaulb, fifty-one, stood behind his desk with another bouquet filled vase in his hands. He set it on the sole empty shelf, which still had room for a few more. While it may seem as though I'm intruding on his recreation time, that's not the case. In fact, he's been expecting me.

"More hydrangeas?" I asked. "At this point you're going to have to start placing them on the floor."

"Yes, that might have to do," Javis said, glancing over his shoulder with a full toothed smile. "I do wish I had more space."

"More space? Earlier this year you had three shelves of flowers. Now you've transformed into a bloody florist."

"Like I told you before, one hundred and nine, Gwendoline loves hydrangeas. It's my way of spiritually having my heart with me until it's time to go home."

Javis placed his hand toward the faux leather orange chair settled in front of his desk. I took my seat, wary of the potential imminent weariness due to the sheer comfortability this chair wielded. The way your body slowly sinks into its marshmallow-like cushions is swift, and the immense cosiness that derives from your body practically becoming one with the chair is truly potent. To combat the comfort enough to keep myself aware, I retrieved a pen from a mug on Javis' desk and continually tapped it on my thigh.

"You're the one person who always tries to fight off the power of these cushions," Javis said, taking a seat and leaning back as much as he could.

"Of course, I do. Considering how you splash drinks on those who drift into a slumber, I have good reason."

"My superiors demanded full attention no matter the occasion, even if their way of getting it was disrespectful. I do what they did to me, but only because it worked so well." Javis said while chuckling. He then eyed the glass of water on his desk, swimming through his thoughts.

Born in Jamaica, Javis and his parents immigrated to England by the time he turned four. He's expressed to me that his interest in the military was stoked by his father's scrapbook of battleship photographs. While his father, a baler, had bought the antiquated book out of mild curiosity, it was Javis who'd spend hours studying and memorizing the various details of each battleship. The book was ultimately passed on to him, who's told me that it now resides in his home library.

Javis' passage into the skeletal clutches of Her Majesty's Church, let alone the military itself, wasn't an overnight occurrence. After completing secondary school, he was employed as a night watchman by the Sheffield-based Pointshure Security Services. He's since admitted that the position was relatively mundane, but that Pointshure was known to hire almost anyone. As a teenager, it was his best bet if he wished to land a job directly out of school. When he left Pointshure after a couple years, he continued in the line of service by joining the then-called Sheffield City Police.

It wasn't until the age of thirty-four that he enlisted in the Royal Navy. Despite my reverence for protocol, I've tried my damndest to convince him to disclose at least one detail from his time with the Royal Navy. He is one of the few employees whom I've met here that stemmed from those ranks instead of the Royal Special Forces Unit. And although he's disclosed why he enlisted, saying that "it was bound to happen eventually," there's a mystique revolving around his years of service. The bloke is so composed and amiable, compared to how others allegedly are. Many of my colleagues have been in contact with servicepeople currently enlisted in the Royal Navy, and the stories they've divulged are quite raucous. However, perhaps it depends on the era of service. Nevertheless, Javis refuses to violate protocol, which must be respected.

I am aware, however, of how he ascended to his current position with Her Majesty's Church. His tenure in the Royal Navy lasted around six years before he, like the field operatives, was scouted by Minister Esprine. The then-head of the Weapons Department was preparing for retirement and, as that role is directly underneath the Ministry of Combat's purview, Minister Esprine had to locate a successor.

Once the combat minister and assets minister have settled on necessary artillery and other assorted equipment, it's stored in the office of the whoever heads the Weapons Department. Serving in that role means you're the one who's in charge of supplying this paraphernalia for anyone who's employed by Her Majesty's Church. It doesn't matter if they work in my field or if they're low-level staff, this department distributes *everything* to all of us. Also, the head of the Weapons Department has the authority to build bespoke arms and gadgets. While this craft isn't mandatory, it's an art that has been forwarded to each successive head since the organization's founding.

Laurence Quinturry was the head of the department before Javis. He was a Scotsman who, at the time, had just turned seventy-five and chatter of retirement loomed over him with each passing day. Though I'd never met the man, by all accounts he was impatient and overworked, the latter because he held an obsession over the job. This obsession led to his refusing to cede his position to a successor, which vexed Minister Esprine. Though Laurence apparently recognized the imminence of his retirement, he was displeased that his supervisor would select *his* successor. Even though that was simply protocol, he didn't believe his replacement would hold a beetle to his tenure.

Being that most existing applications reside in the classified documents of the British Armed Forces, why Javis managed to secure the nomination of weapons head over his peers remains a mystery. Having known him since my induction into the organization, I'd personally assume his unruffled demeanour aided him significantly. The impression he gives off is the extreme opposite of Laurence's crotchety air. And yes, though Javis does tend to splash drinks in the faces of those who doze off, it's done in a light-hearted fashion without an ounce of maliciousness.

When Minister Esprine introduced Javis to Laurence, their encounter was rather off-putting and exasperating. He fondly recalls his soon to be predecessor refusing to make eye contact with him and responding to remarks and questions with incoherent grunts. So Javis, understandably wrung by displeasure, asked the old bloke why he was expressing such hostilities. The bitter man, without hesitation, shouted "because you're taking away me livelihood, ya sumph!"

The rigorous trials Javis endured under Laurence's eyes aren't a secret to anyone here. For exactly one year, just like a field operative, he underwent extensive training so to be moulded into the model employee. Firstly, he had to memorize the names and designs of the *entire* arsenal. Then he had to become adept at constructing and disassembling each of the arms. Finally, he discovered how to equip everything with fingerprint scanners so he could track the whereabouts of weapons that'd been loaned out. If that wasn't stressful enough, Laurence would test Javis at random, berating him incessantly if he answered anything incorrectly. He'd also require him to work extensive hours, splashing liquor in his face if his eyelids grew heavy.

Laurence came off as a true bastard, but Javis has surprisingly expressed his appreciation for the man and his methods several times. While he believes it's more appropriate to handle this position with more composure, he's also admitted that Laurence's non-stop aggression made his personal devotion to the job profounder than it ever could've been. And though Javis says his apprenticeship under the old bloke led to a mutual respect between the two that lasts to this day, he's adamant to ensure his tenure as head of the department is seen more favourably than his predecessor's. To some, such an ambition might be deemed a dot petty. But, if that's the case, they just don't know Javis.

"Could you hand me your files?" he asked.

"Of course."

I handed him the folder containing Abraham Scobretti's documents. Though Trailsby will usually alert Javis of forthcoming assignments before operatives are summoned to HQ, specifics are commonly scarce until he meets with us. Scanning the first page, Javis tilted up his bronze-tinted glasses as though he came across bewildering articles.

"Forgive me. I'm so used to reading about morbid souls trying to destroy this planet that your assignments always stun me, one hundred and nine," he said. "The illegal trade of exotic sea animals seems so tame."

"While nothing compares to saving the planet from some brilliant fool, these operations still have purpose."

"They absolutely do. Tame might not have been the right word, as what this man is doing is disgraceful."

"I'd say that those scum who my colleagues handle are heinous. Those who I hunt—" I stopped myself, a sudden twinge rocketing in my chest once *hunt* had slipped from my mouth. It was as though an invisible foe had rammed their elbow through my lungs. Releasing a modest if not mortified chuckle, I continued with "my apologies, err, those I *pursue* are downright sickening."

Such was far from the correct word to describe how I contend with my assignments. Unfortunately, *hunt* was only word readying itself to raid my speech. Javis, thankfully, remained focused on the files and an inquisitive expression hadn't gripped his face. While it was merely a fair slip up, it's safe to say no one particularly cares for a word as vicious as *hunt* to be used while conversing about assignments. Besides, that word is utterly vile. I'm not a bloody animal, therefore I don't partake in any sort of *hunting*. I *pursue* these targets, just like any of the other operatives. That word, *pursue*, is a much more appropriate description.

"They are downright sickening," Javis said, his voice seemingly engrossed in his own thoughts. "Also, I see that you're going to a gala. Do you need any tracking devices? Suits?"

"No tracking devices. You know I never use them, so it's best they're not squandered. However, I do need a tuxedo for the gala."

"Excellent." He handed the folder back to me. "Let me grab one of your tuxedos and then we'll go over other needs."

"Thank you."

Though Javis' area of expertise might appear to be weapons, given his job title, he's even more gifted in the art of tailoring. Yes, bloody tailoring of all skills. He's mentioned how, when he was a child, his mother would earn extra income by sewing clothes for friends. He admitted that, while studying his mother's needlework, it spurred titanic revelations. So, he asked her if she could teach him the craft and, after some quizzical reluctance, she obliged.

Originally, Her Majesty's Church required its members to purchase their own formal apparel from shops. As with all the other privileges the members are given, these suits and dresses would be paid for by the organization through the assets minister. One day, a former field operative entered Javis' office while sporting a rather raggedy dress and he offered to mend it for her out of kindness. When he mentioned his proficiency with tailoring, she readily went to Lord President Trailsby with the news and Javis got saddled with the unofficial supplementary title of expert tailor.

Javis only tailors a suit or dress when there's a new member joining the ranks. Upon submitting your soul to Her Majesty's Church, we're given a form that asks us to specify our personal design preference for formal attire. It also states, clear as Tuesday, that each item of clothing is plain in style *unless* we wish to have them enriched by vogueish modifications. Quite hysterical, isn't it? So, if someone fancies polka dots, they'll jot it down. A preference for florals? Jot it down. One of my female colleagues, Vivienne Roathey, boasts several dresses with a horde of cartoon moose splattered on them. In my case, I wrote of my penchant for darker colours and, not knowing any better, also requested an addition to my tuxedo foolishly believing it'd still be *sophisticated* six years later. After submitting our forms, Javis will conjure up at least ten different outfits based off what we listed.

The clothing that is personally sewed for us is utilized during assignments and must be brought back to Javis upon completion of our obligations. This is because we'll wear this apparel up until our eventual exit from the organization. Of course, if someone faces any bodily transformations during their time here, then new garments will be produced for them. But their former items will be stored away in case they revert to their previous appearance.

I'm grateful that Javis sews suits that could be deemed *in-style* no matter the occasion. They're all sleek and devoid of additional padding or the extreme bulkiness of the power suit I'm currently sporting. Now, he did tailor all the power suits in my possession but that isn't another special perk we're allowed. No, I had to commission him to design those suits for me. It all derives back to conformity but mother of mercy those suits are comfortable.

Each outfit is housed in a room on the sixth floor, so I'm waiting as patiently as I possibly can until Javis returns. It's not as though I need him to get on and leg it, as that would be rather impolite. However, there are deep growls deriving from my stomach that are vying for my full attention. For most of this year, skipping a meal every two days has become an unhealthy routine that's been complicated to shake. The brain inevitably sinks down the foggy trash chute while this occurs, which signals the voices for a feeding frenzy. Right now, however, they're off being menaces elsewhere so the pleading of my vacant stomach is as apparent as it's ever been. The cafeteria on the second floor has countless options to choose from, so this damn hostility will be righted in due time. Just need to subdue it as much as possible, even if this surfacing headache is revelling in the fact that it's bouncing on a colossal trampoline.

The door behind me opened and Javis strolled in, carrying a black leather garment bag that contained my tuxedo. He handed it to me as he went around his desk, though not returning to his seat.

"A standard black tuxedo, complete with an artificial rose boutonnière," he said. "Why on this sacred land you thought a boutonnière was a good choice I'll never know." He chuckled softly before adding, "and on *all* of your tuxedos?"

Stifling my own laughter, I agreed that the addition happened to be downright dreadful. And, unfortunately, if you decide to add any sort of decoration to your outfits, such as a boutonnière, it is not allowed to be removed for any reason. Whatever the cost, the clothing must never be tampered with. As Javis tailors plain outfits that are devoid of anything that might outdate them, I'm almost certain he devised this rule with a pint of mischief. He knew six over blue that some of us would want to have clothes that were more in line with the current times. I happened to be one of the many duped but, luckily, I rarely have the misfortune of wearing one of my tuxedos.

"In my defence, I'm not the only one still stuck with an asinine add-on," I said.

Javis grinned. "I know. You don't have a suit that's powder blue with frills."

He was referring to Oswald's tuxedo and damn did he wallop poor Oz in the jaw by throwing his name beneath the river. Still chuckling, Javis slid his hand under the desk and pushed a button. This contraption causes the hydrangea-stocked wall behind him to slowly retract from us, complete with a bellowing noise like that of a hefty conveyor belt. The plants jostled initially but regained their composure as the wall trudged further away.

Both the wall and the bellowing stopped abruptly, signalling the completion of the journey, though more raucous racket decided to begin its set as a new wall sluggishly lowered itself down. This one reminds me of an industrial sliding door and, good mercy, do I wish these ancient appliances were scrapped along with that dreadful wallpaper in the hallway. The clamour isn't deafening, thankfully, but it's still aggravatingly thunderous.

While the mechanics are tiresome, the substitution of the walls is still a captivating sight, and all too necessary. The replacement wall, after all, is a tactical one. It's impressive too, as it contains such a vast assortment of weapons that it'll take a good season to take note of the whole lot if you're new to the organization. And that's even with pieces of the collection absent, as they're currently being put to work by some of my colleagues.

"From flowers to Her Majesty's arsenal," I said.

"Duplicity at its finest," Javis said. "And I'm not sorry for my fondness of both."

"You shouldn't be. It also helps that you're sensible. That alone puts you in a cup above the rest."

Searching through the assortment, it took no time to locate my preferred choice staring back at me, chuffed to be reunited. See, when Javis asked me to select an arm for the first time, I had no preference for any one brand. Part of this stemmed from a yearning to brandish as many pieces as I could while running amok. These chiefly included various types of handguns, such as Automags, Berettas, and the Hardballer. Pistols happen to be the most practical of arms, in part because it's quite elementary to be able to tuck them away while traveling. Mightier firearms I've employed, such as the Smith & Wesson M76 and Stoner M63, must be concealed inside of inconspicuous flight cases and can be a bother to lug about while seeking to be cautious.

After I'd been afforded the pleasure to dabble with an array of arms during my early assignments, Javis introduced me to a handgun that he'd specially designed: the Matilda-C70. Invented by Javis in 1977, this handgun is blued and wields an elongated barrel on par with a narwhal's horn. It also includes the valuable and obligatory fingerprint scanner on its handgrip so that its whereabouts can be tracked. The handgrip also showcases a stamped line art icon of the Queen's crown directly on the grip panel.

Named after the Queen, this weapon had never been taken off the rack during its three-year existence, much to Javis' disappointment. You could say there was an immediate and glistering draw that the C70 issued, though that very well could have stemmed from its pristine condition. Electing to magnify the man for his steady counsel, I commenced what has been a blissful partnership with the gun. It's been such an extraordinary companion that the C70 is now the lone weapon I'll handle.

As I stand at six foot one and sport, what one fling of mine has said, a body like that of former American football quarterback Moe Fraymeth, I find the full-sized handgun, even with its nine-inch barrel, easy to conceal. Its fifteen round magazine is reliable, but I never have to load it up to the tee. Whether it's from skill attained from years of practice or an egotistical refusal to add more than five cartridges, unearthing a clear answer is futile.

Removing the C70 from its mounted rack, I hastily pressed my fingers against the grip scanner. When my eyes are awarded a view of the masterpiece that is this handgun, then the sooner we must meld together. There's a harmless symbiotic magic in our pairing. The handgrip vibrated before emitting a low buzz, which indicated a successful pairing.

"I was so certain you'd choose the C70 that I'd already loaded the magazine with your usual five cartridges," Javis said.

"Always appreciated, Mister Macaulb," I replied.

"However, and you know I must ask this because it's my responsibility to confirm every one of you are fully prepared for an assignment. Are you sure you *only* want five cartridges? And are you sure you don't want *any* type of tracking devices or gadgets to aid you?"

"Yes, to both."

"Absolutely certain?"

"Without a shadow of a doubt. Five cartridges haven't failed me, I'll never have a use for tracking devices, and you know how ridiculous I find gadgets."

"Explosive Aqua Net may sound like the work of a jester, but I assure you it's been a known success."

Chuckling softly, I was adamant in my refusal. No matter how much of a success it's been with my colleagues, immensely lethal hair spray and all these various arrays of tampered household items will always be a waste of time to me. Aqua Net is more refreshing when it's being used by someone like my ex, Darla, or those countless pouty rock bands swarming the television. I'll take hair as enormous as a mountain over gimmicky gadgets any day.

Without saying a word, Javis retrieved a leather shoulder holster from a cabinet in his desk and handed it to me. Like how Francine keeps a stash of ties for me, Javis does the same with holsters. My colleagues have rather awful tendencies to forget them upon arriving at HQ, whereas I repeatedly tell myself to purchase one already and then forget. It's like my absentmindedness with regards to ties, but a holster is more of a priority if I had to choose.

Swiftly slipping on the holster, which is designed to position the handgun vertically, as is my preference, I performed a final inspection of the C70 before securing it in place. As I donned my jacket, Javis extended his hand.

"It looks as though we're all done here, one hundred and nine," he said. "As always, safe travels and best of luck to you."

Thanking Javis, I shook his hand before gathering my belongings and heading to the door. Before exiting, a recollection suddenly circled before my eyes, causing me to stop and look back toward him.

"I almost forgot. My sincerest congratulations on ten years here," I said.

Javis, who'd been preparing to raise up the tactical wall, grinned in response. "Thank you, Mark," he said, unexpectedly removing himself from formalities for the first time I could recall. "All of you have taken the time out of your days to congratulate me, whether in person or by phone, and I'm truly appreciative of all the kindness. I'm fortunate to work here, that's for certain."

8

Greencaster Airfield is a compact private airstrip owned by Her Majesty's Church, located fifteen minutes away from HQ. The Royal Air Force initially made use of the site during the Second World War, before allocating the entire area to Her Majesty's Church once the organization began gathering private jets for its field operatives soon after the war ended. There isn't much to explore at Greencaster, as the entire area is made up of grass and runways. Guards roam the grounds as well, with some perched at the entrance gate and others keeping a close eye on the hangars that store the planes. There's also a massive, awkwardly shaped air control tower that gives off the impression of a microphone. It's a dreadful view, enough to make one's eyes sore if they stare in disbelief for too long.

The Saldrake Corporation, an English aerospace manufacturer, has a partnership with Her Majesty's Church in which they supply us with jets. We bestow them damn all in return, not out of discourtesy, but because Saldrake refuses to accept anything from us. They believe they're aiding in the betterment of our country through working with an intelligence organization, and that is more than enough for them.

Each jet is an ATC-6608 model and is the only such business jet designed by Saldrake. It seats up to ten people, plus two crew members, and contains standard appliances such an in-air television and telephones. There's also small refrigerator that's always and only ever stocked with non-alcoholic beverages, something that had been implemented a few years ago as some of my colleagues tended to arrive at their destinations entirely unfit to perform their tasks.

Unfortunately, as with some aspects of HQ, the mass produced 6608s have not had their designs updated for at least a decade. It's miserably obvious, as some jets have vibrant yellow and green seats with cotton candy blue interior. Or, and this is downright embarrassing, both the seats and the carpet are made of rich purple velvet. While most contemporary styles follow the mundane cult of pastels, even I would prefer that over the sheer hideousness of that damned velvet interior. Whereas Her Majesty's Church has flawed reasons for preserving their outdated designs, it's truly perplexing that Saldrake seems even more aghast over having their interiors modernized.

Saldrake graciously supplied us with twenty jets, all of which reside in two separate hangars on the airstrip. We have five extra jets for insurance purposes, as you never know if a malfunction may occur. While rare, it's better to be mindful of such an ordeal taking place. Something that I am thankful for is the fact that none of us operatives have assigned jets. Personally, I deem owning a private jet to be a haughty trait. An aggrandizing symbol of wealth exuded by people who're able to drop whatever they're doing at any time and vacation whenever they wish. It's not that I'm against it, as if you're fortunate enough to afford such luxuries and have a desire to own a personal jet then by all means do it. But it's just so bloody pretentious.

They are, on the other hand, highly convenient in the case of this job. We're simply able to arrive, board, and take off with ease versus having to go through all the checkpoints at an airport. On no occasion are you hassled by a child who's bawling over pinched candy or an irate imbecile having a pitiful fit, screaming at flight attendants because they're upset about an immensely unimportant issue. So, maybe it's hypocritical, and it probably is, but the stain of conceit doesn't stick to me knowing the jets are all interchangeable.

Upon boarding the jet that's been waiting on the runway for me, I'm immediately welcomed inside by the velvet interior, something that doesn't surprise me. Jet selection is entirely random, though almost always are my assigned jets the ones festooned with velvet. For as abysmal as they may be in terms of viewing them, they're about as comfortable as the chairs in Javis' office. That's a plus at the very least.

A black suitcase rested toward the back of the jet, but this isn't because the previous occupant forgot their luggage. Her Majesty's Church is consistently five steps ahead of their employees and, when they know for certain they'll be sending an operative off to a destination, they'll do a great deal more than simply creating fake identification cards and compiling documents for the upcoming assignment.

Harking back to past conversations with Javis soon after I joined the organization, he told me that once the Lord President was ready to inform an operative of their assignment, he'd ask Javis to pack them a suitcase full of clothes and other necessities. He would then deliver the luggage to a secretary, who'd send it off to Greencaster while the operative is meeting with the Lord President. This protocol is both convenient and necessary, as the location and details of our assignments are confidential until the meeting. Therefore, packing would be both a waste of time and a chancy game of prediction regarding required attire. Instead, we have the ability to get up and go to HQ without any additional hassle.

Before making my way to Greencaster, I stopped at HQ's cafeteria and picked up a chicken salad sandwich on rye. The food they serve is, well, hardly above a five but it's still more delectable than the slop that's fed to schoolchildren. Even if the food had no redeeming qualities, I'm not one to stop somewhere for a bite when there is urgent business at hand. Even if there were no other options aside from food that's gone off, it would've been feasted on. Well, that might be a bit of a stretch, but at this point just about anything would subside this bloody headache. Preferably the answer should've been medicine because eating is a drag. But hopefully this chicken salad is my saviour, because the unpleasant fumes rummaging about in the cabin of this jet are readying to fully decimate my head.

Setting my briefcase and the tuxedo garment bag on the seat across me, I began to unwrap the sandwich from the cling film that secured it as an unfamiliar redheaded man stepped out from the cockpit. He sported the standard uniform worn by pilots employed by Her Majesty's Church: a white short-sleeved button-down that's tucked into grey slacks, an olive-green necktie along with a tie-clip, a black belt, black dress shoes, and a Royal Air Force flying badge. Female pilots wear almost the same outfit, except they're usually in skirts instead of slacks and sport a bowtie instead of a necktie.

"Good afternoon," the man said. "My name is Simon and I'll be your pilot for today's ten a.m. trek to Howslip Township."

"You sound more formal than most other pilots here," I said. "Are you new?"

"It's actually my first day on the job, sir," Simon said, a grin emerging as he appeared to lift his chin a tad. Perhaps to demonstrate boldness or something.

"Congratulations. You're in luck, having me as your first passenger."

"Yeah?" Simon's face rapidly transformed from bold to quizzical, with one of his eyebrows jutting up. "What's got you saying that?"

"Just wait, Simon," I said, knowing full well the bloke hadn't a clue how to adequately supervise some of my colleagues. "Some words of warning for you. My lads and lasses are a great bunch, but you'll be in utter disbelief over how disorderly they can be."

Judging by his blank stare, Simon's confidence had entirely eroded, and though I carried regret in knowing such happened to be my fault, it's certainly for his benefit. He should be aware of how his imminent journeys would play out. Several of our pilots entered this profession brimming with poise, only to watch all of it evaporate because of the foolery committed by the others. None of them have quit, amazingly, though they have become weary to the point they'll revel in relief when they discover *I'm* their passenger. Not to rattle my drum or anything, but I merely utilize my flights as a sanctuary to unwind as much as possible. The others, well, they take *pleasure* in their flights on their terms.

Simon chuckled and straightened out his tie some. "I appreciate the warning, Mister McGarriff, but I'm certain that I'll be prepared when I meet them," he said.

"I believe it as much as you do," I said.

"*Right*," Simon said. "I hope you enjoy your flight, sir."

With that, Simon returned to the cockpit. I'm admittedly eager to interact with him again once he had experienced the splendour of my rambunctious colleagues. It's not an exaggeration, continuously lumping all fourteen of them together as a mad lot. Each of them have their idiosyncrasies, to the point one would think *I'm* the sane bastard. Such is false, of course, but it seems that way because my dark mannerisms are properly concealed.

I took a bite of my chicken salad sandwich, immediately tasting the mild sting of jalapeños. This sandwich had been selected at random in a hurry, so the inclusion of the pepper was a satisfying surprise. With each bite, my headache gradually lessened somewhat. As expected, food accomplished its task but only my perpetual fix would complete the job. Truly disappointing that Saldrake failed to consider the inclusion of stewardesses on these jets. Oh well, this is suitable enough…for now.

One of the guards outside pushed the jet's door up in place and fastened it. Soon enough, the jet ascended to the skies for its voyage to New Jersey. Now that we were off, I decided to close my eyes and take in some rest. Mercy knows it's desperately needed.

***

Upon awakening, I asked Simon how much time had elapsed since we'd taken off. He told me that it'd been about four hours, which is sufficient for me. I'm more energized than usual, which once again showcases how poor my sleep habits are. Attaining four hours of sleep, alone, is quite a feat and something that's rarely ever matched. Having someone like June in bed with me is more comforting and assists me in achieving decent rest. Unfortunately, the prospect of sleeping with some woman isn't always dependable, especially when on assignments. Maybe that'll change while in New Jersey, and this headache can finally be eradicated for the time being.

Flights to the United States are in the middle of the pack when it comes to how lengthy they are. A merciful lack of layovers is also convenient, allowing us to arrive at our destinations without any prolonged delays. I suppose that's yet another positive feature of private jets. Anyhow, to pass the time on flights, I'll read over the paperwork in the folders again and study the photographs until they're fixed into my memory.

Music is another friend of mine during these journeys, and I always strive to keep a cassette tape player in my briefcase. For this trip, I brought the most recent album by Gerald Mancs, a quiet storm musician. Mancs, a former astrophysics professor, is far and away my favourite artist. His clever lyricism, the smooth clarity of his vocals, and the magnificence of the musicians backing him makes for an unbelievably tranquil listening experience.

Plugging a pair of headphones into the tape player, I then cracked open the cellophane seal of the album, *Pelt Sink*, and placed the tape into the music device. Immediately after pressing play, the sound of electronic drums and slap bass nearly knocked me for a six. Even Mancs couldn't avoid toying with a more modern production, much like almost everyone else who'd started making music in the sixties or early seventies. Though the music itself followed trendy patterns, the lyrics and vocals were still as superb as could be, and I slowly found myself warming to the record.

The photographs taken by the CIA were of Hooking Up, the Nesmith Docks, and the ballroom where the gala would be taking place tonight. Photos of the first two locations featured Scobretti or his brother Sergio with the other associate, Abruzzoli. All of them were photographed outside of Hooking Up, which dwelled in a relatively inconspicuous strip mall that wouldn't stand out if I'd taken a passing glance at it. Sergio Scobretti and Abruzzoli were photographed at the docks with a figure whose sunglasses and scarf completely obscured their face, wisely rendering them impossible to identify. The image of Sepia Harvest had to have been included for reference purposes, as none of the three were anywhere to be seen. The building is certainly fit for a gala, considering its expansive size.

One of the strangest emotions to possess is that of detestation toward another despite never meeting them. However, it depends on how this emotion is employed as it's quite effortless to abhor a well-known tyrant, dictator, or terrorist due to their notoriety. Like many others, I'm not fond of the vile dictators who've tormented countries and civilians with their banal ideologies of antagonism and submission. How they exercise despicable actions to cause widescale suffering throughout their wicked supremacy. What Abraham Scobretti does is nowhere near that level, but it's nevertheless unquestionably horrid. And he more I scan his face…the more wrath intermingles within my veins.

None of the files explicitly detail who he transfers aquatic wildlife to, only that he acquires them from sources who'll most likely be lurking around at tonight's gala. But the odds are that people buy these animals from him for heinous means, such as alternative medicine. Ludicrous how some are oblivious to the blatant deceit of such a bloody sham. It's devasting, revolting, and despicable but more commonplace than most realize. Considering how Her Majesty's Church and the CIA have been scoping this bastard out for some time shows he's among the worst of this type.

This atmosphere of ire is not unusual for me to explore. Scobretti may operate in the field of illegal animal trade, but he's just like all the other scum I'm routinely forced to deal with when on the job. When comparing him to others I've encountered in the past, there's nothing different. They're all just a boat of meaningless lowlifes who dabble in illegal tripe up until they face me. Before working for Her Majesty's Church, I never would've thought twice about all these operations taking place because I lived obliviously just like so many others.

An enchantingly mellow duet between Mancs and Deondra Stossell, an emotive vocalist who I'm moderately familiar with, played as I placed my briefcase on my lap and opened it. What resides inside are extraordinarily confidential files that are never to escape its clutches. These files are precisely the reason I'm so paranoid over someone like June discovering them, and why I'll restlessly check the briefcase's combination code numerous times before someone visits me.

These files are just like the ones of Abraham Scobretti and his associates. Bursting with information about the other scum I've had the pleasure of connecting with during past assignments. There's a stark dissimilarity between these files and Scobretti's, however, though such a difference won't last for much longer. See, each of the photographs included of those I've pursued have a puncture through the person's forehead, which derives from a prized possession of mine: a silver spitzer bullet gifted to me by Bart soon after becoming a member of Her Majesty's Church. Though it's become a habitual practice of mine to jam the pointed tip through the photographs of my targets once an assignment has concluded, it's a recent custom that only commenced a few years ago.

Retrieving the spitzer, I slowly dragged the tip of the bullet around Abraham Scobretti's forehead in a circular motion, careful not to accidentally puncture the image. To explain how calming this ritual is would be both challenging and incomprehensible, which is why I'm the only one who has any knowledge of this. It's another facet pertaining to the handling of my position that would undoubtedly concern the rest of the organization.

The duet ended, concluding the A-side of the tape. Its ending also caused my circling the spitzer on Abraham's image to cease. Taking a deep breath, I set the spitzer and all the manila folders, old and new, back into my briefcase and returned it to the seat across from me before switching to the B-side of the tape.

***

I've never stepped foot in New Jersey before. None of my prior assignments ever involved targets located in or based out of the state, and even while living in the United States way back when, there wasn't any reason to visit the area. Between family and the very few people I'm still in contact with from my younger years, none live in New Jersey. That's a plus as unexpected encounters with someone you might know while on an assignment are highly precarious. You must be incredibly crafty with spewing falsehoods or excuses, anything to get them as far away from you as possible to ensure their safety. Thankfully, such instances are exceedingly rare as we're all required to run incognito the entire duration of our assignments. We're not permitted to venture out of our hotels unless we're engaging in work-related activities. This makes satiating my vices nearly impossible, but I've found ways to sneak around these rules in the past and the same *will* apply this go around as well.

As the jet landed on the runway, I remained in my seat and waited for it to come to a full stop. Once it was safe to get up, I made sure all my belongings were packed away and that nothing had been left scattered about. Realizing that the numeric code on my briefcase hadn't been randomized yet, I tampered with the numbers until it formed an incorrect combination that was amiable to my eyes. Glancing out the window, I found this runway to be almost exactly like Greencaster's, as all that appeared in the surrounding area were trees and unkempt grass that probably hadn't been tended to in ages. Even the grounds of Greencaster were occasionally cultivated.

Simon emerged from the cockpit and unlatched the staircase door, signalling the conclusion of our journey. "I hope you enjoyed the flight," he said.

"I did," I said, shaking hands with him. "Hopefully you're less flustered now that this flight is over."

"Flustered? Oh no, sir, I might have been a bit overwhelmed at first but after this flight I'm sure every other will be absolutely painless."

"Even with what I told you about the others?"

"Even that."

Simon's grin did appear as though it reclaimed the initial daring aura that he displayed upon our first interaction. If he's truly prepared to fly with my colleagues, then I give him a whole boat of credit. Otherwise, he's not even going to comprehend his future misfortune until it smacks him on the back of the head. Hopefully that doesn't *literally* happen, but you just never know with those mischiefs. It just might.

Shaking hands with Simon, I departed the jet and proceeded to a limousine waiting nearby. I greeted the driver, a stocky middle-aged man who hastily opened one of the doors for me. This proved to be another example of faux affluence that never ceases to make me a tad uneasy. Her Majesty's Church truly goes above and beyond in cramming as many high-class amenities as they can down the throats of their employees. Thanking the driver for his courteousness, I settled in the backseat of the limousine. The driver nodded and shut the door before placing my suitcase in the trunk. He then looped around to the front seat, and we drove off.

As I stared out the window of the limo at the encircling sights of Howslip Township, there was a noticeable internal emptiness that startled me. Earlier in my tenure as an operative, there was a distinct awe upon arriving in a state or country that I'd never been to before. It was mesmerizing to absorb these locations as an outsider, uncovering various traditions and dishes foreign to me until entering this profession. Even a state as outwardly dreary as Utah, and that's said with affection, hypnotized me with sites such as their utterly gorgeous national parks. But as the limousine travelled through the Garden State, the joys of exploring new regions no longer exhibited the same mystique.

It's not a knock on the Garden State. Everything that rolls out of my pupils is distorted, though that's because I'm so bloody detached from this wretched world. It's not shocking, I suppose, considering my relentless aversion toward my job. But even during the assignment before this one, traveling to the enthralling country of Greece, there was a marked difference. Every single sense of invigoration possible coursed throughout my entire being throughout the duration of that assignment. Sure, maybe comparing Greece to New Jersey is unfair, but I'm almost certain this utter lack of exhilaration would've persisted even if the assignment took me to somewhere like New Zealand, a country I've always wished to visit.

The driver pulled the limousine up to the front of the hotel, which displayed a gorgeous spouting fountain with water soaring in every direction. A sizeable sign near the fountain displayed the hotel's name, Nouveau Rêve, in gaudy gold and black letters. Upon parking the limo, the driver came around to open my door. I exited the vehicle like a has-been Hollywood star, conveying a ridiculous attempt at haughtiness while striding around outside. Might as well play the lute when you arrive at such a garish hotel. Rarely do I even dare demonstrate this light-hearted side of my being, but it had to be done because…why not? After scoffing at my own absurdity, I attempted to retrieve my wallet so to tip the driver. However, after hurriedly lugging my suitcase out of the trunk, he rushed back to his seat and drove off. I know Her Majesty's Church frowns on our giving gratuities to the limo drivers, but that was a dot ridiculous.

Nouveau Rêve's lobby continued the theme of gold by means of the paint decorating the walls as well as the marble tiles, which were mostly white with splashes of gold throughout. No doubt this colour scheme is striking at night, especially the walls as they almost certainly give off a golden rod hue when the sun isn't shining directly on it. The current mixture of the gold with the sunshine roaming around clashes violently and simply isn't an easy sight to relish.

There were a good deal of people conversing loudly in both the lounge and dining areas. Almost everyone held either bottles of water or glasses of what I assumed to be white wine in their hands. The men wore polos and khakis, apparel that I'd only wear as a Halloween costume, while the women all appeared as though they had tennis lessons soon. There were no children in sight, which meant this hotel was either designed for childless vacationing couples or mingling singles. I'm thankful for that, as it's a pain in the arse to deal with unattended children running amuck while their parents pamper themselves.

At the front desk stood a receptionist who immediately wrangled my attention away from all the other activities taking place around me. Substantial eyeliner and violet mascara skilfully clothed her all too absorbing teal eyes, a graceful yet mysterious shade. The eye makeup, combined with her bronze rouge, boded especially well with her warm beige skin tone. Most eye-catching, in my opinion, happened to be her long and modestly teased rust coloured hair. Whether natural or unnatural, any shade of red hair on a woman is among my greatest and most fervent weaknesses.

The receptionist wore a white blouse that barely enclosed her ample chest, to the point I could detect the outline of her bra. Though I couldn't tell its colour, the tell-tale lace texture alluded to what she was hiding underneath. Her blouse is tucked in at her plentiful waist by an almost inappropriately well-fitting black pencil skirt that I'm willing to bet ends right above her knees. On both her wrists were clunky golden link bracelets that would've appeared out of place on most anyone else yet accentuated her outfit beautifully.

Strolling even closer to the woman, I made out a golden nametag that rested on the top left of her blouse. It informed me of her name: *Robin.*

"Welcome to Nouveau Rêve," Robin said, flashing me a dazzling smile. "Are you checking in with us this afternoon?"

"Yes, I am," I said.

"Excellent. May I have your name please?"

I hesitated briefly enough to damn Her Majesty's Church for gifting me the name I'm required to use on this assignment before uttering "Basil Courtauld."

Robin nodded, her smile unwavering as she opened a nearby book so that she could find my reservation and room number.

As she surveyed her book, my addictive eyes were deadlocked on Robin. The lively noise emitting from the other guests plummeted away, evaporating into distant echoes reminiscent of planetary sounds. Simultaneously the pulsating beats of my ever-lustful heart crammed my ears. A chance appearance by Abraham Scobretti himself couldn't wrench my sight from its unyielding fix on this alluring woman. Yes, it would be unbelievably appalling of me to neglect an opportunity to apprehend that scum, but it's the truth. A majestic woman will never be unsuccessful in commanding my attention. They bathe my heightened emotions in a bed of aphrodisiacal tea leaves while an invisible hand guides my crazed fervour to their mystifying soul. Dramatic but potent magnetism. And mercy not a bloody thing would be more exhilarating than to be with this woman.

"How long have you been in the realm of hotels, Robin?" I asked.

"About three years." Robin's eyes remained on the book. "Though I've been here at Nouveau Rêve for just under a year now."

"Nouveau Rêve seems a tad high-end. How's the clientele here?"

"Usually, they're a bunch of old stuffy shirted businesspeople." Robin glanced up at me, her smile now showing signs of deviousness as demonstrated by her front teeth slowly prancing along her bottom lip. "But every now and then, there's an attractive guest who shows up."

"Yeah?" I leaned an elbow on the counter of the desk. "When's the last time someone like that checked in?"

Robin's attention now fully drifted away from the book, latching onto me as she reciprocated my posture by leaning closer herself. "Well, he hasn't checked in *just* yet, but he arrived about two minutes ago."

"In that case I'll seal my mouth so that we can both learn my room number."

Though her eyes journeyed back to the book, Robin's smile had intensified to the point I observed her tongue slither on the edge of her upper teeth. She flipped another page and dragged a peach-coloured fingernail down to my drab pseudonym.

"You're in room four-twelve," Robin said. "Let me grab your key for you."

Decorating the wall behind the receptionist desk were numerous rows of key cubbies, with more than half of them empty. Robin turned toward the cubbies and began searching for my room key. As she did, my assumption that her pencil skirt ended right above her knees proved correct. This also allowed me to detect sheer black stockings, a garment that complimented her skirt beautifully.

Robin found my room key residing in the fourth row and handed it to me. The plastic tag on the key had the room number printed in bulky, cartoonish script on one side, and the gaudy Nouveau Rêve logo on the other.

"I hate knowing that you're gonna be up there all alone while I'm down here," Robin said.

"In that case you'll be happy to know that I have an engagement tonight," I said.

Watching Robin's mouth gently gape as she said "oh" in response sent rampant pulses of electricity across my frenzied flesh. Several severe magnets surging within my veins, dangerously daring me to lean closer to her. Those full, flawless maroon lips of Robin's could coerce me to surrender and bow to her control at any given moment, and I would gladly oblige without a hint of hesitation.

Robin gently tapped her fingernails on the guest book, her eyes leaving mine as she faced the door enough for me to catch an impeccable view of her profile. That gripping smile of hers soon returned.

"An engagement? Hmm, well whoever she is she's a very lucky woman," Robin said, her tone struggling to give a snooty impression but failing beautifully.

"Oh, it's nothing like that," I said, recognizing her ploy with ease. "Just a work function that I'm required to attend."

My response caused Robin to turn toward me again, but she did so in a carefully precise manner. The way her eyebrows rose briefly before settling back in place just as her smile curved upward a touch exuded a cunning playfulness.

"Work function? So, you won't be back too late then?" Robin asked.

"Should be back around eleven thirty at the latest," I said.

"And I get off at twelve. I'll see you at twelve-oh-five, Mister Courtauld."

9

Out of all my addictions, the lone romance that provokes shame is the one I've had with tobacco smoking. It's such a repulsive habit, though I'll be the first to admit that my peculiar adolescent self was among the masses who found themselves fooled by the mystique. Yes, smoking does have an initial mystique, and it comes in the form of this manufactured idea we all get of the *generic smoker*. These *generic smokers*, of course, were the glamourous and implausibly successful movie stars who'd graced our lives since childhood. It made no difference if they were performing in films, being interviewed on television, or taking part in publicity shoots for the world to worship. Cigarettes made damn sure their presence was accounted for whenever the opportunity arose.

All those publicity photos, especially, are still as stunning as they are deceitful. Long ago, I owned several photos of my favourite film stars, all of which were bought from some guy on the street when I was around thirteen. These black and white photos, which are probably somewhere in my parents' house, draped a cloak of fascination on top of me when I'd stare at them for hours. And every one of those stars and starlets had a cigarette either dangling from their lips or nestled between their index and middle fingers. The smoke that rose from the cigarettes would occasionally dance in front of their faces, creating an artistic aura that only captivated my childhood astonishment more.

My dealings with cigarettes didn't occur until after I'd graduated high school. Neither of my parents are smokers. What's more, they're both tenaciously against tobacco use and all other sorts of addictive stimulants and substances. So, needless to say, my parents did not fancy the concept of their children picking up the disgusting habit. They knew better, repeatedly telling my sisters and me that the process of someone inhaling smoke into their lungs made for a bloody inane image. My sisters all heeded their words of wisdom and followed their apple of guidance. I, however, *pretended* to understand just how valuable their declarations were all the way until I left for college.

Unfortunately, the fascination and appeal of the cinema star vision blocked me from apprehending just how cheap and unpleasant the habit ended up being. It's one thing to gaze at photographs of people smoking cigarettes in expensive suits and dresses, swathed in jewellery and other luxurious accessories. It was certainly another to see ordinary people, such as myself, lull about with cigarettes in their mouths, completely devoid of the elegance I assumed derived from smoking. The notion of glamourous smoking only exists in photographs or on film. Smoking's true form is merely a mirage designed to tempt the masses.

It took thirteen years to finally make a forcible attempt at kicking tobacco, and the herbal cigarettes that Francine bought for me have been of considerable assistance. Though they're just as toxic as tobacco cigarettes, herbal cigarettes are not addictive and have been immensely helpful in lessening my pining after tobacco. The next step is ceasing the compulsive demand to smoke something. While herbal cigarettes are dangerous if used as much as tobacco cigarettes, I'd rather smoke them than marijuana or those light-up gag cigarettes my nieces and nephews used to love playing with.

During my exchanges with Robin at the front desk, our suggestive conversing barred me from inquiring about in-room smoking. While I'd neglected to see a single *no smoking* sign anywhere in sight while proceeding to my room, I figured it'd be best to wait until the aquarium gala before smoking the herbal cigarettes. It starts at seven, so there's about three and half hours to pass before I have to begin preparing for this trifling event. Being that no one in the lobby offered me one of those luggage trollies, carrying the garment bag over my shoulder proved tricky. It was a great struggle to keep it balanced while also lugging a suitcase.

Room 412 is more than adequate and, mercifully, doesn't continue the gold scheme like the rest of the hotel. Instead, the shades of the walls are a misty white and the flooring consists of grey patterned carpet except for the bathroom, which has generic tile. It's your run-of-the-mill hotel room, and I've had the great misfortune of staying in some places that were either utterly sickening to the stomach or splattered with sunny, blinding colours. While I did expect something a tad more upscale, if only because of that garish logo this hotel shows off, I've no issues with making this room my base for a couple of days.

I hung the garment bag in the quaint closet before setting both my suitcase and briefcase on the queen-sized bed. Opening the suitcase, I rummaged through it to investigate everything that'd been packed. Inside were four dress shirts, four pairs of slacks, an extra suit jacket, and a few pairs of basic blue boxers and black socks. There was also a bag of salt and vinegar potato crisps as well as a gold and silver lighter, surely sweet gifts from Francine. The lighter, massive and shaped like a generic skyscraper, swiftly made its way inside the inside pocket of my jacket.

Not once have I ever made use of a hotel's chest of drawers. It's not out of a wariness or a general fear of leaving anything in them, though I've always questioned whether they're ever cleaned with a sanitized wipe or the like. The usual routine I've been used to, however, has been one of keeping everything inside my suitcase and unpacking what I need when it's duly necessary. In the following days, I'll then place the dirty laundry on top of one of the closet racks.

Retrieving the crisps from the suitcase, I moved the luggage into the closet but kept my briefcase on the bed. Figuring that I'd most likely not be eating at the gala aside from the occasional hors d'oeuvres, I lounged on the bed and enjoyed the crisps while going over the files. Though the prospect of having to attend this gala, not to mention having to scout out another target, still bugged me, there were still several potential positives that could arise while wandering around here. Perhaps an *additional* pursuit would give me the sense of normalcy my colleagues embrace whenever they execute their assignments.

Achieving that normalcy might make me loathe my job less. It might allow me to reexperience the excitement I'd once cavorted with years ago. There are so many satisfying possibilities that could come about this that I wondered why I'd been so aghast about the idea when Trailsby and Pierce informed me of it earlier. And who knows? If this assignment allows me to embrace the human in me that's almost entirely decayed, those bloody voices might finally cease their pitiful existences. I could finally gaze at myself in a mirror because the continued gnarled warping of my face would vanish. Mercy that would be an unbelievably lovely occurrence.

Some time ago, I attempted to chat with Trailsby when my rotting sense of self first began to emerge from the infernal regions of my head. Describing, with substandard detail unfortunately, how this raging fear seared my heart and lungs in waves because of how this job was eliciting a frenzy that apparently dwelled in my mind. A frenzy that was unbeknownst to me until I continued to partake in more assignments. Trailsby promised me that every operative of Her Majesty's Church goes through this period of forgetting themselves as the job progresses, but that it'll halt once you get used to it. He also promised me that I could retire early if the tribulations worsened.

Though I desperately yearn for the serenity that has evaded me once the true purpose of my job became apparent, a great piece of me calls such an act to be a sign of failure.

Although all my mental images became scattered the more they attempted to make themselves the star of the picture show taking place in my loaf, knowing that the potential of normalcy lingered so intensely within the scope of this job made me content. It successfully battled away the voices, as the Phantasms had briefly recognized an opportunity to wreak havoc inside me. Thankfully they were unable to leak out from one of the black holes. Edith the Tempest, on the other side of paradise, was content due to my future plans with Robin. Engaging in ardent conversations or sensual actions always placate her. Admitting that though…how I just wish to escape the never-ending despair that drags around me like a parasitic slug.

***

Galas aren't something I'm well acquainted with, as it's typically the elites who attend these functions. I'm aware that there is most likely a fundraiser involved, though this is mainly through conversations I've had with Bart and Oswald. They've done plenty of assignments involving these events and have described them to some extent. Even with that information, I truly hadn't a clue what to expect from this gala.

There are no additional details amidst the files that pertain to the gala except for the picture of Sepia Harvest and its street address. All else I must accomplish had been relayed to me by Trailsby and Pierce, that there's potentially another party who'll be in attendance. Someone who aids Abraham Scobretti and his associates in attaining these exotic sea animals. With that knowledge, I figure there are a couple of tasks to follow through while in attendance.

The task that takes precedence over all the others is that of keenly scoping my surroundings without being too obnoxiously obvious. There will be several people present who've been around the hedges enough times to identify an outsider lurking in their midst. Surely Her Majesty's Church has already thoroughly established background details for my fake name, enough to give this alias a clear reason for attending an invite-only function. While I'm not sure why they failed to even pass this information to me, I'm guessing they have enough faith in me to not blow my cover entirely. Makes me wonder what kind of data is passed along to the others in the organization.

Trailsby explained to me that the Scobretti brothers and Rocco Abruzzoli will be in attendance so, if I catch a glimpse of them, it's crucial that I deplete all aspects of my usual work behaviours. Under no circumstances am I allowed to apprehend them in the middle of this function, as much as that irks me. How can any of us continue this ordeal of tracking when the targets are in clear view? It makes no sense. If they're in my scope, then they're fair game to be captured. But regretfully, I must keep reminding myself that this potential fourth party that's involved is just as important to apprehend as those in the files.

While venturing through the lobby and to the front doors, fully clad in my outdated tuxedo, I was a tad thankful I didn't catch a glimpse of the alluring Robin anywhere in sight. Strange to think, yes, but this damn boutonnière on my jacket makes it seem like I'm heading to some tacky dance. Wearing a relic of the past decade also flaunts my age more, which is unappealing. On the sunnier side, I didn't ask Javis for flared slacks at the very least.

Several hotel patrons, including a few I recalled from earlier in the day, were still chatting noisily in the lobby. While walking outside, I found the entire front entrance to be devoid of anyone. The spouting fountain in front of the hotel was illuminated by gold lights, which tinted the water well. Within seconds of being out front, a limousine pulled up the circular driveway. A driver exited, this one different from the hurried driver I met earlier.

"One-oh-nine?" He asked, referring my identification number.

I nodded and the driver made his way to my side so that he could open the door for me. Taking a few swift glances around me, making sure the front entrance of Nouveau Rêve remained free of anyone else, I entered the limousine. The driver returned to his seat, and we were off.

All limousine drivers who haul members of the organization around are employed by Her Majesty's Church. Almost all of them, such as this driver and the one from earlier, are immensely secretive and untalkative. With all the confident turns the driver was making, he clearly knew how to get to Sepia Harvest. It's more than possible the drivers practice the route multiple times before an assignment commences, as the drivers all have this robotic precision about their driving style. They stay the speed limit and are cautious with shifting lanes. Her Majesty's Church wouldn't have it any other way with their employees.

"Do you mind if I smoke in here?" I asked, finding this to be an ideal time to finally have one of my cigarettes.

"Unfortunately, I do mind," the driver said. "My apologies, sir, but smoke makes me lightheaded."

My hand had already been positioned on my suit jacket, unconsciously expecting a different response from the driver. Though disappointed, I told the driver that his reasoning was understandable. There's a fifty/fifty chance we're allowed to smoke in the limousines, as they do not have privacy dividers. This is because our drivers are required to keep an eye on us the entire period that we're in their orbit. All sorts of disobedient behaviour, however, are strictly prohibited.

Eventually, we arrived at Sepia Harvest. Though its picture showcased a structure of tremendous size, it failed to do the actual building any justice. Between its astonishing height, the structure had to be at least five stories, and its extensive width, it made me curious as to what all was occurring inside. Galas must be a tad more excessive than your generic party I suppose.

The driver wished me luck but, when I attempted to reach for my wallet this time around, he put his hand up to halt me and shook his head. These drivers deserve more credit than they get, obeying their rules even better than the operatives do. Most anyone else would salivate at the chance of a tip, and I can't blame them considering how downright ungenerous some people are.

A small set of stairs led me up to the front entrance of the stone building, where a well-dressed man with a bushy moustache stood by the closed arched doors. He wore an earpiece, which he had a finger pressed against, presumably to listen to someone from inside. Undoubtedly this bloke is one of the guards for the event, in charge of barring anyone who wasn't invited.

Once I got within reach of the doors, enough to where I could detect somewhat faint music and other assorted noises, the man put his hand in front of me as though he expected me to just waltz inside without care.

"Name?" He asked.

"Basil Courtauld," I said.

Checking his clipboard, the man pinpointed my name before extending his hand out toward me as though he demanded a tip. "ID."

ID? Really? They're doing whatever they can to prevent anyone who shouldn't be here from entering, so I'm quite appreciative of my invitation. I handed the guard my fake identification card. It performed its job perfectly, as the man immediately gave it back to me and moved away from the door.

"Welcome, Mister Courtauld. You may enter."

"Thank you." I returned the ID to my wallet, relieved that I didn't have to go through some body search that could've given away my Matilda-C70, and continued into the building.

Passing through a modest lobby and through expansive open doors, the scenes taking place before me were entirely unexpected. This entire time, I truly believed I had a vague idea regarding what to expect from this gala. It'd be a decent-sized get-together with maybe sixty to seventy people in attendance, a relatively easy base to investigate. Instead, the venue I entered featured a great, boisterous party with hundreds of exorbitantly dressed people laughing, dancing, eating, drinking, you name it.

Vibrant bright green and pink lights illuminated the entire building, which only consisted of two stories instead of what genuinely could pass for five. There was a staircase in the lobby that led to the second floor if you could call it that. That area was in the style of an encompassing balcony, where even more people chatted and partied behind the railings. Such a ballroom was reminiscent of the kind where my fourth oldest sister, Blythe, had gotten married back in 1963. Even that structure, utterly lavish and magnificent as it was, could only bow in humiliation to the exuberance of this hall.

Fluffy haired women in skimpy leotards swivelled on ribbons dangling from the extraordinarily high ceiling. Middle-aged men and women in tailcoat jackets carried plates full of hors d'oeuvres and thin glasses of bubbly champagne. Up-tempo synth-pop music blared from loudspeakers that rested on a grand stage in the far back of the room. Hanging above the stage from the balcony was a gigantic banner with the words *Friends of the Grand Howslip Aquarium* printed on it.

Amidst the considerable amount of circular dining tables that filled the room were all the guests. The volume of people partying on the dancefloor, combined with the music and lights, was a lot to take in at once. There's only one sizable gathering I have a weakness for, but I'd rather not think about that one right now. All that can be disclosed about that gathering is that it's more of an underground get-together than a thrilling party, which is what this event was. And, aside from those exploits, I tend to avoid such altogether because I've never been one for crowds.

Some people fancy these engulfing crowds that are crammed with a multitude of strangers moving around frantically. They'll engage the shrill collection of noises, whether its music or thunderous chatter, that thrust through them like arrows from directions even they wouldn't think of glancing toward. But, if you're someone whose preference for the mundane madly trounces any want or will to attend these events, you'll be utterly tormented and restless to the point your soul insists on stripping away from your damned body.

These strangers, though they're pleasantly indulging themselves in the entertainment, don't make being swallowed by their swarm any easier. The charged commotion caused dozens of my nerves to jitter, and all the random nudges made my body progressively tenser. My chest decided to swap my heart and lungs for an abnormally sized discus, and my throat began to shut, all due to the surging distress raging across my being.

Making matters worse was my previously dormant headache gradually shoving its way to the forefront of the uproar. While the troublesome array of agony stemming from this gala was a trial that must be tolerated for the sake of this assignment, the headache was more of an unnecessary fiend who arrived without an invitation. To combat it, I painted faint images of Robin from Nouveau Rêve, reminding myself that our later rendezvous would decisively vanquish that headache.

A tailcoated woman presented a tray of champagne to me, bowing her head in an act of servitude. While the spectacle came off as a tad bizarre, I thanked her and immediately gulped down two of glasses, setting them back on her plate before she could leave. The scene caused her to giggle some as she moved on. She probably comprehended that this wasn't my favourite environment, nor one I was all too familiar with.

Alcohol is my sole companion when I'm trapped in an ocean of strangers but having to yield to the beverages isn't all that common anymore since I'm often able to avoid being stuck in crowds. It's not like when I'd be forced to make a speech in front of a class back in my youth. That's how my apprehension for enormous clusters of people started and it's nauseated me since.

Occasionally a few swigs of alcohol would be necessary to fulfil those speeches during my college years, but I usually avoided the temptation because of a staunch refusal to succumb to yet another vice. The prospect of overcoming my anxieties while clearheaded was another reason as well, but that proved to be considerable failure.

I wandered around the expansive, packed ballroom, trying my damndest to locate both the Scobretti brothers and Abruzzoli despite being ambushed by the now flashing colourful lights and the swarm of people. All the men I've spotted are either in my age range or older, so finding the three scumbags somewhere in this gala should be effortless. Unfortunately, all the activities running rampant in this room made it bloody impossible to pinpoint any of my targets.

The last event I attended that was remotely like this was forever ago, when I was in my late twenties. Similarities between the two were substantial, as both events included large parties dancing enthusiastically underneath multicoloured lights. Had the synth-pop been replaced by that archaic psychedelic rock that never gets played anymore, and the guests here been younger, I'd almost be convinced that the clock decided to rewind time some to make me relive that frenzied experience.

Suddenly, soft fingers delicately grasped my wrist. Before I even had the opportunity to retaliate, this person spun me around and I found it to be some woman who was *maybe* in her fifties. She had an empty glass in her other hand and, judging by her lopsided smile, was beginning to experience the sway of the champagne a smidgen.

"Let's dance," she said, struggling to stifle her giggles.

"No thank you," I said. "I'm quite all right."

Evidently unable to process what I'd told her, the woman yanked me over to where most of the guests were dancing and began shaking her arms and upper body wildly, as if she'd been electrocuted. This woman has guts, that's clear as a ghost. I am not a dancer, and I never will be one. The dance floor is to me what insect repellent is to a mosquito. Not wishing to stare awkwardly at the woman, I figured there was no other choice than for me to move along with the music as best I could. This woman also kept her distance from me enough so that I could slip away without difficulty if need be.

Apparently, the good graces decided to cut me a break as the music gradually lessened. The pinks and greens faded away as traditional lights emerged to overtake the room. At this point, the other guests became easier to observe and I discovered that almost every woman in attendance happened to be a blonde. Part of me deeply wishes they were all redheads, brunettes, or raven-haired. That would be the personification of my own private paradise. At the same time, that would merely render me incompetent and incapable to complete my job so in a strange way I was thankful all these women were blondes.

Over on the stage, a young woman with long, full, teased and very obviously bleached blonde hair was walking across it. She wore a glittery, button-down red dress with long sleeves, shoulder pads, and a matching red belt around her waist, as well as white heels. The guests had started clapping for her even before she made it to the microphone that stood in the middle of the stage. In response, the woman waved with both hands while beaming an incredibly perky smile.

"Hello everyone, and welcome to the Friends of the Grand Howslip Aquarium gala," she said, her voice animated and cheery.

Everyone continued clapping and cheering, so I followed suit. Carefully, I glanced around the room to try and pick out either of the Scobretti brothers or Abruzzoli. To my dismay, they were nowhere in sight.

"In case we haven't been introduced yet, my name is Stella Pescaghi, and I'm the Director of Strategic Partnerships for the Grand Howslip Aquarium. As president of the Friends of the Aquarium Foundation, I'll also be your hostess for this evening. Just so that everyone is aware, we'll be starting the auction in five minutes so once the music turns off, please take a seat. If you have any questions, please come to me or talk to anyone wearing a nametag with this little dolphin on it." Stella pointed to the paper nametag on the top right of her dress. "For now, please continue having the time of your lives!"

Stella began waving with both her hands again as she walked away from the microphone. The sounds of applause combined with the music increasing once more swiftly engulfed me. Seeing that the woman who'd pulled me over to dance had all her dizzy attention on the stage, I managed to slip away from her so that I could continue searching for my targets.

Those damn colourful lights didn't re-emerge with the music, so it was no longer as complicated as it had been to examine everyone's faces. Stella did mention that the auction would be taking place very soon, which made me ponder whether the targets were arriving solely for that part of the event. It was logical, being that every person I sifted past in this sea still happened to be of the older variety. At this rate, I had little doubt the Scobretti brothers and Abruzzoli would be among the youngest attendees here.

I made my way to a table that had been neatly arranged with an array of desserts on it. Chocolate cake, sugar cookies, and wide muffins were among the sweet snacks that adorned the table. Rich, sugary scents radiated from the desserts, with the muffins producing the mightiest aroma. Those scents were tempting, but being that I'm not much for sweets, there was little need to indulge in anything. Instead, I continued my observations which, by now, had grown tiresome. What if my targets were at that fishing shop Abraham Scobretti operates? Imagine that. Such a scenario would make me unthinkably incensed. I could be finished with them by now instead of lolling about this raving party with all these rich and rowdy businesspeople.

Doing another scan of the crowd, a pair of eyes met mine. They belonged to yet another blonde woman. Though her bottom half was obscured by some of the other guests, the majority of her fashionable outfit could still be made out. She sported a long-sleeved white coat puffed with shoulder pads and fixed with sizeable winged collars. Underneath it was a forest green dress that possessed a loose collar.

Her eyes were fastened onto mine, but in a manner dissimilar to that of Robin's from earlier. This woman's eyes were studying me, with glints noticeable from afar that seemed to give off the impression that she recognized me. The swirling bright greens and pinks from above dazzled on her face, which was gingered up by a coat of sweat. A stimulating sight. Mercy how I fancy the sleek, sensual magic of a woman who's drenched in sweat. This woman must've been dancing until she fixed her sights unto me.

The woman's jaw drooped a tad and the edges of her lips darted up. Her eyebrows were raised as high as they could go, accentuating this display of pure…memorisation? Part of me found her to be attractive, yet there was something very disconcerting about her studious gaze. I've observed faces of lust, maddening attraction, and general curiosity. The woman's face contained none of those hints. Ultimately, I presumed she must've been as intoxicated as that woman who tossed me onto the dance floor.

For some reason, however, a demanding energy bellowed at me to keep this woman in my view. There was something so starkly magnetic about her that it struck me as odd. By now I was more than certain this gaze wasn't brought upon by allure. Many a drunken woman had approached me before, but this woman merely stayed put and stared. The confusion and peculiarity of our mutual locking of eyes took its toll and I decisively broke off our eye contact. This woman can present those unnerving stares onto the others while I focus on my job. And since my targets are all but undetectable at this level, no matter where I've meandered, perhaps the mezzanine will be the answer to my troubles.

I began to head back toward the entrance but a tailcoated man holding a tray of fried shrimp blocked me. He held it out to me while bowing. I respectfully declined, but still thanked him for offering the hors d'oeuvres. The man sighed deeply as he walked away, seemingly disheartened by my refusal. Maybe he prepared the shrimp himself? If so, that would be means for an apology but how was I to know that?

More well-dressed invitees entered the front doors of the building as I began to walk up the stairs. However, I caught that intoxicated woman with the dreamy eyes briskly moving by the front as well. Her eyes hadn't trailed away from me. I slowly continued up the stairs, watching as the woman moved closer to the entrance. As I expected, she began hiking up the stairs too. Her pace made it seem as though she desperately wished to break into a full-on sprint. I'm sure she would've if it hadn't been for her heels.

Did this woman see through me and realize I didn't belong at this function? No, that's ridiculous. In no way has my demeanour been out of the ordinary here…or has it been? No, of course not. A more logical explanation is that this woman is the fourth party that I'd been warned about. But even then, there's no possible way she could sense the blood in the water as being me. I told myself a couple times that my initial deduction, intoxication, was the most likely answer. She's too jogged up on champagne and is unaware of what she's doing. That *must* be the reason she's lethargically staring at me as though I snatched her keys and am now engaging in some teasing game with her.

The mezzanine wasn't as overcrowded as the downstairs area was, but I still couldn't identify any of my targets from where I stood. That woman was still climbing up the stairs, and at this point it's best to try and lose her before resuming my pursuit. The last trouble I ever want to deal with while working is the possibility of a bystander getting caught in the middle of what has the potential to be an unpleasant ordeal.

Initiating a diversion might help me lose that odd woman...if it's performed organically that is. As I began to swim through the groups of people relaxing and dining together, Stella, the hostess, happened to be headed my direction. She might be beneficial in my crafting this diversion. Better to engage the hostess in meaningless chatter than vaulting into a random conversation with strangers.

"Hi, Stella," I said, extending a hand.

"Hi there," Stella said, shaking my hand with a smile. "Do I know you?"

"Oh no, I'm just a guest who's enjoying a wonderful time."

"You have no idea how happy I am to hear that." Stella placed her other hand on mine and patted it before our hands parted.

"However, now that I've got you, I do have a bit of a trivial question. Where is restroom?" I asked, successfully batting away my using the customary term of *loo* in place of *restroom*.

Stella pointed across to the other side of the mezzanine floor, directly above the stage. "Right over there past those doors."

"Thank you very much," I said.

"Of course! I hope you continue to enjoy yourself!"

We exchanged smiles before I rounded the balcony to the doors Stella had pointed to. I glanced back and noticed that the peculiar woman had remained near the top of the stairs. Of course, the moment my eyes dropped like a bomb onto hers, the woman proceeded to move in my direction. Her hasty body language now indicated a desire to rush me like a cheetah erratically stalking its more conscious prey. This was now becoming a tedious game that should've ceased after heading up the stairs.

Though my conversation with Stella took somewhat longer than I was hoping it would, the woman's decision to wait by the stairs apparently meant she didn't wish to cause a scene. After all, she could've easily have approached me while I was with Stella. This piqued my interest even more than it initially had been. This woman wasn't some champagne-filled guest who had an itch to cause drama. No, somehow, she must've recognized me.

Arriving at the doors Stella had told me led to the loo, I entered the one with the word *Gentleman* printed on it. Aware that a precarious situation might be forming, I made sure not to lock the door. It'd be pathetic to lock it when the likelihood of a scuffle was on the rise. The bathroom was larger than I expected, and contained a single toilet, a sink, a kitchen paper dispenser, and a trash can. Nothing out of the ordinary, sure, but still vastly important for me to survey.

There weren't many people hovering over in this section compared to the area near the staircase, so if this woman wished to try anything, she could do so without causing a scene. In preparation for any sort of incident, I stood against the wall next to the door, positioning myself on the side where I'd be obscured if she so brazenly entered.

Now, there's also the possibility that she simply lolls about outside the loo, waiting for me to exit before she proceeds with her attack like an animal. Whatever the case, I'm keenly interested as to what this woman plans on attempting. And I know damn well she's plotting something risky. A person's eyes can define their demeanour more than any other facet of their face, something that I've long been mindful of.

Personally, I sincerely hope she chooses to enter. So far, performing this assignment with the same approach of my colleagues has been nothing more than a bore. This normalcy approach is, lamentably, uninteresting and I'd much rather be back at the hotel with Robin. But...if this strange woman decides to finalize her fate by entering the loo, this assignment will have shedloads more appeal.

My left hand snuck into my jacket, fingers calmly gripping my C70. Emotions that were once overwhelming and smothering thanks to that oversized crowd gave way to a familiar and eager frenzy that swelled up rabidly. This atmosphere hadn't reared its head since the finale of my previous assignment, and as much as I struggled to diminish it there was this furious thrill that laughed and told me not to lessen the rage.

This frenzy, mother of mercy, this frenzy is unsullied. The notion of turning the tables on someone and becoming the sole, true unhinged beast that exists in a space is everything about this job that I detest yet adore because it fulfils me. The widespread frenzy dragged my hand away from my C70, not allowing me to proceed this easily.

The handle pushed down, and the door slowly cracked. My heart pounded more recklessly than a sledgehammer working a nail, and my eyes were so intensely wary of sudden movement that they refused to blink.

A bush of blonde hair materialised ever so slightly from the past the door frame, and I failed to bless her with another step. I yanked the woman forward the moment her arm came into view, slamming the door shut with my back at the same time.

"Hey!" She shouted.

The woman grunted as I flung her across the room without warning or issue. To my surprise, she managed to gracefully roll back onto her feet. All while wearing a dress *and* coat to boot. At this point my hand reached back for my C70 but the woman was quicker, kicking the handgun out of my grip just before I could aim it at her. The tip of her heel stung the back of my hand, but I still responded by throwing a kick of my own at the woman. To my dismay, she dodged it.

"What do you think you're doing?" The woman asked. Though her voice bellowed with rage, her startingly hurried voice caught me off guard.

"Don't play the fool with me," I said, grabbing the woman by her shoulders. Spinning around with her in my grip, I thoughtlessly slammed her against the wall. "You know damn well I saw you following me."

For a moment, the woman's bewilderment melted into another doe-eyed stare. Her glamourous chestnut eyes raced around my face as I continued to pin her to the wall, unable to comprehend what on earth she could be thinking about. Eventually, she snapped out of this daze and those eyes of her suddenly charged with a velocity of venom.

"How dare you," she said.

My grip on the woman's shoulders tightened, causing her to squirm some. "How dare I? I know who you are. You're involved with Scobretti. I don't know how the bloody hell you managed to figure out who I was, but you have five seconds to give me information before I fully lose my temper."

The rage this woman carried tripled, and it was evident by her viciously contorted facial features. Her sweat-drenched face was a blistering shade of crimson and steam would've been bursting from her ears had this been a cartoon. The woman's open mouth exposed clenched teeth that were most likely barely able to keep her from shouting a pile of obscenities are me.

"You absolutely pathetic moron," the woman said. "You clearly have no idea who the fuck I am."

"You're running out of time."

"And I'm running out of patience! How you do you not know me? Didn't your organization give you my files?"

Her words, bizarre enough as they were, caused a rapid decrease in the frenzy that raged within my blood. My tight grip on her shoulders loosened as my hands retreated from her gently. This act was unsuccessful, however, in that it didn't lessen the hostility any because the woman shoved me with enough might to send me back a couple feet.

"I'm Debi DeLaise, CIA. You…you damn imbecile, are Mark McGarriff of Her Majesty's Dauntless Church of Secret Intelligence."

Debi proceeded to fling her hands up to her head, ripping off what was all along a blonde wig. And underneath that wig was a sight that converted all that drained rage of mine into, out of all possible emotions, utter allure. Debi possessed one of my most potent drugs. Her actual hair, though partly concealed by a wig cap, was a stunning shade of dark auburn.

10

I've been employed by Her Majesty's Church for seven years and never has mortification been as prevalent and jeering as it is now. Sure, there'd been times where utter unease slithered up my sleeve, but they tended to fall in the garden of modest predicaments that were uncomplicated to escape. For example, early on in my career I'd accidentally attempted to check in to a hotel using the wrong pseudonym. The receptionist explained to me that there was no one under that name listed in their books, but I shamelessly argued until the realization of my mistake struck me with an iron. See, that sort of humiliation certainly wasn't agreeable, but it was swiftly alleviated due to my crafting a somewhat believable tale about why the error occurred. But this time around? Roughly handling my contact in the manner that I did? If Trailsby ends up ordering me go inactive for a period, I'd take that reprimand directly on the chin. This is an unforeseen level of atrocious that I'd never experienced, nor ever imagined I'd undergo.

Almost every time I'd been saddled with a contact, there were two outcomes to our partnership. The first, which was not only the most frequent occurrence but also my personal preference, was that I managed to avoid the contact the entire duration of the assignment. Regarding how my regular assignments are handled, they're able to be accomplished in less than three days. Never has one lasted any longer than that, and I take immeasurable pride in that. Even with the target I dealt with who frequented eight bases, the number of locations didn't matter because I still apprehended that garbage heap twelve hours upon the jet's landing.

The second outcome was rare in comparison, so much so that it's been around an eternity since I can even recall standing face to face with a contact. That outcome involves actively working with them, and I'll admit that such idiocy was briefly attempted upon first joining Her Majesty's Church. Did I cross paths with any contacts I truly enjoyed working with? Never, but they were accommodating enough when it pertained to dealing with a new operative who'd surely be more of a drag if it weren't for the beauty of discipline.

The two contacts I ever cooperated with were men in their mid-fifties who'd been working for the CIA for so long that they were heavily lacking in personality. Their personalities were, unfortunately, so maddeningly intertwined with their work that I honestly cannot tell the two blokes apart from each other. Despite this, they were courteous enough to put up with the questions I'd ask them in my futile attempts to better acquaint myself with them. But they never gave up too much personal information. They preferred to focus on the job, which I respected but also found horribly dull at the time.

A year of employment passed before Trailsby explained to me the true purpose behind my position versus the positions of the other operatives. And, after expounding the brutal details of my *higher purpose* inside of my mental facilities, he made a vow. He swore to me that, unless it was imperative, I could proceed with my assignments without the assistance of a contact. Rare as it is for Trailsby to overpromise and underdeliver, that is precisely what happened in this case. Some months after being assured that I'd never be hindered from my responsibilities by having an officer or agent breathing down my neck, he called me into his office for something even more rare: an apology.

Trailsby explained that, while most allied foreign intelligence agencies were willing to abide by his proposal, the CIA steadfastly knocked it back. Donald Ganderman, who'd been confirmed as the new Director of Central Intelligence in January of 1981, informed him that every operative of Her Majesty's Church is obligated to be assigned a contact while executing jobs on American soil. Undeterred by Ganderman's refusal, Trailsby reassured me that he would do everything in his power to have this legal matter amended for the purposes of my assignments, but that I was required to *at least* meet and share intel with my assigned American babysitter.

Like contacts from any other agency, those from the CIA aside from the director were not aware of the certain *horrors* that detail my position, and the distinct permissions my organization has granted me as it pertains to the completion of assignments. This made Trailsby understandably perturbed, so he vowed to help maintain some distance between myself and these inadequate add-ons as much as legally allowed. For example, he would make reservations for me at a hotel different from the one where my contact would be staying at, which aided the fulfilment of my tasks. However, the expectation of still meeting with them was too much of a bloody drag to obey. So, I made a conscious effort to simply avoid contacts at all costs. Oh well. It's truly so much easier to do my job without being hampered by some random bore and their incessant craving for tracking a target.

This Debi woman, from everything I could gather in our exchanges, possessed no similarities to the previous contacts I'd dealt with. If only that were a positive, because instead of being a bloody lug she's viper mouthed and has a disdainful, volcanic personality. She's the type of contact I desired to leave in the dust. Alas, Trailsby was more adamant about my working with her than he'd ever been regarding a contact, so I suppose I'll have to be fused with her the rest of our time together.

Debi was positioned by the loo door, arms crossed tightly and muttering inaudible words that I only imagined were the vilest one could spew. Although not the least bit thrilled about the fact that we had to continue collaborating, I detected multiple words within my

For Josephine

Acknowledgements: Excerpt by Michael Benedikt, from *For An Architecture of Reality*, copyright ©1987 by Michael Benedikt. Reprinted by permission of the author; Excerpt by Anne Carson, from *NOX*, copyright ©2010 by Anne Carson. Reprinted by permission of New Directions Publishing Corp; Excerpt by Moyra Davey, from *INDEX CARDS*, ©2020 by Moyra Davey. Reprinted by permission of New Directions Publishing Corp; *Index Cards*, Moyra Davey. London, Fitzcarraldo Editions, 2020. Copyright © Moyra Davey, 2020; Excerpt by John Kelsey, from *Rich Texts*, ©2010 by John Kelsey. Reprinted by permission of Sternberg Press and Institut für Kunstkritik.

First published 2024 by Vagabond Press
www.vagabondpress.net

ISBN 978-1-925735-73-4

This project has been assisted by the Australian Government through Creative Australia, its principal arts investment and advisory body.

Australian Government

being that I ached to tell her. But how in the world am I supposed to apologize for my inappropriate and reckless actions when there's no conceivable circumstances where she'll forgive me? Most would never take such vicious interactions flippantly. However, it's crucial that I do apologize, and I must say something because she's refusing to speak.

"You haven't a clue how—"

"How sorry you are?" Debi asked, keeping me out of her sight.

"Yes."

Debi chortled. "Right. *So* sorry. You know, I feel like I know exactly what I want to say to you. But there's just so many different options that I don't know which feels best."

"Just speak your mind, Debi."

"For starters you're an unbelievable moron."

"You said that already," I said, pointlessly trying to improve the mood.

"I called you a *pathetic* moron," Debi said, finally facing me again.

"Ah."

"Look, I have so many questions for you that I can't keep track of them all. I'll tear into you more later. Right now, we have a job to do."

There were likely a handful of decent responses I could bestow unto her, but none were successfully unearthed. Debi gently shook her head, beads of sweat springing from her forehead in response. She lazily tossed her wig onto her head, likely bothered by my failure to speak, and swiftly proceeded to exit the loo without waiting for me.

Picking up my Matilda-C70, I returned it to my holster as potential questions I yearned to bombard Debi with decided it was *now* the safest time to arise. Why did she practically skulk after me, especially into this loo, when she very well had several opportunities to approach me? Why did she think it was a smart idea to enter the loo without knocking or asking for me? I'm not sure and, the more I ponder it, the more I'm beginning to care less about any rationalizations.

I'm still irate over her spewing off like a bloody banshee, and if she thinks she can spout on like that again she's mistaken. She doesn't care for my actions, fair, but I respond just as poorly to being called a bloody *moron*. For now, we'll just continue with our task at hand and hope that our unfortunate misunderstanding will blow over come morning.

When I finally exited the loo, the music had begun to decrease until it ceased entirely. This, I guessed, marked the start of the auction. I approached Debi, who had her elbows resting on the railing, and mirrored her pose. We both watched as Stella returned to the stage, receiving a wave of applause fit for a celebrity once more.

As Stella began expressing gratitude amidst the cheering and animated guests, Debi tugged on my arm. She motioned her head down to the main floor while pointing at a group consisting of four men and two women situated near the dessert station. They were engaged in a chat and one of the men was more energetic than the others, gesturing a dot but not enough to draw attention away from Stella and the stage.

A facet of this man's appearance that stood out the most to me happened to be his hair. Even though Debi and I were quite far from this group, the lights satisfactorily helped capture his noticeably dark hair. Until now, I hadn't come across a single bloke in this entire building with hair as dark as this man's. Nearly every person in attendance had light brown, blonde, greying, or white hair. Both Scobretti's were listed as having black hair, so this was a positive step.

"One of the Scobretti brothers?" I asked.

"Just wait until he turns around," Debi said, her voice monotonous but almost certainly exaggerated given the manner that she stretched the words out.

Debi must've foreseen the ending to this group's conversing, as the whole lot abruptly dispersed to nearby tables. Everyone except for the dark-haired man. He pulled something out of his back pocket that instantly made my fingers itch for my C70. However, my instincts were peeved when the man started running this object through his hair a few times before returning it to his pocket. Must've been a comb. The man then glanced toward the stage, allowing me to scan his profile. Within seconds, everything clicked into place and Debi's suspicion was revealed to have value. The man was unmistakably Sergio Scobretti. Mercifully my wild interaction with Debi hadn't dragged out any more than it did otherwise we would've missed this chance sighting, especially because Sergio proceeded to make his way to the now shut lobby doors.

None of the other guests appeared to follow Sergio, and at that moment I recalled that the lobby was entirely closed off from the ballroom now that the doors were closed. The staircase had access to the lobby, so I hastily made sure none of the other guests were contemplating whether they needed to go downstairs. Of course, there was always the possibility of bystanders loitering in the lobby, but I casted that idea out because the auction had just begun. That's the gala's main attraction, so everyone's probably fixed on the activities occurring on the stage. Everyone except Sergio, but that doesn't knock me for a six whatsoever. Surely, he's not here for the auction. He's gathering intel for his brother, who is, with any luck, also in attendance.

"So, Mark," Debi said, applying this condescending emphasis on my name that deeply irked me. "How would you proceed? We should've gone over this earlier, but someone apparently decided that would be a waste of time."

"I'd cease that unnecessary conduct if I were you," I said.

Debi scoffed. "Fine. *But* we have to work on the fly so just lead the way."

Obviously, I'd be the one taking the lead here, even if Debi hadn't mentioned it. If she thought otherwise, well, I suppose all faith in her would've gone totally adrift. I began to head to the stairs but before even two steps could be taken, Debi snatched my upper arm and firmly pressed her fingers into my bicep.

"But if you start any bullshit downstairs, you're following my lead," she said.

This woman has got a lot of bloody nerve with her poor attempts at challenging me. Debi glared at me with boatloads more scorn than she had possessed during our initial confrontation, and I merrily returned her spiteful expression. Our mutual glowers lasted several seconds before I tore my arm out of her grip. Continuing, I tilted my head toward the stairs as a signal for Debi to follow me. Despite all her aggressive remarks and confrontational brashness, Debi did *ever so sweetly* gift me the lead so if that's what she asks for, that's what she gets.

There's no doubt that the CIA presented Debi with a file containing my information, so her perception of me, as an operative mind you, should be fully established. Of course, the CIA's file on me almost certainly does not fully enlighten others on how my assignments normally conclude. However, she should at the very least possess enough gen to recognize me as not one to stealthily waltz downstairs when a target is in plain sight. Unfortunately, the guidelines of this assignment bit the rat and forbid me from acting in such dodgy means.

Deplorable bastard, dutifully surrendering to the barmy decree of an ignorant old bloke. Don't adhere to his feeble guidance. You know it's imprudent to repress your pestering insanity.

Oh mercy, there's another voice jostling to expel its asinine opinion. Grotesque in its tone, brittle and low-pitched, it evoked a startling snarl akin to how a deformed neanderthal might've vocalized. Voices like this one are relatively distinguishable from the Phantasms and Edith but are identical to the multitude of scoundrels who frolic in the beastly ocean that is my brain. And, though brushing aside the nit's comment should be undemanding, they don't take kindly to such disrespect. They'll unleash a flock of heinous insults, which commonly compose of rabid yet almost incoherent barks of animosity toward me. Once that initial onslaught of antagonistic babble has concluded, the voices will then recover their composure enough to chastise me for attempting to disregard their words. The derogation of my mental health is utterly agonizing and callous. It's too detestable to definitively defy. Therefore, there's no option but to comply with the voice and...not adhere to Trailsby's instructions.

Unwillingly, I scurried down the steps like a peckish jackal so to reach Sergio Scobretti before he had an opportunity to vanish. This was a bloody inappropriate decision, but the momentarily reduced decomposition of my sanity was paramount. The clacking of Debi's heels on the steps echoed from behind, and she's undoubtedly a touch slower than me because of them. That's no issue. I'll just set the scene up and she can be a mere background player for now.

Once closing in on the final three steps, a sudden mental twinge coerced me into carelessly jumping past them as though I was ten years younger. At least at that age handling such actions with the athletic grace of a kangaroo was a full sail. My subsequent attempt to land on the carpeted lobby floor unfortunately devolved into a stumble that was utterly devoid of poise. I expected to hear Debi either chuckle or groan at my barmy behaviour. But she didn't and, for her sake, it was appreciated.

Sergio Scobretti, twenty-seven, was standing in the middle of the lobby with a notepad in his hand. His attention was pinned on me, however, no thanks to that abysmal landing of mine. Cocking an eyebrow, Sergio smirked as he chuckled. He set the notepad inside one of the inner pockets of his satin black tuxedo jacket and asked, "you miss a couple steps there, guy?"

In hindsight, never have any of my numerous targets been younger than thirty-five or so. On average, they're around five years older than my current age and have put years of depraved dedication into their tawdry line of work. The crueller the profession, the more creases and marks adorn their faces. It tends to apply to their associates too. Even their ages are normally advanced too, and sometimes they're *older* than the target themselves. This is usually an indication of someone hardened by their profession, though it's not uncommon to challenge some henchman in their fifties who's utterly inept at what they're paid to do. And yet there's Sergio. It was difficult to believe this bloke could be part of such an atrocious operation.

For someone nearing thirty, the man owned a youthful appearance. If, by chance, I'd bumped into Sergio on the street, my guess would've been that he'd just graduated university. It's one thing having to refer to a black and white licence photo, as still images do love misleading people if certain angles are captured. But finally facing him in person made this whole situation vastly uncanny.

Debi's phrase of "just lead the way" circled around me as I tidied up my jacket and shook off a stinging sensation in my knee. A nagging tweak that could've been avoided had that joker not convinced me to cause a stir. The conduct that I intended to proceed with was going to further incense Debi, as if that were possible, but it was padlocked and unalterable. To try and ease my nerves, I mentally repeated to myself that it was going to be tolerable. One of my targets was mere feet away from me, and if this were any other assignment then it could be dealt with in this procedure.

Precisely. You must waste him, Mark. You won't be reprimanded for doing your job.

Yes, that's true so why fret about *modifying* the plan a tad? Trailsby might be flustered if word travels back to him, but at least there's one bastard knocked off. So, does it truly matter? No, and damn anyone who claims that it does matter because they're bloody liars. And that includes the version of me who initially thought it'd be the logical decision. Damned fool. All of them would regret not advancing in a guise like my regular approach. Besides, I've earned something that the lot will never acquire. Not the police, not servicepeople, and not even my contemporaries in any intelligence service including my own. No, I earned the right, as invested by Her Majesty's Church, to be as deranged as I dare desire.

Wasting no time, I promptly approached Sergio while drawing my C70 out from its holster. The handgun's sudden appearance scrubbed that nonchalant smirk off his face. However, an intense glare formed from the wreckage as Sergio continued to stand where he was. Absent were any signs of dread and, even with his eyes planted on the C70, he didn't cower at the sight of the weapon that was itching for him.

I jabbed the gun into Sergio's stomach with the vigorous intensity of a brawler's prizewinning strike. The impact caused him to bowl over and grunt. Though the rapid slosh successfully winded him, Sergio was able to cough out "are you serious?"

"What are you doing?" Debi's venomous voice whispered in my ear, her hands snatching my drawn arm.

"I'm not someone who can be reasoned with, Scobretti," I said, ignoring Debi's question. "So, the only choice you have is to listen to me."

"Is that right?" Sergio asked, his hostility now drenched with a wave of incredulity.

"I have a job for you," I said. "You're going to take us to your brother's shop. Questions aren't permitted. And don't fight me on this because I won't continue to be as warm and caring as I am right now."

Sergio chuckled with an emerging smile, which alluded to his persona now shifting entirely from fury to disbelief. He proceeded to say, "I don't know how you know me or my brother, you psycho. But let me tell you this. I'm not taking you anywhere, so you oughta put that gun away before someone fucks you up."

Debi took a stab at yanking my arm away, but all that derived from her poor attempt to halt me was my bestowing her an utterly brief glance. Mouthing "no" to her, I immediately refocused my concentration on Sergio. His arrogant air was infuriating so, to rectify that, I drove my C70 into his stomach even more relentlessly than the first time.

"It's pitiful that you even remotely believe some nit can save you," I said, litres of my own arrogance lining each successive word. "Though, frankly, it's worse that you *require* reinforcements. Are you *that* daunted? If so then call someone, you bloody coward. Call them so you can watch me singlehandedly ravage this whole lobby. Whatever happens to them, well, their blood would be on your hands."

"This bad cop routine is getting out of hand," Debi cruelly whispered in my ear. "Stop it. Let me take over."

Sergio must've caught my eyes momentarily race toward Debi because he seized the opportunity to shout "Rocco!"

A faint clamour developed from above, like that of distant stampeding bison. The noise rapidly revealed itself to be thunderous footsteps that were bombing across the upper half of the staircase. Then came a drop of silence that disabled my senses. Glancing upward, my ability to respond was in vain as my view became obscured by a burly figure that plummeted in the guise of a seasoned skydiver. The shape collided into me like an anvil, the severity of the impact sending me several feet away. My body roughly rammed against the ground, which caused my C70 to soar out of my grip.

The spreadeagle figure that had ambushed and staggered me was, as expected, Rocco Abruzzoli, thirty-three. He proceeded to lift my collapsible frame up and landed a powerful, and lucky, strike to my stomach. The extent of the strike's potency propelled my feet off the carpet before I slumped to my knees, gasping for air that was wary to return to me.

Debi made an effort to place Abruzzoli in a headlock, but a now unrestricted Sergio shoved her from out of his way and opted to slingshot himself against the door. A peculiar signal of distress, perhaps? Sergio's exaggerated exit drew the attention of the guard with the bushy moustache, who barrelled into the lobby like a raving rhinoceros.

Abruzzoli's hand was clenching the collar of my shirt, so I decided to manoeuvre the control of the situation toward my deck. I hastily repositioned my body enough to cast my assailant along the path of the guard. Failing to halt his vexed charge, the moustached bloke accidentally struck Abruzzoli with all the might intended for me. Evidently, this guard had quite a few faulty wires tangled in his brain.

The bodies of Abruzzoli and the moustached guard careened into the doors that led to the ballroom. Though the doors didn't fly open, the might of the collision delivered a roaring clang. This, predictably, resulted in some people to rush inside of the lobby. Luckily for us, however, it only happened to be the tailcoated servers and not any of the guests. Maybe those champagne-filled businesspeople and their spouses knew better than to venture toward such brutal racket.

Initially, the arrival of the servers came off as understandable. They were probably curious about the sudden commotion and simultaneously fretful over the lobby being trashed. Then, much to my sincere surprise, the servers attempted to detain both me and Debi by arranging us in poses that would make a martials arts grandmaster shed tears of hysterical shame. Two of them were gripping at my legs and struggling to pull me to the ground. Judging by their shoddy efforts, these lousy middle-aged hors d'oeuvres peddlers absolutely hadn't a clue what they were doing.

"Forget those psychos, Rocco!" Sergio shouted, his head peering through the doorway of the building's entrance. "Let's go!"

Abruzzoli, who'd flung the immobile and possibly unconscious moustached guard off him, returned to his feet. "Deal with them," he told the servers while wiping off his shoulders. "Call the cops, toss them into a river, I don't give a shit. Just deal with them."

As he hiked to the exit, Abruzzoli took a brief detour and approached me. He snatched my collar and rose a fist, which prompted me to inch my chin up a touch. If this bastard desperately wants to hit me again, then I might as well assist him. But, after glaring at me for several seconds, the bloke ultimately released his grip. Interesting. Miscreant must've believed another strike wouldn't be worth the effort. So, to my chagrin, Abruzzoli rushed out of the building with Sergio.

It was almost comically effortless to break free from the timeless takedown abilities that were skilfully modelled by the servers. Straightening out my hands, I carefully whacked the necks of the two clods who were handling my legs. Due effort was made to land each hand precisely where the carotid artery was located. Upon impact, both of them groaned and sagged to the ground, releasing me in the process.

Debi rolled her body forward, which sent a different server gliding off her back. The servers who weren't yet seeking to challenge us merely retreated after witnessing this scene. Surely the ease of how we removed ourselves from their comrades' pitiful grasps was enough to dissuade them from following Rocco's commands.

As I recovered my poor C70, which had now absurdly left my grip twice in a single night, another booming racket rocketed violently throughout the lobby. This stemmed from Debi, who'd departed through the front entrance without saying a word.

***

The dismal sky was rather eager to let Debi and I know just how displeased it was with us by concealing itself under clouds. Streets that could've been painted by the lustre of the moon were instead ornamenting itself by lampposts and traffic lights. We'd very likely be mocked and denounced as voyeurs if we'd asked to view the moon, which was showering behind that barrier of clouds. Had the moon been out, these streets would've brought forth an enchantingly haunted ambience. One that, no doubt, had the potential to remind me of Vrycastle's sullen nature while basking in the dark. Alas, the mixture of the golden hues with the traffic lights brought about a grittier air that enunciated the emptiness of our surroundings.

We were in Debi's car, a pale blue Volkswagen Polo Mark I. The cosy vehicle, once parked in a five-hour public car park near Sepia Harvest, exhibited a predominantly dark interior that corresponded with what I presumed was the starkly negative nature of Debi's thoughts. Once we'd left the gala, she'd been silent and immensely icy toward me considering she'd nearly driven off before I'd even settled into my seat. Part of me desired to express ample aggravation with her in return, but why bother? Her life was put in danger tonight because of me and while I proceeded as I would during any other assignment, I'll admit fault in my judgement. An inability to refute orders from one of my mental captors.

Personally, I bloody detest questioning hypotheticals but what if Abruzzoli elected to finish us off before leaving the building? What if the guards and servers were capable *and* armed? There have been innumerable instances where I've willingly journeyed into these situations fully aware that my behaviour was asinine. And though, at least then, I vehemently champion those prior actions, it should've never been instigated with Debi in tow.

My ferocious desire to perform this assignment in my usual approach consumed my judgment. Fear of mental retribution only enhanced the decision. That, right there, is my one regret from this evening. There shouldn't be additional qualms compounding that grand mistake. Absolutely not. That single regret happened to be the domino that commenced the downfall of the evening's entire purpose. We didn't learn the identity of the potential fourth party and got trounced on top of that. That's more than enough regret to serve a table of twelve.

Debi began to say, "just so you know" and her voice, for the first time this whole evening, exuded calm. She continued with "I'm not going to let you complete this mission alone. We're going to stick it out until we've arrested Abraham Scobretti and his allies. But even with that being said, you have no idea how disgusted I am with you."

"Right," I said.

"I mean, damn it, I just wanna scream at you right now. I wanna tell you how your presence in my car is making me shake because of how enraged I am with you and your actions. How I don't even know who in the world you are aside from the most basic details in a damn file and yet I can't stand being near you."

Out of the corner of my eye, I captured Debi swipe a glimpse of me. Her face contained none of the rage she spoke of. It was as blank as her voice was calm, which very much conveyed just how horribly I'd spoiled the evening.

"Maybe the oath you took doesn't respect the purpose of working with contacts, but mine does. And we have to do this together."

Whether racked up by pure guilt or realizing there was no other choice but to answer accordingly, the words that uttered from my mouth happened to be "I agree."

"Good."

Debi parked the Volkswagen in one of open spaces of Nouveau Rêve's lot. Turning the car off, she took her blonde wig off and hurled it into the back. I accepted that there was a near zero percent chance of Debi reaching over to strangle me, though that didn't keep me from bracing for it. It never came about, however, as Debi unlocked her doors and the two of us strolled into the hotel donning deserted expressions that might've matched if examined closely enough.

In the lift, my body stiffened and paused when Debi reached for the buttons at the same time I did. Please, for all that's good and glorious, tell me she's not on my floor. Fortunately, Debi pushed the button for *three* and that was satisfiable enough. The last thing I presumed either of us hankered for was to be sharing a floor, let alone lodge in adjacent rooms. When the lift dinged, Debi turned to me and said, "I'm in room three-oh-six. Meet me downstairs at nine. We'll get breakfast and go from there." With that, she went on her way.

The ominous tension that'd been looming like a torrential rainstorm above my bonce since the moment my eyes met Debi's finally dissipated. I emitted a heavy sigh of relief, which was followed by a random, silent chuckle. Appropriate for such a dismal evening. Experiences this poor seldom occur and the last one, while bleak, doesn't hold a sabre to this wretched muck.

Even though England is five hours ahead of New Jersey, my mental facilities are still as energized as they'd been upon waking up from that nap on the jet. The concept of *jet lag* has never affected me all that much, which is one of the most beneficial abilities you could possess when your job requires you to fly through multiple time zones. The first time this knack was truly documented was when I'd travelled to…bloody California on an assignment. That journey took me back eight time zones and yet becoming acclimated with the Pacific Time Zone happened almost immediately. Not an ounce of exhaustion settled in until it was nearly midnight *in California*.

It's incredibly possible that jet lag never manages to detain me because the nature of my profession stirs up every one of my nerves. Once I've been dispatched by Her Majesty's Church, the voyage to my assigned destination allows me a final opportunity of possible slumber before the remainder of my time is absorbed by the prospect of briefly mapping out my strategies and executing them.

Every now and then, I'll find myself unable to even fall asleep while on the jet, but it's not all that worrying. Sleep is already a stranger, so the concoction of thrill and despair that inevitably roams inside of me once on the pursuit is never too alarmed by my inability to secure rest. It's another drug that's slowly destroying me and only makes the voices, which are at bay as of now, more sadistic and vitriolic.

Stepping out of the walk-in shower after savouring the pressure of the hot water, any residual tension from this blissfully unenchanted evening evaporated with the steam that spun around in the loo. Grabbing a towel from the neatly folded collection on a rack near the sink, I instinctively pressed it against my face and appreciated its soft and comforting sensation.

The rectangular mirror began its predictable begging of me to observe my worn face. They don't suppress their hatred for me. They feast off the torment I stumble on when compelled to examine a face that they've mangled and maimed. However, upon wrapping the towel around my waist, I meticulously glued my vision to the tile. While the voices are heinous and mighty in their persuasion, the sway of the mirrors have never been able to rival them. They're more persistent, the magnetic nagging occasionally mustering a side glance from me. But, unlike the voices, the mirrors are easier to reject.

A gentle knocking rang three times and, though briefly exasperated that the visitor might've been Debi itching to berate me more, sudden remembrance of my late-night lust eased those concerns. I opened the door and there was the gorgeous Robin standing before me, still dressed in the same clothes as earlier and with a cunning smile on her face. In her hands were two glasses and a bottle of white wine. How blissful it is to have her accompany me for the night. Had it not been Robin, seedier means would've had to have been undertaken. Though American sex workers are judged as disease-riddled harlots, that's the fault of trashy forms of media. Nevertheless, my preference is for the shapely woman in front of me.

Robin slowly eyed me up and down before saying, "doesn't look like you forgot about our plans."

"Of course, I didn't," I said, unsure if that were true or not.

When Robin entered, she set the wine and glasses on the desk near the closet. But she didn't open the bottle or even return to me. Instead, for some reason, she began roaming around my room. She peeked under my bed, scoped out the loo, and studied every trifling aspect as though she'd never been in one of these rooms until now. Highly doubtful, being that she's an employee.

"Is there something wrong?" I asked

"Oh, no," Robin said, briefly eyeing the closest before ambling back toward the bed. "I'm just wondering where you're hiding her.

"Hiding who?"

"When you returned not too long ago, I saw you walk in with some other redhead. Both of you were dressed to the tens." Robin picked up my tuxedo jacket from one of the lounge chairs and examined it.

"Ah yes," I said, trying to pick up if Robin was merely teasing me or was truly suspicious that Debi was in here with me. "She's a work associate. I'm afraid I can't call the lass anything more than just that. *Especially* not an acquaintance. Through conversation I learned that she was staying here as well, so I asked her for a ride back."

Robin began to step closer to me, but she still remained a couple inches away as she asked, "you stand by that story?"

"You can continue searching, my darling. Tear this room to pieces if you wish. But my associate went right to her room once we returned from the event."

"Just making sure." Robin finally entered my realm and grabbed my hand. "Wouldn't have blamed her though." She led me to the desk where the wine sat. "After all, it's not every day you encounter an attractive man with an accent as soft and deep as yours. You're British, right?"

"Not quite," I said, cracking open the bottle before pouring wine into each of our glasses. "I'm a Welshman. Well, partly that. My mother was born in Wales while my father is from Massachusetts."

"Where were you born?"

"Wales," I said as my hand crept onto Robin's back, slowly hiking upward.

Robin reached for the glass that was presented to her, but I refused to fully surrender it to her. The hand placed on her back had now reached the end of her hair, which I gently pulled. Robin's chin tilted up as the glass, still in my grip, touched her lips.

"Hmm." Robin smirked as she took a sip of the wine. "Then you're Welsh to me."

"Well, I can be anything you desire."

Admittingly, I cannot claim myself as a genuine Welshman. While I was born in Wales, I grew up in the United States of course. See, my parents had been living in the United States for about fifteen years before I was conceived. When my mother was about seven months pregnant with me, she received word that her mother, a true example of the Welsh people and a pillar in her community in the south of Wales, had fallen ill. She's explained in the past that she only intended to be gone for about a week to help her aging parents through this harrowing time, as she's an only child. My grandmother, tragically, ended up passing away from what started as a small virus, and my mom stayed in Wales much longer than that seven-day deadline. She had to help plan the funeral arrangements and support her father as he adjusted to this new life without his wife. Things took longer to settle than expected, as things always do, and suddenly Mom was far too pregnant to be permitted on a plane. Thus, I was born in Wales.

Robin recaptured my priorities, as her curvaceous body was now practically attached to mine. We left no room for even a family of particles to pass between us. Her fingers caressed my hand, gripped it, and brought the glass back so that she could take another sip.

"Anything I desire?" She asked.

"I'm your servant, Robin," I said. "That's my purpose."

Robin didn't answer me. Rather, her face flushed and her breathing rapidly intensified to the point it resonated through my body.

Regardless of my partner, I'll make damn sure she hears me utter those words when we're together for the first time. This enables her, whether she's a regular escort or a mere fling, to anticipate an evening where she's royalty. An evening where she assumes supremacy, in certain aspects mind you, and most anything she desires shall be granted.

Of course, there's a few wishes I'll outright decline because even my lust-craved vices have standards. And if she aims to dominate me, well, that's a farcical mistake. Practical pleasures, however, make for a lively evening. Of course, that's my opinion as I refuse to speak for her. While lovemaking is a grave addiction of mine, so much so that it's *never* been less than satisfactory, claiming every frenzied rendezvous has been perfect *for her* would be arrogant and foolish. All that can be said is that I never fail to give her my all and my only hope is that my partner is satisfied by the end of it.

The wine glass found its way back to the desk as our mouths solely craved one another's. With every animalistic kiss and lip bite, an article of Robin's clothing sailed off until she was left nearly bare. She wore her green lace bra as well as baby blue satin knickers that had a black lace trim at the legs and a tiny bow at the top. Her hands impatiently gripped at my towel, but I seized them and whispered "no."

Robin cocked an eyebrow, but I made sure she understood my intentions promptly as our bodies dropped to the bed. Lifting onto my knees, I admired Robin's dazzling figure for a moment, specifically the artistic design of her body spread on my bed. She was showing off a full smile while moving her rust-coloured hair out of her face. Taking snapshots of conquests is a droll kink, one of which I'm not friendly with. However, several mental photographs have been snapped and I'll be damned if they melt away.

Her superb thighs were pressed together, but this wrong was fixed as I slid a hand between her knees and spread them out. She stared at me, her expression feverish, hungry, and seemingly in awe of what she was about to receive.

"This is first, Robin. Your pleasure comes first."

11

If the masses were asked if they had a *type* as it pertains to who they're sexually attracted to, a titanic majority would reveal that they most certainly do. Some probably unearthed it upon the commencement of their maturation. Others, such as I, might've discovered their type at a very young age. For me, the dawning of my adoration for redheads developed while in elementary school. My first-grade teacher, Ms. Clothilde, whose image is still unmistakable after over thirty years, was a stately woman in her mid-forties. She had long, vibrant, and natural red hair and mercy was my erotic outlook on women forever determined. Between that hair and her constant smile, never fleeing no matter how unruly some of us petulant children could be, the woman should've been in movies. Ms. Clothilde was just too affectionate and sweet to be involved in *that* world.

For the most part, I'd like to say that while I possess a *type*, it's not as though I'll eternally pursue partners who fill that image. For example, while redheaded women might be my drug of choice, my ex-wife Darla is a brunette. There are certainly shedloads of other factors that come into play here, and it can range from pure mutual attraction to my fix simply not being concerned if the woman is twenty-five or seventy-five.

Surely all my peers, and especially my entire family, would judge me if they were aware of this range and that judgment would be welcomed with barbed arms. They have no business criticizing my choices, just as I've never maligned their personal decisions either. Most importantly, other ranges unfortunately exist that are horribly despicable for someone around my age to hold. Therefore, my preferences honestly sit in a rather tame league.

Speaking of being judged, there are people out there who irresponsibly consider it wise to confuse *type* with *fetish*. That's an issue, and one that bothers me more than it probably should. This stems from a salivating infatuation I have for a certain design of women who're unjustly ridiculed by the absurd public. Here's the truth. Not only do I believe all bodies are attractive, apart from ones that are twig thin, but my favourite female body type is one like Robin's. Shapely. How the dictators of mass media would bawl over my disregard for thin and temptation for curves.

This fondness for buxom women, mother of mercy, brought about so much scorn during my youth you'd think I clubbed a baby seal. It arose in high school, specifically at...bloody prom, an event so asinine that the mere thought of its artificial merriment causes repulsion to this day. Due to the overwhelming persistence of my parents and sisters, I begrudgingly attended it and even though the company of friends was decent, most of the experience was unbelievably banal and insincere.

When the romantic ballad started, everyone scurried onto the dancefloor and swayed together. Lacking a date as my most recent relationship at that time had ended a month before, I ended up dancing with a girl who was hardly an acquaintance of mine. We had mutual friends but never conversed much at all. Her name was Virginia, though her last name escapes me aside from the fact that it began with a *P*. She had a charming, round face as well as a very shapely figure. Our dance lasted the entire two-minute song and, though we both appreciated the moment as a friendly affair, this spurred my passion for buxom women.

Throughout college, Mom used to have this aversion to my walking out with girls who possessed these figures out of insensitivity that stemmed from our dreary society. Mom was staunch in her beliefs that men who found buxom women attractive were obliviously eroticizing them because they shunned society's rules. She, along with several old acquaintances of mine, would try explaining to me that this attraction was a *fetish*. Yes, that *absolutely* makes sense.

Mom's judgment has improved considerably now, though reminiscing of her previous beliefs have made me ponder more about certain situations. For example, neither of my parents were initially pleased when I married Darla, but my firm belief is that Mom coped with it sooner than expected because Darla was slender. This anecdote is interesting to recall because Darla's now on the buxom side.

Though I haven't been in a relationship not based around sex in over ten years, the few women I've *sort of* walked out with after my marriage ended were also on the buxom side. Just because someone's type may not be what society ignorantly pressures us into worshipping, to desire a certain kind of woman doesn't mean it's a fetish. Unfortunately, adolescents are amped up on society's nonsense, so only those not infected by that cult-like mindset can see beauty in its countless true forms.

Women wearing uniforms, now that is a fetish of mine. Yes, if a woman adorned in theatre blues crossed paths with me, that would be unquestionably alluring. To ramp the table, I know someone who's admitted they're madly tempted by the image of someone swimming or merely basking in water. If that person is in water, then the bloke is utterly enamoured. That, in my opinion, is a fetish. Possessing a sexual attraction toward a shapely woman, on the other hand, is *not* a fetish.

Rolling onto my back, the startling shimmer of the sun's rays cracking through the blinds signalled a new day. Attempting to sit up on the bed and stretch out, a swarm of aches coursed throughout my upper body and the resulting torture was ecstasy. The aches are a characteristic of lovemaking that never fail to bring immense gratification, and these were no exception. Part of the soreness might be the result of getting older, but that comes with the territory so there's no choice but to request it doesn't worsen anytime soon.

Robin wasn't in the bed, but that hardly surprised me. There's a strong likelihood that she must work again today so she probably had to hurry out of here some range of hours ago. I do recall turning onto my stomach around five in the morning and catching of glimpse of her slumbering close to me, which was nice. Seeing a partner resting in serenity after our liaison, her nude body touching mine, is strangely soothing.

Checking the digital alarm clock on the bedside table, I groaned upon making out the number as eighty-forty. Debi told me that we were to meet downstairs at nine and there was no doubt a late arrival would nark her all over again. Unfortunately for Debi, it seems as though she'll be playing another joyous round of the waiting game. At this rate, it must be impossible for her to abhor me as much as she already does.

***

Entering the lift, I exchanged "good mornings" with a couple who were probably around my age. They were dressed identically in all white: polos, shorts, crew socks, sneakers, and visors. And even though we were all indoors, they both already had sunglasses on. Like most of the other guests at Nouveau Rêve, it's evident they're rather affluent. These two have "tan" skin, but the sections of their foreheads that close in on their hairlines display lighter skin tones. They're also standing so straight they're practically stiff. The soft smiles they're showing off are rather satisfied, and I'm guessing this means they haven't an iota of worries plaguing them.

The pair stood closer to the doors while I pulled myself to the lift's rear and slumped against the wall. After our initial "good mornings," we didn't speak again and that was perfectly alright with me. Lift conversations are normally forced unless someone has a pet that'll ease the awkward nature of standing around with strangers for some time. Speaking of time, in my head the lift trip took ages to complete when it was almost certainly descending at its normal pace. The persistent soreness preoccupied me so much that it made me yearn for that comfortable bed, not to mention Robin's secure embrace.

For as much as I strangely love the excruciating sensation of muscle aches, it generates drowsiness and makes insignificant tasks trickier. It was enough of a struggle to put on this grey dress shirt that I decided to forgo a jacket for the time being. Rarely will this be the case when strolling out in public, as I tend to follow strict guidelines with my clothing. But my shoulders can barely lift enough without wanting to stretch to the point of tearing like taffy. I should've caught the time before leaving the room but being neglectful of it was probably for the best because it would've given reason to rush. The shower lasted longer than necessary, but the ecstasy of cold water eagerly attempting to lessen muscle soreness was far too divine to cut in half.

Usually, a Stork watch would be latched on my wrist, but it remains upstairs in my jacket. And for all that the couple in front of me were clad in, identical watches were not among the accessories they flaunted. It is what it is. Debi's undoubtedly going to ram the current time into me while reminding me of our nine o'clock arrangement.

Stepping into the lobby after the couple, the scene was much less frenzied compared to yesterday's nonstop social gathering. The area, which still contained a decent assortment of guests, presented a more controlled atmosphere as most of them were sitting around reading newspapers while taking swigs from their mugs. Those who were conversing did so in tones much fainter than prior. The lack of wine glasses freely circulating probably aided in this calmer environment.

Amongst the crowd, in one of the beige lounge chairs near the dining area, sat Debi. Her chin rested on a clenched fist that was elevated by one of the chair's arms. Due to the placement of her chair, I was non-existent to her unless she decided to glance toward her left. It's a tad surprising that she refused to sit on the nearby loveseat that directly aimed at the lift, though if that had been the case, she absolutely would've greeted me with a malicious scowl.

Debi's dark auburn hair, finally exempt from the confines of the wig cap, was short but impressively teased on top. It's not precisely what I predicted her actual hair would be when not restricted by that cap. There was no doubt it'd be a shorter cut, but my first guess would've absolutely been a bob. This style, however, reminded me of all the upstart soap opera actresses who've rocketed to fame in this year alone. It's also sported by those video-ready and interchangeable young pop singers who've made the radio utterly unlistenable. At least there's a positive and a negative with such a style.

Moving closer to Debi, I observed her eyes blinking at a ferocious pace. It was as though her eyelashes repeatedly took part in botched parachuting attempts. Debi's head began tilting forward but immediately darted back up, the blinking refusing to cede even after such a full-bodied jerk. That's when it became apparent that she was all but ready to nod off.

Would it be best to gently say her name to seize her attention? Most certainly but, upon taking an extensive scan of my exhausted *partner*, maniacal jesters materialised atop Debi's head. They pleaded with me to be surlier in my methods before vanishing as instantly as they'd developed. Abysmal attempts at justifying my lunacy, I suppose.

While my embarrassment over yesterday's poorly judged actions have subsided, the venom that leaked from our words still incited aggravation. But, for as much as last night has left the most abhorrently bitter taste in my mouth, coming off in a surly manner will do damn all to salvage our already fractured partnership. So...instead of giving in to those jester bastards, perhaps giving off a cheeky impression would soothe any tension that might trickle out today.

Deciding on this morning's performance was an effortless undertaking. A classic trick that used to leave me rolling in the aisles during my youth. Executing it now, at my age, was admittedly absurd but you never know. Maybe it'd give Debi reason to laugh at the pure foolishness. And if it was to fail, well, at least her non-frazzled, authentic personality would be revealed in mere moments.

Near Debi's seat stood a column that marked the end of the *lounge* section. With that in mind, I gradually morphed my casual walk into that of a discreet stride. Approaching her from behind, my index finger extended and carefully advanced toward her shoulder in a painstakingly drawn-out manner. Debi continued to operate in that unending cycle of nearly nodding off before abruptly awakening for a tick. One of her sudden jolts occurred just as my finger reached her shoulder. Fortunately, I'm entirely incapable of flinching anymore, and that's due to the year of combat training with Minister Esprine. How proud he'd be to see me utilize my techniques as adeptly as I am at this very moment. When Debi's head began to inevitably tilt forward once more, the time had come to conclude this quest. Smirking at my madness and unable to halt myself from acting like an unadulterated joker, I swiftly poked Debi's shoulder a few times.

Just as I'd hoped for, Debi's entire body propelled up at least a few inches from her seat. Witnessing her arms and legs flinging around as though she'd ejected all her bones from her body was hysterical in of itself. But then there was the theatrical manner of how she shouted the word *huh*. Almost in the guise of a cartoon character. Debi must've elected to succumb to the demands of sleep the precise moment of the poke because the first sound that emitted from her mouth happened to be a shrill snore.

Perching myself behind the nearby column, I quietly chuckled. Mercy was that the most idiotic game someone my age could partake in. Though, despite the insanity of the situation and how unlike me it was to perform such an action *now*, it harkened back to my childhood. Those entertaining days when I'd tease all my sisters with a whole shedload of practical jokes. Popping out of their closets while sporting unsightly rubber monster masks, waiting under their beds for hours on end just to snatch their unsuspecting ankles.

The supreme prank, however, involved fake blood capsules I'd chew on during dinner. When the dining room was devoid of conversations as everyone was preoccupied with their food, they'd all become alarmed by my sudden howling in pain. Whichever sister was sitting closest to me *always* asked if I was alright, only for me to spit the fake blood onto her blouse. Each of my sisters fell for this every time, to the point my parents began to laugh at their expense as well.

My sisters would curse me to the depths of the abyss for my being a nuisance then, but they all ultimately found the humour in it as we aged. Those thoughts, well, they honestly made me think less negatively about what I'd just done to Debi. Oftentimes we all could use a hearty laugh to take pleasure in. Makes me question why I don't seek these pleasures out more instead of rotting away in my mental prison cell.

"You're a barrel of laughs," Debi said, the volume of her voice increasing with each word.

When Debi took at peek at me from the other side of the column, her face initially bore frustration. Her rose lips had crafted a firm frown and those chestnut gems of hers eyed me as though I had behaved like a disobedient dog. This reaction, much to my satisfaction, failed to stand pat for more than two seconds as the edges of Debi's lips began budging up.

"That was ridiculous." Debi stifled a laugh. "And you should be ashamed of yourself."

"You needn't worry about that because I'm always ashamed of myself."

The two of us moved away from the column and back to where Debi had once sat. She leaned against the back of the chair and adjusted the floral purse she had slung over her shoulder. Debi then tried to place her hands into the pockets of her baggy grape-coloured trousers though the various silver bracelets on both her wrists made the process problematic. They both displayed charms of the classic playing card suits: silver hearts, spades, diamonds, and clubs.

"Looks like you overslept, huh?" Debi asked. "You're at least an hour late."

"I did," I said, "but thankfully I'm *well rested.* Was your bed not comfortable enough?"

Debi scoffed. "It was fine, but I have my reasons for not getting enough sleep. I'll tell you over breakfast—"

"Not exactly sure I fancy to hear those reasons," I said.

"Oh, how you frustrate me. As I was saying, I'll tell you everything over breakfast. There's a lot we need to talk about, but I don't wanna grab anything here. Never liked hotel food. Anywhere in particular you'd wanna go?"

"Maybe there's a Waffle Lodge nearby."

"What?" Debi stared at me as though I'd personally insulted her entire family. "Waffle Lodge? We don't have any of those up here. I'm shocked you even know about Waffle Lodge. Aren't you from England?"

"Yes, I *live* in England, but I lived in the United States most of my life. And a good portion of it was spent in Georgia."

"Ah, Georgia. Where there's a Waffle Lodge on every street. I'm guessing you never spent much time up north, huh? Waffle Lodges are a southern thing."

"Damn," I said, rather stunned by my obliviousness to such a distinct fact being that Massachusetts was technically my home state. "Well, that's unfortunate."

"Yeah, I guess. Have you ever been to Dunk Your Donuts? They've got the best coffee I've ever had."

"Never heard of them, but I do enjoy a good coffee."

"Perfect." Debi dug through her purse, retrieving her car keys. She tossed them to me and motioned to the front doors.

Following her lead, I instinctively glanced over at the front desk as the two of us neared the doors. Robin was nowhere in sight. Instead, a male receptionist stood behind the table. He waved to me, and I reciprocated the gesture. Perhaps Robin works later in the day. And besides, it's best she doesn't see me departing the hotel with Debi. Obviously, Robin and I have nothing more between us than a mere fling, but I'd rather not be deemed a *two-timer*.

***

With their upbeat yellow and orange lettering, Dunk Your Donuts could've been a product of this zany 1980s obsession for colours. However, Debi explained during the drive that it'd been around since the 1940s. Apparently, the chain launched in New Jersey and the first location is still fully functioning as well. She told me that she's visited that location numerous times, but that her first visit was almost surrealistic. How she could visualize the history of the store upon stepping through its doors, especially as the building was lacking customers while she was there. In that emptiness, she described how she detected the presence of people who are now most likely around my parents' age lined up to order food. Hearing the lively chatter of patrons and staff throughout the entire building. The way she spoke about the chain so highly did dramatically raise my expectations, though it also justified why she's adored the place for all this time.

I followed her stories up with tales of my experience at the original Waffle Lodge which, unfortunately, became non-operational a few years before I left Georgia. Rather than appreciate how relatable our stories were, Debi proceeded to wonder how someone with my accent managed to end up in Georgia. If that wasn't enough, she also questioned how southerners didn't laugh me out of buildings because of my accent. To be fair, those questions weren't out of the ordinary as the whole lot of my old schoolmates in both Ludlow, Massachusetts and Spotsylvania County, Virginia marvelled at that topic. Even I reflected on it for years after moving back to England. Though no solutions were unearthed in the case of the adolescent epoch, my ability to persist in Georgia had to have been bolstered by the clout wielded by Darla's family.

It was almost comical, the sheer quantity of doughnuts situated on the racks behind the worker. This establishment seemingly offered every variety of doughnut ever invented, and it knocked the spots off the modest shops in Vrycastle. A small sign close to the register advertised pumpkin flavoured treats and beverages that were to be available next month. A shame, truly, as I used to revere pumpkin flavoured items and would've been keen on trying one of their doughnuts.

Debi ordered the both of us hot coffees. Hers was crammed with cream and sugar, whereas mine was black. "Figures," Debi said at my choice. She also chose to have hash browns, but nothing else. Being that I was unable to decide on a food item, that choice was allocated to the worker. He first asked if we wished to have a dozen, but that suggestion was declined. Just one would do. With that established, the workers seized a doughnut topped with strawberry frosting. Not a ghastly choice by any means.

"If you're truly sorry about last night, you'll pay for our food," Debi said in a playful tone.

"Shocking," I said, not taking issue with it in the slightest. Luckily my wallet had been transferred to my back pocket instead of lingering about in my jacket with the Stork watch.

Taking our food and beverages, we found a table by the windows at the front of the rich, coffee-scented building. Upon sitting down, I noticed Debi's hash brown packet only contained two. Perhaps we share the same shoddy habit of food neglection, though that's merely speculation. We all have our reasons, and it's none of my business so I'll leave it at that.

"It's crazy how we've been getting along shockingly well this morning, because you have no idea just how pissed off I was yesterday," Debi said with an unwavering stare. "And I'm not going to apologize for anything I said."

"Fair," I said.

"I've worked this job for seven years and *never* have I been paired with someone like…like…you. And this isn't even my first time working with someone from your organization either. While our first encounter may have been harsh, I'm willing to say it was also excusable. Maybe I should've just gone and calmly approached you instead of…stalking you…" Debi paused for a tick. She coughed, which brought upon a sniffle. "I…the flashing lights and loud music were disorienting so my logic was messed up. But you'd already skipped out on me at every turn that I thought you were playing some dickish game."

For as exhausted as Debi was before we departed the hotel, she's certainly more active now. She's only taken a few sips of her coffee, so it's doubtful this stems from the caffeine. Maybe yesterday's drama is cause for an adrenaline rush? Who knows, but it's a possibility.

"I'm sorry but skipped out on you?" I asked. "How?"

"Your file should've explained that we were to meet in the lobby at five-thirty," Debi said. "We were going to introduce ourselves and then figure out our course of action. Simple as that. Then we'd leave together. But when I saw you exit Nouveau Rêve and hop into your limo without even bothering to find me, it was beyond confusing.

So, I learned early on that you either didn't read the files or did and neglected to follow protocol."

"I read everything but your file."

"Ah, well there you go." Debi sighed as she nibbled on her hash browns. "That leads us to the lobby of the ballroom. Your approach was reckless, your attitude cavalier. It was as though I was watching some cheap police drama. Had there been actual guards around that building, we could've been killed, and it would've been on you."

What joy it's been to savour in this whole "dressing down" of me. It's far from ideal to listen to. After all, only a sadist would bathe in this degradation barrage that has no end in sight. In some ways it's relieving that Debi's expounding on this now. It might very well allow us a clean slate to work with for the remainder of our assignment. But mercy on hearth could she just get on with it?

"And I'll be honest, Mark, I called headquarters this morning and told them about your actions."

Debi paused, almost certainly in anticipation for me to do the same. For my face to drop. For me to roar "you did what?" Unfortunately for her, she'll have to be perfectly content with being utterly disappointed. What Debi's oblivious to is that I'm, of course, quite aware of the countless advantages my job tolerates of me. Her Majesty's Church is far more lenient with me than any other intelligence agency would be with their employees. This lenience has its limits, like anything else, but my actions in regard to the handling of Sergio Scobretti last night were protected by my position. And no matter how dreadfully the whole ordeal may have gone, all the other agencies are aware of my privileges as well.

"I talked to the Director." Debi glanced around the table, possibly to make sure no one could hear her, before leaning in closer to me. "The Director of the goddamn CIA and do you know what he said? The Director of the CIA told me, verbatim, that Mark is an enigma compared to others in his organization. That he's a problematic operative with a tendency to shun his contacts, even after his superiors were given instructions that stated he *must* work with them. But," she paused, taking a deep breath, "Director Ganderman then told me that, while we may think that you're a loose cannon, your employers have talked big about you. How you've always successfully completed your assignments. And, despite our partnership, the CIA has *no* authority over you. So…I'm forced to let you call the shots."

Her voice sounds as though it was teetering on perplexity, how she seemingly wished to shout "call the shots" at me but simmered the volume after the first syllable. While that occurred, her arms had jerked up an inch from the table, possibly to make an exasperated gesture. However, Debi glued her arms back to the table, most likely recognizing that such an action would've not been apt in this moment.

"I was *also* informed that there's been so many complaints about you lately," Debi continued, "so the Director pushed your employers to have you work with me on this assignment. But, because of the CIA is unable to reprimand you, we're powerless here. Absolutely unbelievable. So, you oughta tell me what exactly it is that you do. Why are you so different compared to everybody else?"

Setting my coffee onto the table after a rather large swig, I immediately responded with "are we going back to the hotel after this? Or are we going somewhere else?"

This response noticeably caught Debi off guard. It could've been due to the words, but it's very likely the shifting tone of voice did the job. Emotion drained out of every successive word that came out of my mouth, until it ended up as a mere drone. Debi gradually backed away from me, her mouth dropping simultaneously.

"We're going somewhere. Why?"

I rose from the uncomfortable plastic chair while grabbing my half-empty coffee and unfinished doughnut. There are some conversations that aren't appropriate to partake in when out in public, even if there's no one around who could eavesdrop if they so wished.

Debi can discuss CIA matters wherever she chooses but talk of my position or Her Majesty's Church in general while having a meal in a place like Dunk Your Donuts is *strictly* prohibited. That's precisely why I lie to my family and June about my profession. And why conversations of this degree, in my opinion, should only ever be carried out in discreet spaces. Basically, aside from within headquarters, I've always stood by the rule that if you can delight in a rendezvous somewhere without the risk of being caught, then you can discuss these matters *with associates* in those locations.

"Then we'll talk about this in the car," I said.

An unexpected growling in the air swirled above me, issuing a stern warning that conversing with Debi about my job was a repulsive idea. And even though my words had been spoken with a coating of truth, the growling exposed the actual lie that was concealed. Everyone at Her Majesty's Church is conscious of my role and how I'm assigned to handle my targets. I'm also of the understanding that CIA Director Ganderman comprehends such because Lord President Trailsby explicitly passed that information to him with instructions that any partners were to be kept in the dark about this. That's why he gave Debi such vague answers and orders as to how she's to work with me.

Eluding most of my previous contacts has vastly aided me in accomplishing everything in my own specialized manner. And if Debi learns what I do, that's the equivalent of admitting to myself just how bloody wretched my trade is. To admit that is to reveal the wrath of the cruel beast that dwells within me. It almost surfaced at the gala last night, with both Scobretti *and* Debi. Telling myself that this animal does indeed exist is perfectly alright if it's performed mentally, but I could never permit myself to verbally state it.

Adrift in my anguish, my senses snapped back into place like building blocks when Debi's soft hand clasped securely around my wrist.

"Wait a minute," she said. "You're being all short with me. Why can't you just tell me now?"

Either I unmask my agony or give Debi some sort of bullshit excuse. And, in my weakness, the latter claimed victory. She would not be satisfied by my answer, but all that comes to mind after careful deliberation were lies that desperately demand they be declared.

It's abhorrent, how comfortable I am with lying. Lies are almost a defence mechanism of mine, as miserable as that sounds, because slipping into the practice is as graceful as ballroom dancing. The second a falsehood recognizes that it's the most advantageous time to arise, it'll latch onto my tongue and be the first announcement that spews out of my mouth.

From the air conditioning vents swelled a ghostly aura that swiftly floated beside me. Then, without warning, it united with my entire being. Face muscles stiffened. Eyesight amplified due to a strenuous stare that formed. This plague is distinct compared to my demented daydreaming. That's desire. Compared to the voices and the mirrors that mangle my face. That's self-hatred. It also has nothing in common with the damned beast that emerges when I'm prepared to complete an assignment. That's ire. No, this occurs out of the dormant misery that's finally protested for, and has been granted, its release.

"I lied, Debi," I said, sedately shifting my body in her direction. "My apologies but there's actually nothing for us to talk about. My organization forbids me from explaining the purpose of my employment. We'll work together just fine as long as you heed the directions of your director. Follow my lead. And though I vow to never put you in danger again, you are not to question me."

Debi's grip automatically loosened, and I pulled my wrist away before she could fully release me. Deprived of any inclination to speak about these topics again, I quietly strolled away from the table. The scraping of Debi's chair against the tile floor did damn all to lessen the mental hell, but at least she was following me. At least she appeared to see the daylight instead of starting another row and insisting upon answers. That's good enough for now.

12

Most people would readily admit that it's disconcerting if a random, unknown individual decided to stare at them for a prolonged period. Intentionally directing their eyes at them, taking notes of all their actions all the while the other person is entirely in the dark about their being observed. Unconsciously ignorant to their surroundings because they're simply performing daily routines. Routines that don't require much thought such as walking about a grocery shop or attending your child's sporting event. Unless they were meticulously mindful of their environment, and some people are, why would they possibly have any reason to think they're being watched?

Now, this does not pertain to the act of cheekily ogling someone. If I'm out with my colleagues and an attractive woman walks my way, she'll unquestionably steal a decent bucket of gazes from me. But that's also where it ends. Once she's passed by, every bit of my focus returns to the discussions taking place at the table. No, while that can also be manipulated into a more underhanded variant by scoundrels, this pertains to someone *staring* at another with an unrelenting, vacant expression. That's bloody bizarre and will cause all the white flags to scream until they're red.

Uninvited stares have vexed me since childhood, and the story behind it is rather preposterous. But it's one of those thoughts that curiously remain perfectly clear after several decades, despite being such an insignificant tick. Honestly, there are plenty of these obscure film reels from my youth that'll stage viewings for me to re-watch, but this one is a special case.

Mom, throughout the entirety of my youth, had this routine where she'd take an excursion to the grocer's every Sunday. For reasons I cannot remember all too well, there used to be this thrill about wandering through a supermarket. Aisles lined with foods and condiments that were adorned in vivid and imaginative designs. Cereal boxes, especially, were extraordinarily captivating to my seven-year-old self. And the produce section reminded me of when we'd be shopping for toys, with the variety of fruits that presented themselves in different colours. Somehow, that sight was reminiscent of the figurines that were also designed in multiple colours.

Once, while out in the store, Mom allowed my sisters and me to visit the bakery so that we could decide on a dessert to go with the meal she would cook that evening. She put Liane, my third oldest sister, in charge of overseeing the lot of us because she was seventeen at the time. Liane was the oldest child in the house, as the elder two sisters had already gone to and graduated university by this point. When it came to deciding on a dessert, my sisters were the ones who had more clout in terms of selecting an item due to my being the youngest. So, while they were scouting pies, I ventured to the cakes and took in the exquisiteness of their designs.

Standing by the cakes were a few older women, none of whom seemed to know one another as they were all silently inspecting the desserts. When I waltzed up to the same area they were, each woman simply stared at me for a lengthy period before resuming their search for the right cake. Six pairs of eyes, staring at me as though it was utterly mystifying that a child could also view cakes. None of them asked me where my parents were, though that could be justified by their noting the interactions I had with my sisters. They just eyed me like some sort of delinquent. And ever since this utterly laughable slice of perdition took place, it's made me loathe unwelcome staring from unknown individuals.

Debi hadn't unglued her pairs from me since we left Dunk Your Donuts. It was obvious, as I could steal glimpses of her out of the corner of my eyes. Her waist was twisted in my direction, head tilted like a curious animal. Although her stares were born from inquisitiveness, the fact Debi hadn't withdrawn her focus from me for countless minutes caused those ancient memories to intensely reappear. They would've returned yesterday, when Debi's stares were in the guise of maliciously off-putting glares, but an assortment of other hassles stemming from the event barricaded the visions of the unpleasant supermarket women.

No question she was thoroughly analysing me. Pondering questions that she desperately craved to ask, though fully mindful that she wouldn't receive any valuable responses. Frustrating, isn't it? How Debi could disclose so much more regarding her occupation because she probably has nothing to hide from her contacts. Of course, I'm in the dark as to whether that's true or not. But even if she does in fact store skeletons in her closet, they're not as wicked as those that are decaying in each of my rooms.

Somehow the car trek isn't leading us to this side of nowhere. Debi might be fixed on me, but instead of telling me where we were going to, she began muttering directions to our destination the instant we entered her car. She continued this whenever I arrived at a light or a stop sign. Maybe she's scoped the region out extensively before this assignment commenced. It's rather impressive, how she's able to robotically direct me while not bothering to unbolt those frozen gems.

"If you're trying to be discreet with your stares, you're doing a particularly atrocious job," I said.

"There's something *off* about you," Debi said without hesitation. "You just…you're an enigma. You violate protocol, disregard files, and everyone brushes it aside. I guess I'm still in disbelief that my own boss admitted that you're on this elite level where you're untouchable."

"It's just how it is."

"You don't get it. If I even dared to act as irresponsible as you did, you have no idea how severe my punishment would be."

"You'd probably be terminated."

"Probably." Debi clicked her tongue. "Yet you're given the longest leash ever manufactured. How? What is it about you that makes you the chosen one?" Debi snickered, probably out of disbelief rather than her remark being humorous. Her voice then returned to the stern air it'd initially been. "Why are you allowed special treatment?"

"First off," I interjected before Debi had an opening to continue, "it's not special treatment. It's my role. Yes, my failures in regard to that disastrous apprehension attempt weren't what either of our organizations hoped for. But the higher-ups know damn well it won't happen again. And…the only way that I would've faced consequences for my actions yesterday is if you'd been maimed."

"So, putting me in danger is fine, but actually being injured *or worse* is where the line is drawn? Don't you see how flawed that is? Also, you didn't answer my question. How come you're given privileges no one else gets?"

"I refused to answer that question because I told you at the doughnut shop that my organization restricts me from discussing those matters."

Debi sighed. "Such a load of bullshit, Mark." She finally twisted her body from my direction and returned to her proper form.

She's not wrong in that my response *is* utter bullshit, but we'll leave it at that.

This is the first time I've truly taken note of Howslip Township. Yesterday's ride from the airfield to the hotel was a blur, while both excursions to and from the gala were shrouded by intense contemplations. Finally, being consumed by the bustle of the community was sublime, as it glaringly clashed with the melancholic atmosphere of the apathetic moodiness Vrycastle presents.

Scores of vigour infected the masses who went about their late morning hours. The sheer cluster of civilians who both crammed into and squeezed out of the countless shops was staggering. Everyone who managed to exit carried multiple paper bags of food, appliances, or comics that were just about ready to plunge out from their safety. These shop owners must bathe themselves in bloody cash each night because their businesses were truly flourishing. This was entirely unanticipated from a township that boasted a population of barely over twenty-five thousand. That information stemmed from the files. Rich.

"Turn here at Morris," Debi said, her silver bracelets jangling as she pointed a French manicured fingernail at the street sign.

A joke slithered to the tip of my tongue, desperate to impishly remind Debi that she's supposed to be following *my* commands. However, not only would that remark bomb brilliantly because it wasn't even high-quality humour, but Debi could easily perceive that comment as my being discourteous even if I was to explain that it was meant to be a droll remark. So, instead, all Debi received from me in return was a slight nod.

"Coming up on your right," Debi said.

Plastered on a cream, half-moon, wooden shaped sign was the name Howslip Plaza. Composed of spindly red and blue lettering, its design catapulted me back to my childhood once more. But these recollections had damn all to do with the trivial images from earlier that just revel in incessantly plaguing me. No, these memories were not only superior, but it'd also been ages since they'd bobbed up and the films were coated in hordes of dust.

Before Dad began serving in federal government, he was the commissioner of the Massachusetts Department of Environmental

Management. Though he was extraordinarily absorbed in his work throughout my youth, and especially once he was tapped to be interior secretary, he still strived to make adequate time for his family. Every Friday, for instance, he'd unfailingly get home as soon as he could so that both he and Mom would greet my sisters and me when we arrived home from school. While Mom would run herself rabid preparing dinner, Dad would bring me along on errands. Occasionally one or two of my sisters would join us, but they tended to be preoccupied with their own varied interests.

Most of the stores Dad tended to rootle around in resided within Ludlow Plaza, another ordinary strip mall with a design akin to Howslip Plaza. As my sisters would often ask if they could paint their rooms a different colour, one of the shops we routinely visited was a hardware store where Dad would search tirelessly for whatever colours they were craving.

Two stores down was a second-hand shop. We'd spend over an hour in there, basking in the new items that'd arrived in the week since we'd been there last. As the items there were so inexpensive, Dad would prefer to buy stuff for my sisters and me here. Some might deem it cheap, but it didn't trouble me. I'd often leave with a house of trading cards, still in fantastic condition, that would only cost Dad a few dollars. Not once did new toys or clothes ever appeal to me. It wasn't saintly behaviour from a child. They just weren't compelling enough for me to bother asking for, I suppose.

Those Friday afternoon errands were the most time I'd ever spend with Dad, which is a shame because we'd always have a blithe time together. Alas, my growing older shoved me into the arms of rebellion. But that's a banal topic fit for any generic made-for-tv film involving teenagers finding fault in damn near everything.

Underneath the Howslip Plaza header was a list of the ten stores, separated in two columns, that inhabited the shopping centre. The still maddeningly humorous name of Abraham Scobretti's fishing shop, Hooking Up, rested in the second slot on the left. It, like the names of the other shops, grinned in the same blue hue as the one that adorned the word *Plaza*.

"It's going to be on the left, by that nail salon," Debi said. "But I want you to park closer to that massage parlour while facing the street."

Hooking Up dwelled near the end of the strip mall's left side, three down from the parlour and one away from being the last. We passed by Scobretti's shop, and everything practically decelerated as I gazed at the spirited, bold, wine-tinged lettering that hung above the entryway. This *deceleration*, however, was a mere mental trick. The speed of the Volkswagen hadn't shifted a touch and doing such would've been utterly apparent.

After Debi guided us to the ideal spot, she swiftly unbuckled her seatbelt and extended herself toward the rear of the car. She yanked away a pale blue cloth sheet that concealed the backseat. As Debi tossed the clump of cloth below where she sat, I examined the bulky piece of machinery that had been resting underneath the sheet. It had the appearance of a VCR, between its charcoal tones and burly rectangular shape. However, this equipment was ornamented with several switches and possessed a sizeable speaker directly in its centre.

"So, as you know, I barely got any sleep," Debi said. She grabbed the machinery and set it onto her lap. "And you wouldn't be wrong if you guessed that it was the fault of last night's crap. Since I quickly realized there was no chance of sleeping with a spinning head, I decided to do some work."

"Work?" I asked.

"Yeah. Around two in the morning I left the hotel and came over here. Luckily the lot was empty. I surveyed this entire area until I was certain he and his associates weren't here. Once that was done, I slipped into his shop."

"*You* infiltrated his shop? I asked, utterly astonished by Debi's admission. This sudden outburst was not the product of ire or frustration, but of sincere confusion. "How could you have possibly achieved that? Clearly you didn't shatter a window. Was a door unlocked? Did you enter through the roof?"

"No, a door wasn't unlocked, and I never thought of entering from the roof. How I entered *does* involve windows though." Debi pulled out a white and green striped tube that could've easily been mistaken for toothpaste. "This is Mordglu. If you apply it to the edges of a window, it'll loosen the pane from where it's been installed. I had to be so damn careful that I didn't accidentally smash it when I set it against the door. I've got another tube in my purse that does the opposite. You set the window back in place, apply the paste, and the pane reconnects without leaving a trace."

Debi's explanation reduced me to a state of incredulous disbelief. She handed me the tube and, upon retrieving it, I rotated it in various directions. This surely gave the impression of a curious infant experiencing a way of life for the first time. Unable to truly process much else aside from utter awe.

"Where did you get this?" I asked.

"CIA Gadgets Department," Debi said. Her eyebrows shot up, and her gems widened in pronounced amazement. "Wait, I'm willing to bet your organization has a gadgets department. How could you be so startled by this?"

"Our gadgets department is intertwined with our weapons department. It's ran by a sterling lad who, singlehandedly, produces every device as well as many pieces of artillery. He endlessly asks me if I wish to utilize the gadgets, but I always decline. They're just not for me."

"Not for you?" Debi snatched the tube from me and shoved it into her purse. "You've been looking at this like it's some foreign elixir."

"I'm just knocked for a six as to how extraordinary these appliances are. But…they're simply not valuable when it pertains to my methods."

"God, you're unbelievable." Debi scoffed. "Anyways, I explored the shop for a few minutes with the help of a flashlight. Standard stuff. Miniature aquariums and accessories for 'em. All kinds of fish food. Tons of fishing tackle. There's a public restroom and Scobretti's also got an office in the back. There's another room attached to his office, but all that's in there is a steel table like one you'd see in a morgue."

Pointing to the machine on Debi's lap, I asked, "so where does this figure in?"

She didn't take kindly to my question as she glared at me. "Be patient, Mark. After searching around the shop, I placed bugs in every room. They're as big as a sprinkle you'd find on a doughnut, but they're able to pick up noise in a room no matter how far away the person is standing away from them. This machine will allow us to listen in to whatever conversations are happening."

Debi deserves credit for exercising her time wisely. What she accomplished is something I'd have done if those gadgets had any strip of use to me. Though the whole basis of this assignment has been alien to me, Debi's deed enabled us to *hopefully* continue along on the correct path. And though we're still not quite sure there's a fourth individual who's conspiring with Abraham Scobretti, I'm confident that we'll uncover a potential identity much sooner now.

The five switches that ornamented the listening device were colour-coded and had numbered stickers underneath them. Debi clicked a button on the device's side and immediately flicked the first switch, a red one. From the speaker emitted what sounded like an air conditioner intermingled with faint music. Probably from the main area of the store. She must've planted that bug in an abysmal spot.

It's likely Debi realized her mistake as well, as she muttered "oops" and turned that switch off. She then moved on to a blue switch. This time, whistling arose the from speaker, indicating a potential success. However, it was soon followed by the sound of what I believe was the whistler urinating. Debi grumbled and promptly selected a green switch. Almost immediately, voices in the midst of chatting sprung out of the device. We glimpsed at one another. Green was the victor.

This was honestly somewhat of a thrill, but I'd be a bloody fool to concede that truth aloud. It certainly fails to contend with the dangerously formidable ecstasy that swells during my typical assignments. But, for the purpose of this job, mercy on rye was this listening device the bearer of pure bliss. As Debi twisted a knob to increase the volume, the subject of the discussion intensified. By nonsensical chance, the voices were conversing about the mayhem that ensued during the gala.

Unlike facial features and distinguishing marks, the act of identifying voices is not at all crucial to my assignments. And it's understandable. The files provide us with an image of the target's face as well as their base of operations. So, if that face is lurking about in the correct locations, that's just reason for me to apprehend the target. But there's this distressing tendency of mine where, during the apprehension, I might order my targets to speak to me. Listening intently to the turmoil within the voices of contemptable swine who are normally so confident…it's bloody paradise.

I recalled Sergio Scobretti's distinctly mellow North Jersey tone, so distinguishing him from the other male was unproblematic. That person possessed a very similar voice, but it was a touch deeper and more nasally. Also, whereas Sergio spoke at an average pace, the other man talked as though he was participating in some sort of speedreading competition. What was intriguing about his speech patterns, though, was the absence of either frustration or frenzy. This rushed pace was merely his normal voice.

Any irrelevant noises, such as the car's engine, the hiss of the air flowing from the vents, crackles from Debi's device, dispersed. They were rendered non-existent as the brothers' discussion conquered my attention. Every word that expelled from their vile mouths was logged in two shakes.

ABRAHAM: Give me more details about this lunatic who approached you (pause) what do you remember about him? Anything is helpful.
SERGIO: For starters, would you believe that he's some British guy?
ABRAHAM: (pause) No (chuckles) you serious?
SERGIO: Had the accent. No reason to see why he'd fake it.
ABRAHAM: Or why he'd choose a British accent. How can you go around acting like some sorta big shot with that accent? *Especially* in this town. Okay, what else?
SERGIO: Tall…six-one maybe. Dark hair. That's really it, Abe. Oh, and his composure. The guy pulled out a pistol in public…zero hesitation. He didn't seem to give a shit if one of the guests walked in.
ABRAHAM: Right. Well…look, I'm sorry youse had to deal with this maniac but the answer is pretty damn clear.
SERGIO: Yeah?
ABRAHAM: One of our rivals probably got a new goon to search through our turf. How he knew you'd be at the gala, fuck if I know. Either way, he tried to intimidate you but failed (pause) Rocco, you have anything to say?
ROCCO: I do.

Right, must've been Abruzzoli who we accidentally heard relieving himself in the loo. Despite how he was the de facto *heavy* in Scobretti's operations, his voice strayed from stereotypical buffoonery.

Abruzzoli's baritone was rooted from somewhere in New York, and he possessed a silver-tongue as judged by his judicious selection of words.

ROCCO: He was not alone. Accompanying him was a blonde woman and, if you're still set on the Brit being a hired goon, she was most certainly his partner.
SERGIO: Partner? Like work partner or lover?
ROCCO: Work partner. They did not arrive together, and they each spent the first twenty or so minutes wandering instead of engaging with other guests. It was unusual, but at the time I didn't give it a second thought.
ABRAHAM: Did you lose track of them after those twenty minutes?
ROCCO: Yeah, briefly.
ABRAHAM: Where were you when my brother was in danger?
ROCCO: The mezzanine. I saw them up there too. The woman followed the guy into the bathroom, which was (pause) bizarre. After that, I paid no attention to their whereabouts until Sergio called for me.
ABRAHAM: (sighs) Damn it, Roc. These incidents, they're rare so I get it. But you've gotta keep an eye on my brother. Our enemies can spot his face out of a fucking crowd much faster than they can spot yours. For the *love* of the divine, please don't let this happen again.
ROCCO: You have my word, Abe.
ABRAHAM: Good (sighs) now I don't want the two of youse to worry about this British goon. I don't know how yet, but I'll handle this *merda*. The gala is one thing, but I'd like to see that fuck enter my store (pauses) and youse gotta focus on tomorrow. Sergio, you know what's going down?
SERGIO: We've got an appointment at the docks in the morning. Eleven sharp.

ABRAHAM: Just making sure you remembered. Keep your focus on that, not the Brit. And remember that youse gotta pick up Stanley on the way.
SERGIO: Yeah (pause) you sure Stanley ain't gonna back out?
ABRAHAM: I'm positive. Stanley's our cousin, and you know the word of family is supreme over all else. With that being said, I *still* made him swear to me that he wouldn't retreat.
ROCCO: You know, you never explained why Stanley wanted to work for us.
ABRAHAM: There's not really much to talk about. We're all aware that he and his wife got a kid on the way. They need some extra cash. I'm happy to help. Just don't bring him back here when the deal is done.

Unbelievably brill. Happening upon their conversation at this precise moment was sheer chance, and in mere minutes we unearthed multiple factors that'll benefit our assignment tremendously. Firstly, Abraham Scobretti appears fully committed to this notion that I'm employed by a rival faction that also deals in illegal trade. It's mystifying, honestly, how the man can operate so flawlessly under this "store owner" guise. Otherwise, there's reason to believe he'd be more troubled by law enforcement than rivals.

Also, while my questioning of Sergio Scobretti last night has been incessantly maligned by Debi as well as myself, it's pleasing to now ponder whether my approach aided us or not. Law enforcement would be damned if they even dared conducted themselves in such a bestial fashion. So, by rousing my inner wrath, the ordeal might've seemed a tad too sadistic for the Scobretti's to even consider me as an affiliate of the law.

Tomorrow, at eleven in the morning, Sergio Scobretti and Abruzzoli would be arriving at the docks. However, they wouldn't be alone. Now this is somewhat perplexing to me in that Her Majesty's

Church strongly believes that there's a fourth member taking part in these operations. Stanley, the cousin, will be participating, yes, but he's nothing more than a hired hand. Unless there's a detail that is still eluding us, Stanley has scant knowledge regarding the private workings of Scobretti's business. This potential fourth member was said to be aligned with the aquarium. Perhaps they'll be present at the docks tomorrow as well.

Satisfied by the encouraging progress, I took a tick to glance away from the device. But, without warning, the atmosphere in the Volkswagen altered. The persisting discussion between the rogues, one utterly crucial to this assignment's success, discarded itself into the distance. Scheming that was once discernible to my ears were now trifle echoes. Just about every bit of required essential data had already transpired between these bastards, and prompt reminders of such eased me to some degree. But witnessing the erosion of my once intact concentration left behind an anticipated amusement.

Senses remained vigilant as they acknowledged the modest breeze that discharged from the AC vents. The breeze, however, had intensified into a maddening warmth that bombed itself into this space. Warmth so mighty and devious it was captivating, despite my disdain for muggier climates. Yet, strangely, neither of us instigated this temperature shift as our hands dawdled nowhere near the dials.

I'm mindful of this cognitive fault. It's one that was contemplated upon arriving at Nouveau Rêve. The frustrating yet one-sided scuffle between work-related affairs and riskily indulging in vices. And the vices will not only triumph, but they'll then roll in the aisles at my ruin. Have I cavorted with vices since my escapades with Robin? Of course not. But they enjoy this animalistic desire that's forever prepared to ambush me with fervent aches. And it'll make sure to surface at the most inopportune of times.

At some point, I'd leaned closer to the listening device as my absorption with the chat increased. And my momentary glance from the device led me to a full, close-up view of Debi. No doubt a dangerous barrel of preoccupations forbade me from intimately taking in her face until now. After all, first impressions ran astray and her tainted attitude that stemmed from such all but generated shoddy judgement on my part. But…mother of mercy…now that Debi is baring her true colours, nothing could've prepared me for the unmitigated magic that is her portrait.

Substitute her teased, in vogue hairstyle with a short, wavy bouffant and she'd be a dead ringer for several 1950s movie starlets. Her long eyelashes, exquisite yet gaudy enough to be artificial, glistened with calming ease as she continued to concentrate on the device. Faint pink rouge clothed her cheeks, and her bottom lip dropped a touch, which accentuated the soft roundness of her chin. Hints of tropical passionfruit drifted amongst the heated breeze, a distinguishable scent…*Tropiques Étranges* by Marion Marie.

It was at this moment that Debi pulled away from the device herself and caught me amid my muses. She stared at me with a vacant face that dragged on for weeks. All remaining and worthless strands of the conversation that had lingered in my ears disappeared without remorse. What reared was not silence, though it featured a similar sensation if that made any sliver of sense. Noises were still somewhat audible, but they had merged into a low, garbled buzzing that reverberated throughout my entirety.

Up in my bonce, I damned myself for failing to even contemplate the extreme likelihood that Debi would end up catching me. It'd be laughable, juvenile even, to pretend there was an air of subtleness in my studying her. To try explaining that it derived from anything but blistering attraction. On top of that, though we'd been successful in whittling down some of the ice, we hadn't yet managed to clear all the air between us. No matter the sparse pleasantries we'd exchanged today, there's no doubt Debi's still vexed about the gala, the numerous freedoms that are permitted by Her Majesty's Church, and *me* in general.

To my utmost surprise, Debi didn't scoff or berate me for my display of unprofessionalism. Instead, she developed this quiet trace of a smile. And that was it. Her silence persisted as she refocused on the listening device. Perhaps this was a lucky break and Debi failed to notice any variety of desire within my face. Relieved, this sudden and overwhelming magnetism toward Debi decided it might be best to terminate itself.

As I proceeded to also return my attention to the listening device, however, the corner of my eye detected a peculiar display. It had to be a mind game, as they were keen on toying with my conscience. But Debi appeared to have shifted herself closer. Our shoulders were now brushing against one another's. And her cheek was mere inches from me.

13

Being shoulder to shoulder with Debi created a myriad of pictures from my youth. How even the most insignificant connection of flesh between myself and some girl would alter the shifting ruby spheres. And all because of that momentary touch, a spontaneous development of desirous and profound allure would sprout. It would send the two of us tumbling into a relationship, though that word is honestly too…mawkish. Perhaps "starry-eyed attachments" more accurately suits what those partnerships were. After all, usually within weeks, the appeal would pop and rarely would we speak to one another again. That was the pattern for each of my heedless, unsavoury, and ill-fated starry-eyed attachments throughout my schooldays, an unfortunate cycle that concluded upon meeting Darla. But, of course, it resumed to some extent *after* Darla…though in the most lascivious variety possible.

If my recollections were accurate, my ventures into these squalls came about midway through eighth grade. They were certainly delayed in comparison to a good deal of my peers, who'd embarked a year earlier. That was by the design of my parents. While they didn't outright forbid me from having a girlfriend, they wholly believed it'd distract me from my studies. To make matters worse, both my parents would only ever refer to a girlfriend as my *friend*. It's clear neither of them believed those attachments of mine were significant, and that caused me to be less willing to even mention any girlfriends, Due to this, most of my flirtations during those days were "school-based," meaning I'd seldom loll around with a girlfriend outside of school.

There's one entanglement that, at this tick, stood out more than the others. This was mainly because the circumstances behind its instigation were parallel to my current...*blend* with Debi. It just so happens that this attachment was also the first I'd ever stumbled into. However, compared to all the "relationships" that ensued, this romance was undoubtedly the most platonic and insipid of the whole lot.

Her name was Penelope Kruithof, and she was a quiet, pale girl with thin desert brown hair that reached her mid-back. She also wore dental braces, which I clearly remember weren't the most tender ally of hers. It was customary for the metal to carelessly scrape up the inside of Penelope's cheeks, and every time she'd have to excuse herself so that she could spit out blood in the restroom.

We shared no classes and were only familiar with each other through an assortment of chums at our lunch table. I haven't a clue who initiated the inaugural conversation, but we soon unearthed a mutual fondness for...the director J. Sven Egot. It's rather bloody droll to recall my past appreciation for Egot's unsophisticated and horrifically low-budget material. The man merely scribbled out the most outlandish plots, messily compacted it into an incoherent synopsis, hired drab individuals who were devoid of any flair for acting, and deemed it cinema.

Yet the bond between Penelope and I expanded as we further discussed the nutty pictures that Egot drooled onto the big screen. So much so that we'd both block out everyone else at the lunch table as we rambled about our favourite scenes from his various films. Surely the others must've deemed us loons, especially when our ramblings morphed into outright re-enactments of said scenes.

Ultimately, these moments escalated in their intimacy as we'd be huddled together while spouting lines. Our shoulders touched, as did our knees, and eventually our hands followed suit as well. Truly twee in the most laughable guise. But, especially when you're a newly minted teenager, these instances are pure bliss to your green and dreadfully mediocre self-esteem. So, with a flag of vigour, I ended up asking Penelope to walk out with me when lunch was over. To my jubilance, she simply smiled and replied "sure."

Unfortunately, I was unsuccessful in discovering her favourite colour, the food she relished most, any iota of her personality even. In retrospect, we were merely friends who referred to one another as our *partner*, though "friends" was truly a stretch in of itself. Our physical contact never extended past hollow embraces and, even then, they were certainly not front facing. I'd drape her shoulders and give them a squeeze while walking to class, and Penelope once hugged me from behind while I was seated. That was it.

So, after an "amazing" run of two weeks…our connection ceased to exist. One of us moved to a different lunch table and we never spoke to another again…until a random yet cordial encounter at university about four years later. But, even after that, she once again vanished from my life, and I haven't seen or spoken to Penelope in twenty-four years.

After Penelope, each successive relationship mushroomed from these unbelievably inane conditions. We'd go from barely being acquainted with one another to walking out in a matter of days or months depending on the amount of time it took for our flesh to inadvertently touch. There were never conversations that allowed us to unearth anything deeper than our skin. Sure, there'd be a commonality we'd share, such as the adoration of B-movies between Penelope and I, but at the end of the day my "starry-eyed attachments" were all vacuous. And, honestly, apart from Darla, everyone else was interchangeable. Penelope included, even if she was the first person I…sort of walked out with.

Departing from the drivel that was my adolescence, I decided to gaze at Debi a final time before permitting my concentration to revert toward the listening device. Considering the rubbish that discharged upon brushing against her, there was an unquestionable rationale for such remembrance. A rationale that both astounded and concerned me due to its abruptness and sheer potency. And that was because they unleashed sentiments that hadn't existed for over a decade.

Studying the magic that was Debi's beguiling, tanned ivory face, my loaf voiced its intensifying ardour for her almost immediately. But the ardour wasn't in the form of the sullied lust that has imprisoned my carnal aches since the conclusion of my marriage. No, the electric currents in my head were interpreting an itch for more than such tawdry sleaze. But why? Why were these asinine reactions being elicited after they were dormant for what should've been eternity?

For some reason, I wasn't gazing at Debi and solely ruminating about all the animalistic positions she could be put in. No, what began to ascend from the depths of the red-hot coals that made up my psyche was a frantic pining for *more*. And that *more* was the prospect of…a future with Debi. Having the ability to share laughs with her over a candlelit dinner, caressing her cheek while reviewing the morning paper, or crafting breakfast plans together.

These contemplations confounded and bothered me. At least with Darla, we'd spent enough time in each other's company before comparable thoughts had awakened between us. In this case, Debi was still nothing more than a stranger to me. We weren't here to take up with each other, which meant that her true colours would have to continue plugging away in uncharted territory. And baring those mystery colours would be detrimental because, judged against our assignment, it palled in importance.

The fact that I was so utterly blinded by a hasty, spurred magnetism toward her, to the point of deeming her the brill model of a romantic partner, was purely asinine. But, then again, there were a few fragments of these desires that somehow held a peppering of water. See, any time that I've acted on my…carnal needs, such as with June or Robin, or even pondered extensively about them, such as with Francine, dilemmas such as these have been non-existent. For as maddeningly attracted as I might be toward all three of those women, they simply don't meet *any* of my prerequisites when it pertains to preferred significant others.

With June, she's an enrapturing woman with a blithe attitude, a welcoming presence, and an arousing fashion sense. On top of that, it took no time at all for her to learn how I take my tea. The downside, however, is that her occupation effectively eliminates her from contending. Of course, she can toil in whatever line she so wishes…but I could never walk out with an escort. There's far too much baggage there…though who the bloody mercy am I to talk in that regard?

As for Francine, she too is a striking woman. Her optimistic attitude is utterly appealing, and her loyalty and work ethic surmounts everyone else's. I'm also infatuated with her flirty disposition, and how it ceaselessly goads me into surrendering to her allure. But her sole flaw rested in her inability to comprehend the emotional depth of a committed relationship.

And finally, there was Robin but she, of course, was merely nothing more than a one-night stand. I don't fancy regarding her in such an insensible manner, but at the very least we were *both* aware that such was an accurate statement. What we shared was a passing fling that stemmed purely from intense physical attraction and not a splinter more.

Debi, despite the few dots of information I've gathered about her, has shown signs of being someone who's career-orientated, meticulous, perceptive, and prepared. And that's not to say June and Francine don't possess any of these traits. There's just a sense of experience in Debi's mastering of these traits that boost her over the lot.

All these tame passions...they're certainly spirited. Yet, when all is said and done, they're not practical no matter how relentlessly they attempt to sway my decision. I still firmly believe that romance, especially at my age, is harmful. Romance isn't for me, not anymore. The door to its grievous chamber closed once I took Her Majesty's oath and, as the years drudged on, such has only solidified.

Contact between Debi and I will terminate upon the conclusion of the assignment. Neither of us have much of a defence for continued correspondence. That's the nature of this occupation. Besides, even if she possessed the same aspirations and we gave it a try, there are numerous reasons why a potential romance between us would ultimately languish.

To start, she's a redhead, so there's an intense possibility that my longings have been trounced or exacerbated by that physical aspect. I go mental as a mantis over redheads, even though that penchant has kicked me in the arse quite a load. So, it's not inconceivable that my thoughts have been blurred by that potent fact. Her hair colour might very well be what's causing me to slip into her oblivious spell.

Before the second thought could formulate, one that I believed was more crucial to contemplate, Debi began to sharply nudge my arm. This was probably in an attempt to garner my attention. She also flicked off the switch that controlled the listening device.

"We gotta start heading back to the hotel," Debi said.

"Hmm?" I mumbled. The smog in my bonce hadn't entirely vanished. "Head back to the hotel? Why?"

"*Why*? Mark, we got every bit of information we needed to get. Besides, didn't you just hear Sergio? He and Rocco are leaving now. I don't know about you, but I don't wanna take any chances if they happen upon us loitering out here."

"How would they? We're not the only car in the lot. I also doubt that these blokes are paranoid enough to search every vehicle on the off chance that we're here. They sounded more…frustrated than apprehensive."

Debi's face collapsed into a state of suspicion, her eyebrows shifting pointedly. "So, are you saying you don't want to go back to the hotel? I don't understand. There's nothing else for us to do here."

Damn, what *exactly* is it that I'm doing right now? Of course, we should go back to the hotel now. Like Debi said, we've acquired all that was necessary. The correct response to her explaining that the two bastards were leaving should've been "okay, let's get a move on." But now I've senselessly stumbled into a boggy reservoir by speaking without thinking. Perhaps that was a remnant of my tripe dwellings that hadn't departed. Subconsciously attempting to stall time so that I could continue mingling with Debi. How bloody daft of me to drown in these pathetic reservoirs.

A sudden proposal manifested, one that surely had its flaws but was also the most suitable cloak I could scrounge from the dreadful void. It would no doubt pry Debi from off my back, and that was the cardinal reason for me to go on and run with it. Even if the likelihood of it bombing was, admittedly, bordering on red level.

"There is something else we could do…more precisely something that *I* could do," I said.

"Like what?" Debi asked.

"When Sergio and Rocco leave, I'm going into the fishing shop so—"

Debi wasted no time with interrupting me. "You're doing *what* exactly? Going into the fishing shop? Uh-uh. No way. After how you handled yourself at the gala, there is absolutely no way that's happening."

"Debi, listen. I recall my behaviour at the gala well, no thanks to your constantly reminding me. Yes, it was shoddy, but it will not happen again. If you don't believe me or you're so aghast over such a plan, then you can listen to us converse over your device. Or, better yet, you could certainly accompany me into the shop. That choice is yours, but you know damn well you can't stop me from going in there."

Debi sighed, probably because she once again found herself in a futile joust. Exercising this advantage over her doesn't bring me any sliver of jubilance, though in some respects it should. Instead, I'm merely assisting her in attaining a common goal by putting my privileges into service as effectively as possible. And though this scheme might've been created under grimy circumstances, and the perils remained apparent, the more it dawdled in my bonce it truly appeared to be the correct choice.

"Okay. I'll stay in the car and listen. The checkout area is in the far back, and I planted a bug underneath the counter. It connects to the yellow switch so, if you make it back there, I can pick up your conversation," Debi said.

"Perfect."

"Go on and explain this plan though."

"Right. As I was saying, I'm going into the fishing shop so that I can interact some with Scobretti. I have no intentions of proceeding with any investigations of my own, as yours were quite perfect. But I'd like to…analyse the bastard. After all, you've had time to examine him and his operations. I'd like to see for myself who exactly we're dealing with."

"That's…a fair reasoning."

In a flash, Debi's gems shifted to her right and out the window. I barely had a chance to notice them freeze in place before

Debi hurled her hands at my head and forcibly jerked my entire upper body toward her lap. Though the seatbelt's polyester material demonstrated no mercy as it brutally dug into my body, it came as more of an afterthought compared to my utter incredulity over the circumstances.

"What the bloody hell is going on?" I asked.

"Sergio and Rocco are leaving now," Debi said, "and their car is directly behind us. If, for anyone reason, they peered into my car I don't think they'd recognize me without the wig. But they'd recognize you, so you have to stay down until they're out of sight."

A verbal acknowledgement of the circumstances was incapable of escaping my mouth. And, well, that was because my eyes were steadily glued to Debi's groin. Though affairs such as this were usually greeted with pleasure and an eager removal of clothes, this unconventional instance gave off a rather sleazy atmosphere. I was a common degenerate, my face inches away from Debi's…well, *you know*. This was an unforeseen predicament, and one that wasn't appropriate…as stuffy and unlike me as it was to admit. Certainly, an interesting changing of the hare, being that my thoughts of her were a dot more passionate not even a couple minutes ago. But, as taxing as those musings were, at least they were less lecherous. After all, our current proximity to one another was far too close and wholly unprofessional. Debi might be a ravishing redheaded woman but, alas, she's my colleague.

"They're gone now," Debi said.

"Good," I said, beginning to raise my head from Debi's lap. However, to my bewilderment, her steady grip endured without weakening.

Debi continued by asking, "you're sure you're willing to take this risk? There's always the chance that Scobretti's guys will come back because they forgot something."

"I'm aware of that, but it's worth the risk. These sorts of chances are *always* worth it," I said.

"Well, there's one other thing, Mark. They all know you're British. How exactly are you going to con that card?"

I stifled a chuckle. "That, Debi, is child's play for me."

***

Upon stepping foot into the fishing shop, I was greeted by an overhead shopkeeper's bell that rang merrily like a chipper bird. That was just the first of several interior aspects that caught me entirely off guard. My expectations of the interior were tilted more toward grimy and suspicious. That it was a shop rarely frequented by the public, so it had no excuse to stay hygienic and organized. Granted, these dismal expectations were induced by the wicked individual operating the business, but prior occasions also played a part in shaping such anticipations.

When it pertains to some of the immoral scum that I'm assigned to, those who "run businesses" very obviously use their buildings as fronts that mask their actual services. It's rather evident that most everyone keeps away from those places for reasons such as it being in a rundown area or that the "store" promotes useless trades such as "alkaline battery repair." Some are truly that ludicrous, but the police never plot any raids because they're told that *the agencies* will handle it.

I envisioned the walls to be an icy monochrome in dire need of repair. That they were full of cracks, potentially even with a damp spot somewhere that indicated a leak. Instead, they were a garish lemon yellow that produced a vat of liveliness. Sitting on the racks of lengthy rows were shedloads of fishing line, bait, and sunglasses that should've been soiled and cheap. But they were pristine, neatly packaged, and marvellously laid out.

Inobtrusive rock music whirled from square speakers that were positioned just above me. Featuring animated synth horns and a soulful, raspy vocal track, it sounded like that recent hit record by Dewey Hubris and the Facts. The agreeable, parky air was refreshing and subdued, not as harsh as I was presuming it'd be after hearing it through Debi's listening device. A citrus scent meandered about, adding a parade of crispness that enhanced the overall sense of comfortability within the shop.

And then, out of the corner of my eye, I captured Abraham Scobretti, thirty-five, toward the rear of the shop. His checkout counter was obscured behind the assortment of fishing tackle, but there was surely a direct line of sight between him and the front door. There was no doubt he spotted me as I entered. Unfortunately, the interior had knocked me for a six, so my preoccupation with such had rendered me unsuccessful in detecting *him* upon entering.

Prowling around the shop like an unsettling lunatic would stir a cause for alarm, as would leaving without purchasing something that I had no use for. Fishing has never been a hobby of mine, despite the great effort that *both* my parents went through as they attempted to reel me into it. In order to alleviate any potential issues, while also enabling myself to further my familiarity with the target, the most beneficial course of action was to initiate conversation with Scobretti.

Ambling out of the row of tackle I'd been dallying in, my vigilant strides led me to the counter where Abraham Scobretti stood. He was on the phone, his head slanted to his left so that he could keep the handset positioned against his shoulder. A massive Italian flag hung behind him, a decoration that proudly alluded to his heritage. As I approached him, Scobretti glanced at me and nodded as he raised a finger. The generous gesture was reciprocated, especially since it allocated some time for me to discreetly listen in on his conversation. To diminish any blatancy, however, I toyed with some of the simple one-dollar plastic items in a nearby plastic bowl.

"Yeah...yeah," Scobretti said, "lasagne is a great choice, baby. Okay...yeah, I'll be home around six. And I gotta get off the phone now. Got a customer. Okay...yeah, I love you too, baby. Bye." Scobretti set the headset in the receiver. He then presented a relaxed smile as he fixed his attention on me. "Hey there, how ya doing today?"

"I'm doing fine, thank you. How are you?" I asked, adjusting my accent into that of a Bostonian one. It's a relatively entertaining dialect for me, one that takes no effort to segue into, though at the same time it never ceases to startle me. My dad has a distinct, sophisticated Boston accent and, whenever I utilize my variation of it, we sound almost entirely alike.

"Ah, ya know, no need to really complain. Anyways, what are ya looking for?"

Making a conscious effort to blurt out whatever sort of fishing accessory came to mind first, I said, "some of that fishing net."

"Okay, and what are ya trying to catch?"

My voice nearly quavered as the word "trout" left my mouth. It, like fishing net, came to me out of the blue. But, unlike fishing net, there was no confidence in this mentioning of trout. I hadn't a clue what sort of fish roamed the waters of New Jersey, but trout had the most appropriate air to it.

"Trout? Easy. You're gonna wanna grab the smaller net. It's gonna be in the last row to your left." Scobretti tilted his head in that direction. "There's only two sizes and you'll see the packaging has the sizing on it and all."

"Perfect. Thank you."

Scobretti patted the counter. "Not a problem."

I walked to the row that Scobretti mentioned and immediately located the fishing net. It was packaged in this rather appalling yellow and green plastic pouch, with the sizing positioned to the left of the pouch's front. Seizing it, I hardly shook my head at the fact my brass would be spent on something so inessential. Even worse, it'd be going to *Scobretti himself.* But, in order to duly execute an activity with first-class precision, sometimes you haven't a choice.

Returning to the counter, I found that Scobretti had closed his eyes, slouched his body a touch, and was nodding his bonce to the music. He must've heard my footsteps and realized he had to tend to me once more, however, as he hastily reformed his posture to one that would've made Queen Matilda unbelievably proud.

"Must be some fancy event you're going to, huh?" Scobretti asked as he scanned the pouch of fishing net.

"Fancy event?" I asked.

"Well, yeah." Scobretti stared at me in a bemused manner, with one of his eyebrows arching up as his mouth produced lopsided grin. "Guys in suits don't just wander into a tackle shop looking for fishing net, ya know?"

"Oh, it's for a sta…bachelor party," I said, correcting myself before my preferred phrasing of *stag party* could be formed. "My buddy loves fishing, so all the groomsmen are taking him to a lake and celebrating on the water. Unfortunately, I waited until the last minute to purchase something for him."

"So ya got him…fishing net? Strange, but hey if it makes the guy happy, right? Still, I gotta thank ya though."

"Yeah?" I chuckled. "Why's that?"

Scobretti chuckled too. "Because *my* groomsmen are gonna know about this. And they're gonna know better than to set up some boring fishing trip for my bachelor party."

"That's fair." I cautiously took out my wallet and scrambled around for some cash. "Are you engaged?"

"No…not yet. I've been with my girl for over three years now, so it seems as though the time is right for popping the question, ya know? So, I'm hoping to do it soon. Probably take her to Italy. All my grandparents live in a small village outside of Tuscany, so I'm gonna get their blessings and propose while we're out at night somewhere. They've all met my girl before and they adore her so, seeing them and being in Italy, it's sort of a double win."

"Certainly sounds like it. And it may be premature…but congratulations." I handed Scobretti a five-dollar bill. "I hope your plan goes smoothly."

Scobretti took the brass and said, "much appreciated, guy." He finished ringing me up and set the brass in the register. Scobretti then sifted through the coins before retrieving a few that he handed to me, along with the pouch as well as my receipt. "Also…where ya from, guy? Massachusetts? No way you're from Jersey."

"Yes, I'm from Massachusetts."

"Yeah, I knew it. You sound like one of those Ivy League preps." Scobretti handed me a plastic bag. "It stands out compared to a Jerseyan yuk like me. Anyways, enjoy that bachelor party. But next time…if you wanna get your pal some *fishnet*, just get a stripper, huh?"

"Absolutely. A stripper would've been a much wiser option." I gathered my items together and placed them in the bag. "Have a great rest of your day."

Scobretti waved. "Same to you, guy."

As I made my way to the entrance of the store, the affable façade that had been projected throughout that conversation vanished. It was replaced by a sheer perplexity over the situation that'd just occurred. My initial belief was that Abraham Scobretti, my debauched target, would be fidgety, irked, harsh, and generally unpleasant to correspond with. And how could he not be? The vile scum that Her Majesty's Church has me pursue are devious cretins devoid of morals. They represent the worst of society. The sinful, corrupt, and downright roguish.

Our banter should've lasted for maybe a minute or so before the discomfort would settle in and inform me that it was time to leave. But Scobretti was relaxed and cordial. Our interaction was…decent.

The filth that I imagined would be distant and ill-mannered was surprisingly open about his personal life. Optimistic even. It was bloody terrifying, as the man was more *human* than my previous targets.

Opening the door to Debi's car, I settled into the seat and captured her confused gaze. The deer-eyed stare and luscious gaping mouth. She was gazing at me as though I'd just spewed a barrage of repulsive curse words at a vulnerable elderly person.

"Holy shit that was scary, Mark. You two spoke as if you were…buddies," she said.

"I'm afraid I'm aware," I said, putting the Volkswagen in drive so that we could leave the car park.

"It's insane." Debi positioned the listening device in the backseat and placed the sheet over it. "I would've never thought that Abraham Scobretti would be so…polite. The man trades sea animals for entertainment. He has no remorse for their wellbeing, the pain he's causing by removing them from their natural habitat."

"Have you ever been assigned a target with this sort of…temperament?"

"Never. I'm talking zero, Mark. They've all been shameless, cold assholes who are violent and insult everyone, even their associates. What about you?"

"Same. None of them have ever been as sociable as Scobretti."

"Really makes you think, doesn't it? It's always scared me…how some wicked people can wear a friendly, caring mask yet have such sinister darkness hidden inside them."

Yes, the notion of a savage sporting a mask covered in righteous jewels is quite frightening. So many wretched individuals roam this sickening planet, presenting themselves as saintly warriors of society. The most compassionate of Earth's otherwise insane flock. And yet, it's all a deceptive game played beautifully by the beast.

They, too, are part of that flock and so much more despicable than the rest.

14

Whenever I'm able to obtain even a few hours' worth of slumber, eighty-five percent of the time the internal realm is vacant and lacking colour. This has been the case for around five years, which is a damn shame because my dreams would routinely calm my nerves. The ounces of sorrow that would form out of constant stressful days found itself transforming into unflustered mental pictures the second my body jumped into inactivity. Subject matters of the dreams varied but the most common involved taking in the magnificence of an endless forest. It was a vibrant, green area with droves of thin, towering trees as well as dazzling, unblemished and cloudless skies. Crisp, earthy scents flowed through the environment, soothing any drops of tension that'd attempted to pervade this terrain. Though I've toured through many a forest in my life, I'm certain that this was one that existed solely in my mind. None were anywhere near as impeccable or bliss as this forest.

My other reoccurring dreams were in the guise of carnal crazes, as if that's any major revelation. Settings rotated on a mill, generating scenes as customary as a romantic cabin or as raunchy and smutty as a battered bathroom in a dive bar. Personal penchants of mine tended to emerge at some point during the duration of these dreams, since my partners were anonymous to me. Glasses of red wine, chains, paddles, bites, sizzling candle wax…even in that lewd dive bar scene each of those existed as further tools of indulgence.

Rarely am I able to luxuriate in the splendour of dreams now. It's not as though they're simply unable to generate anymore…but at this point it'd be bloody preferred that they discontinue altogether. This is because my brain has been sabotaged by those damn visions that plague me. Stressful, horrendous nightmares have now taken the shape of *dreams*. They're diabolical enough to possess such a grip on my slumbers that it's impossible to unlock my eyelids at night to end them.

Unlike some common nightmares, the visualizations that arise in mine are incidents I've, in fact, lived through. Well, *suffered* through is a much more fitting term. They're incidents that've haunted me since they first transpired. Allowing those miseries to feast on the lingering tatters of my sanity is yet another instance of my being wasting away. It's plausible that the Phantasms, particularly, play a substantial part in this continuous ruin. The Phantasms very well could've incited the episode that caused the nightmare that's currently swelling. Anxious to taunt and prod me into conceding that I'm more depraved than we all realize.

The third of February…three years ago. My eldest sister, Nell, celebrated her fifty-fifth birthday and the whole family convened in Minnesota, where she and her husband live. I was supposed to stay in town for several days. However, an incident ensued on the night of Nell's party that forced me to fly back to England three days early. The incident did not involve any of my family, which I'm of course thankful for. No, this whole quandary occurred some hours after returning to the hotel I was staying at.

I had switched the television on and began to remove my suit jacket. That's when the late-night news began playing, and I should've coerced myself to fetch the remote and change the channel. But that failed to happen. The anchor dove into a story involving a salesperson in a department store who'd been beaten with a wrench by a disgruntled customer. Repulsive report. Its abhorrent nature, however, hauled me to one of the chairs so to survey the television. The anchor talked at length about the incident, and she described the events as comprehensibly as possible. Then she continued with a following story, which dealt with another heinous crime.

All forms of mass media do damn all aside from stoking the already hectic rage that broods in me. But watching those revolting reports kindled an unanticipated reaction from me. The menacing rage, aching scowl, it all quietly dissipated into an emotionless vacuum. My thoughts fizzled down until they were no more than a barren plot of land. I was glued to that chair in utter silence for such a period that, upon finally standing, the news had ended, and some movie had taken its place. Once up, I snatched my keys from the bed and ambled out the hotel.

I'm still unsure as to why the drive led me to an expansive car park outside a Huge Lots store, especially since they were closed. Everything was progressing on autopilot and the car acted as though it performed all the actions necessary to bring me here. For whatever reason, there was a maddening itch that demanded my presence in this exact location at this precise moment.

This Huge Lots shared a car park with a few closed stores, as well as a twenty-four-hour launderette. Upon parking, my rental car was amidst about four others that were scattered about. Without thinking, I chose a spot that faced the entrance of the launderette before shutting off the car, ruminating in silence. My sights were fastened to that entrance for minutes on end, examining the five individuals who dwelled inside the facility. Not once did I question their mundane activities, nor my own. Instead, a transfixing aura coated me in its muggy intrigue. And as irrational as this scenario seemed, the itch was expressing patience with an assurance that the wait would be justified.

In due course, two individuals exited the launderette. Mercy, even if this scene didn't continuously haunt me in the guise of a nightmare, I wouldn't have forgotten them. Especially the woman. She was likely in her late twenties, with short light brown hair done in an asymmetrical bob. Her attire consisted of a blue, floral dress with a white cardigan draped over it. Black flats completed her simple yet nurturing attire. Then there was her most distinctive feature: a noticeable pregnancy bump.

Accompanying the woman was a bloke, walking some feet behind her. They were together, and the key indicator of such stemmed from the identical blue baskets they each carried. The man was barely taller than her, adorned in an orange t-shirt and jeans. As these two strolled to their car, I observed them chatting about who knows what. And the closer they approached their vehicle, it became obvious that the man was incensed about something. His eyebrows were furrowed harshly, and a turbulent glare was glued onto the woman.

Then...the bloke demonstrated just how bloody worthless of a human being he was. In two shakes, he dropped his basket and charged at the woman, shoving her to the asphalt in a violent rage. She landed hard, her own basket gliding from her hands as clothes spilled out. The vile subhuman then crouched down and began striking the defenceless, sprawled woman. Her aggressor had swiftly proven to be the embodiment of a reprehensible, infantile bastard suffering from abject inadequacy.

A thick air that comprised of charcoal and smoked meats greeted me as I left my car. Trudging toward the two at a brisk pace, muttered words resonated in my ringing ears on a loop. *You know what to do*. Every step grew weightier, every breath stormier due to the blistering rave that streamed in me. The closer I got, the more a demented fragment of myself tore itself from chains that tried with all their bloody might to keep it incarcerated forever. This fragment wore my figure, an image that became evident as it ripped and clawed itself out of my body. It was not like a snake shedding its skin. The sensation had more substance than that. When that identical persona surfaced from the shreds of old, my head became freer than it'd been in years. It was as though the true manifestation of my existence had finally been unshackled. This was *me*.

The man stopped his sickening assault when he got a decent view of me, screaming at me to "back off."

His words weren't going to interrupt me, and if he had thought they would then that was bloody comical. The face of the subhuman became more discernible at this point. Deep set eyes, severely receding brown hair, wispy beard, ivory skin with a laughable tattoo of a bowtie underneath his Adam's apple. His face twisted up in a blister of frustration when he realized my casual disregard of his petty threat.

"I said back off," he screamed again, emphasizing *back off*.

Again, I ignored his wretched attempts at deterring me.

His eyebrows contorted even further downward, which was quite fascinating being that they were already as sharply arched as seemingly possible. "Stupid clown," he said as he tried to stick one on me.

The man's fist drifted in slow-motion as my mental grasps became cognisant of an impulsive conversion. A conversion from mere human to maiming machine. Without an ounce of hesitation, I sidestepped the strike. Grasping his wrist while smartly positioning myself in front of him, I hammered the man's elbow over my shoulder. His subsequent agonizing bellows were brasher than anticipated. The man's breathing intensified, and he muttered incoherently as he sought to check his elbow. It had been shattered, courtesy of my admirable yet meagre strength. And do you know what was, by now, feeding into my increasing pique? The fact that this bloke was entirely unaware that a broken elbow *wasn't* my end point.

Snatching the collar of his orange shirt, I headbutted the man three successive times with uncanny might. It should've administered a ruthless headache but, even when the adrenaline winded down in the coming hours, it was unsuccessful in developing. The impact of the headbutts wounded and dazed the aggressor, however. He slumped to the asphalt near the woman, who was frozen as she watched the entire ordeal with amplified eyes.

This is where the savagery *should've* concluded. The fallen aggressor writhing in agony, hopefully recognizing that his malevolent actions were, frankly, unacceptable. And me, resolving an abhorrent incident by defending an innocent woman. That's where this whole situation *should've* stopped. If only the circumstances played out in that lacklustre fashion. What happened next could either be deemed an act of unwavering heroism or sheer dishonour. I'm still bloody torn after all these years, even upon re-evaluating these nightmares again and again.

As the aggressor laid on the asphalt, his hands shielding his battered head, I heaved him up by his collar again. His once perturbed face was now stupefied and drowsy, nefarious bloodshot eyes barely able to fasten themselves to me. Blood messily ornamented his nose, cheeks, and beard. He made several attempts at grabbing onto me, but he could hardly keep his arms up.

Scum like this shouldn't be allowed to exist. Those who'd assault innocent civilians, such as this pregnant woman. What's more, she was probably *his partner*. Despicable. It's utterly infuriating that these swine dwell among our wicked gardens. Prison is much too pleasant a residence for them. They deserve consequences much, much severer than what they dish. That's a bloody fact no matter what muck the misinformed spew. They're both mistaken *and* insensitive.

Both of my hands clamped around the man's neck. My grip intensified enough to inflame my veins, which were bulging within the flesh. The guilty face of that garbage heap rummaged nervously to paint a pleading expression. His eyes filled with aggrieved mercy and skurried gasps searched for any apologies he could muster. How pitiful must one be to even believe an *apology* would be enough to erase his sins? In the end, such acts of desperation went unanswered as the ghastly crunching of bones finalized the scene. The bloke's head bobbed backward while his body became limp in an instance.

I released the garbage from my grip, my hands sullied by touching pure grime. Adrenaline still swam millions of laps but decreased enough that the magnitude of my actions became stronger with each second that I gazed at the man's body resting on the asphalt. As it continued seeping from my system, the phrase *unlawful death* echoed in a bellowing buzz. Though such an act wasn't unaccustomed to me, in this scenario it was. Unless I'm on assignment and the British government has granted me the right, this ordeal was forbidden. This was motivated vigilantism.

The pregnant woman still hadn't tried rising to her feet. I wouldn't have doubted if her interpretation of life on planet earth had altered that very evening. Turning to her, I asked if she was okay. A streetlight illuminated her face, which highlighted a purplish bruise on her right cheek and a gash on her bottom lip. She could only manage a few slow nods.

When it came to pondering my subsequent steps, there were two options that jostled for position: call for help or bolt from the car park. Nearer to my car stood a payphone so, refusing to submit to cowardice, I told the woman to stay put and jogged to the spot. Were the police dialled? Absolutely not. That would've been the same as signing off on my own demise. To be fair, had I been detained there's reason to presume the evidence would've played in my favour. But emotions had irresponsibly intensified. Stakes were dramatically heightened. And judgement had been skewed. So, there was simply *one* person who could've lent me a hand at the time: Pierce Laughton.

Getting a hold of Pierce through his personal office number, it was a damn struggle to explain the whole situation while cramming in as much abundant detail as possible. A horde of words were all eager to trounce over one another, so much so that he had to stop me several times and ask that I repeat myself. It took him aback at first, how terrified the ordeal seemed to have made me. That was until I confided in him the truth about my fretful tone, namely the frenzied clashing between just and unjust actions.

The Deputy Lord President, in confidence, expressed his endorsement of the experience's outcome. He said that, if he were in the same position, it would be utterly impossible to stand by and twiddle his thumbs while such horror was unfolding. Pierce then informed me that he'd pull some strings, so to speak, but refused to disclose what exactly would be executed. All he revealed was that this incident would never reach anyone employed by Her Majesty's Church. Especially not the Lord President. Pierce also said that there'd be a jet waiting for me at an airfield that was in the area.

When I inquired about the pregnant woman, noting that she'd been lingering on the ground in shock, Pierce made me promise to stay with her until law enforcement arrived. Hearing that set off quite a load of alarms and made me question why a jet would be summoned when I'd still have to deal with the law. However, upon asking if that was a safe idea, Pierce's vigorous Australian accent produced a haunting frost that has stuck with me since. He merely said, "Mark…stay with her." And the line disconnected.

For ten minutes, I sat with the pregnant woman as we waited for law enforcement to arrive. Small talk was briefly employed to console her, but it was futile. The woman barely had the ability to form words. Her body was quivering from the reverberations of fear. She'd switch between sitting up and stretching out on the asphalt over and over. It was possible she was aiming to ease herself. Whatever the woman did, however, she was careful to keep her eyes off both her assaulter and me.

Two patrol cars pulled up to where we sat. I remember thinking it was sheer luck that no one else entered the car park while we waited. No one else left the laundrette either. Imagine witnessing a sight as traumatic as ours. Me, an injured pregnant woman, and a deceased body all situated together. How could anyone explain that? Is there any explanation aside from revealing the truth? I didn't believe there was.

When the officers approached us, two of them helped the woman to her feet. As they walked her to their car, she muttered "thank you." The three of them left and, of course, I never saw her again. She has emerged in my loaf a decent amount since. Perhaps it's careless optimism but I prefer to imagine she healed well and gave birth to a healthy baby some months later.

The other two, I thought, were priming themselves to arrest me. It was possible that Pierce's request fell into the sometimes-neglectful arms of the law. But, to my utmost satisfaction, one of the officers informed me that I was free to leave. He stated that they were aware of the situation but that I'd been granted immunity by the United States government due to my line of work. The officers did warn me that this was a one-time occurrence and that, while they understood my rationale, any future acts of vigilantism would result in my incarceration. Their instructions were acknowledged, and they let me go.

Before leaving for the hotel so that I could retrieve my belongings, my eyes caught the two officers desecrating the body of that subhuman. Kicking and spitting on the ghastly carcass while shouting expletives at it. While the thought of participating in such improper actions is inconceivable, there was a sting telling me that such was completely warranted. And all the while these officers behaved as jackals, it was still remarkable that *no one* else exited the launderette.

My youngest older sister, Sybil, was staying at the same hotel. Though it was rather late, I rang up her room and expressed dismay that my job required me to terminate my trip at once. The excuse was full of weak bullshit about how sudden business proposals desperately demanded my approval. Like the rest of my sisters, Sybil's never appreciated my shadowy explanations for abrupt departures. Funnily enough, she's the one who's held the most animosity toward it, which made the call loads grimmer to make.

Sybil's tone was exasperated and disappointed upon listening to yet another bucket of my paltry excuses. She knew convincing me to stay would be nothing more than hopeless fuss. On numerous occasions she'd run the hills, pleading for me to refrain from returning to England so soon. To her credit, Sybil never utilized guilt in her appeals, but she always enunciated how much she missed me. Anyhow, in between yawns Sybil said she'd tell the rest of the family for me. She then hung up before I could thank her.

Throughout the trip back to England, the war between honour and misconduct continued to rage. Why are these procedures appropriate if the government bestows the privilege unto me, but illegal if executed off the clock? There's no bloody difference. Misdeeds involving death, physical abuse, sexual corruption, children, venomous racists…they merit the same consequence. People who walk those dismal sides of this planet shouldn't exist. Execute them, rid the planet of their sickening lives.

It should be carried out through the means of capital punishment, not through vigilante activism. But…damn it…eliminating that subhuman was crucial even if the means are prohibited. Still…what if it ceased at the headbutts? There'd be no unlawful death and…well, there's the possibility of mere imprisonment which is a sham. No, his revolting deeds saw him rewarded with precisely what he warranted.

Honour and misconduct, in situations like these, are bonded together. It's morally wrong but it would've been unspeakably worse to have let that man…that ogre…continue breathing. Yet, why is it that despite my vehemence for recognizing this honour I'm still bloody tormented? Is it because there's no justification for unlawful death? Is it because all the targets I've been assigned to apprehend are just like me? Not because of the fact we both commit immoral deeds, but because there's that unending thirst for blood. The thrill of deranged pursuits. Where's the distinction? Tell me…where's the bloody distinction?

***

I awoke in a bomb with sharp, uneven breaths that took their time to rediscover their natural frequencies. Getting up from the bed, I turned the nearby lamp on while shaking out the reverberations of "bloody distinction." Reliving that episode again wouldn't have happened had there been someone else to share this bed with. Warm embraces from an enchanting woman are the only remedy for nightmares. Unfortunately, that just wasn't in the plans for this evening.

Upon returning from Hooking Up, Debi and I parted ways with plans to reconvene tomorrow morning at eight. She had wittered on about how she refused to wait over an hour like she did this morning. However, Debi said this with a spirited tone that, mercifully, implied that she was being playful with her remarks.

Before heading to the lifts, I had approached the front desk. The well-dressed male receptionist from earlier was still supervising the lobby, so I inquired as to whether Robin would be here later. He explained that she had the day off but that her next shift would be tomorrow. A dispiriting response for an overwrought sex addict, though it was understandable as well. Robin's enjoying an off day that she deserves and there was no fault in that. It wouldn't be fair to deem otherwise. Thanking the man, I brooded on my way.

It'd be foolish to assume some semblance of slumber would transpire soon, so I contemplated various paths that'd pass the time. A favourite pastime of mine is to embark on a long and aimless walk, but that didn't seem plausible right now. Whether out in a town that's still unfamiliar to me, or around the hotel, neither were very appeasing options. The latter, especially, might make me appear as dismally morose as the few ghouls that might be skulking around at this hour. If I had more knowledge as to the town's more *indecent* sites, then that'd be a preferred choice. That's a statistic that should be planned out in advance of assignments.

Then I wondered...perhaps Debi's still awake? After all, she was occupied with assignment-related plots for a good period last night. Enough to leave her exhausted by the following morning. Sure, she could very well be recouping lost slumbers now. Still, why not give it a whirl? The worst that could arise is she's sound asleep...which means that she'd secure yet another reason to pester me if I rouse her. Then again...what else is new?

The lift was a cheeky bastard, as it decided it was going to operate at an exceptionally slow rate this evening. Not an issue. Instead, I trudged down a flight of stairs before reaching the third floor. Public staircases are somewhat relatable. Forlorn, colourless, and vacant. A destitute location in need of vibrancy and zest that fails to congregate no matter where they've been constructed. How they stand out against the cosiness that inhabits every other sector.

A faint hint of music emitted from beyond the door of room 306. That's a positive sign, and it compelled me to knock a couple of times.

"Who is it?" Debi called, her sing-song voice sailing over the music.

The bounciness in her voice at this hour caught me off guard, so it took a second to respond with "Mark."

The music minimised a touch, though Debi presented no immediate urgency to answer. She didn't say "just a minute" or "I'll be right there." She *also* didn't say "go away." I figured she probably wasn't modest, that her attire was inappropriate, and she was changing into clothes that were. Figuring there was damn all to do aside from giving her some time, I loitered by the door and stared at the pure golden wallpaper that Nouveau Rêve savoured.

Debi, at long last, answered the door right as the particles in my vision began to creatively mingle with the gold colours. Her outfit of choice for the dead of night was…intriguing though also quite captivating. She wore an oversized short-sleeved silk, cheetah-print nightshirt that was unbuttoned and revealed a black bra underneath. Debi's knickers were also black but with the addition of a pattern of purple leaves. Her jangly silver bracelets were still adorned, and she also sported a necklace with a black triangular pendant. The most curious piece of her nightwear, however, happened to be the sea captain's cap she had on.

Delicate beads of sweat scampered across Debi's forehead in the guise of a liquid headband. A few beads had also trickled down to her cheeks, still peculiarly clad in rouge at this hour. She rubbed her nose before violently inhaling.

"Don't get any ideas," Debi said. She moved away to allow more space for me to enter. "Aside from the hat this is just what I wear to bed."

"I wasn't going to ask," I lied.

There weren't many dissimilarities between our rooms aside from how Debi's had papers and clothes strewn around it. The sheets on her bed were in a clump and so towering that they could put Everest to shame. A radio rested on a nightstand, and the bouncy synthpop that emanated from it was extraordinarily peppy to a rather artificial degree. However, there was an aspect of the rather conventional tune that attracted my attention. It was the singer's animated, melodious, and recognizable tone.

"Is that Eldritch Hawn?" I asked.

"Yeah. Not bad, huh?"

I responded by saying, "I suppose," though the sugary sheen of the hyper track wasn't my cup of tea. Apparently, if an artist initiated their musical endeavours over a decade ago, they weren't safe from the seduction of processed instruments. And, miserably, Eldritch was yet another causality of the barmy fixation this decade has on these twee baskets of modern records. "I don't believe I've heard this record before."

"You haven't," Debi said as she tampered with the radio, ejecting a translucent cassette from the deck. "These are unmixed demos of songs that'll be on his upcoming record. He's thinking of calling it *Denim Scarves*."

I stared at Debi with stripes of perplexment. *She* owns a copy of Eldritch's new demos before they're to be released? Preposterous. I mean what an utterly laughable falsehood. Debi had to be pulling some dense wool with such a daft comment. It was more likely this record was a recent release that hadn't introduced itself to me before. However, instead of tossing Debi's claim in a rubbish bin, I pried her a touch to see if she'd relent and admit the truth.

"Right," I said. "How did you, of all people, manage to secure his new record this early?"

"Well," Debi began with a smile, "when you're in the CIA, you do get a special treat. All the top artists in the world have a special instruction written in their contracts stating that they are to loan promotional demo tapes of new releases to us officers. There's one rule we have to abide by though. The collaboration between the CIA and participating record labels includes a strict policy that forbids distribution of the music in any form. If word gets out that some asshole ran around flaunting these tapes, then we're fucked."

Admittingly, acquiring demo tapes from top-tier musicians is certainly a unique privilege. One that appears to snow Debi under sheets of exuberance. However, the concept also comes off as rather lacking due to its general…uselessness. Perhaps it's just me but possessing a tape for personal recreation while maintaining confidentiality doesn't exude entertainment. It also has limited value in that tapes not only wear out from repeated listens, but hasty overuse can diminish the initial zest.

"Seems like you're going to be in a whirl of trouble, considering how you're flaunting this record."

Debi scoffed. "*Flaunting*? By playing *my* record in *my* room? This isn't flaunting. I'm *explaining* the situation. Besides, you're the only person who's heard this tape aside from me. I doubt *you* of all people will run around Jersey and announce that you just heard Eldritch's new record. Do you always waltz into people's hotel rooms and accuse of them of a fireable offense? Or is it pleasure saved just for me?" She placed the tape next to a pocket-sized, portable television that lounged on a cluttered desk near the edge of the bed. The television was switched on but must've been muted. "And sorry about the mess. I don't prepare for visitors."

"Are you normally this shambolic?" I asked, ignoring her insignificant question while searching for a place to sit.

Debi sniffled as she glared at me, pointing to the chair by the desk, instructing me where to sit. "If you mean messy, then no. Not at all. I just feel unorganized because of this assignment. We still don't have a course of action. That is, unless you do, and you just haven't been upfront about it."

"I have an idea. You'll see after our excursion to the docks tomorrow."

"Can't wait." Debi's sarkiness couldn't have been any clearer. "When I heard it was you at the door, I really thought you'd come to finally spill *something*. If you're not hear to talk about the assignment, then what do you want?"

"Couldn't sleep. Figured I'd take a gander and see if you were up."

Debi took her nightshirt and swathed it around her body as she crossed her arms. "See if I was up? With what goal in mind?"

"Would you believe me if I said I just itched for someone to chat with?"

"No, I wouldn't believe you. Besides, what's the point of talking if you can't answer any of my questions?"

"Answering your questions is fine. Just as long as they don't pertain to confidential matters."

Debi sighed. She splashed onto her bed, flattening the clump of sheets. "I don't think you're being honest about this *confidential* crap. So, I'm sorry if this sounds cold but that's really all I'm interested in learning about you. And if you still can't spill anything then you oughta just go, Mark."

Her words weren't unkind. It's much preferred to keep my issues locked up versus admitting them. There's no joy in allowing someone into your darkest realm, only for them to conclude you're a wicked mess. Has it ever occurred before? No, but I'll be damned to invite others into delirium they simply will not be able to cope with. If I must be alone with those dire nightmares, the voices, and all those demented streaks of spiritual destruction then so be it. However, there's an option that might permit further conversation. Though it might be a vain attempt, it's worth pulling out all the stops.

"You do realize this isn't all about me, right?" I asked. "Why don't you divulge some details about yourself?"

"You're joking," Debi said. "There's no way you're actually interested in hearing me talk about my life."

"You've never allotted me the chance to inquire."

"Hmm…I mean…where's the lie in that?" Debi rose from the sheets. "Fine. Go on and ask. Maybe watching me answer your questions will get you to reveal your casket of secrets."

"A casket of secrets, you say. How suitable." I reclined in the desk chair. "Early life."

"Starting off *strong*, like a college boy struggling to learn more about a girl he's crushing on."

Debi's quip did no favours as I gestured for her to get on with it.

"I'm a New Jersey native who was born in Brick," Debi said. "And before you make any silly jokes it's a township. I was raised by my Aunt Paula. Don't have any memories of my parents. To be honest, I don't know anything about 'em at all. My aunt has never liked talking about 'em. Do I wonder about 'em? Occasionally. But I consider my aunt to be my mother. She raised me and I'm indebted to her." Debi slouched some, setting her elbows on her thighs as she appeared to become more introspective. She focused on the nightstand as memories surely migrated to her head. "I graduated from Rutgers with a degree in Criminal Justice—"

"My apologies for interrupting you, but what got you interested in Criminal Justice?" I asked.

"Fair question. Damn, I haven't talked about this in ages it feels. When I was a kid, I used to love visiting the library. The librarian was this old guy, sixties maybe, and he was what comes to mind when you think of some sweet, little old man. Receding hair, beady eyes, large glasses. He was always so kind to me. Would give me lollipops and ask me what books I'd be reading. They *were* great memories."

"Do I even have to guess what comes next?"

"No. All that news came out when I was sixteen. Seemed to shock the adults more than the kids. Having to realize those memories were forever tainted, having to deal with the fact that I was fortunate while others were left without their innocence…it's bullshit. I was pissed. And I wanted justice. So, there you go. My reasoning for getting into Criminal Justice was kinda personal. Didn't think it would lead to me joining the CIA."

A rush brought upon by vehemence required more information about this scenario. Did the bastard meet a deserving end or did the courts coddle a bomb as they tend to and offer the monster an utterly pathetic sentence? None of those ponderings came to fruition as my following question kept the conversation on the tracks without issue.

"And what led you to join the CIA?" I asked.

Debi's expression transferred from focused to one more sombre. Her face relaxed as she sniffled, though it took some time for her to gather her thoughts. "I started off working as a court clerk where I did mostly dull tasks, such as setting up appointments for judges. Crap like that. Wasted five years with that position, until I met someone involved with CIA who ended up recruiting me. Can't disclose that information, unfortunately."

"That's it?"

"Sure is. The nature of how the CIA recruits its personnel is very discreet. They *truly* will not allow us to talk about that information. But I've been part of the organization for seven years and I'm grateful. Simple as that."

It's amusing, how she'll pepper her words with hints that'll try and loosen me up. For as admirable as Debi's persistence is, her attempts at persuading me to budge will continue to disappoint her. I think she's mindful of that truth but continues with her futile bids because of that beautiful phrase: *you just never know*. That, right there, is precisely why I respect her goads.

"Hopefully you'll see that it's not hard to share information, Mark," Debi said. "At the end of the day we're on the same side of the coin. Who cares if you're able to act like a loose cannon?" She expelled the last sentence through almost gritted teeth. "While I still *sorta* loathe you for it, you're not going to scare me away by revealing the privileges your organization allows you. Sleep on it. But for now, my show is on." Debi pointed to the television. "I missed it earlier so the I gotta catch the re-run."

Debi removed herself from the crowded bed and went to the television. She hadn't told me to back my chair away, so I was honoured to study Debi up close as she turned up the volume. At first, I prepared myself to marvel at her body. From the initial impressions, before seeing her so underdressed in her nightwear, it was splendid and reminiscent of June's svelte figure. Couple that with her dark auburn hair and there's a drug so pure it amplifies the carnal amphetamines forever coiling in my blood.

Surprisingly, my first impressions were a dabble off. As Debi twiddled with the knobs on the television, her nightshirt loosened and allowed her body to become exposed once more. And, in all honesty, I was quite staggered by the unusual proportions. They were unlike any I'd ever seen. See, Debi's arms were skinny, not dangerously so, but comparable to lead pipes. Her wrists, in particular, were tiddly and conceivably fragile like that of a plastic javelin. On the contrary, her torso was modest, blessed with a waist that would toast the ecstasy of a corset. My observations, of course, would also be bloody barmy to ignore her delicate peach-sized chest so divinely enveloped by that black bra.

"You're welcome to stay and watch, if you'd like," Debi said. "Don't know if you've ever seen shows like this though."

Snapping out of these fascinating bodily examinations produced a sensation similar to that of an out of body experience. The simple, sluggish act of tilting my head up to view Debi's face elicited a reaction from my physical being, but not my soul. And the two were split as they determined which corroded bucket my concentration should be loaded up in. My physical being contended that I respond to

Debi's comment, while my soul desired to continue its immersive figure studies. Ultimately, the former prevailed and I uttered "what is it?"

An unassuming disclaimer indicated that the following show would feature strong language and adult content. Amusing. Isn't everything in today's day and age brimming with that nonsense? Might as well glue that warning to the intro of every bloody form of visual art that exists now. Anyhow, the disclaimer faded into the beginning of the show, which featured a dark-haired man walking down a set of stairs. He sported a full suit as well as a comical grin. Surrounding this man was an enormous audience, all cheering and applauding him as if he was this mystical idol. Some of the men were bowing to him, while women were blushing and twirling their hair as this bloke kept walking.

The lad certainly appeared to apprehend the sheer command that he exerted over this television studio. He raised his fists in the air before spinning toward one of the male audience members. The two slapped hands before the suited man, who I'm guessing is the host, yanked the audience member into a headlock and proceeded to grind his knuckles over the man's head. I expected the roughed-up bloke to be incensed by the action. Instead, he got even more boisterous with his cheers.

"Why is that man so thrilled over his mistreatment?" I asked.

Debi stifled laughter. "Keep watching."

The host made his way to the stage, which was encompassed by blinding lime-green walls, where he shook hands with two men and a woman who were all seated in a row of charcoal chairs. He began gesturing to the audience to quiet down, signifying this by darting his flattened hand across his neck like a knife.

"When someone with an idealistic worldview thinks of religious leaders, they picture people who've lent their souls to their places of worship for the benefit of the greater good. Priests, ministers, rabbis, bishops, pastors, imams, they're all here to bring you closer to your beautiful beliefs. So close that you can practically taste the cottony clouds that their deities amble on. But jaded individuals, such as I, know that there's a deceitful, corrupted side to *plenty* of religious leaders. Those who love pocketing money from unsuspecting fanatics who think they're throwing cash to aid the enhancement of their place of worship. But little do they know that *these* religious leaders are using that money on the cheapest prostitutes and the purest cocaine immoral cash can buy. So, what happens when these two divisions meet? Stay with us, and you'll find out. Hit the music, you son of bitch!"

Synthesized horns and drums played as the opening credits launched. What ensued was the most rum, unconventional yet also hysterical show introduction I'd ever witnessed. A man dressed in full Nazi regalia, complete with that reprehensible armband, was being dragged into an interrogation room by the wild host. He then proceeded to shove the Nazi's head onto a table as someone off-camera threw him a meat cleaver. Whoever hurled the cleaver must've had some experience with weapons because the manner of its rotation was gorgeously artistic. As expected, the host then smashed the cleaver through the Nazi's neck, severing his head with the assistance of astonishingly gory special effects.

While the Nazi's head rolled off the table, patriotic confetti sputtered out the neck wound. Apparently, all this took place before an audience because the scene shifted to show three individuals lined up against a wall in the same room. They consisted of a Soviet soldier, a Klansman, and a moustached man adorned in extravagant military appeal complete with rows of medals. My hypothesis is that this person was generic representation of various military dictators currently decimating their countries. Regardless, all three were shivering and animated sweat beads were hopping off their bodies. The host then, with a gleeful yet mad smile, proceeded to rush the three frightened fiends as confetti showered both him and the screen. At this point, the title card finally appeared as the live audience cheered like they'd all simultaneously won life itself. This was, undoubtedly, an introduction that encapsulated American television at its finest hour, and that's irrefutable.

"*The Hugh Wreyford Show*?" I asked aloud. "That name sounds familiar."

Debi raised a finger and pointed to the television.

"Here's my nightly reminder," Hugh said once the title card faded away, "for everyone who's not aware, that Catch Heusley, creator of Mollin Maus and other happy-go-lucky anthropomorphic animals, and all the most beloved cartoons of all-time, was actually a racist, anti-Semitic, communist bastard."

Bloody hell this man doesn't restrain his boxes. If he'll chop away at the legacy of Catch Heusley of all people, he must attack everyone. To be fair, what he said about the illustrious animator was unfortunately true. The masses, however, are simply too horrified to acknowledge such reality if it means shattering their sappy childhood bliss.

"Sorry," Debi said, "but I just really wanted you to hear that part. Anyway, how old are you?"

"Forty-one," I said. "Why?"

"I've been a fan of Hugh's for years, so I'm familiar with most of what he's done. Now that I know your age, I can think of something you might remember. So, if you're forty-one, do you remember that old soap opera called *Erstwood's Game*?"

I nodded. "Yes, my…*I* used to tune in every now and then. It's been years though. Haven't heard anyone mention it since Georgia."

"Remember the male lead? The guy who played the character Strom Claever?"

Debi was asking quite a lot in this regard, but it's not as though she was aware of such. Watching television has never been a major recreational activity of mine. On top of that, soap operas are all interchangeable and blend together too much. However, this one was a favourite of Darla's, and we'd watch it together often during our marriage.

Swimming through the few, various clips that still somehow lingered in my head at this point, it took a couple moments before a clear scene from the show formed. The two lead characters were in a cabin at a ski resort, though the content within the scene had been lost with time. The reason this scene stood out more than others was because I recalled watching this episode with Darla, coincidentally, at a ski resort an eon ago.

"That's right. That is him. But I thought he'd retired? One of my sisters had mentioned that at least a decade ago."

"He did. He'd gotten married and had kids, so he wanted to spend more time with them as they were growing up, which I can respect. But two years ago, he made his return to television as the host of this unbelievably loony contest show called *The Million Dollar Odyssey*. It's geared toward teenagers and young adults, but I loved it. Would you believe it if I told you that Director Ganderman's son, Richard, was on the show?"

"Not a single bit," I said, attempting to process each facet of information Debi was rolling at me.

"He was. Richard didn't win, but Director Ganderman said he was pleased with how much the show matured his son. I'm getting off-topic. Anyway, after *The Million Dollar Odyssey* ended, it wasn't renewed for a second season, which was odd because the show got good ratings. But Hugh moved on to this show and, honestly, it suits him perfectly because he just lets loose."

"You don't say."

"Keep watching," Debi said. "There's no way you're prepared for what's to come."

How right she was. From everything that'd previously occurred, my expectations were heightened. However, they were still unable to process the extent of the madness that ensued. Hugh, upon inviting his guests to the stage, immediately began lashing out at a "pastor" who was being investigated for fraud. From what Hugh explained, the man had squandered every cent of his donations into an Olympic sized swimming pool he'd installed in his mansion. The so-called preacher accused Hugh of following "the hounds of media" and that he'd "never be able to wash away the sin of the sheep," whatever the bloody hell that means.

"You invited me on this show under the premise that I could clear my name," the man shouted, his face a blistering crimson like the shade of his necktie.

"I invited you here to show the world just how much you *care* about those who *care* about your church, you weasel," Hugh retorted.

The accused man leapt from his seat as though animated by a spring and began shouting "wash his sins" repeatedly, as well as "he will be damned." He then looked directly at the television, eyes glistened with tears of rage, and shouted "I'm the only one in this room who walks with those who are righteous. I have never sinned."

Hugh strolled to him and, without any hesitation or signs of restraint, made a fist and struck him across the chin. The man tumbled off the stage like an underpaid stuntman as Hugh shouted for security to retrieve him.

"Get off my set," Hugh barked.

Observing this entire debacle, I began to laugh more than I'd ever done so in my life. Plain truth. So much that my stomach cramped, my ability to breathe became hampered, and my body temperature swelled to the point I started sweating. This was truly one of the zaniest interactions I had to pleasure to witness. And it was ridiculous because this show seemed like it would be utter garbage. In a way, it *was*, but the initial thought was atrocious, unwatchable garbage. This was hysterical, entertaining garbage.

From the corner of my eye, I caught Debi in full hysterics too. However, she appeared to be more amused by my reaction than by the antics on television. Her eyes were stuck on the sight of me barrelling over and, each time my laughter became so much that it'd clench itself inside of another wave of laughter, she'd giggle even harder.

Since even in fits of merriment the cruel reality of my sorrow still dwells, I couldn't help but once again note Debi's fragile frame. It made me question how I didn't accidentally break her when I held her against the wall at the gala. And I don't mean that in a figurative manner. No, how did her bones not shatter from that? Debi's form was concerning, but there was no possible approach to questioning her. First off, how does one go about such? Secondly, and most importantly, it's simply none of my business.

So, instead of worrying about my partner, I resigned myself and shut the blinds so to live in this tick of hilarity. To be content in this shared amusement between Debi and I because we were finally baring ourselves to one another. That's what the takeaway should be at this very moment…right? Right?

15

When the sun peeked through the blinds and whispered "good morning" in its usual, dreary drawl, I immediately made out the sight of my hotel room. The haunting blankness and sheer lack of personality that wandered the area stood in stark contrast to the disorganised air of Debi's room. The blurry shears of thoughts that didn't disappear from last night failed to provide any answers. We continued watching Hugh's unstable yet uproarious talk show until, I suppose, my constant laughter helped a bed of slumber overtake me. I'm not certain as to when exactly Debi ended up giving me the boot, or *if* she did in the first place. But somehow my body slugged its way back here in the dead of night. And what's more? I managed to secure enough slumber to recharge to, at least, a decent thirty percent. For a frenzied insomniac, that'll do. Especially with what was to occur today.

Surely both Debi and I had differing beliefs as to just how crucial today's *surveillances* would be. No doubt she's been awaiting this stakeout for as long as she's been attached to this assignment. As for me, the stakes weren't nearly as high…nor as essential. Our excursion to the docks would bring us another step closer to apprehending our targets, and to identifying the mysterious yet alleged fourth member of Abraham Scobretti's operations. I'm so bloody deprived of the thrill at this point, but the finish line has emerged in the vague distance of this murky desert.

As I finished preparing myself for the day, my eyes roamed to the clock more times than they needed. "Nine-fifteen," I muttered before making an effort to cease these glances. It should be mentioned, at this point, why I'm such a stickler when it pertains to keeping a close eye on time. After all, it's become so habitual it's practically embedded in my mad personality.

When one grows up with five siblings, you must cope with the prospect of arriving to events late more often than on time. No matter the occasion, my dad and I would be the sole members of the family dressed and ready for hours on end. So, we'd have to wait and wait while my mother and sisters all dragged on with their routines. Their hair had to be so perfect that a single misplaced strand would cause an uprising. Outfits would be swapped three times on average. Mom tried exacting this level of precision with me and, admittedly, it succeeded while in grade school. But by middle school I'd become unruly and she all but gave up on persuading me to conform to her meticulous standards.

As for my sisters, well, as expected, their shoddy preparation habits escalated as they aged. It was to the point where my family almost missed my high school graduation because all five of them were unable to stumble upon the right outfits for hours. Of course, I'd stressed this importance to them days prior, going as far to ask that they had their outfits selected the night before. Even my eldest sisters who'd flown in to attend had decided their selections weren't up to snuff, so they chose to borrow from my younger sisters' garments. Had I not caught a ride with some lads, that would've boded poorly on me.

The awkward shadows of late arrivals haunted me enough to strive for a difference upon reaching adulthood. Only recently have I regressed to "sometimes on time, sometimes not," and the blame is entirely on me and all these bloody issues I juggle. With yesterday, there were facets of regret rounding me upon learning how late I'd be to assemble with Debi. It's just that they've been buried underneath mountains of other attentions.

I was in the middle of lacing my usual bland black shoes when three light knocks rang from my door. Upon answering, the woman who stood before me wasn't Debi despite my certain anticipations. No, it was Robin, the shapely receptionist.

She wore a beige blouse that was tucked into a black skirt. Other than her outfit, everything about her remained unchanged from our previous encounter. The artful dusk of her violet eye makeup, the lively nature of her teased rust coloured hair. It was perfection. She continued to define perfection.

"Surprised?" Robin asked with a light smile.

"More than you realize. I at least expected a note," I said.

"Do all your girls usually leave notes?"

"If they leave early, then sure," I said, stepping closer to Robin in an ever so sly manner. "But I suppose this…lack of communication is something you'll have to make up to me."

Robin's gaze travelled me up and down with a certain gentleness. A fixated precision. Her smile loosened, though this derived from lust and not indifference. How am I able to confidently discern this? Simple, seeing that Robin's hands were slithering around my waist.

This was, of course, an unforeseen dalliance. A type that is considerably rare, as second cavorts with partners are scheduled in advance. It's not like the first, where it just happens to fall upon you like destiny enveloped in a gaudy, glittered bow. And I'm not confident enough to pretend there's a magnetism within me that works like a charm any given time. One that enables situations like this to be commonplace. No, what happened with Robin the other night was a general one-night stand, or at least that's what I believed. But I'm quite content with being so maddeningly wrong.

***

Once my colleagues began learning of my…frequent liaisons, they were rather hasty in generating a suitable nickname for me. A nickname that subtly alluded to that facet. Anyone who has served as one of the fifteen members has one, though it took a full year and a half until I was awarded such a prestigious title. My good lad, Bart, was the bastard who established my official epithet amongst Her Majesty's Church: *Mister President*. Now, it doesn't make much sense without context, which is what everyone was aiming for in the first place, but it's also a bit antiquated too. On top of that, though I don't mind the nickname, the person it refers to is my antithesis when it deals with views on liaisons.

Mister President refers to Roy C. Paisenduil, the 51st President of the United States who served two decades ago. Youthful, handsome, charismatic, he was immensely popular with almost everyone even if they disapproved of his policies. However, despite being married to an elegant, enchanting if not robotic model, Paisenduil engaged in hundreds of affairs. Not only were these liaisons highly publicized, but he also had this brazen quality of demanding he be photographed while in the midst of being absorbed in smutty behaviours. And the women ranged from escorts, to housewives, to socialites, to celebrities, and even to those involved with politics. Needless to say, his end game, assassinated while in office, was one of the most unsurprising events in world history.

I think my colleagues are aware, or at least with any luck they are, that my dalliances are more meaningful than indecent. That, while being an addict, I am not a sexual deviant. For as exhilarating as the ecstasy may be, the most vital aspect of the dalliance is that we're both satisfied. There's no need to justify this to myself, but the fear of negative connotations is unquestionably harmful.

These ponderings floated around me as I relaxed in the passenger seat of Debi's car. She was focused on the drive to the docks. When we met up in the lobby, with me *still* able to arrive on time, she merely said, "let's go," and we embarked. Like most occurrences pertaining to this assignment, Debi had everything set in place. I was just along for the ride, which could be grating but ultimately was the ideal situation unless a reprise of the gala wished to rear its mad grin again.

With Debi taking the reins of my attention, what previously roamed in me converted to stressing observations of my partner, namely the outfit she sported. Between Debi's collared mauve shirt and the white sweater over it, the combination proved bulky enough to shield any evidence of her thin arms. Those frail wrists. Was it because she realized how exposed she had been last night? Who knows? But I told myself to let it go and, regrettably, that's what must be done.

"I still can't get over how much Hugh's show did you in," Debi said. She giggled some before sniffling. "You're finally less of a robot now."

Snapping out of my blue haze, I replied, "how sweet you are," with enough frost to build a snowman. "But," I continued, "yes, I still can hardly believe it. I don't tend to laugh at foolishness like that."

"Until last night, I would've never guessed you could even laugh like that in the first place. But it was nice. You're so guarded, so it was fun seeing you in a good mood."

I chuckled tersely. "Glad to be of service."

"Oh, I almost forgot, are you hungry? I brought some chocolate covered expresso beans. They're in the back. Got 'em from the hotel snack bar but didn't care for 'em. You can have 'em if you'd like."

Though I'm not one who gets pleasure from chocolate all that much, the idea of chocolate covered expresso beans sounded decent enough. I retrieved the plastic cubed container, which was seated on the sheet that covered Debi's listening device. Taking a handful of the marble shaped beans, the resulting blend of flavours was unlike any I'd ever had the fortune to experience. To go and say they were merely "delectable" wasn't enough to do them justice. These beans were potent enough to compel me to scoop more from the container.

As I view food as a nuisance instead of as a necessity, nothing I've ever eaten has ever had *this* commanding of an effect on me. One could make the argument that I was famished and desperately in need of nourishment. Is that any surprise? But I've been dangerously starved before, and *nothing* ever seized me the way these expresso beans had.

Debi smirked. "Glad you like 'em. They're yours."

After a third handful, I placed the lid back on the container. That was enough to hold me until dinner, as dreadful as that was to admit. Besides, I refused to act like some sort of glutton in front of Debi. That would provide her with more fodder to crack wise about me. I mean, there's not an issue with that, but bloody mercy she's got plenty of ammunition now. Why add to her stockpile? Well…actually...it'd continue to decimate all her previous thoughts of me. The apocalyptic images she possesses of my deranged actions in full rage. Those would be replaced with scenes showcasing a more humane side of me. It does exist when it wishes to.

We soon arrived at the Nesmith Docks and, even though I'd viewed the picture in my files, the area wasn't what I had been anticipating. For some reason, the location appeared in my mind more along the lines of industrial docks with cargo ships. Suppose this confusion was warranted, being that those files haven't been touched since my first day in New Jersey.

This area had more in common with a marina, as rows of identical white houseboats were situated on the water. A steel ramp ranged from the docks to the sidewalk, and a thin rectangular strip of asphalt contained one of the car parks. Debi had parked in a different lot that led down to the area, but it was perched up on a meagre hill that overlooked all the sites. Though pine trees were scattered on the grassy knoll in between the two sections, Debi smartly found a spot that allowed us a clear view of the area down the hill.

The sun struggled to make itself present behind a wall of clouds, which gave the area a beautiful sense of gloom. This was somewhat unfortunate, as I could only imagine the gorgeous scene of the sun bouncing off the water like one of those miniscule rubber balls. But, knowing that such a dock, err, *marina* was routinely infected by Sergio Scobretti and his illegal transactions sullied those pictures. Perhaps it wouldn't have been as brill as it could be.

Debi pulled a pair of binoculars from behind her seat and had them pressed against her gems. She pointed a finger to a section of the car park, though I wasn't entirely sure whether that was the correct location she was identifying.

"Right there. Every time Sergio Scobretti comes here, he always chooses that parking spot," Debi said.

"Which one?" I asked.

"That one," Debi said, gesturing her finger some.

I sighed. "May I see the binoculars?"

"Oh," Debi said, possibly realizing her error. She handed me the binoculars as she said "sorry" with a low chuckle.

Upon observing the car park through the binoculars, I followed where Debi's finger was and discerned a number that marked the apparent spot. "Number thirty-seven?" I asked.

"Thirty-four," Debi said, her cheek close to mine.

With almost imperceptible movement of my head, the correct spot was detected with ease. Removing the binoculars, I prepared to return them to Debi as I began to say, "thank you." Debi, however, was planning to say something herself, though none of the words ever formulated into anything intelligible.

Our faces had spun toward one another as we both began speaking and, with Debi's cheek having been almost pressed against me, our bottom lips accidentally brushed together.

There's a distinct alteration in the universe when you happen upon this very situation. When people mention that the world disappears, they're not necessarily wrong. Everything that surrounded Debi and I, the entire *marina*, became a blur and fizzled like tonic from existence. It's not as though everything around us faded to black, but the colours melted together to create a pile of bizarre art. Almost like a psychedelic illusion.

Those scenes, however, didn't matter. I watched Debi's lips move, though words failed to figure out how to exit her mouth. Or did she say something, and the intensity of the ardour ended up overriding all sound? Regardless, Debi's hand crept to my jaw and the softness of her fingertips pranced to my chin. Her face drew closer, and my nostrils became crowded by a surge of sensual, emphatic jasmine. Debi's lip-gloss, on the other hand, produced hints of cherry that asked me to take a journey on coral-coloured clouds. When our mouths touched again, the syrupy sensation of her sweet lips suctioned onto mine.

Bloody mercy, admitting these corny comprehensions were wholly unlike me but to disregard their presence would've been the card of a fool. These sudden kisses raised my body temperature far past a reasonable heat. Like venturing into dodgy territory and revelling in the exhilaration that arises when you've outdone yourself. It'd been decades since I tumbled over piles and rows for kisses like Debi's.

But…to my dismay…I detached my lips from Debi's and relocated them down toward the ground. "I can't," I said.

Debi's breathing had intensified to the point I could barely decipher the word she'd mumbled, which happened to be "what?"

"I can't."

Though our lips were no longer attached, Debi's hand remained on my jaw. When I trekked back to her gaze, her eyes gave the impression of stunned disappointment. They were broader, curious yet the same expression would've been provoked had she run over a cat.

"Upon taking Her Majesty's oath, I upheld one particular rule: that I would never get involved with a colleague. Whether a fellow member of Her Majesty's Church or someone from another intelligence agency, the rule is still one I abide by. And, Debi, I respect you far too much to violate that rule…no matter how challenging it may be."

"Oh," Debi said, her hand leaving my jaw. She reset her body back into her seat and took a deep breath before drawing out her exhale. "I…appreciate your honesty."

"Honesty" …well, there's that beautiful word again. Everything that I told Debi, it's fact. After all, that's precisely why I'm incapable to bring myself to romance Francine. But…when I first took my oath, that personal rule never traversed my mind. It sprouted after an acrimonious separation from a colleague, not that we were ever walking out with one another. No, our "relationship" was sex-based, yet still a separation in a way.

It began mid-way through my second year with Her Majesty's Church. Without going into specifics as to how everything progressed, being that it's unimportant, all I can say is that I entered a highly carnal "relationship" with Apollonia Libhriwar, who had three years over me in terms of tenure.

Apollonia, a six-foot spectacle of grandeur who exemplified the incantation of pure eroticism, was of Scottish and Kenyan descent. Her skin was an enthralling honey bronze. Her lips were plump, soft as marshmallows, and always swathed with gloss. As for her personality, well, the confidence she had was almost unmatched. Apollonia knew how to exploit her gifts while cautiously downplaying her faults. A brilliant mind, with brilliant moves, brilliant form…

Alas, our involvement lasted three years but, again, never became more than frequent rendezvous'. That, understandably so, is a key reason as to why we didn't last. She desired shedloads more than I planned to provide. How we even attained three years is a shock in and of itself, but the ensuing split soured my views on colleague relationships being that we still had to be cordial with one another.

All is better now, as she's put aside her ill-will while I've expressed disappointment in my actions and attitudes. But that initial fallout, and the jokes from other colleagues, convinced me to strictly hold myself to a higher standard with anyone I work with. Even when the green light is begging me to just say "damn all," like how it is with Francine…or even with Debi.

Thankfully, all the circumstances that were building up to a pool of awkwardness evaporated once Debi's eyes perked up. She motioned for me to use the binoculars. Two black sedans had entered the car park. They drove slowly before positioning themselves in spots thirty-four and thirty-six. Doors opened and, lo, the transaction was commencing.

Sergio Scobretti exited the passenger side of the car in thirty-four. Rocco Abruzzoli came around from the driver's side, while a third man emerged from the backseat. This must've been Stanley, who we learned yesterday was a cousin of the Scobretti brothers.

From the backseat of the other car emerged a man with grey hair who was adorned in a dark suit complete with a trench coat. He was the sole occupant who left the vehicle. In his hand was a briefcase. Classic. One can imagine just how much brass occupied that briefcase. The older man handed the briefcase to Sergio, who signalled for Rocco to take it. Sergio proceeded to shake hands with the older man, before Stanley approached him with an outstretched hand. In between Stanley's fingers was something I couldn't quite make out at first.

"I believe he handed the man some sort of card," I muttered.

"It's one of Abraham's business cards. They'll be meeting later in the afternoon for the transfer of the animal," Debi said.

"Quite foolish how brazen they are to do this in public."

"You have to remember that the cops don't have a clue about these dealings."

"What about the situation at the gala? Surely that would've put everyone on high alert."

"I guess not."

The four returned to their cars before the vehicle carrying the older man drove off in a somewhat hurried manner. Not enough to capture unwanted attention, discounting myself being that I'm trained to identify such, but enough to disclose apparent discomfort in the seediness of the ordeal.

Sergio's car hadn't yet driven away when an idea bid me hello. The idea was, undeniably, poor and unreasonable. But, if everything somehow managed to take shape in the format I believed it might, then it'd be worthwhile. See, the conversation Abraham had with Sergio and Rocco yesterday, it started to play back in my bonce right when the latter two exited their car. Memorizing each sliver of dialogue wouldn't have been feasible unless it was required, and Her Majesty's Church does a decent job at training its members in the craft. In this case, only select words and sentences were indispensable.

Abraham mentioned, moments before Debi's exalted splendour sailed me away, that Stanley was invited to partake in the transaction as a blood favour. Apparently, the miserable slug was in desperate need of cash, so Abraham relented and allowed him to join in. However, Abraham specifically told his associates *not* to bring Stanley back to the fishing shop once the transaction had concluded. This...presented a chance opportunity. One that could crack certain, unresolved matters, while also permitting me to savour some personal merriment.

"When they leave, I want you to follow them," I said.

"Are you joking?" Debi asked. "Why?"

"Don't ask any questions, Debi. Just do it."

Debi sighed. "Son of…I already don't like this idea. But…there are too many reasons to name, and they'll just fall on deaf ears anyhow. So, fine. But only because Director Ganderman *insisted* that you're the shot-caller. That you're allowed to take over when you want. Look at that. I have rules of my own to follow."

The declarations of a jilted partner. This response was anticipated. I had subdued suspicions that Debi would be dissatisfied by our disastrous share of heightened passion, and how I halted something that could've been potentially stimulating. Besides, no sane person takes pleasure in rejection, and though I don't believe that obeying my rules instigated *rejection*, per say, it's still hurtful. If only she was aware of how regretful I am over abiding by that damn rule, but this is another one of those situations where it's best to just let this one wane.

When the car containing all three of those bastards left, Debi followed suit. The two car parks were attached by the exit, in that whoever was parked on the hill had to yield to those parked near the water. Keeping this in mind, Debi wasn't in much of a rush to go downhill. The wise option, as we had to maintain a low profile. Easier for her than I since Sergio and Rocco would be more likely to remember me than her. After all, she's no longer sporting that inane blonde wig.

As we trailed Sergio and his associates down the road, we were careful to allow other cars the opportunity to cut us off. Remaining behind them the entire car ride could very well be detrimental in that they could detect us if we were glued to them for too lengthy a period. The roads today were light on cars, so the silent pursuit was easy enough. All their movements were visible no matter where they ventured.

Debi convinced me that it'd be preferred if I lay myself down. This was to avoid any potential glimpses the scum might catch of me from the rear-view mirror. I agreed and believed she wanted me to recline my seat as far back as I could. After all, it certainly would've been the most suitable method. But, without warning, Debi snatched my arm and yanked my head toward her lap. This must be her preferred approach when it comes to prompt safeguards, considering this was exactly what she'd done yesterday when we were staking out Scobretti's fishing shop.

"You realize I'm blind down here, right?" I asked

"Tell me, Mark, where do you think they are going?" Debi asked.

"This might come off a touch daffy…but I have a hunch. There's a chance they're going to drop off Stanley."

"A hunch, huh? If you were some bozo, I'd call you an idiot…going off a hunch. But what the hell. Worst case scenario they'll return to the fishing shop, right? Or they somehow noticed us and are leading us to "happy trails" of sorts."

"Okay," I said, discounting her unimpressed sarcasm, "and answer me this question. You told me that you've lived in New Jersey your whole life. Do you still have a place here?"

Debi nodded. "I do. It's maybe forty minutes from h—" she paused, her mouth still open judging by the position of her bottom lip. She finally uttered out "I know what you're planning to do. Damn, Mark…are you sure that's what you want?"

"I'm certain. So, keep following them and see if my hunch is correct. And if I'm wrong then we'll merely circle back to the hotel."

Debi did as I requested. She followed them for what might've been ten minutes or so while I remained hidden from view, head in her lap and with a searing pain in my waist because the seatbelt was embedding itself into me. With this hunch I possessed, there was an intense likelihood that it could fail. Where it derived from was entirely unknown, but it was reminiscent of the one those demons planted years back. The ones who convinced me to venture down to that Big Lots. There was motive behind this madness. If they were, indeed, correct then perhaps a side career as a detective was in my future? Of course, that's a joke. No bloody chance I'm wasting my time as some sleuth when it's so devoid of manic action.

"We're in a neighbourhood now," Debi said, "and they're parking on the side of the road in front of a house. Address is ninety-eight Hickey Lane"

"Park in a nearby driveway," I said.

"Okay. Wait a minute. The back door is opening and...Mark, you detective fucker. I don't know how you called it, but Stanley is exiting. Just him." Debi placed her hand on my shoulder and began patting it harder than she must've recognized. The tone of her voice grew animated, louder as well. "And the car is leaving. The car...is leaving."

I could tell that Debi's breathing had sped up, as her slight stomach was expanding and shrinking rapidly against my head. Can't exactly fault her. It's all part of the thrill. "Tell me when they're out of sight," I said.

Debi's eyes were fastened to her window. "Going...gone. They're gone, Mark."

"And where's Stanley?"

"He's walking up the driveway."

At that point, I sprung up from Debi's lap like the undead after having been struck by lightning. After unbuckling my seatbelt in a hurry, I unlocked the door. As Debi said my name in a startled and almost confused tone, I left the car.

This neighbourhood was pleasant in a classically suburban aspect. Rectangular brick houses all of a similar build, though with identifiable touches that enabled them to stand out among the scores. One had a porch; another had a lengthy walkway. A brush of nostalgia fluttered, though not because I'd once lived in a neighbourhood like this. See, as a teenager, I knew that this neighbourhood was the model for my future. A close, cosy, tight-knit area that would be perfect to raise children. Those plans didn't *quite* end up in such a manner, but that didn't halt the nostalgia from rising.

These neighbourhoods have always presented a serene quality of safety as well. The image of children playing in the streets without any issue was one of the prevalent features that arose. Men on lawnmowers or working in their garage, complete with a stereo nearby that was blasting music. Women tending to the gardens or walking their dogs, sunglasses on to fend themselves from the outside world. And then there was me, rushing down the sidewalk on a pile of feathers before flinging myself like a poison dart barely above the ground.

One of my shoulders drove into Stanley's back, causing him to grunt as we collided onto the grass. He struggled to lift himself to his knees so I, being the level-headed bloke that I am, generously assisted him. Snatching the collar of his long-sleeved denim button-down, I heaved Stanley up and struck him in the face with a fist. The impact sent him tumbling to the sidewalk, his body unable to stay upright as he toppled over. Stanley was unsuccessful in remaining entirely on the sidewalk, however, as the nature of his topple led to his upper body landing on the asphalt.

As entertaining as this ordeal was shaping up to be, it regretfully had to cease. No one was visible in the surrounding area, so no time was as opportune as now to conclude this irrational business. Grasping Stanley's shirt once more, I sprinted him back to Debi's car. The haste was enough for Stanley's dark blue baseball cap to fly from his head, though I saw him seize it within seconds.

Opening the door, Debi had already done me a grand favour in assisting my crazed idea. She had pushed my seat upward and also moved the listening device directly behind her seat. After shoving him into the back, I retook my seat and demanded that Debi "take us to her place at once." She obliged.

16

There are two actions that, when enabled, will cast me off to a castle in the desecrated red mist – a location still in existence yet sinking into a mirror of disconnection. One of these actions deals with carnal affairs, and how the sheer intensity of heated attraction will cause me to transform into my partner's model servant. In doing so, I'll abandon the mental erosion for a section of time and luxuriate in the blissful passions of the flesh. What emerges from this period of disconnection is a form of myself that is the most parallel to the one who existed before Her Majesty's Church entered my life. To be fair, the reason for this is not due to a similarity of actions between me and this form. Instead, it is because there is no presence of collapsing woe attempting to wrench me from the fervour of lovemaking. And while I might still be connected to my partner in all aspects of the self, my servitude to her disables a true association to *my* actual self.

Then there's the second action, that of consuming and unhinged ire. When it first erupted during that night in the Huge Lots parking lot, it set off a startling sensation that horrified me. Recognizing, at that moment, just how ghastly my behaviours could grind down to if I'm not cautious enough. Of course, that wasn't the first time I ventured down that murky path, considering my profession empowers those methods. But it was the first time they surfaced without being under the guiding eye of the United Kingdom's government.

Since then, there's been an evident shift in my customary methodologies. More along the lines of how I charged Sergio Scobretti at the gala while lacking discretion. Sure, it's careless and asinine, but there is no longer a humane connection with myself while on assignment.

Blaming the voices entirely for this indifference would be easy but it would also be ignorant. They've certainly exacerbated the degree of my lunacy, the way they dangle me like a hopeless marionette. But I take full responsibility for what occurred in that parking lot. Same applies to my handling of current assignments.

At this state the bestial yet identical figure that resides in me, the one that tore its way into reality on that bloody night, is consuming me. It hasn't yet decided to come into view, but it's on the brink of becoming known. Right now, it's not worth the hassle, but when it knocks on my fragmented gate…I'm prepared to liberate it.

***

We've been in the car for around forty or so minutes, and I believe we're nearing our destination. My torso is twisted toward the backseat where Stanley sits. His apprehensive eyes were darting back and forth between mine and my C70, which I have levelled at his chest. It's discreet, low enough to avoid detection from any wandering glances of other drivers. Stanley's blue baseball cap is also helping to conceal the gun, its barrel nestled through the back slit of the cap.

Initially, upon lobbing Stanley into Debi's car, my design was to render him unconscious the second Debi sped out of his neighbourhood. This would've been accomplished by smacking him in the bonce with the butt of the C70. Debi, who's been giving off an unnerved impression throughout the drive, was quick to talk me out of this suggestion. She never uttered an explanation as to why she preferred to keep Stanley alert, though it might be chalked up to avoiding any "unnecessary violence." This is speculation but, recalling her attitude toward my conduct during the gala, it makes enough sense.

At the same time, it's preferable that such is not the case. Hopefully Debi is not one of those sickeningly drab passive types at the CIA. The ones who prefer all tasks are accomplished without the use of excessive force. She's never explicitly admitted such, but the assorted signs that've appeared since we began working together all lean toward that. Sure, I wasn't anticipating a more invigorating and crazed reaction when she revealed her apparent comprehension of my plan. But, at the very least, I was expecting a certain willingness. For both of our sakes, I hope that Debi isn't of the belief that this is merely a routine detainment for the purpose of interrogation. Otherwise, it's best that she doesn't flip her lid when the already sullied colours of my palette darken entirely.

After Debi convinced me not to strike Stanley with the C70, the bastard attempted to utter something that was most likely along the lines of "what do you want from me?" A typical and obvious question that's regularly spat out by some pitiable nit who's been entangled in this mess. Before any intelligible words could even be formed in his mouth, however, I halted Stanley in his tracks. Whatever he had the urge to say did not matter to me then, and it doesn't now. Even if he was willing to tell all right then and there, he's not escaping the talons of justice that easily. Therefore, I demanded that he keep his mouth glued.

Once Stanley had shut his mouth to *literally* keep his life intact, the remainder of the trek was immersed within an ominous vacuum. Very few sounds twirled about inside the Volkswagen. They included Debi's sniffles, which reoccurred every couple of minutes. The number of times this has occurred, plus the innumerable instances she'd done it while we've been together has convinced me that she has a sinus condition. The other sound that addressed us was the steadily increasing volume of Stanley's own nasal inhalations.

Unlike most of the targets I've dealt with, there was a distinct lack of confidence in Stanley's demeanour. It was plain non-existent. Reflecting on my previous adversaries, some had cackled the instant they witnessed the unsheathing of my weapon. Stanley's entire being instead began to tremble in an almost cartoonish fashion. So much so that the vibrations that emanated from his rattling shoulders gave the impression of shockwaves. A few of my other targets had cursed me for telling them to glue their mouths shut, incensed that someone as lowly as me would speak to them with such a rosy attitude. Stanley, on the other hand, had kept his lips tight and unmoved since the demanded was given.

Stanley was probably in his mid-thirties and had a face that was arguably more unique than those of the other rogues. He possessed a square jaw and distant eyes, the latter of which was instigated by his eyelids. They gave Stanley a weary appearance, something that came across even through his trepidation.

As my sights refused to wave from Stanley, the outside realm was unclear. I could, however, tell that we were now lugging up an incline. Figuring that we must've been arriving at Debi's, I tossed Stanley's cap toward him. He was immobile as the cap bounced off his chest and settled on his lap. Witnessing the impressively statuesque stillness he emitted as his hat landed on him, not even daring to glance down at it, and certainly not moving an inch to retrieve it, it's doubtful that a scenario exists that would compel him to budge. Even a rabid Doberman, amped on amphetamines and barking in his face, would prove ineffective. I staunchly believe that.

"We're here," Debi said, turning off the car.

"Debi...go to the front door and unlock it," I said. "Then go inside. Stay there. We'll be in momentarily."

A surge of control parades about me when I can sense someone's eyes on me without connecting with theirs. This, of course, doesn't pertain to the unwelcome stares of a stranger. No, this is about dominion. How someone watches you upon being given a command, and they're incapable of rebuffing such. In this case, Debi's were latched to me like magnets, and I desperately yearned to read her thoughts. She's probably questioning me again…or questioning whether or not she ever expected to be intertwined with this kind of rot when she joined the CIA. Ultimately, Debi left in silence so that she could follow my instructions.

With her presence now absent, the mood of the Volkswagen became markedly austere. I continued to assess Stanley, my C70 still happily aimed at his chest. Her Majesty's Church imbedded in me an important rule of thumb during my initial training - that you never let your guard down. Such a rule is one that should be taught during childhood, a matter of common knowledge. See, it doesn't matter if there's a commotion stirring up in surrounding areas, a rioting crowd, or even a bomb threat. You always keep your bloody eyes on your target until you're one with them.

"Watch her," I told Stanley. My voice began to display signs of self-disconnection, none of which occurred during my encounter with Sergio. The most apparent facet of this trait is that my voice lowers into this cauldron of gloomy ice. It's vacant of rage even though such continues to ruminate in me. "Tell me when she's inside."

Stanley's tense eyes gradually removed themselves from me and struggled to relocate to Debi. They raced back to my weapon every now and again due to what I'd assume were jumps of panic. Once they'd finally reached the window, the dread of speaking even though he was ordered to caused Stanley to sputter out "s-s-she's in-inside."

"Good. Now…I'm an easy bloke to get along with. So…follow my instructions and you'll find yourself in a much better standing than those with cross me. Is that understood?"

"Y-Yes…"

"I'm going to exit the car. You'll follow. We'll then enter the house together, with you leading the way. And…if you dare scream…if you even attempt to run…I assure you that you won't get very far. And the last sensation you'll experience will be the rushing build-up of blood swallowing your lungs after you collapse."

The colour in Stanley's face dwindled until he was pale as a corpse sunbathing in a tundra. Though I partly expected him to ask me a question of some sort, something along the lines of "you're mad…you wouldn't do that in broad daylight," he instead nodded slowly. At this point, I must admit, there's something peculiar about the extent of his unease. It's almost…human compared to much of the insanity I've dealt with throughout these seven years of doomed wrath.

The two of us proceeded to follow the line of my orders. Even though the possibility of being spotted by wary bystanders was astronomical, I brazenly kept my C70 pointed at Stanley as he trailed out of the car after me. How "unprofessional" and "disturbed" must one be to act in such a careless fashion.

Stanley hesitantly ambled before me on the concrete driveway, his quivering body seemingly trying in vain to calm itself. He clearly understands the necessity of keeping himself poised, despite the marked difficulty. It was at this point that the warm August weather that I'd managed to abate since arriving in New Jersey finally slapped me in the face with a pie. It's far from perfect, but I brushed off my discontent as the agreeable surroundings overtook my focus at long last.

When Debi told me that she still owned a residence in New Jersey, I somehow mustered a tick to paint the faintest mental portrait of its exterior. Granted, its presentation was brief as her recognition of my true intent ended up jolting me back to our conversation. But the image still made enough of an impression to linger for some time. It's a pity, however, that my picture of 47 Turtle Hill Road shared nothing in common with the abode I hastily crafted.

The chief distinction between my creation and Debi's actual residence was that I believed she lived in an apartment. Had that been the case, this undertaking would've turned out a dash more complicated. I could only imagine the struggle of bringing Stanley to an apartment, and the possibility of him causing a scene so to compel dire consequences for all involved. Thankfully Debi had a house, one that's quite delightful in my opinion.

Perched atop a modest hill was the one-story brick building with a coral hued concrete tiled roof. An apple tree partially obscured the right side of the broad house. To reach the front door, a classic snow white that was just visible enough behind the tree, we had to scale a few wooden stairs. This brought us to a porch generous enough to fit a single white rocking chair…and nothing more.

Stepping into Debi's living room, peaceful hints of oak traced my nostrils. This was the entrancing scent that I'd always believed belonged to houses of this design. Surrounding me were paintings of oceanic scenes that decorated pale yellow walls. Enriching the walls was a sofa with a golden and green floral pattern. It sat atop a circular, mustard yellow cotton rug that featured a pattern of rotating circles all a lighter yellow. Absolute madness, the amount of bloody yellow all at once.

Before the sofa was a wooden cabinet that accommodated a television. Gracing the shelves to the right of the television were an assortment of pictures. They were all of Debi and, I'm assuming, her Aunt Paula. Aside from the oldest photos, which were in black and white and featured a very young Debi, most of them were rather alike. They were in the guise of those family portraits people would take at a Meares department store. Debi and her aunt were situated in front of a cloudy pastel blue background in every image.

In the earliest image, Debi had to be around five or so. She was sitting on the lap of her aunt, a radiant woman with a confident smile who sported an appealing dress and pearls. Debi wore a dress as well and had a neatly placed bow atop her shoulder length hair in that photo.

When it pertained to what I'm guessing was the most recent photo, Debi was probably college aged. Her hair, which was about the same length in each photo, now had a part down the middle and was pumped with more volume.

Debi's aunt, however, was certainly a striking woman. She must've had access to beauty secrets because she didn't appear to age a touch in any of the photos. Though I don't fancy blondes, hers was lavish and fluffy. The presence of crimson lipstick and another gaudy necklace that reached her cleavage…it almost made me lose track of the task.

I'll also admit that, since my twenties, I've had this bizarre fascination with viewing old portraits of familiar people. Scanning their faces and comparing them to the person they used to be, older or younger. For example, upon catching a glimpse of Debi in her youth, grand smiles crossing her face in every photo, it's quite intriguing that she evolved into this CIA officer. That the little girl in the outdated frilled dress would be working to assist the country in seizing worthless wrongdoers. How that girl was gearing up to assist me in spoiling this man's day. *Yes*, I'm aware that my quirks are out of the ordinary.

"Now what?" Debi asked. She was standing near the television.

"Lead me to the basement," I said while pressing the C70 directly into the lower section of Stanley's spine. While she'd never mentioned it, there's absolutely a basement in this house. Sometimes…you just know.

Pursing her lips, Debi used her finger to motion us toward her as she began walking. The three of us ventured to the left and down the hall. Out of the five doors that stood around us, Debi stopped at the first of the two to the right.

"After you," Debi muttered as she opened the entrance to a soon-to-be faux netherworld.

The stairs led to a chamber of nothing. Utter oblivion. The light that would've brought a sense of calm to such a dreary space was predictably off. It was merely an unwelcoming pit, though it would've been much more satisfying had there been rusted spikes at the bottom.

Though he'd courteously heeded my directions to this point, Stanley hesitated. He refused to venture into the void. Pressing the gun into his back with more pressure did nothing to encourage the reluctant man into moving. It appeared he now wished to take part in a ridiculously daft game. Unfortunately for him, that's just not the way these procedures work. Besides…I have a severe aversion to games.

Summoning the vigour of a riled, charging bull, I shoved Stanley into the darkness. He exclaimed for just a split second…before the repellent thuds of his body walloping the multiple steps below eclipsed his shouting. When it ceased, indicting the conclusion of Stanley's excursion, my instincts urged me to remain standing at the top of the stairs. To stare at the void, conscious of the batty terror that was to come. Allowing the escalating parasites of menace to envelop me. Listening to the snickering Phantasms, invisible but whose hyena-like tone of their despicable voices began to whisper *do it* repeatedly.

"Mark…I-I don't think I can go through with this…approach," Debi said. She was no longer directly behind me. After the shove, she had backed a couple of feet away from me.

"Are you quitting on me?" I asked, not bothering to turn toward her.

"Of course not. I could never, and would never, abandon an assignment. But…this…I don't feel comfortable with—"

"Amplified interrogation methods?"

Debi scoffed. "I hate that term. But yes. I'm sorry, Mark, but I'm not going to help with you with *this* part. You can do what you want. You *were* given the green light after all. But I'm staying up here."

"As you wish. If I need you, I'll come for you." I finally glanced at her with a smirk so slight it's impossible that Debi caught it. "But you'll find yourself skulking down here in no time. The curiosity will be too maddening. So don't be startled."

Debi placed clenched fists on her hips and turned her head away from me as though she refused to accept my words as truth. Evidently, she's a nonbeliever, but it won't last. Even the sanest humans own a glass shard of inquisitiveness when it pertains to their inner degenerate.

Hiking down into the blackness of the abyss, the thick gelatinous dark clung to me. The submersion was slow, a purposeful tactic to stir anxiety within Stanley. Hearing the haunted creaks emitting from steps only added more joy as I continued to submerge myself. Before long, the soft light from upstairs was a remote tunnel that minded its own business. I expected Debi to close the door, but she never bothered to make an appearance as I finished my journey.

Stanley grunted as I took my first step on the basement floor. Well, in all honesty, it was his body that I'd walked on before my feet touched the actual ground.

"The light is switch is on the wall to your left," Debi called from above.

With my hands stretched out, they acted as scouts as I followed her directions. Thankfully it was rather easy to locate the switch, as the wall wasn't all that far from the stairs. Instead of immediately flipping the switch on, however, I wasted some time by taking an exaggerated breath. It seemed inane but turning the light on was another signal of liberating myself from reality. So many bloody obstacles that are as fragile as they are sullen. Aching for this liberation so to eliminate the final shackles, my finger flicked the switch upwards.

Debi's basement was unfinished and cluttered, its walls and floors grey and devoid of life. It was used for storage, as dozens of old cardboard boxes loitered about in every corner of the room. One of the boxes had the words *Debi's old clothes* etched on it, while another contained *Debi's baby photos*. There were also around eight dolls lying next to a battered yellow dollhouse that had been knocked over. A small purple bicycle rested near the dolls. The only other items of note inside the basement were outdated pastel orange lounge chairs.

Stanley was trying to lug his body across the ground in an attempt to seize his cap, which had flown off during his tumble. Setting my gun back inside my holster, I went toward him and used my foot to swat the cap away just as it was in his reach. An unnecessary choice by a callous bastard.

Grabbing the bloke by his collar, I dragged Stanley away from the steps and to the middle of the basement. His weakened body demonstrated no will to start a scuffle or defend himself, which was miserable but more beneficial for me. I dropped him against the ground with intense force and he again grunted. The lounge chairs jovially offered themselves as assistants, which was pleasing because they were precisely who I would've recommended in the first place. Unfortunately, only one was required, so it was brought to the middle of the basement as well. I heaved Stanley up onto the chair and set my hands on his shoulders.

"You've been good," I said, "and I *need* it to remain that way."

Stanley stared at me, his face weary and eyes struggling to remain open, but said nothing.

I decided to thoroughly examine the basement to see if there were any useful items hiding around. Otherwise, I'd have to go upstairs and ask my unwilling partner for assistance. Her behaviour is rather bizarre, this disdain for amplified interrogation methods. Until now, I would've been willing to bet that all CIA employees satiated in these moments. Perhaps my beliefs were skewed due to my disinclination to work with partners, so what would I know? But all my colleagues are proponents of these methods because they are effective and essential. To shy away from an indispensable technique is to submit yourself to cowardice.

Amidst the boxes and toys strewn about the basement, there was a black duffel bag hiding in plain sight. I unzipped it and, after battling a sudden scent of must from the timeworn bag, found an array of mystifying tools. The bag was filled with hammers, a drill, screwdrivers, pliers, three-strand rope…everything one could wish for at a time like this.

Returning to Stanley with the rope, I managed to secure him to the chair without issue. The rope was tightened around his torso, his arms pinned to his sides and unable to move. For safe measure, rope was applied to his ankles as well.

Even though Stanley was behaving better than most, it's important to be as meticulous as possible when dealing with any targets. The last predicament any of us would want to face is the possibility of the target gaining the upper hand. Does it happen? Yes…but it's exceedingly rare. And when those rare ticks occur, it's routinely against some young upstart who believes they're already top-tier because they entered an exclusive organization.

Only one last precautionary method was needed. See, he needs something to bite down on because no matter what happens…he will shout, and I'd prefer it to be muffled. Rope could be used, but that didn't seem to be *enjoyable* enough. What would be appropriate, however, would be something…cruel. Cruel in that it's hysterical to me yet humiliating to him. No additional searching was required, though, as I already had the most brill idea for that item.

One of Debi's old dolls passed the audition, so I went to snatch her. It was one of those Bararella dolls that every girl since the 1950s seemed to be obsessed with. This particular doll wore a long flowing green dress, which made it ideal for my plan. Removing the dress, I gently set the doll back with the others and returned to Stanley.

"What are you doing with that Bararella dress?" Debi's voice called out.

In no time, she was right behind me. I hadn't even heard her descend those creaky steps. Debi snatched the dress from my hand and placed it by the doll that was once wearing it. Before I could answer her question, Debi asked another.

"Were you gonna make him put that in his *mouth*?"

"Sometimes you have to make do with what you have, Debi," I said.

"Well, you could've asked me for something like a towel."

"It's less demeaning. Also…you were watching from the stairs…weren't you?"

Debi, though she'd been up in arms over the doll's dress, said nothing.

"I knew the curiosity would overtake you."

"S-Stop it. You don't know how wrong you are."

"Whatever you say. But if you think a towel is what's best, then we'll use a towel. But get it fast. We need answers and then, because you're still antsy over this, we'll get rid of him."

"Get rid of him?" Debi shouted, louder than she probably intended.

"No…no, not like that. We'll…let him go."

"Wait," a soft and low yet drained voice spoke up. It was reminiscent of Sergio Scobretti's voice, but less self-assured. Of course, that could've been from the pain being that it was Stanley who had interrupted us. "What is it you need answers about?" He coughed. "Does this have to do with Abe?"

"Yes." Debi sniffled. "Yes, it does."

"You his rivals?"

"You can say that," I said.

"Well…it hurts me to say this…but I'll spill whatever you need to know."

Though I couldn't view my own face, its muscles twisted itself into a mixture of surprise and rage. Those battling emotions were churning as they struggled to process Stanley's willingness to speak. Sure, it made our job easier but…damn it, why is it that this assignment fully lacks merriment? Why must the ire be poked like a dazed bear but never be allowed to fully rise? At the same time, why can't I just be pleased that this assignment refuses to let me sink into those despicable thoughts?

"You'll speak?" Debi asked, her own voice more satisfied than it'd been for a while.

"I will," Stanley said, "and not because I hate Abe. He's my cousin, and I love the guy. But what he's doing with the animals…I hate that."

"Then why are you assisting him?" I asked.

Stanley sighed. "A couple months ago I met some people who were shelling this lucrative job opportunity. One of those too good to be true gigs. So, I up and left a well-paying job at a food processing company for that other job…which turned out to be a load of crap. And some other guy got my old job…so…I've just been trying to make ends meet. I got a baby on the way with my wife. It'll be our first. I needed some money and…Abe was the only person I could think of who'd help. I thought I'd just help with the tackle store, but he wanted me to get more involved with "family business" shit. Knowing that the people I love are out doing shady, illegal stuff…it pains me. But they're family and I need this."

Never had a mere henchman been as obliging as Stanley when it came to letting loose like this. It might be asinine, but…I believe him. If he's casting Debi and I as the fools in this production, then give the arse an award but…it's doubtful. Everyone else follows the same old pattern of being a pseudo-tough guy who relents once the pain that's been inflicted becomes too much to bear. But this bloke…he's talking out of remorse. Or fear. Perhaps it's both.

I went toward Stanley while drawing my C70. The muzzle of the gun pressed against his chin, which caused his subdued body to become fidgety again.

"Mark," Debi said.

"Debi, not now," I said. My focus turned to Stanley. "As for you, this isn't new to me. I've done this before. Are you being honest about everything you've said? Yes or no?"

"Yes," Stanley replied, hesitation entirely absent.

"And what do you think you get out of this? Telling us this information. A reward? Your life?"

"A r-reward? No. But…yes…I-I would h-hope you s-spare me," Stanley replied.

"Hmm. Maybe. I'm not so sure."

"Mark," Debi said again. The tone of her voice was more forceful.

I ignored her. "How much do you know about your cousin's operations?"

"H-Honestly, more than I-I should."

"Tell me this. We heard that there's someone else who assists your cousin in securing those sea animals. Someone who, quite possibly, works with the Grand Howslip Aquarium. Do you know who this person is?"

"I do."

"Is that right? Tell us then. It's utterly *imperative* that we know who this person is."

Stanley froze for a tick, which convinced me to ready the C70 by both cocking it and dragging my antagonistic finger against the trigger. If he does, indeed, know the identity of our mystery partner then we'll have our long awaited go ahead. Stanley's hesitation with revealing this person's identity, however, says so much about the power they must wield.

"Is it t-that important?" Stanley asked. He slowly began to regain control of his anxiety. "You've already k-know everything you need to. If you're trying to hire this person for your own gain, I'm sorry but there's no way they're budging."

A sharp twinge resonated from my left eye as I swiftly swivelled away from Stanley. He must realize that there's barely any chance I'd pull the trigger in this basement. Especially with Debi nearby. But that didn't hinder me from reorganizing the C70. With the barrel now in my grasp, I spun like a mechanical screw and sloshed the butt of the weapon against Stanley's nose.

The harshness of Stanley's subsequent shout was almost as immobilizing as the impact of the strike against his nose. He squirmed a bit and shook his head while facing down. Despite the angle, it was easy to discern Stanley's inflamed nose.

All of a sudden, the scene of Stanley clutching his nose began to greasily melt to the point it'd been entirely erased. In its place arose a memory that I hadn't replayed in some years. It was serene memory too, which was rather rare for me to relive. I was attending a carnival with my family, and my parents were fanatical about taking photographs of their children. Specifically, they always had us line up in birth order for any photo they took of us. As the youngest, I'd be at the far right of the image and next to my sister, Sybil.

I watched as my dad motioned for me to scoot closer to Sybil. He wore one of the extraordinarily conservative dark suits he had a fondness for throughout my adolescence. My mom spoke to us, but the audio in this fleeting memory was muted. She must've been signalling for us to say one of the many phrases she'd like us to call out during a photoshoot. Dad then snapped our photo on his trusted Arcticoid camera.

This memory evaporated as Debi gripped my bicep. Sniffling, she yanked me away from Stanley, who was grunting in distress.

"Damn it, Mark, please *don't do that*," she pleaded.

"Sometimes…there's nothing else you can do," I said.

"Mark, you *hit* him with your gun just because he refused to give you the answers you wanted. Do I want them too? Yes, but why can't you just approach this calmly? Why is it so hard to do that?"

"I don't care if he's just a pawn in this game. The fact that he got involved with this immoral activity makes him just as liable as Abraham Scobretti and the others. He had two choices. He could've reported his cousin and been deemed a bloody hero for single-handedly thwarting an unlawful operation. Or…he could've played along and turned a blind eye to it. He chose the latter, so he signed his own warrant."

Debi re-placed both her hands onto my shoulders. "I understand that it can be difficult dealing with these immoral types. Some want to inflict pain onto them, and sometimes they're inflicting their own pain onto these creeps. Others see the bad but still try to be humane. *You* need to be more humane."

"Don't preach to that crap to me."

I brushed off Debi's hold and approached Stanley once more.

"B-Before you do anything," Stanley began, "I'll talk. I'll tell you who it is just…please don't do that again."

"Your call. Talk to us, Stanley. It's that simple. That's what we yearn to know. So…tell us what we've been raring to hear. Who is this person?"

17

The concoction of the glaring, displeased sun and the strong white warehouse in the distance made for a scene too intense to cope with. The sheer might the two shared was enough to make me a dot nauseous. It's funny, to be honest, as the setting before us in this form was not exactly how I envisioned it to be. First off, I was positive we'd be roaming here when the moon reigned instead of the sun. It's rare for the major confrontation to take place in the daytime. Though some of the former operatives have experienced it, neither I nor any of my current colleagues have ever found ourselves in such a predicament.

Night gives off an appropriate impression because there's an apparent covert sense about the dark. Everything looms behind a sheen of mystery, and it's easier to skulk about as you track your targets. Going about this under the sun seems more unconventional, as though you're set up for failure. You're more susceptible to be spotted when you're lurking without the duvet of night. And the world itself is still relatively awake at this point, whereas at night you're as ghoulish as a ghoul gets. Right now, there's a harassing sense of everyday life taking place around me that's creating a distinct amount of apprehension.

Each member of my family is going about their lives as I'm here in New Jersey without their knowledge. They're out running errands, having lunch, or taking part in recreational activities. And again, unbeknownst to them, here I am planning to conclude an assignment for the Government of the United Kingdom. Perhaps it seems more imaginary when I'm operating at night because those who love me are most likely asleep. And they have less of a reason to suddenly become fretful because they develop a rush of panic…knowing a loved one is partaking in debauchery. At the same time, it's very well that paranoia is manifesting itself.

I must admit that I'm thankful for Stanley's cooperation. Once he revealed the identity of the heralded fourth person involved in Abraham's schemes, my personal aggravation with this assignment finally subsided. Frankly, though I never once took any guesses as to who this person might've been, the revelation did amaze me. Still, it was one of those admissions that should've caused more satisfaction than it ended up doing.

The reason I believe such is because, until now, this assignment has gone through as many ticks of jubilation as experiences of exasperation. Between the botched romantic inclinations and our radically differing beliefs regarding interrogation methods, Debi's downright clocked out of this assignment. Her emotions border on a muddle of exhaustion and irritation, to the point she won't make eye contact with me. Nor will she utter a word to me. She hasn't since we dropped Stanley off.

What did her in was my…*reward* for Stanley due to the immeasurable aid he provided. As we returned to his neighbourhood, he received a parting gift of a single gunshot to the ankle with the addition of a warning. That warning was to never reveal the truth of his whereabouts unless he desired a worse ending. Personally, I found this to be justified because leaving a mark such as that will scare him away from ever participating in such wicked trades again.

Debi, however, revealed her disgust with that action after we left Stanley writhing on the sidewalk in front of his house. Though no one caught us, as far as I can tell, Debi tore into me by expressing her disdain with my performing "an irresponsible and unnecessary action." Even when I sought to give her my perspective as to why it was done, she told me she was done reasoning with me. That she'd had it with my "violent nature" and that she just wished to conclude the assignment and never deal with me or my "disgusting green light" again.

Her biting remarks stung yet they also brought about a realization. Director Ganderman is, unquestionably, aware of the *allowances* of my position. So are my own superiors, the ones who bestowed this wretched curse onto me. Do all CIA operatives behave in such tame, unaggressive manners? Do they ever actually get anything accomplished? And more importantly, if every decision maker on this case knew of the stark contrast in methods between Debi and I, why were we still assigned as partners? Why did Trailsby and Pierce all but coerce me into working with someone with such utterly conflicting views?

Well, there's the possibility that Debi was saddled with me to tone *me* down. Do both of my superiors recognize the ferocity of my mania? Are they finally trying to reel it in more to save me from myself? For some reason I believe there's no chance at that being the case. They've built me into their own personal destruction machine. Why reel it back in when it's almost honed? Unless...that's precisely the reason. They didn't plan on it...me...becoming this merciless.

We continued to trudge toward the warehouse, which was still several hundred feet away. Though New Jersey isn't known for its walkability, it would've been absurd of us to drive right to the front of this location. Especially because Stanley told us that there would very likely be a chance of armed guards wandering around. We did know for certain that Abraham and all his associates, including the fourth person, would be there. And if they weren't, well, Stanley should've known better.

The area surrounding the warehouse was crowded with greenery, though beyond the trees we saw the full magnitude of a massive car park, capable of holding hundreds of vehicles, if not more. That was pure open space, so the moment the trees and other bits of greenery no longer provided us with our neat cloaks, we would have to be discreet and swift. As far as I could tell from this distance, none of the guards were situated outside the warehouse. The building's side was facing us and painted across the grey wall were three navy blue rectangles. An interesting design choice.

Both Debi and I had our weapons equipped just in case they were to be demanded out of the blue. My C70 now had only four bullets, so the remainders each had to be used wisely. Debi carried a Colt Combat Commander and, although it did look out of place in her petite hands, she gripped it with assurance. Seeing that she's willing to possess a handgun makes her appear less passive and, as I pondered earlier, more inclined to use only *necessary* means of force when needed.

As the two of us snuck around the greenery, I tried my damndest to reject any forethoughts of what might occur once we entered the warehouse. The voices were still concealed by a considerable number of bricks I'd constructed in my head, but their snickering was echoing in my ears. They were enthusiastic about the probable ending to this assignment…because they were desperate to devastate the surviving tatters of my sanity. I tried to shrug them off as the final bits of greenery began to wind down, but those bastards never relent. They're gaining supremacy by exhausting my capacities. Staying on track while concentrating on the warehouse were the sole devices that forbade the voices from unleashing at random.

When we emerged from the foliage and entered the car park, I took a tick to survey the building itself from afar. The photograph did nothing to explain how elongated the building was width-wise. Even with it being a two-story building, it looked like a regular house had been stretched out like taffy and left to suffer with its poor dimensions. As someone who lives in a narrow terraced house, it was by far one of the most peculiar buildings I'd had the displeasure of observing.

There was a single, colossal window on the side, as well as six more of the same at the front. They were each blacked out and I was concerned that they were the types of windows where one could observe the outside from inside, but not vice versa. To my relief, the glare from the sun revealed the blackness to be the product of a tarp from inside.

When it pertains to a location's excellence, this warehouse might secure the victory. Hidden from the main thoroughfare by the luscious landscape, there were also no other buildings in this general region. Debi had to park by a bank and then, using a map which was now in the pocket of my jacket, we had to plunge ourselves within the forest to arrive here. Of course, there was a road that led down to the warehouse but, again, we had to be discreet about our movements. While life continued to masquerade beyond the greens and several upon several hundreds of feet away, this warehouse was in its own domain. Thankfully it meant the events that were to transpire here would be alien to civilians.

"There's no place we can enter aside from the front entrance," Debi whispered, having gone around to the back while I was assessing the car park.

"If that's our only point of entry then we might as well get on with it," I replied.

"What?" Debi spewed through gritted teeth. She jabbed me in the chest with her free finger. "Do you hear yourself, Mark? Even with all the bullcrap you've pulled until now, I *still* thought you were a *professional.* But now you want to go into a building that we're barely familiar with? And the only entrance is, suspiciously enough, the front door? That doesn't feel like a trap to you?"

"No, it doesn't."

"That's it? That's all you have to say?"

I nodded. While the remark was rather terse, it was still what I believed. Stanley, after revealing the fourth person's identity, continued with some further explaining. He told us that Abraham and all his associates, including this particular person, would be reconvening at the warehouse soon to finalize the transaction with the older man from the dock.

Now, there's still a chance that Stanley called Scobretti after we'd dropped him off. That he spilled varying complaints about his wonderfully woeful detainment. But it also seems implausible because of how effortless it was to get him to talk in the first place. And what nit would put themselves in the position of having *two* people coveting your head on a stake?

"Wow," Debi said, "I may not agree with all your tactics, but that sure as shit doesn't mean I want to be cleaning your blood up off the floor."

"Damn it, Debi, we're right here," I erupted. Even despite the sudden spewing of my own, I still succeeded in keeping my voice faint. "What are we supposed to do? Abort the assignment and leg it back through the wilderness? Return to the hotel and twiddle our bloody thumbs until we twig out a new plan? No. That's a coward's romp. In my field, you face dread head on. You remind yourself that you swore to your government that you'd complete your assignment regardless of any conditions. That it's *forever* country above self when on active duty."

Debi glared at me. The darts of poison in her gems were lashing at me with unforgiving antipathy. Her face had plunged into a raging crimson, the type of facial shade where even the gentlest breeze would accidentally incite an unadulterated rampage. The amount of frustrated fury that circled her made me ponder whether she would *finally* point her gun at me. Considering the extent of rancour that has evidently swam up to her mind now, would it be that surprising?

Turns out it would be, as those questions were immediately dusted away. The plausibility of Debi aiming her Colt at me were next to nothing. Her entrance into my life is recent, yes, but it's been made rather clear she's not *that type* of person. Most aren't. And although she might've ascended to one of the highest stages of wrath, even at her heights it wasn't as though she'd approached my scorching levels.

"You know what?" Debi began. "Bravo. Great speech, *captain.* Who gives a shit if this is a matter of life and death? Let's just move on and capture our targets even though we're underprepared."

Her pitiable comments did nothing to dissuade me from placing my hand on the matte industrial door handle. We'd already wasted enough time conversing about directly under the disinterested sun, and right in a plain field of vision. If we so dared to continue this petty bickering, it'd be at the cost of our lives. And I, for one, would much prefer to be massacred while engaging in combat than by means of an ambush during a chatty moment. That would be far too embarrassing to mull over.

I pulled the door ajar slowly, as well as meticulously enough to forbid the hinges from squeaking. The unlocked entrance demonstrated nothing more than a sign of arrogance in Scobretti. It was shocking to have witnessed the lack of care his associates presented while performing the transaction at the docks. How they transferred a briefcase out in the open the way they did. And then there was the fact that Scobretti assumed I was a rival in this sea animal trade. That the notion of my being any sort of law enforcement employee never crossed his mind. Seeing how uncomplicated the process of entering this warehouse was happened to be the epitome of his confidence.

With the door cracked to some extent, I peered inside and commenced a rapid yet conclusive visual sweep of the warehouse's interior. Steel crates and enormous fish tanks were tidily displayed in alternating rows. A tinge of the area's unpleasant, nautical odour rushed out the gap and bopped my nostrils with a mallet.

Sweeping off that unfortunate scent, I then pressed my ear to the crack and listened for a tick. Amidst the churning rumbles that the tanks spouted, the hardly detectable echo of chattering voices rang out. Judging by their volumes, it appeared as though everyone was to my right and most likely on the second level. Pleased enough with my observations, I titled my head toward Debi and mouthed "the coast is clear" before sliding through the door. But, once my first foot stepped inside the warehouse, my consciousness rotated like a ravaged globe.

Entering the warehouse through that insignificant gap caused my body to encounter a perplexing sensation of a sludgy material. Glancing at both my sleeves, then my legs, there didn't appear to be anything *on* me. Yet this syrupy, mud-like substance still encased me like a cast nursing a broken bone. The heaviness of this imperceptible matter made each step I took seem as though any additional weight would sink me through the concrete.

A searing sting like that of a needle impacted the left side of my chest, close to my heart. The initial jab was then followed by dozens of successive prickles that skittered in surrounding sections of my torso. I gazed down in a sluggish fashion; my sight now obscured by wallowing rainclouds. Spreading out my jacket, I predicated that there would be a display of blood splattered along my shirt. But it was still clean. Even with my unexpected and mystifying disorientation, it was clear that something wasn't adding up.

Developing in the netherworld of my stomach were the befuddled stumbles of nausea. Blaring commotions that obstructed my ears soon followed. The collection of varied noises embodied my prehistoric hallucinations of eternal damnation and the apocalyptic fantasies that'd been exaggerated throughout this decade.

From the rancorous whirls of helicopter wings to the barrage of submachine guns firing in a chaotic storm, these commotions amplified until they overshadowed the rumbles from the fish tanks. Shrill alarms decided to have a go at adding to the bedlam…and through their piercing shrieks I heard those hyena-like cackles. Those damn Phantasms…cruel as ever…have casted yet another one of their charming spells on me from afar.

Debi was moving toward the left of the entrance, while I'd been ambling closer to the voices. Did she tell me we were gearing our surveys separately? Did I accidentally disregard any plans she might've had in terms of us infiltrating this warehouse together? I'm entirely at sea.

Beyond the rainclouds, I detected the two windowless rooms that Abraham and his companions must've inhabited. They were accessible by what appeared to be a set of steel stairs that also connected to a nearby catwalk that overlooked the entire building. This must've been where the guards, if they existed, were prone to hike while on patrol.

Although my body feels as though it's hauling a boulder with a dandelion atop it, I'm not at all sure how my steps are *normal*. It would've been more likely that I'd be walking as though those merry alcohol goggles were snug over my eyes. The fact that, outwardly, my perceptions of the warehouse were still relatively inconspicuous despite the internal hysteria that was brewing meant the Phantasms must've mustered some sort of sway over my figure. It's all speculation, but perhaps they were unable to conquer my loaf, so the only other option was to *genuinely* craft me into a marionette.

Without warning, a cold object positioned itself on the back of my neck. A chill skated down my spine, causing my body to stiffen like a mummy being caught fondling its sarcophagus. This uneasy tension did not occur as the product of apprehension, but instead out of disbelief. Someone had pulled a gun on me, and the air of aloofness had clouded my awareness.

"You lost, pal?" An unknown voice spoke behind me, raking away the onslaught of noises in my ears.

As my C70-wielding hand had subconsciously retracted to my chest during that miserably aimless wandering, it was possible this man was oblivious that I was armed. His comment was stern yet casual, while his voice wasn't loud enough to cause alarm.

Situations like these were among the first I was trained in during that first year with Her Majesty's Church. It's mandatory that you produce a swift response as you scour for any sort of combat technique to subdue your opponent. Sure, using the C70 in some manner would make the ordeal less stressful for the time being, but it wouldn't last. That would automatically incite a riot in this warehouse. More importantly, my weapons aren't meant to be used on low-level trash such as this faceless individual.

"No. I was invited," I said.

The man chuckled as though he'd heard a shoddy joke. "Right. Do me a favour and get the fuck outta here. Don't come back either, cause I'm not gonna be this nice next time."

"Who said you were nice the first time?"

The man firmly pressed the muzzle against my neck. "Wise ass, huh? You wasted your chance at—"

His pseudo-tough guy performance was wasted when, in a blink, I sharply elbowed him in the ribs. It's as easy as counting petals when you're saddled with a talkative opponent. Their chatter is their weakness, because their scrambling to roll words off their tongues distracts them from impulsive movements.

Grunting, the man toppled over and clutched his side. Clearly, he was a tried and true professional, as he'd dropped his pistol as he fell. He was an unremarkable fellow with short, sandy hair and a scruffy face. Better to have encountered this clown instead of Abruzzoli or either of the Scobretti's. Surely my good fortune would've not been purchased had any one of them been so blessed to have discovered me.

One of the many differences I share with my colleagues is that they would've proceeded to knock this man unconscious before moving up the ladder to the holy grail. While that may work fine and dandy for them, that's simply not how I perform my business. Lord President Trailsby, Deputy Lord President Laughton, and Minister Esprine all instilled one principal rule that *I* was to follow while on active duty. The one…fatal rule…was that of exhibiting no mercy to any fiend I confronted.

Kneeling over the fallen trash heap, I hammered him with my C70 repeatedly. Each successive strike came down like a blacksmith crafting his finest weapon. There was absolutely no holding back regarding the sheer intensity of these strikes. This wasn't a situation like the one that ensued with Stanley earlier. He played his part and, not only that, but he also never posed a threat. But, as this man had pulled a gun on me, the obvious answer was to defend myself. Even if he was on the ground and no longer held a weapon, this was *still* an action of *defending* myself. And since wasting my bullets was not an option, this was the next best decision aside from utilizing my bare hands.

Continuing my battering of this guard, more vivid memories of the past, like those that were summoned after I'd walloped Stanley with my C70, flickered before me. The visualisation that played featured my mom talking to me at my family's old dinner table. This memory had to be from my teenage years, as her hair was distinctly shaggy yet sculpted. This short, full hairstyle was one she sported immediately after she'd fallen in love with Italian cinema. It was modelled after one of the actresses who'd starred in this movie my mother obsessed over, though its name escapes me.

This was the second instance that a stray memory from long ago decided to stream into my consciousness. And, for some reason, it too had surfaced during a moment of excessive brutality. The question now was…why? Why was this occurring? For what reason should memories of actual bliss be interspersed with these current actions of callous insanity? There should be no connection between the two. And, even if it's not a matter of *connection*, I'd rather not examine any contrasts now. Reliving peaks while wheeling in perdition. Whatever this peculiarity is attempting to tell me, it needs to bloody terminate at once.

Words started to spill out of my mouth, forming an affable phrase that was not new to me. It was a phrase that I'd began telling myself about a year ago, always after partaking in a deed such as this. Call it an inane practise of faux rationalization but I whispered, "what I'm doing is for the furtherance of all nations. That is what justifies my actions."

Another unrecognizable voice shouted "we've got intruders" from above. Glancing up, I saw a bearded man glaring at me with the pale face of one who'd accidentally walked in on a spiteful apparition. Surely, he never expected to behold the unbelievable spectacle of a madman reigning over his fallen comrade.

The man had a rifle, which I identified as a Ruger M77, slung over his shoulder. He scrambled to aim it at me as I groggily scurried away from the other man, taking refuge behind yet another steel crate. This location wouldn't be effective for long, as the catwalk had the ability to peruse the entire building. But it provided me with enough time to plot my next moves. Hopefully Debi would be able to hold her own as I navigated through this maze of brooding madness.

With the understanding that Abraham Scobretti didn't appear to be too rattled by the prospect of the law, I'm certain that there aren't many guards roaming the building. Though they're all on red alert now that the bearded man spotted me, I predicted that there would be five at most. And, with one already offed, there were three courses of action to pursue. One was to reconvene with Debi at once so that we could have each other's backs. Then again, she'd be more than willing to feed me to the starved wolves now. Two was to hunt, *yes*, hunt the remaining guards. Third, of course, was to successfully capture the main targets.

Gunfire rang about, and the assaulting uproar also overtook the still grating collection of noises that lounged in my ears. Those noises were, thankfully, lessened though they were now causing a vein in my neck to throb. My distorted vision also bestowed no favours. Those damn Phantasms weren't planning on ceasing until this bloody form of purgatory concluded as well. They'd waited far too long for me to enter this orb of destruction. There was no other card that could be played in my favour, as they'd all been damaged beyond repair.

What could be played in my favour, however, was if I could exploit this expansive maze of crates and tanks to my advantage. There were approximately one hundred and twenty containers in total, give or take, and their enormous sizes were indeed valuable. They could shield me just enough as I concocted a plan to reach that upstairs area while evading any other guards. That plan had to be established *now*, however, as I heard the clanking of the bearded man's feet rushing toward where I positioned myself.

There were steps that led up to the catwalk about twenty feet away from me. I wasn't sold on the outline of the warehouse that I'd drawn up in my head, but it included similar steps closer to where Debi had gone. If I could dart to those steps while duping these guards, that would offer a brill opportunity to zero in on those upstairs rooms. If Abraham and his associates were to leave the rooms, they'd be putting themselves at risk of standing in my direct aim. For a plan, it had some considerable flaws but I'm at my most lethal when moulding one on the fly. Now was my chance to experiment with that bloody gamble.

Even with the lethargic behaviour that billowed in my being, I sprinted toward the nearby steps as though my legs were powered by high-tech bionics. Shots from the Ruger breezed over my head as I patted the steps before dashing back into the maze of illegal dealings. The bearded man on the catwalk was too close to the steps near me that racing back to the other end would've been futile. Of course, those other steps could still be non-existent, but we'll see.

So far, the plan was operating as intended. Slipping past the fallen guard, I used my time wisely as I stepped *on* his body rather than over it. However, more footsteps were clattering on steel, but whoever was causing those roars was not above me. I then recalled the additional steps that led straight to the rooms above. Another guard must've used them instead of following the bearded guard. The latter hadn't yet descended the stairs as more gunfire zoomed at me from above. A few of them shattered one of the fish tanks, which exploded right as I'd leapt past it. The water streamed at a rapid pace, reaching my feet in seconds even though it'd now been left in the dust.

"You asshole!" Someone yelled.

It was the voice of yet another guard. He must've just exited the room as I failed to see him while scanning the upstairs just seconds before.

"You hit a tank," the guard continued, "and you know Abe's taking it out of your paycheck!"

"I didn't mean to," the bearded guard said. His voice was no longer emanating from above, indicting his arrival to the bottom floor.

Another gunshot rang out from the where I was running toward. This caused me to pick up my speed, even though the grogginess made it impossible to move any brisker than this current pace. But Debi was in that direction, and, despite our fragile partnership, she was still my *partner.* If she were maimed…or worse…that'd be something impossible to cope with. That's some sentimental rot, but it's still the unrelenting truth.

My foggy eyes peered up and succeeded in seizing this guard. The man was stocky and the lines on his face indicated he was older than the other guards I'd encountered. His hair was light and receding too. The guard appeared to have caught me as well because, even with my weary vision I saw the utter disgust that crossed his face once he pinpointed the person who'd initiated this horror show.

"He's in my view," the guard said, "and there's some broad running around here too."

The older guard began to run, but the route he took also led to the stairs that the other guard journeyed down. By now the possibility of another set of steps being in that spot I'd envisioned were dwindling. There were now three individuals chasing after me, and there hadn't been any more clamour from where I was facing. Debi still wasn't anywhere in my range. There were some tanks and crates I hadn't navigated through yet so, with any luck, she's somewhere in that sphere.

Circling around another display of crates, I stumbled across Debi at long last. She was standing over a fourth guard, this dark-haired man with bloodshot and glassy eyes. Debi had a foot on his back and held two weapons, her Colt and another handgun. Blood was on the floor, most of it draining by the man's right shoulder.

"Are you okay?" I asked.

"Now's not the time for small talk," Debi said.

Fair point, but it was still a courtesy to ask. How was I to know whether she'd been wounded or not. Yes, she was standing over this guard like a lioness with her trophy, but some people tend to dust off any injuries they might sustain as a power play. Well…that's something I usually do on the off chance a weapon wallops me and draws blood.

Selfishly apprehending my attention, however, was situated a couple feet beyond Debi. It was the glorious steel structure that was highlighted in those bonce sketches from earlier. That staircase on this side of the warehouse did, in fact, exist. A rare example of just how sweet some of my mental images can be. They guided upward and, if utilized the way I planned to, would lead me down to the room where Abraham and the others were.

Debi looked as though she possessed an idea akin to mine as she nodded her head toward the stairs. Returning her gesture, the two of us scrambled to the steps and hiked them. While climbing, I sharply resigned myself to a rather unfortunate recollection. See, this was one of those ticks where the accomplishment of the assignment meant more to me than my own personal aversions. The reason being is that, since my teenage years, heights have never been much of a friend. Merely scaling these steps was enough to cause involuntary shudders, ones that were not comparable to those the Phantasms were nudging.

As we reached the top of the catwalk, more bullets zipped past us. Those bloody guards were gaining on us, so we continued away from them and toward the rooms. It was a tad mortifying to fathom that, had our small talk continued even a dot, the three fiends would've arrived where we were. That would've been a violent, and reprehensible, end to this assignment. I ought to understand that, sometimes, there's no time for hindrances.

Then Rocco Abruzzoli stepped out of one of the rooms. His Model 1200 was clenched in his hands as he stood in place like a statue. For an unknown reason, he didn't budge. Making the ordeal more distressing was the expression on his face. It had a solemn air about it, a blank detachment almost. Those faces are easy for me to classify, being that they tend to haunt me as well. His eyes, interestingly enough, didn't seem to be latching onto either Debi or myself. They were staring into the distance, well past the two of us. He proceeded to lift his Model 1200 up and aimed it in our direction.

Both Debi and I were brought to a standstill. The clomping steps of the guards were beginning to charge up from behind us. Now this was a disastrous bind. There was no escaping from either end, and leaping from the catwalk would cause assured death, especially for me and my aging bones. Only two options arose. Either eliminate

Abruzzoli or turn my C70 on the guards. Of course, the first option was the only ideal choice. Looking away from him would end in me being massacred before having the fortune to take aim at the guards. Also, Abruzzoli has more trophy points than those nameless guards.

Forgoing any chances and accepting this calamity, I directed my C70 toward Rocco but…in twisted fashion, Debi swatted my arms down.

18

Since becoming a member of Her Majesty's Church, the concept of a partner double-crossing you was nothing more than a dotty fable. It was so unfeasible, in fact, that most senior members all but laughed at the notion that such an inexcusable incident would occur. Granted, there *was* a critical rationale as to why this sort of episode was so illogical. See, when Her Majesty's Church elects to cooperate with foreign intelligence services around the world, the organization takes several precautions with selecting the proper partner for one of their own. In most instances, the person we're partnered with has already been ingrained into the assignment. It's their pursuit, that is, until one of us enters the scrap. Then we take over, usually with far less information on the targets, much to the chagrin of the other… like how it was with Debi.

An extensive background investigation is undertaken into the life of our prospective partners. It is administered by both Her Majesty's Church and the other agency to demonstrate unity. If, for any reason, Her Majesty's Church takes issue with even the most trivial detail in the contact's life, they'll decline an assignment and move to another. As there are innumerable assignments that are assumed by foreign services, it's not as though this leaves our fifteen-member party devoid of jobs for lengthy spans. On top of that, it's excruciatingly atypical for Her Majesty's Church to deny an assignment.

The Lord President divulges this information to new members before we're presented with our first assignment. This enables us to recognize a procedure that's calculated without our input. We're not permitted to request any specifics, whether it's the gender of our partner or something inane such as their eye colour. Same applies if we ask for assignments in certain countries. Such requests are scorned by the superiors, and none of us are quite sure whether it's to dwindle bias or because it's simply unsustainable. Regardless, it's out of our jurisdiction.

Debi was one of those officers who was thoroughly researched by Her Majesty's Church. She was designated, by both our organizations, to be *my partner*. Me…the one operative in this bloody organization who loathes the burden of having a partner. My colleagues would be falling about if they were punters to this shindig. After all, the irony of my debacle is certainly evident. Unfortunately, it's also mind-bogglingly enraging.

"Debi!" I exclaimed. "Are you bloody mad?"

My "partner" failed to respond to my outburst. Instead, she yanked me out of Abruzzoli's line of concentration. Being that my body is considerably bigger than hers, Debi lost her balance and tumbled to the steel while still grasping my arm. This sent me plummeting straight on top of her. The clanging of our bodies smacking the steel wasn't appealing in the slightest, especially because Debi had taken the entirety of the blow.

Another gunshot flew over us, but…for some reason…the subsequent cry of pain came from my left. Turning to look, disbelief trickled down me like sweat as I witnessed the bearded guard soar into the guard behind him. Despite my muddled vision, a hefty and bloody wound was discernible, sitting directly in his chest. As the one guard flew backward, he collided into the other one who'd just reached the top of the catwalk. The older guard, however, was nowhere in my field of vision.

Switching my focus onto Abruzzoli, the muscle of Abraham Scobretti's group remained in position with his Model 1200 still at the same level it'd been when he first got into this stance. Smoke discharged from the muzzle of his shotgun.

"What in the name of the gallows are you two doing here, Deb?" Rocco asked. "We weren't supposed to make the bust for another day or so!"

So, this wasn't a double-crossing after all? That's somewhat of a relief. But Debi *still* withheld vital information from me since she knew he was on our side this entire time. Her Majesty's Church withheld this information from me. Why in great oasis was I not informed about this *until* we were fully immersed in this utter frenzy? How can one be so underhanded in failing to disclose informants, or whatever the bloody mercy Abruzzoli is, who are critical to our assignment? That's just…infuriating to even comprehend.

"Mark," Debi grumbled as she struggled to push me off her. "Go into the room and apprehend whoever you find in there. Also grab any files or pieces of evidence you come across. We'll secure this area."

"But what about the Scobretti's?" I asked, removing myself from on top of Debi.

"They're not here, but they will be soon," Abruzzoli said. "So, make it quick."

Trudging along the catwalk, I exchanged glances with him. The bastard certainly was a decent actor, as his aggressive nature during the gala was utterly believable. How he lifted me up by the shirt to slug me in the jaw, frustration crossing his face. In all honesty, recalling that thought made me want to toss him over the railing even if he was on our side. But that's just my unstable male ego making a futile crack at clawing out of its marred cage.

The room I entered was the one Abruzzoli had walked out of before his *major reveal*. It was set-up like a makeshift office, complete with file cabinets and poorly hung paintings on its grey walls. A bulky wooden desk sat to my left. Tidily arranged on it were a computer, piles of paperwork, and a wire container full of pens. To my right was a brown two-seater sofa that had seen better days, especially pertaining to this day. And right in front of me was the older man who'd met Sergio, Abruzzoli, and Stanley at the docks earlier in the day.

He was still dressed in a trench coat, even though the temperature in the warehouse was miserably warm. I could read his face now compared to earlier this morning, even though my vision still hadn't quite cleared up all the way yet. Besides, there wasn't much more than what could've been predicted while at the docks. He was your standard middle-aged male with grey hair who waved around wealth and used his brass for malevolent purposes.

"Whoa there." The man raised his hands. "Take it easy with that gun, pal. You've made your entrance, and it was a fine one. But I'm sorry. I'm not in the business for another associate right now. You're too late to be considered competition."

Even this man was numb to the possibility that the law could ever discover these dealings. It's astounding, the level of discreetness that's been employed by all those involved in this horrid trade. Part of it probably dwells in the location. As far as I'm aware, it's not as though New Jersey is a breeding ground for offences of this type. However, I can say with optimism that, after this operation is shut down, New Jersey won't have to toil with these dilemmas again.

"And who are you exactly?" I asked.

Gunfire reverberated from out on the catwalk.

The man's face became perplexed, as though he was displeased by my failure to identify him. "Just a minute. Who am I?" He asked. "Who are *you*? I'm the supplier. If you're not here to strike up a deal with me, then why are you here?"

How I dreadfully yearned to respond with some sort of caustic remark. Or present a reaction like one of those steroid induced heroes cutting a witty quip before proceeding with their affairs. Unfortunately, neither option was suitable enough to be used. They'd either fly over this scumbag's head or come off as unnecessarily humorous. On top of that, there was a much more appropriate retort that could function more pristinely *without* requiring words.

Approaching the man, my free hand recoiled back before lunging at his face. It glued onto his nose and upper mouth, which succeeded in shutting his confused, gawking expression. My velocity failed to decrease as I went on to slam the bastard against the nearest wall. The back of his skull banging against the surface created a pounding clank that was harsh, revolting even.

Like a loon painted in red, I began to solidify the pressure of my grip. The man threw his hands onto my wrists, struggling with such might to tear my one measly hand from his face. Unfortunately for him, his strength was nowhere near sufficient enough to challenge me. And, with the man at my mercy, I upped the ante by tightening my grip even further. Blood gradually streamed from his nose as a twisted turmoil of crunching maxilla and vomer bones, among others, intertwined with his unintelligible stammers. The uninviting sounds of his bones splintering were reminiscent of those a carnivore would produce while messily gnawing at its prey. What a soul-stirring comparison.

To my dismay, my mental torture decided *now* was a superlative occasion to spur another rich memory from the past. The visualisation that sprouted was another one from my youth. But, like the memory of my mother during dinner, this one didn't present much else aside from momentary sedation. Rewinding into my younger days yet again, I was with my dad in his car, a black 1957 Mercury Monterey. This had to have been soon after his tenure as interior secretary had ended, as he didn't purchase that car until after my high school graduation. He adored that Mercury, and so did I. These visuals served as a reminder of that adoration, as well as the general joy that would arise whenever we went around on errands. Memories of crooner music trickling out the radio peacefully drowned out the continued stammers of the vile bastard before me.

Finally, after hours had seemingly dawdled adrift, the man's grasp weakened before coming loose. Removing my hand from his face was not a doddle in any shape. My palm had been embedded into his bones, so it took some significant effort to detach myself from him. It was like uprooting snarled weeds, a fitting comparison for this bastard as he was undeserving of being compared to a tree. Mightily jerking my hand once more, it mastered the art of escape as it freed itself from the man's warped and crumpled face. He slumped to the carpet, his body collapsing like the devastating detonation of a child's building blocks.

I was relieved that he'd settled face-down as I honestly couldn't bear to stare at that mangled profile much longer. And that's saying quite a lot from a bloke who's used to this crap. Yes…there you go. Crap. Oh how…I *loathe* performing this *crap*. That's already two and it's beginning to agonize and antagonize me all over again. Just like it does during every bloody assignment Her Majesty's Church heaves at me.

With the conviction of a robot, I once again repeated the phrase "what I'm doing is for the furtherance of all nations. That is what justifies my actions" aloud.

Stop lying to yourself, Mark.

Oh, bloody mercy…no. Not now. For the love of seared racks, why now? The Phantasms had returned. Their voices swelled with crackles like those produced by dusty vinyl. Such an addition made the tone come off as artificial and ghostly. Nevertheless, it *did* include hints of deep, floral femininity. It *also* displayed a melodic, dark masculinity.

The two were fused brilliantly, to the point they seemed almost genderless.

"Lying?" I asked, though accidentally for all to hear due to sheer bemusement.

Precisely. You're lying, Mark. Which, of course, comes as no surprise. You've been masquerading under this false impression of "honour" and "nobility" since you dug yourself into that wretched grave inside Her Majesty's so-called Dauntless Church of Secret Intelligence. Why can't you finally seize the orb of honesty that has been pleading for you to notice it since your first assignment? The one that aches for you to admit who you genuinely are.

"How dare you deem my actions as anything but noble. Serving the United Kingdom in my capacity has brought nothing but positive results for multiple nations."

Really? Do you believe, beyond doubt, the falsehoods that you spew? That hunting down underground felons advances this garbage heap of a world.

"Your loathsome bias aside, let me first say that I do not *hunt* these rogues. Yes, the word has slipped out of my mouth a few ticks in the past, but it has *always* been used inadvertently. And yes, I am adamant that my *authorised* activities restore betterment in this world. Underground felons or not, they're a major ingredient in the decomposing magnificence of our world. What else are we to do aside from disposing of them? Send them to prison? That would be a mediocre disgrace."

Here's your issue. Though the United Kingdom provides you this free and legal pass, your conduct is nonetheless parallel to that of the scum you claim you're eradicating. You possess a monstrous side to you, Mark, and it's one that you've been mindful of since you joined the Royal Special Forces Unit. That is precisely why you were scouted for Her Majesty's Dauntless Church of Secret Intelligence. Your victory over the others during training, though indisputable, was guaranteed by the higher-ups. They had faith in you because they sensed the depraved soul that dwells in you. As such, the government has moulded you into the perfect extermination machine. You're startled by that truth, Mark. And you drudge through every faulty excuse so to claim valour when, in fact, you're merely a batty butcher.

"Silence! Your barefaced lies insult me. I am not this *batty butcher* you speak of. There are no commonalities between me and those sinful rogues—"

But what of your sanity? You've expressed to yourself over and over that your sanity is all but tattered. That you're unhinged. Acknowledge it! Acknowledge your dodgy spirits. After all, you're so damn willing to admit your other vices. You have no qualms accepting your addiction to vile cigarettes. And don't goad us into mentioning your untamed fixation on partaking in incessant carnal relations with scads of women, you deviant. Your gynephilia is exceptionally chaotic, and yet you'll serve those depravities any chance you get. Why not do the same with this dishonourable reality? Declare it, Mark. Acknowledge your bloodthirsty urges!

"Not a chance in the shades, you bloody nit."

Hmmm…very well then…

As the words "well then" were uttered, the voice gradually dissolved. A faint cough dinged, like a cartoon bubble bursting, which appeared to signify the conclusion of whatever the broom that madness was. The scenario was discomforting to say the least, so much so that a residual slimy substance coated onto my spine like an unnerved parasite.

Being a chance participant in unsettling circumstances is routine with this job. The whole predicament with Rocco and the guards, before the former revealed his true colours, was nothing out of the ordinary for most operatives. It might be a treacherous, daunting quandary for most, but it's relatively effortless for me to devise evasion strategies instead of succumbing to possible terror.

But there's something indisputably horrifying when you're listening to voices tirelessly contend that you are literal swine. Finding myself blind with wrath as I debated that nuisance over their heinous lies. And countering those despicable claims aloud, even though there was clearly no one in sight. Bloody mercy, have I finally lost it?

To my contentment, the halting of the voice came hand in hand with the fading of the fog that had been smothering my vision. The slow and weighty movements of my body were also abolished and reversed to their normal state. With full control of my body now restored, a generous serenity befell me. And though the trepidation over that cursory bout with invisible spirits remained at hand, it failed to overwhelm the newfound stillness that'd infiltrated the aquatic air.

This harmony, unfortunately, began to unravel its once splendid sundress. Rampant nausea amplified in my stomach, skipping rope at a rapid rate. Frigid pins injected themselves into every portion of my ambushed body, which proceeded in doubling me over onto the carpet in severe pain. Clutching my stomach, it appeared as though the serenity was merely a façade to keep me at bay until the spirits could wallop me yet again.

Glancing upward, gasping like a fatigued rat for air, thousands of diminutive pixels swarmed above the desk and rotated like straw stirring powder into a liquid. Pausing in the form of misshapen structures, a bar of extraordinarily incandescent light surfaced. It started glide up and down like a painter's brush to design the pixels into two figures of short builds with bluish grey skin. White lab coats with ragged ends adorned their bodies. Faces constructed themselves in mid-air before a magnet pulled them onto the blank canvas that was the front of their heads. Upon settling in place, the faces were revealed themselves as androgynous and blank.

Those bloody Phantasms had returned in a fashion unlike any I'd ever experienced before. The regeneration of their existence was utterly surreal to behold. Normally it's a one and done emergence. They'll magically pop into the world and initiate their terrorization before vanishing again. But this…this was startling. For them to have wrestled their way from oblivion and enter this office with the poise of a creature in a B-movie…they were probably peeved.

It must've been because they were shackled in the pits for longer than necessary. I'd been doing such a decent job at subduing most of the voices for the majority of this damn assignment. So decent that it deserved at least a bloody bronze medal! But such is life because the Phantasms are back. Whispering those defamations of my identity. This was most certainly the beginning of retribution for my refutations of their demands.

They wasted no time in setting their fevered attention on me. The two raised their hands up, commencing a vigorous tug that lifted me to my knees. They then jutted their arms out from their sides, creating the letter *T*. A torrent of barbed chains dived through the ceiling from the sacred celestial city, two of which locked around my wrists. The chains compelled me to reciprocate the pose, and my arms were unable to lower themselves. Seeing that I was impaired, both of those raving lunatics proceeded to trace a circle with their crooked fingers, which carved an agonizing red-hot sensation into my torso.

As the Phantasms continued to wield this authority over me, a human arm that sported a jacket sleeve like the one I had on tore from out my blistering chest. It used the strength of a battalion to wrench itself from out from purgatory. What was occurring wasn't wholly unfamiliar to me, but it was entirely unlike the previous predicament. See, the diabolical beast that bore my person was executing its grand reappearance…just like in the car park of the Huge Lots years ago.

The sheer pain was abominable, as though each bone and muscle in my chest had been split apart by barbaric foreign death traps. I was unable to verbalize my suffering as my vocal cords were stifled. But, had I been able to release even the most subtle bellow, it would've been enough to plants seeds of sorrow in the reaper.

A compact numbness penetrated my head as I rose from my knees. The excruciating discomfort vanished, though my arms, thighs, and stomach were all throbbing. Taking a glimpse at the floor, I gazed at both the older man's repellent corpse as well as another body that laid adjacent to it. That…wasn't desecrating the floor earlier. I turned to stare at it, and found that body to be the leftover, smouldering carcass of humanoid flesh. An expansive cave conquered the chest area. Closer examination found the body to have been a three-dimensional self-portrait. I was staring at what was once the organism that portrayed me, even though this spectacle was utterly impossible.

Out of grim curiosity, I approached my alternate body and reached down to touch its legs. However, before my finger could graze the limb the original body dissolved into summer's snow and wafted away from me. Whatever was occurring had all the aspects of a psychedelic crisis minus the actual hallucinogens. Though my being took solitude in being refreshed and more energized than it had in decades, there was a lurking emptiness that shrouded me in its ruined coat.

More barrages of gunfire resonated right outside the room, followed by a male's deep voice roaring out and a heavy thud clanging on the steel. The door swung open and a frazzled Debi skurried inside, lugging a fallen Abruzzoli by his shoulders.

"The Scobretti's are here! Fuck…look at what they did to Rocco," Debi said.

Abruzzoli's dress shirt had blotches of crimson smeared around his chest and left wrist. He was breathing through his nose at an accelerated pace. "They arrived with two other g-guards. W-We got most of them, but Abe g-got me. Family r-revenge," he coughed out.

Debi gently eased Abruzzoli to the carpet before slamming the door shut. As she let out a drawn exhale, her eyes shifted and widened with the dread of an injured bird. She'd noticed the body of the older man and, no surprise, it must've terrified the mercy out of her.

"Mark…" Debi said, unable to finish her thought.

"He attacked me first," I lied, glancing at Abruzzoli then back at Debi. "More importantly, how come you never told me about his allegiance?"

"I didn't think we'd be in this bind today. We were aiming to detain them tomorrow, so I was going to tell you about Abruzzoli this evening."

"Tomorrow? With what cause? What did you think we'd learn tonight that would've aided us tomorrow? Not only that, but if Abruzzoli has been mingling with these bastards then surely he knew of the bloody contact that Stanley tipped us off on."

"W-Wrong," Abruzzoli said. He coughed again as Debi returned to tend to him. "I-I found out who it was when w-we a-arrived this morning. A-Abe's best kept secret, t-that's for certain."

The temperature in the room ascended to at least eighty degrees. Whether it stemmed from a faulty air conditioning unit or my expanding aggravation, who bloody knows? I discarded my jacket and threw it to the floor, anxiously craving responses for the shedload of questions that swayed in my head. But, as there's no telling who'll burst through that bloody door next, they'd have to be postponed until this condemning job's been fulfilled.

A jagged object poked my shoulder twice. It was the fingernail of one of the Phantasms, who were still crouched atop the desk. They smiled as they began to point at the desk like children playing silly, meaningless games. Inquisitive about their gestures, I went over to the desk and peeked underneath it. It was there I unearthed the illustrious object of clandestine malice. The individual coveted by Her Majesty's Church, and who Stanley exposed earlier. Someone *amiable* and *courteous* who I'd previously met and spoken to.

There, hunkering beneath the desk, was Stella…the person who orchestrated the correspondence between the suppliers and the Scobretti's due to her Grand Howslip Aquarium connections. To Stella's credit, had it not been for the Phantasms I'd never have guessed she was hidden in this office. She'd demonstrated a rare talent in remaining silent throughout incidents of carnage and the destruction of one's personal identity. Surely those were not common episodes for her to loll around with whatsoever.

Stella trembled as she peered up at me. She wore a long-sleeved cherry red dress with a black notched collar, nylon stockings, and black heels. Her dress was enhanced by shoulder pads that thrusted up the ends of her long, bleached blonde hair. Stella's arms were tightly secured around her knees, which were pressed up to her chest. Mascara garnished her impressive eyelashes, and the shade of her lipstick was identical to that of her dress. The emotion that cascaded across her dolled-up face was almost certainly that of apprehension, as though she'd been cursed by the kiss of Satan.

I snatched a handful of that teased blonde hair and impetuously wrested Stella from her sacred hiding space. She cried out as I towed her to her feet, most likely due to a combination of discomfort and panic. With regards to the former, I'll admit that the yanking of her hair was a touch excessive and unnecessary. Some might even deem it as barbaric. But to apologize for such would be the ludicrous work of a jester.

Stella, the bubbly and perpetually smiling hostess from the gala, was the crux of Abraham Scobretti's occupation. She was the facilitator in transferring these sea animals to him, so whatever front she exuded while at the gala had now been erased from actuality. Stella was just as guilty of sinfulness as everyone else who ploughed their cruddy bloodstained fingers into this despicable operation. So, if anyone was naïve enough to claim my judgment was unmerited that was their own bloody fault. Whether or not you're the trader or the facilitator, the supreme leader or dependable deputy, there is no disparity in your sheer atrocity.

Debi, who was sitting on her knees by Abruzzoli, watched as I positioned Stella in a steady headlock. The confusion that raced the length of her face, mouth agape and all, was predictable. Although she was nearby when Stanley revealed Stella's identity, Debi had initially responded with scepticism. Whereas I was able to trust Stanley's admission after pondering the possibilities some, Debi was less convinced.

All she'd thought about, too, was Stella's spirited demeanour. She even said, aloud, that it was unlikely someone like that could be involved in Scobretti's schemes. And while I understood her reasonings, that's precisely why you can't have faith in anyone *until* they've proven their loyalty.

"What are you going to do?" Debi asked.

"She's *bait*," I said.

"You're not funny."

"*Yes*...I am." I offered Debi an inconspicuous smile as my comment was sarkier than intended. "Also, it's of grave importance that you ring up your superiors now." I gestured toward the rotary phone on the desk. "Get in touch with Her Majesty's Church. Inform them of our location and that our assignment is nearing completion. They'll send personnel here to assist Abruzzoli and...tidy up the muddle."

I lumbered to the door with Stella in tow. She seemed resigned to my control, and surely the corpse of her associate in the path of her feet didn't help matters. I had my C70 situated on Stella's left temple, muzzle buried in a jungle of blonde and touching flesh. My finger was experiencing a severe anxiety attack due to its delirious eagerness to pull the trigger, making it rapidly drum.

"Where are you taking me?" Stella sputtered.

Debi answered, in a murmur, for me. "You'll find out." Her gems were planted on me. From her words to the semblance of unease that washed her face, it appeared as though she'd spotted something that'd left her beyond tense. Like she was an altar girl who'd finally discovered Satan for the very first time. Perhaps she realized she was incapable of prohibiting whatever was to come, and it shook the living mercy out of her.

Without worrying about whether there were rogues outside the room, I stormily kicked the door with such vehemence that it glided off its hinges. The door played the part of a veteran stuntperson, exaggeratedly clattering over the railing upon taking in the kick. It then descended, a shrill smash indicating its excruciating arrival.

Someone to my right shouted "shit" in an animated manner. It was the grail himself, Abraham Scobretti, positioned with a Beretta Model 84 pointed at Stella and me. He appeared bewildered by my vicious entrance. Surely the fact he had his gun pulled on the "man from Massachusetts" he'd met a day before only exacerbated this sensation. It's full circle for me as well, facing the scumbag in his natural form compared to the cordial bloke I'd interacted with from previously.

"Abe! Get him off me," Stella pleaded. "Please!"

"He's not gonna hurt ya, baby," Scobretti said. One of his eyebrows twitched. "That *stronzo* oughta know if he tries anything, I'm gonna kill him."

I'd never partaken in a, how would you say, old fashioned standoff before. Everything about this was reminiscent of the entertaining westerns I'd watch with my dad decades ago. Two foes confronting one another, guns drawn, and willing to prolong the suspense by standing in silence…anxiously anticipating the other's guard to give out. In this case, however, a first-time viewer would certainly be puzzled if they attempted to guess the identity of the villain. After all, I was holding Stella hostage, a common mannerism for the *rogue*. How staggered they'd be upon discovering Scobretti to be the actual rotter.

"What is it you want, Massachusetts? Huh? Clearly you and my brother-in-law are partnering against me. Fucking Rocco…stained our family bonds. Disgraced my sister…" Scobretti almost began to ramble on about Rocco before he seemed to snap back to reality. "So, what is it? You wanna do business? You tryin' to send a message? Whatever it is, we can gab about it *without* all this violent shit. But first…you've gotta take your hands off my girl."

"Not a bloody chance," I said.

My response appeared to incense Scobretti, whose already focused demeanour hardened. His lips thinned out and grazed against gritted teeth, while his grave stare deepened. Scobretti was probably imagining how delightful my body would look if it were riddled with bullets. Personally, I don't believe it'd be among the finest, but it'd still be worthy of placing within the top five hundred most gratifying bullet-riddled bodies.

A rapidly escalating warmth bombed throughout my skin. I wasn't sure if the air conditioner in this warehouse was malfunctioning, or the boiling friction was nudging me to get on with the presentation. White noise developed in my pounding ears and my body had become the literal embodiment of the long-awaited nuclear Armageddon. All else that was required was for the warmth to sizzle my flesh off the muscle. My weeping heart rammed its cranium against my chest in a sickening attempt to convince my non-existent psyche that any potential actions would be flawed. So much so that they would only prove the Phantasms' disgusting claims to be truth instead of the unhallowed fabrications they truly are.

Stomping footsteps sprinted on the catwalk, their clattering emanating from behind me. Apparently, this was about to morph into a reprise of the ordeal I'd been damned into earlier, stuck between Abruzzoli and the guards. Only, in this case, there was no uncertainty in discerning who was also on the catwalk with Scobretti and I. Debi had mentioned that the *Scobretti's* were here, plural, and…until now, Sergio hadn't come into sight. On top of that, Abruzzoli divulged his actual allegiance whereas it's exceedingly doubtful that Sergio would perform the same stunt.

Of course, twisting myself toward the stomping commotion would end in my demise. So would remaining fixed on Scobretti. It's certainly a spot of bother, especially since my C70 hadn't detached itself from Stella's temple. It declined to move from that spot, and it was a decision that I respected. The handgun wasn't planning to separate from Stella anytime soon, not even for the substantial opportunity to zero in toward more *valuable* targets.

Stella, in a probable *and* vain effort to distract me, jabbed her modestly sharp hot pink fingernails into my lower arm. Though the ensuing and sweeping stings that stemmed from her ten distraught nails made me grit my teeth due to its abruptness, there was no loosening of the grip that glued her under my reign.

"You're stuck, you piece of shit," Sergio called out.

"You sure as shit are," Scobretti added. "So, like I said, you let Stella go and we'll let you go."

"Don't lie to me," I said.

"You," Scobretti shouted, though he gathered his composure before continuing with "don't hurt my girl. You got this much of a problem with us? Then we'll sort this out, the three of us. But don't make Stella part of this. Let her go…and drop your gun. *Capito*?"

Stiffening the headlock that I'd secured on Stella, I responded, "you simply don't understand. She's just as much a sinner as the two of you."

"*Sinner*?" Scobretti asked. "What do you mean by *sinner*?"

"Shit!" Sergio exclaimed. "Abe, that accent. It's that British fucker from the—"

It's a bloody shame that Sergio was dreadfully unable to keep his mouth cemented. Sure, his unbelievable unearthing of the crazed individual before him was worth expressing. But damn…it's pitiable that he couldn't supress that outburst from billowing through. It might've allowed Stella more time to wallow in the despairing amazement that is one's mortality. To hark back to the bliss of working for the aquarium...her seemingly brill romance with Abraham...or to deliberate the circumstances that led her to my unremitting, maniacal grasp.

By electing to speak up when he did, Sergio proceeded to betray his brother and "would-be" sister-in-law. His comment disabled his defences while also distracting him from his objective. It seized Abraham's attention as well, as I'd caught his eyes shifting past me when Sergio began connecting the dots. That was precisely the line of action I was bargaining on.

During our training sessions ages ago, Minister Esprine taught me how to conduct my movements if I were in this precise predicament. Combined with the multiple other troubles he cast me into, such as underwater bomb defusals or infiltrating the *actual* White House, I was convinced the man was madder than originally imagined. None of those gambles appeared likely to my ignorant self, especially not the one I was currently in. But lo it'd risen from the graveyard of my education...primed to be of worth.

Before Sergio could finish his statement, amid the mutual distraction of the two brothers, I made the irrevocable decision to pull the trigger. The sharp eruption that enthusiastically generated from the gunshot did wonders for my unfortunate ears due to the proximity between myself and the gun. They began to ripple in a rage, causing me to shift my jaw some in a peculiar attempt to wobble the residual jingles away. These instances can be disorientating, especially because my C70 rarely has a silencer attached. Silencers are futile to me. My distaste for them is out of a dotty lust for exhibiting carnage in its natural beauty, that of graphic grandeur. There's simply no point in subduing those captivating moments of ruthless expression. If only the motion picture censors could engraft such into their non-existent loafs.

Stella uttered a hushed groan as her bonce slumped, the muzzle of my C70 surfacing from the jumble of her blonde locks. Her once fixed and desperate grasps for grace slackened and her arms proceeded to drape down like shabby wind chimes. The weight of her *dearly* departed figure, slender and lacklustre, hung sorrowfully from my forearm.

Sporting the carnivorous disposition of a lion, I continued to maintain a steady clasp around Stella's neck even though she'd converted into a pouch of haunted bones. This animalistic exhibition was arranged to top up the volume of dominion I now wielded over the two Scobretti's. Minister Esprine had disclosed, from the onset of my employment, that one must forever exercise raw supremacy over their foes no matter the circumstances. Concurrently, we must never permit a sliver of indecision or apprehension to cross our judgement while confronting them.

It was very likely neither of the brothers had ever encountered such an unstable individual to this point, considering their incensed and mystified attitudes toward my arrival. Even after…bumping off Stella…they probably *still* believed I was some sort of loony rival in the trade game. That's preferred, in my opinion, as it adds to the covert identity that I'd comically cultivated in the loafs of these bastards.

Abraham Scobretti remained in place, statically aiming his Beretta at me. His aggressive and readied stance hadn't changed but his expression was one of unrest. Scobretti's olive complexion noticeably lightened, his eyes were expansive and barren as the moon, and his bottom lip had slouched. One could only speculate, merrily, what could possibly be scampering about behind his gaze. Was he reliving the graphic carnage he'd unwillingly witnessed? How he was unable to protect the life of woman he adored and spoke of wedding soon. Must be a humiliating scenario to be subjected to…

With Scobretti effectively neutralized by shock, I wasted no time in circling around toward Sergio. The younger Scobretti had failed to conclude in his sentence after my actions halted him. He was also in a stupor, complete with an almost identical expression to his brother's. The sole difference laid in his mouth, which was closed and stretched in a fixed line. By sheer chance, his gun, also a Beretta Model 84, was slightly lowered and levelled toward my knees.

Taking advantage of such an opportune situation, I released Stella's dead weight while also shooting at Sergio. As her body collided with the steel, the two bullets that tore from my C70 slugged Sergio in the chest. The pitiful bastard shouted like a shattered mug as he stumbled over. His Beretta slipped out of his hand, which then soared to his chest to vainly soothe his wounds.

In spite of this achievement, I swiftly identified my impending demise. By incapacitating Sergio, I left myself vulnerable to any hostilities that Abraham Scobretti might choose for revenge. It's the facet of this job that'll never be prevented. No matter how capable or remarkable the operatives of Her Majesty's Church are, we will forever encounter obstacles that are might be too formidable to conquer.

However, to be executed by Abraham Scobretti was the favoured of my two routes. If you're caught in a web between the grail or a subordinate, you eliminate the latter. Yes, trouncing the grail might seem like the ideal move because it technically signifies a triumph. However, it's also quite disconcerting to submit to the violence of a subordinate because they're the lesser of the two. Even worse is if an unnamed henchman was granted such an opportunity. That nearly occurred with Abruzzoli and the guards earlier, but the contrast between subordinates and henchmen are less significant. Anyhow, if you're eliminated by the grail then you've accomplished all that you could. It's a rule that Her Majesty's Church has us abide by, and one that I brandish with honour.

But, as I kept my sights on the wounded man before me, no gunshots rang out from behind. My body didn't suddenly rip to shreds from a frenzy of bullets. It didn't crumple to the steel in a cloak of excessive gore. Curiosity urged me to turn back around, but my pride compelled me to stay where I was. If Abraham Scobretti wished to send me to perdition, then this was his opportunity. Otherwise, he was signing *his own* contract to enter perdition because the bastard was not going to have the satisfaction of glaring at me during the butchery. Only my hypothetical hooded executioners were entitled such a right.

"*Che cazzo...che cazzo...che cazzo*!" Scobretti erupted.

The flustered tone of Scobretti's voice didn't come across as a ploy to seize my attention for his gain. It sounded genuinely agitated to the point of ire. Perhaps the toxic combination of both his girlfriend and brother being massacred right before him had taken its inevitable toll on the wretched man's psyche. A wonderfully morbid trial if there ever was one. That was enough to convince my crazed curiosity to take the reins.

Abraham Scobretti was frantically clicking the trigger of his Beretta. With each successive click, the hastier his fingers became. The Beretta must've been out of bullets, but the antagonism that swelled from the man had likely conned him into believing otherwise. It was a miserable display from a weakened and devastated sub-human. Clearly, he hankered for my body to be among the bloodied that lay upon the steel. But his plodding fairy godmother who could grant such a request was busy soaking in cherry wine somewhere.

One forlorn bullet subsisted in my C70. That was enough to finalize this bloody assignment and obtain another twisted, triumphant tale for my personal records. I could finally jab my silver spitzer bullet through the forehead of Scobretti's photo. He'd become another footnote in my unhallowed catalogue of rogues. And if more continue to accumulate in that bloody catalogue then this damned planet will be untainted for all eternity. That's not too far a stretch, because what I am doing is for the furtherance of all nations. That is what justifies my actions. To commit *inprobicide*, the execution of the sinful, will only enhance our world.

"Their blood has smeared your hands," I said. "And it's because you betrayed them. They weren't given an option to choose between survival and mortality. Neither will you. There's no escaping the grim abyss, Scobretti. Sinners cannot negate their anticipated paths."

My C70 elevated to Scobretti's head when, to my astounded chagrin, clattering footsteps atop the catwalk successfully diverted my attention from the man. Arms swaddled my torso from behind and constricted my upper movement. As this occurred, the sudden jostling accidentally compelled my finger to pull the trigger. My last bullet clanked against the steel near Scobretti's left thigh before ricocheting up. The poor bullet had been, regrettably, squandered. And with these arms locking me in place, any further usage of my distraught weapon had been momentarily disabled.

"Abe, for the sake of what's good, kill him!" Sergio coughed out.

Damn it. I truly believed those two bullets to Sergio's chest had finished him off. The scumbag had been struck in his right pectoral muscle and left extensor oblique muscle before he toppled over. While it may have not been enough to dispatch him immediately, my expectation was that the leakage of crimson would've been too extensive for him to continue. Of course, I could've used that wasted bullet on him, but that would've demanded an improvisation for my subsequent steps with Abraham. My vulnerability would've been as extreme as it currently is. Thankfully, one can't confine an engine of demolition for that long.

Being that my strength was *surprisingly* superior to that of the weakened man, I jutted my arms out like wings. This relatively simple technique succeeded in severing Sergio's latched arms from my torso. I spun around like a poor man's discus thrower and belted the bastard in the nose with my C70. Snatching Sergio by the collar of his red dress shirt, I then exerted minimal effort while heaving the maimed and stupefied bastard over the railing.

Sergio Scobretti's yelling reverberated as he plunged to the first floor. His arms and legs flopped like those of a time-worn toy, seemingly to halt the inevitable end. Maybe his flopping was a possible act of desperation, an attempt to summon the abilities of an albatross so that he could glide to safety. Or perhaps he was too debilitated at this point to brace himself for the termination of his sins. Regardless of the reason, it made nary a difference whatsoever. Sergio ploughed into one of the steel crates on the ground level, the impact of which was so thundering and jarring that it even knocked me for a six. His body had scrunched up upon contact and it slowly lolled off the crate.

With that nuisance put out of his misery, I placed my C70 in my holster as it had been rendered useless before reverting to Abraham Scobretti, However, I was again knocked for a six upon noticing him backing away from me. My target, the grail who headed these illegal animal trading ventures…who'd been so intense and blistering with fury, was skulking away in utter horror.

He must've finally realized that he'd met his match. That the prospect of fighting would leave him like his loved ones. So, what else was he to do aside from flee? That's what he was preparing to do. After all, Scobretti was devoid of any other choices that could salvage his security. And the way he was moving backwards while observing my movements…this was a man who was alone and unable to continue waging a war. So, he, after cautiously taking several steps backward, abruptly bolted to the end of the catwalk. He dropped his Beretta and scrambled down the steps to return to the first floor.

Wasting no time in following suit, I began to climb down the steps myself. But, upon reaching the bottom, the ghouls of good fortune were kind enough to bestow me a gift. Instead of chasing after him through the maze of crates and tanks, I found the man planted face down on the ground. He nearly had the perfect clearing to start sprinting around to the entrance, except for the fact that he'd accidentally tripped over the downed guard who'd been battered by Debi earlier. That's merely what occurs when you're in an agitated rush. Everything else melts into the landscape and your lack of awareness makes you susceptible to endangering yourself.

I yanked him up by his t-shirt and, taking advantage of his state of confusion, pondered my next move. What would be an excruciating ordeal for scum to graft through? Something cruel yet bloody deserving? Something that could even make up for the lack of...amplified interrogation methods that'd been unjustly underutilised? It had to loiter in those categories because I'm a staunch believer in making the grail endure agony for their corruption of humanity. Any upright individual with an ounce of self-respect would concur.

An exquisite idea that suited all three categories swung in my head. I stayed silent as I arranged to exploit the idea, dragging Scobretti like a prisoner to his grave. This was the culmination of multiple objectives that were to be officially satiated, such as the damned target finally paying for his depraved activities in the most "compassionate" manner. That would, in turn, fulfil this bloody assignment and cause the United Kingdom to rejoice in yet another accomplishment for the British intelligence community.

Scobretti, whether it was out of exhaustion or his surrendering to the significant losses he suffered, didn't struggle nor did he battle his way out of my hold. All my previous targets had carried their defeat in an ungracious display, sometimes out of spite or because they'd given up. He fell into the latter category, the rarer of the two. Almost everyone else continued to brawl until they'd been reduced to a heaping row of sickening flesh. But they also had more to lose. That wasn't the case with Abraham Scobretti, who'd lost both his brother and potential fiancée. Who'd been deceived by his brother-in-law.

When we had spoken to one another, the bastard truly appeared to cherish those closest to him. Losing them probably overshadowed the impending end of his operations. Some find no use in collecting brass when there's no one to share it with. Strangely enough, they're the most humane of the wicked. And the fact that these individuals exist might be among the eeriest facts of life.

With Scobretti in tow, we lugged ourselves to one of the fish tanks. I used my free hand to pry the lid off it before flinging it aside. Effortlessly hoisting the grail over my shoulder like a duffel bag, I stopped for a tick to analyse the inside of the tank. Enriched with pebbles, seaweed, and other water plants, the tank was brilliantly furnished for occupants. However, neither fish nor aquatic life of any kind were present.

"You won, Massachusetts," the bastard muttered. He then chuckled softly before continuing with "was it worth it? Huh? You said something about me having blood on *my* hands. What about you, guy? Yours are soaked in the blood of *my* family. All because of what of I do. This business rakes in, I dunno, maybe a few million a year. Is it *honestly* worth taking lives?"

Finally…some semblance of defiance had risen from the otherwise defeated man. But…those words…they stung me even though they shouldn't have. It's merely venom being spewed from the mouth of the genuinely sinful, attempting to cast me as one *not* on par with him, but *more debauched* than him. What's more, no other target of mine *ever* dared to speak to me in such a vile manner. Then again, that's because I never granted them the opportunity to do so. Their last words would've fallen on deaf ears, and yet Scobretti's are mocking me. He should've known better than to further provoke someone like me.

I restrained myself from verbally responding to his inane question. As a substitute, I vigorously plunged the grail into the fish tank. Water harshly splattered onto me and throughout the surrounding area. Scobretti's lower body thrashed about like a ruffled sailfish, an unforeseen visual considering he appeared resigned to his ultimate fate. Who knows…he very well could've been hoping I'd give him the decency of a more appropriate answer than this.

Regardless, it made no difference in the outcome. My arms declined to cut the grapple that I'd latched around his waist. With every writhe of his body, mine synced with the chaotic commotions. His struggles were venerable, but ultimately ineffective as I realized his body had begun to slacken. Eventually the sole person still in motion was me. Drained but pleased with my feat, I lobbed Scobretti's torso out from my grip. This left the immobile man hanging from the fish tank, his upper half still submerged in the water.

19

Every member of Her Majesty's Church can name the most recent field operative to have failed an assignment: Reiss Muellington. We hardly ever spoke, as he was shedloads more absorbed in his work compared to my other colleagues. He preferred to float on in a more discreet manner, revealing only scarce aspects of his personal life. On top of that, where the others have tendencies to ramble on about their jobs, Muellington would provide the bare minimum when it came to his assignments. Generally, it'd be his target's name, their misdeeds, and the destination. But Muellington was a decent bloke with an affable presence and a primed willingness to honour the oath he took. The prime example of a reliable field operative who had the potential to transcend the rest of us had he pursued an upper-level position. Yet every aspiration he might've itched for had been impeded by his untimely departure at a mere thirty-seven.

He was on assignment in Canada when the entire operation collapsed into alleged ruins that the Romans would scoff at. That's all the information any of us operatives are aware of. Lord President Trailsby keeps all records of unsuccessful assignments locked away in an unspecified location within HQ. The only individuals who have any knowledge regarding how the former operative arrived at the celestial city are Trailsby, Pierce, and the ministers. And rightfully so, though my sombre curiosity has occasionally requested that I attempt to locate those blood-stained records. Surely Trailsby would be livid if such an undertaking was ever attempted.

Since Muellington's death, a medley of rumours have swirled within the halls of HQ. I've heard plenty of them in the three years that've passed, and some certainly seem plausible. Francine, an immensely credible source considering her closeness to Trailsby, presented a claim to me not long after the incident. She told me that he accidentally shot himself with his own gun. How the bloody mercy that's possible is utterly up in the air, but I'm inclined to believe her. After all, Francine is among the last of my associates who'd even dare spew falsehoods to me.

Then there are rumours from unreliable sources, such as what my madcap colleague "Fulch" Fleppings asserted during the annual dinner we operatives delight in together. He tried to convince the lot of us that Muellington was amid a frantic pursuit, his target trying his damndest to get away by hopping over tracks before a cargo train chugged between them. The target was successful in his feat, though Muellington ended up stumbling onto the tracks at an incredibly inopportune time. He tripped just seconds before the train severed him in two. It's highly doubtful that this account occurred, however, as Fulch is notorious for spouting morbid tall tales.

No matter what sort of incident transpired during Muellington's final operation, his dismal finale did enable him to ascend to an echelon few have attained. Like five others before him, he has been deemed one of the revered deities of Her Majesty's Church. It is an exclusive club that is worshipped by *all* members of the organization, no matter their position. These esteemed ranks are awarded to those who've departed this life, selling their souls to Her Majesty's Church and Her Majesty the Queen.

On the second floor of HQ is a pocket-sized chamber that functions like a hospital's chapel. An exquisite, hand-carved ten headed candelabra rests atop a wooden altar table and reigns before a row of pews. And behind the candelabra are portraits of the six operatives who've attained the status of deity. All lord presidents have required their employees to visit this chamber. Once inside, few will pray but most simply pay tribute to those who remained true to their oath until their finishing breath. While the pseudo-religious atmosphere of this room sort of rubs me to the wrong way, I've still entered and honoured them as well.

The last time I visited that sacred chamber was in May of this year. Bart rang me up one morning and invited me to his office in HQ. He wished to catch up on life before he set out on an assignment. Bart's a bloody good bloke and it'd been some time since we last had a good chat. Having the opportunity to loll abut some was much needed, so I immediately took him up on his offer. It was a pleasant occasion filled with plenty of roaring stories and merry jokes. We spoke for well over three hours until he had to catch his jet.

As Bart was preparing to leave, he grabbed a briefcase and slapped me on the back while saying, "hopefully I return in less pieces than Muellington." It was a far more morose joke than even Fulch would make, but it did elicit a chuckle from me. It also provided an impulse to visit the chamber once more before leaving myself.

We got on the lift together and Bart instantly questioned why I pushed the second-floor button. Upon responding that his joke reminded me to pay my respects to the deities before leaving, Bart shrugged and said, "I would join you, lad. But that damn room is as unsightly as your mother's knicker drawer." Such a bloody tosser. When the lift doors opened, we exchanged goodbyes and well wishes before I went on my way.

The chamber was empty that day and it was excessively biting, though that wasn't a surprise as the air conditioner in that room happens to be much more vigorous than in others. I used one of my matches to spur life into the candles before taking a seat in the first row. And, for an hour, I traded stares with each of the six portraits that were presented for all to honour. It was one of the rare instances where my thought capacities were vacant. Entering this chamber was like stepping into a vacuum where nothing existed aside from your breath, your grief, and your responsibility to fulfil their legacies.

Frankly, at this point in my career, I'm astounded that my portrait isn't up in that chamber. It's not out of some egomaniacal hankering to have all my colleagues refer to me as a *deity*. No, after all that's ensued since joining Her Majesty's Church it's quite bewildering that I've ended up on this side of anguish. Certainly, all six of the revered operatives had taken shedloads more precautions before, during, and after their assignments. Surely, they'd used their time wisely to prepare for the madness, mentally and physically, they were about to undertake. And, on top of that, their assignments are without a nymph's doubt far less undemanding than mine. As far as I'm aware, none of them have ever had to finish an assignment in a manner like mine. It's always ended in…actual apprehension.

So how is it that I've lived more life and completed more assignments than any of them? Is it because I'm abnormally skilled in my approach? Doubtful. There's nothing Minister Esprine trained me in that's any different to what he taught them. Pay more attention? Even Debi has noticed my piss poor attention to detail aside from facial recognition.

Why was it them instead of me? That question, which is worth two nickels and a bus ticket, haunts me whenever an assignment had been concluded. When the Scobretti's had me surrounded, it was pure fortune that they never attempted to go on and off me while Stella was in my grasp. That the shock that arose from the gruesome display of wrath they witnessed allowed me to…" secure" Sergio. And, especially, that Abraham's Beretta jammed while my back was turned. Perhaps if I were someone else, that fortune would've ceased to exist, and my name would be followed by *deity*.

But there's also the possibility that something…greater is playing a hand to keep me alive so that it can guide me down a different path. And despite the struggle that arises from all the missteps and perils that maunder about with each step I take, it's somehow confiscated the danger and transformed it into life lessons. Though my blood hasn't been obligated to swim in religion since I ventured off to college, it could all genuinely chalk up to the fact that some higher power in a motorcade has a deranged desire for me to succeed without Her Majesty's Church. To renounce this job and turn my life around. To work a modest job, like how I was a teacher back during the years of martial…*bliss*. I mean who bloody knows if that's the case or if I'm just bowling straws like rocks now. Anything is certainly possible at this point because I've all but exhausted my decomposing cerebral facilities.

A series of stings impacted some of my muscles, each boasting the sensation of flesh being stapled. It initiated in my biceps and travelled down so that it could swarm my thighs. The prickled pains caused me to clutch my stomach as I stumbled against the fish tank where Scobretti remained halfway submerged. Unlike the earlier pains my body…err, the other body of mine suffered, these concluded much sooner. I haven't an inkling what they derived from, but thankfully they didn't linger.

Slumping against the tank, I gazed up at Scobretti's body. His legs were pointed up like the mast of a sailboat while his upper half was crumpled up like a shoddy accordion. Initially, upon removing my grip from the bastard's body, I was prepared to witness the tank topple over and spill all over myself, the floor, and my blood-stained attire. But clearly these tanks were first-rate in their construction, as Scobretti's entire six-foot and brawny build continued to stay static.

A shrill, dense noise screeched from nearby and the brilliance of sunlight emerged into the warehouse like a natural diva. The ear-piercing sound must've emanated from the entrance. It was probably the consequence of the steel door's ancient hinges bellowing upon being forcibly pulled open. Several booted footsteps soon stormed in, the subsequent striding seeming to charge in all directions judging by the clamours that fenced my ears.

One pair of footsteps belonged to a woman who sped around nearby fish tanks and found me hunched over on the ground. She was immensely attractive, with deep sepia skin that possessed rich sunset undertones; round, invigorating lips ornated with gloss; misty, dark eyes; and short, cropped, curly black hair.

The woman wore a turquoise jumpsuit, white gloves, and black combat boots. This ghastly ensemble is the outfit that's worn by the "clean-up" crew who works under the minister of justice. For decades, the jumpsuit used to be a bland charcoal colour with the symbol of Her Majesty's Church on the back in black. The gloves, too, were black. But two years ago, once this decade apparently began to find its footing, Lord President Trailsby surprisingly enacted a modification to the outfits. He claimed that these new jumpsuits were adopted so that employees could be "up to date with the latest trends." The swap of a moody, reserved grey for the gleaming, indiscreet turquoise was horrid enough, but the symbol on the back had also been exchanged for a lemon-yellow variety.

"One-oh-nine?" The woman asked.

"Affirmative," I replied.

"Assignment complete?"

"Affirmative."

"Any injuries?"

"Negative."

"Anything else we oughta know?"

"Well...my target, Abraham Scobretti, is the miserable bloke right next to me in that tank. There's plenty of other garbage strewn about this building. However, more importantly, up on the catwalk are two rooms. My...*partners* are in the one to your right. The male,

Rocco Abruzzoli, he's all roughed up and in need of immediate medical attention. The female, Debi DeLaise…she's tending to Abruzzoli. I believe she's fine otherwise. Make sure she's okay for me, please."

"You got it. We'll send Mr. Abruzzoli to a hospital at once. Give the rest of us a few minutes to tidy up in here. We'll bring you and Ms. DeLaise to your hotel once we're finished."

"Thank you."

The woman patted my shoulder before moving on. It's amusing, in a mundane manner, how all members of the "clean-up" crew are terse in their manner of speech. Their questions and responses are all part of a script that they're not allowed to modify in any fashion unless they're replacing a person's name. The sole difference between this woman and others I've interacted with in the past is that she patted me on the shoulder before going off. That's new. It might've been to indicate a job well done. I'm not entirely sure, but the gesture was appreciated at the very least.

Now that we've interacted, the woman will soon relay the information I communicated to her back to the Minister of Justice. He'll then send that information to Lord President Trailsby, who'll mark my assignment off as *successful*. Once that occurs, Francine will place a sign up on a bulletin board that's in the cafeteria. The sign will have my most recent official portrait attached to it, and it'll say something along the lines of "Congratulations, 109, on another successful accomplishment."

My colleagues will then, one by one, jot down congratulatory messages on the sign. And in the coming days there will be a gigantic crate arriving at my door that's filled with fourteen different bottles of liquor, each selection specially chosen by my colleagues to commemorate the date. It's a considerate gesture, especially when you're celebrating the achievement of systematically executing immoral scum. At least when I'm partaking in sending one of them a commemorative bottle, they've succeeded in saving someone or the world at large.

As I heard the "clean-up" crew chat and work in the distance, nothing compelled me to rise to my feet and move from this hunched over position. For such a grand triumph and having knowledge of the merriment that's to come, the air of inebriation that's applauding me isn't doing so with praise. It's doing so with contempt. The satisfaction that rallied upon finishing off Scobretti had evaporated without notice. The exhaustion that arrived with the satisfaction continued to loiter, increasing in heaviness with every breath that I discharged.

Surrounding me were deceased bodies, all of whom were the product of my devotion. In the past, upon conversing with the crew I'd go and wait by their three vans outside until they had everything seamlessly back in place. There was never any thought about what I'd just done, only that Her Majesty's Church would be proud of my conquest. But there's a dreariness that's enclosing me. A startling sensation of defeat despite success.

Two members of the crew approached me, nodded, and proceeded to remove Scobretti from the fish tank. One of them held his shoulders, the other his legs, and they carried the bastard away. As this happened, Scobretti's voice swelled in my pounding ears, repeating his final words, "is it honestly worth taking lives?" If I dared reply, my impulses tell me that the answer would be yes. That's what my oath entails, that's how it's been for years and years. But there's another part of me that isn't so sure and is shouting "no" over the monotone "yes's" that I hear.

Yes is undoubtedly the answer, Mark.

The psychotic, crackling voices of those damned Phantasms caused a searing throb to strike the left side of my head. How humorous those Phantasms are, always injecting themselves into my realm when the door was supposedly locked. Their voices prompted my heartbeat to hurriedly whirl around at a speed that could've matched the propeller on a motorboat. But, as I searched around the area, they hadn't materialised. At least, not anywhere that I could actively view from my location.

Stop looking for us. We're in hiding again. You know that we're shy around anyone who isn't you.

"Don't you clots ever quit?" I asked.

Quit? Why would we quit when all we're struggling to achieve is your resurrection? It's a shame that you've been so oblivious to our taxing labour. How we've been trying so hard to salvage the slivers of what was once a decent man. Someone who used to be an optimistic, honest, cordial being. Whose true self was misplaced the moment Her Majesty's Church dug their talons into you and decided they'd experiment with your frail psyche.

"It's droll, really, how inaccurate your assumptions are."

Inaccurate? By no means is that the case. Listen to us closely, Mark. Everyone that's ever existed, even the best of humanity, has internal darkness that's stored in the subterranean jalopy that is their mind. Those who discover this darkness overtaking their spirits always go through a trial that enabled the madness. For you…it was joining Her Majesty's Church. They fed into the torment you wallowed in upon abandoning your family for the Royal Armed Forces. They were, and still are, fully aware that you have nothing to lose because your relations with those you love are so poor. With that knowledge, your mentor trained you to hunt, maim, and kill. Why? It's because this organization needed someone with a hunger for demolition. So, you were converted, unfairly, into an extermination machine.

"The audacity of you both to desecrate the name of Minister Esprine disgusts me. Have you no decency? Now I've told both you clots this before and, apparently, your inability to listen is bloody appalling. What I do—"

Is for the betterment of the United Kingdom, blah, blah, blah. We've grown weary of routinely hearing that frustrating sound bite of a lie. You tell yourself that after almost every killing because it's the one phrase that is somehow successful in repressing your malevolence. Your realization of being a monster! As for Nigel Esprine, how is it that you're unable to see him as being sinful? After all, everything that he taught you has been used by you to kill.

The tone of my voice began to flicker with vexation as I continued answering the Phantasms. It was asinine, even bothering to answer the utter rubbish they spouted. But the voices of those blue-grey nutters wouldn't fade away unless I submit to their disorder. That was not going to happen this time around. So, combatting them in this setting was essential, if not bizarre. Whenever the voices would rear up before, I'd never audibly converse with them. Nothing ever compelled me to do such a loony joust, until now.

"Her Majesty's Church," I said, "works to improve society by ridding the streets of the worthless miscreants who dabble in a variety of shameful deeds. If Minister Esprine taught me to rid of them, then what on mercy's grace is the issue? That fails to make me this extermination machine you speak of. It's a matter of bettering this planet. Again, I ask you what there is to do when our civilisation is being corroded by the wicked? Displace them? Lock them away and swallow the rusted key? If someone does what Scobretti *did*...or worse, they don't deserve to coexist with the worthy. Their corpses should rot for all eternity."

How is it that you're so oblivious to the fact that what you do is what many of them do?

"It's laughable how you attempt to tie me to them, when there's a clear difference between moral and immoral. Out of all cretins, you two should recognize that. Stop this delusional effort to persuade me into your beliefs. You shitters have caused so much bloody grief since you first rose from the abyss. And it's all because of this, this...self-hatred ceremony?"

When it pertains to you, there is no difference between moral and immoral. But, most importantly, it's truly pitiful how you've been unable to comprehend the truth, Mark. What's more is how greatly you've misinterpreted us and our mission. Since we first became among your closest acquaintances, you've questioned our expertise and falsely accused us of being the catalysts of your mental rot—

"You've no proof of that."

Wise up, Mark! We have knowledge of everything that drudges about in that decrepit shack of a loaf. You blame us for everything when, in fact, it's all your doing. The daydreams of firing squads...we are not the cause of those thoughts as you claim to have seen. We aren't fortune tellers communicating your future to you. Those images were entirely constructed by suicidal tendencies that you've tried in vain to smother. But evidently, they're devastating and yearning for a break.

The phrase "suicidal tendencies" produced another bitter twinge, this one in my ribcage.

Everything you did to Scobretti and his associates was you. When you're just about set to initiate a termination frenzy, your excessive rage agitates an inner lunacy. Mark, you're just as much a rogue as your targets. Abraham Scobretti asked you if this was worth taking a life, and equal parts of you shouted "yes" and "no."

Sweat from my forehead dripped into my eyes, and the irritation that derived from it was worse than if I'd dunked my face into a vat of hot sauce. A charred blanket of unnatural mugginess latched itself onto my trembling being. Was this the incitement of rage from that assault of lies? Maybe...but my frazzled mind was beginning to have trouble rewiring all its faulty systems. The agitation was impairing my thought process.

"This pathetic attempt to persuade me into believing your falsehoods was already amusing enough," I said, rushing my words in between harsh breaths. "But to claim you're trying to help me? The moment you bloody menaces entered my domain my sanity eroded. It's not my fault. It's yours! You've only *exacerbated* my internal distress. Dejection has ramped up, the visual image of myself has been *sullied*, and now I'm in this cycle of loathing a job that once brought me joy."

As my voice bellowed with rage, the Phantasms were apparently more than delighted to reciprocate the billowing craze.

It's never brought you joy. And your dejection might've been dormant for years before we arrived, but it's only amplified because you're always fighting with yourself and then blaming it on us! If you were wise enough to just acknowledge your dodgy spirits, then surely this wouldn't be the case.

"And what of my warped sense of self?"

Guess what? That is because of us! We want you to see what we see. What you've become. A carefully crafted, tactical monster. A man on the brink of becoming a perpetual, intentional mistake.

Seldom have words managed to inflict as much of a dent on my skin. There were, maybe, three occasions in the past where they speared directly into my heart. Twice they had been expelled from Darla's mouth…once our marriage had decided it wished to sink to the depths of the sea. The other time…it came from my eldest son. With each of those instances, the poison that trickled out of the spear and into my heart caused considerable misery.

In the case of Darla, it's easy to understand why such misery weighed down my shoulders. After all, hearing the woman I held dear to me for four years say, "I'm not in love with you anymore," right upon waking up…it's harrowing. And the sight, tears streaming down that faultless face of hers…how can one possibly take any of that on the chin and bob right back up? And then with my son, he told me a few years ago that he couldn't stand how I "promised to come home but decided that work was more important than family." He's nineteen, in college, and has hated me ever since that outburst. Possibly even earlier than that.

Now there were these words…from the bloody Phantasms of all beings. Regardless, it didn't matter who spewed them. Hearing those crackled voices vilify me was the equivalent of being kicked in the abdomen with a stiletto…multiple times. The word *mistake* trampled on my chest until it caved in and sulked in the corner. My shoulders slouched in utter defeat, like a rag doll whose arm stitches were ninety-five percent torn off. Continuing with further arguments would do zilch in trying to slog out of this predicament.

Yet, allowing those words to fester and devour my mind would cause further self-hatred. I suppose the Phantasms did pinpoint that rather well. Insane, truly, how such could even be possible…*further* self-hatred. Scraping the acidic words off my shoulders with a snowplough, I chuckled softly before saying, "perhaps everything would be worse without your both trying to *guide* me. But I haven't a need for spirit guides. Especially ones who've been as destructive as you. I'm fine without you."

If that's the route you wish to travel, then so be it. We did our best to assist you in seeing the inevitable. But if our aid now comes off as a hindrance, then perhaps it is time to part ways. We refuse to hand out any reconsiderations, as your decision is clear as your bonce is full of smog. Goodbye, Mark, and best of luck. Once our voices vanish from your skull, you'll see just how much we truly relieved that wretched psyche of yours.

Gradually, their voices did diminish…until they were overtaken by an onslaught of white noise that expanded. The shrill wrath of these crackles, which might as well have been the Phantasms screaming as they returned to the inferno where they belonged, sent my hands flying up. They glued to my ears as the white noise finally retracted and puttered out.

The sounds of the "clean-up" crew chatting about, far from me, returned as I remained locked to the floor and doused with sweat. You could've mistaken me for a vagrant who'd just taken a dip in an ale keg. Surely it wasn't an inviting sight, but what more could you ask for from a downtrodden mess?

There's a hopelessness that's entered this warehouse. It climbed an invisible ladder that's somewhere above my bonce, and it's lingering over me like an air freshener in a car. Trying to clean off the bleakness is challenging, as the aura is like honey. It sticks to you, attaches to your hand while straining to wipe it away. You're coated in this disgusting, gluey filth and if you don't succeed in scrubbing it off in time it'll drain your soul until it's mere talcum powder. But even talcum powder has more self-assurance than whatever the bloody mercy that resulting residue ever had.

In this…state, the overbearing corners of my ravaged mind created parallels between me and someone with shedloads more notoriety than myself. None other than Willard Triclun, the 53rd President of the United States. See, after serving as interior secretary two decades earlier, my father was tapped to be Triclun's ambassador to the Federal Republic of Germany. Due to this, my knowledge of the former president is more extensive than I'd like to admit. And what similarities we lack regarding title, family life, and prestige we make up for in an unending cycle of gloom and mental anguish.

Through research I discovered the extent of the excruciating torment Triclun suffered in the wake of his resignation, and the dreary level of desperateness in his blood as he hoped to not succumb to a pitiful demise. Though learned after the fact, it was very apparent in hindsight when my father introduced me to Triclun some months before the resignation. The forfeiture of his initial optimism had betrayed him through the visible bags under his eyes, and the gauntness in his cheeks. And I fear as though the monsters that feasted on him are the same that've massacred me at this very moment. At least my faults didn't come at the expense of the United States.

Being reminded of my faults has some advantages, strange as that may sound. Those faults can make one strive to better themselves because they learned from their errors. And all my loved ones have been aware for ages that I've made plenty of errors. But instead, there's now this sickening negativity that's laughing at me, resulting from an amalgam of these damn faults.

The one actual, successful relationship I'd ever been in was an utter bomb, as it was unable to last "till death." And remembering how Darla decided, out of the blue, that she was no longer in love with me was devastating. It dramatically altered my perspective on relationships and romance. Most importantly, it signified my ultimate failure as a husband. Between being unable to continue loving Darla for as long as I lived, as well as ceasing stability for our children, the heartache that has persevered has no end in sight.

Speaking of our children, it's true that this job has rendered me as an absentee father. I truly believed that my settling in England would last a few years. That personal accomplishments could rack up by my own doing, without the help of either my family or Darla's. Such would've been the catalyst for a successful return to Georgia. Alas, that was not the case and I got involved with Her Majesty's Church. Now my sons either view me with contempt or indifference. And my daughter, though she still very obviously presents her love in buckets…there's no doubt she still wishes our situation was more traditional. As such, there's my failure as a father.

Then, with Her Majesty's Church, what is not to fancy with an organization that provides *everything* for you? Shelter, food, a vehicle, private jets…it's essentially being a wealthy bastard without ever actually earning money. And that's bloody shameful. Even if I indulge in all Her Majesty's Church provides me, there is no leisure that occurs from failing in my own terms. There is a prosperity that pertains to my assignments, and my perfect record as an employee, but now all that is being questioned because apparently, I have no bloody clue whether this is bettering society or worsening it.

How is it not? Do the civilians of New Jersey honestly have an outlandish desire to watch scum like Scobretti wander their streets? Don't the masses at large have an appetite for security so that they're not exposed to bloody nits while going about their business? What good does it *possibly* bring our societies if the world is a dingy, reprehensible confinement centre that gorges on scum and then spews it back onto the already soiled streets? Where's the bloody issue?

There was a final fault that dwelled, and it prevailed over the others with its durable shell. But I had no inclinations in studying or contemplating that fault because, unlike the rest, it was more of an effect brought about by the three aggravating causes. This one could be deemed sinister by some, and unfortunate by others. As for me, I haven't an inkling what it means to me…aside from the subconscious sway that it reigns over me.

I reached for my holster without looking and grasped the C70. Taking a shallow breath while removing the gun, my fingers slithered into position on the grip, my left index finger beginning to rile itself up over nothing. Tilting my head down, I patted the mammoth-sized barrel before lifting it up and inspecting the most minor details this beautiful weapon had to offer. Javis truly produced his finest work with this sterling gem.

The C70 then followed my command, dragging itself up toward my left temple at a pace that would please an elderly slug. I hadn't forgotten that the chamber was empty. Three bullets were wasted by Sergio Scobretti, two of them unsuccessful at executing their job and the other ricocheting off the catwalk after a near detainment. But mercy it just made enough sense to invoke gratification.

No one should be impressed by this scene, for it's a foolish one and by no means courageous. But unfortunately, when you're beaten down, depleted, alone, and wallowing in continual mental rot...sometimes there's an inane method to remove yourself from those twisted ropes. It shouldn't be fulfilled, but bloody mercy some people just do not comprehend the absolute misery others face. So be it.

Without a moment of hesitation to ruin the impending meaninglessness, I pulled the trigger three successive times with the C70 pointed at my head. Of course, due to the lack of bullets, nothing happened. Oh well. My worldview remained imperfectly in place. The colours stood their ground and remained as rich as this dull area could be without blacking out. The sounds of chattering persisted, as well as footsteps thumping on the steel catwalk. I was still on this planet, in this New Jersey warehouse. And though it was unfortunate, there wasn't much else that could be puzzled out. Perhaps I had a dot of an aversion toward the inclination now...but that also didn't mean it wouldn't transform in the future.

I couldn't halt the quiet laughter that emitted while moving the C70 away from my head. Why it began, who knows? Flinging the C70 away from where I sat, my head rolled back as the laughing lessened. Then, catching me unaware, Debi emerged to my right. She strolled over from around one of the steel crates, her mauve shirt covered in what was presumably Abruzzoli's blood. In her arms was my suit jacket. Her widened expression gave the hint that she still hadn't fully recuperated from either my madness from upstairs or the view of Abruzzoli's wounded body. It was as though a war had begun and Debi was packaged far too deep within it.

"Got this for you," Debi said, handing me the jacket as she took a seat next to me.

"Thank you," I said, retrieving the jacket and placing it on my lap. "How are you holding up?"

"Shit…I don't really know, Mark. This day just…it…I wasn't expecting all of this to go down the way it did."

"Me neither."

"Everything seemed to get crazier by the hour. I spent months and months thinking about how this day would play out. And it didn't look anything like this mess."

"What'd you think it'd be like? A simple *got you* bust?"

Debi shrugged and sniffled. "I guess. I also wasn't expecting to see this much blood either. I've never seen so much in one day. It's…hard to explain how I feel looking at my shirt."

"Now that you mention the blood on your shirt, how's Abruzzoli doing? Did our *partner* make it?"

"Your…people or something, they said that he lost a shit ton of blood but that he'll be okay. They transported him to a hospital already. Did you see 'em leave?"

I shook my head. "No. I didn't."

"Have you just been down here this whole time?"

"Yes. Haven't moved. Just…toyed around with my thoughts some. It's a lot to take in all at once."

"Yeah, it is." Debi chuckled but sounded faint and somewhat uneasy since it quivered some at the end. "Oh, here I just remembered this, and I didn't wanna forget." She dug a hand into her crimson splotched shirt and removed my wallet. "This flew out of your pocket when you…threw your jacket off. Oh, and so did this." Debi again ruffled through the inside of her shirt before she retrieved a five-by-seven picture. She handed both items to me.

Upon reclaiming the items from Debi, a faint smile sailed across my face at a gentle speed. Strewn among my expression, however, were particles of unadulterated misery. That photograph was the only one I carried in my wallet. And it was, perhaps, the sole belonging of mine that correlated to treasure. The image consisted of myself, Darla, and our children posing for a family portrait. It was taken at a Meares, of course, in 1970. My comprehension of the specific year isn't a general estimation, nor is it based off the unfashionable, matching floral patterned attire we're all outfitted in. No, we took this photo maybe six months or so after our daughter was born. In addition to that beautiful memory, this was also a smidge over a month before Darla and I officially began divorce proceedings.

Reflecting on that period, I pondered why we even believed this seemingly "wholesome" photograph was the appropriate decision considering the duff state of our marriage. Though the desertion of Darla's love was the catalyst for our dissolution, we went through with the portrait at her suggestion. She persuaded me with the rationale being that we had no photos that comprised of our entire family. As such, this morsel of treasure is the sole image of us with all three of our children. But an enduring internal ache has convinced that there's much more surrounding this photograph's backstory than Darla wishes to admit. And it remains to be seen whether these beliefs stand on a wooden leg or if they're submerged in rattled assumptions. You be the judge.

Perhaps the photograph symbolized the final representation of an irreparable family unit. To bid farewell to astray adoration by retaining a mere keepsake of what once was versus what had happened. Or, on the contrary, maybe it was done out of a vain bid of restoration. A chance to caustically scrub away any inclinations that asserted our marriage would inevitably terminate. Who knows? It's probably best to dissipate these contemplations. After all, regardless of the possible circumstances behind the portrait, it all culminated in divorce.

"Did this actually fall out, or were you prying?" I asked.

"I promise you that it fell out."

"How ironic that is," I said. My smile, once faint and pained, sprouted into a calm sea of harmony. "I was just thinking about them."

"Is that your family?"

"Indeed. That's Darla, my ex-wife. And those three…smart-arsed wolverines…are my children. My crown jewels."

"I never would've guessed you were married and had children, Mark." Debi chuckled. "Never."

"It's understandable. Really. It is."

My eyes trailed away from Debi, though they came to rest at the C70 sitting about a foot away from me.

20

Bedsheets, an arguably inconsequential household item, go overlooked by the public day in and day out. These linens may be tucked in your very own cupboard right now, and without a doubt you would hardly pay them a spot of attention. But me? In all honesty, they were never so inconspicuous in my childhood home. My family possessed an abundant array of both plain and patterned bedsheets. And there was one set that happened to encapsulate much of my adolescence due to my immense affection for it. These sheets did not have some drab sentimental ribbon attached that drooled on it like a starved mutt. No, they were brilliant and lively champagne yellow bedsheets adorned with grinning sunflowers. My parents had owned them well before my birth, and they were specifically bought for Liane. But ultimately, these lustrous bedsheets became synonymous with me. And why? Simply because my mother happened to randomly place them on my bed one afternoon after she'd finished laundry.

I'd never slept with those bedsheets previously and, to six-year-old me, they were the most comfortable of the countless that belonged to my family. It's peculiar, being that they weren't manufactured with any exceptional materials. From what I can recall, they were merely cotton sheets. But they must've been woven by the nurturing goddesses above because the pure warmth was vastly apparent to my younger self. For that reason, those bedsheets would reside atop my mattress for seven years save from when my mother had them in the wash. And yes…those yellow sheets with childish cartoon sunflowers were constant companions through most of junior high.

As a thirteen-year-old, any revelations of possessing such should've guaranteed severe derision from most of my peers. But those who visited my home all but ignored them. With regards to my female acquaintances, however, they would gush about how *sweet* the sheets were and soon shower me with more attention than I merited.

It's quite astounding how tolerant my fellow newfound teenagers were because, at that point, it was utterly ridiculous to still utilize those juvenile bedsheets. That's precisely why I exchanged them for steel grey sheets by the start of eighth grade. It's part of aging…swapping comfort and innocence for the mundane and *excessive* smut. So, for three years my favourite bedsheets toiled about in the cupboard with their reputation mostly intact aside from a miffed ego. Bloody mercy…how I wish that's where they continued to spend their days. Instead, my once unsullied memories of those gleeful sheets are now tainted. Now they're forever intertwined with my first attempt.

My years in high school were, admittedly, as drab as a white padded room. But, somehow, there were still multiple moments of merriment interspersed with the tedious disputes most adolescents are forced to endure. Rousing sleepaway camps, running odd jobs for neighbours, anything that had damn all to do with the school itself was sheer bliss. But if there's a single period that, regrettably, eclipses all other affairs, it's undoubtedly my ill-fated two-month relationship with a girl named Josie Pegosti.

A senior with light brown hair, grey-green eyes, and intense pale skin, Josie initially presented the purest vision of a virginal saintess that has not been equalled by any other since. She spoke in a breathy, higher-pitched voice that safely bordered more toward youthfulness than cartoonish. And then there was the excessive volume of makeup that caked her face, which was her essential hallmark. She applied more than the majority of the other girls, but never in an exaggerated manner that cheapened her. Josie's reasoning for it also held its water well, as she was deathly insecure about the specks of acne that were strewn about her face.

Like Penelope, my first "starry-eyed attachment," Josie and I were initially acquainted because we both assembled at the same lunch table due to mutual connections. We never spoke more than a couple of words to one another until January of 1961, when I made an arse out of myself by asking her if she wished to go to a movie one night. It was my classic attempt at letting the bombs soar in the dark, asking a mere stranger out without possessing a shred of knowledge about her. Josie declined, as she had just entered a relationship, but did so in a gentle approach. It allowed a door to remain ajar as her "relationship" faulted within a month or so.

Once that whole debacle ran its course, she and I accelerated our chatting at an alarming rate. At first, we'd spend lunch raking the remnants of her previous relationship and discuss its ultimate collapse. Suddenly, the chats diverted into provocative territories that led to late night phone calls after school. That, right there, began to plant seeds of negativity into the heads of my mother and sisters. They found her constant calls, which were occurring every night, to be frustrating and off-putting. As for me, I was initially entirely oblivious to their concerns. And, once they hounded me enough to finally secure my attention, I disregarded them without an ounce of hesitation.

Josie and I began walking out together by the conclusion of the school year. Consequently, almost all our days throughout summer were spent obsessively bound together. She'd ring the house every day at twelve on the nose, asking me if I wished to go spend the day somewhere. Unconsciously, my body would dart out the door; into my old, black 1955 DeSoto Firedome; and straight to her house. And we'd be cavorting about at the movie theatre, a park, or a skating rink until eight in the evening.

My mother, still ruffled by Josie's inordinate number of calls, expressed hesitations that continued to be unheeded by my irresponsibly hormonal soul. With each passing day, her aggravation intensified and smouldered through vexed facial expressions and limited speech. There was never a dot of thoughts put into the fact that my mother had justified reasons behind her qualms. Josie was, quite clearly, an emotionally dependant girl…but the hearts stapled over my eyes were too mystified by her allure to apprehend the adverse flaws in this "attachment."

Then arrived August, which signified an impending conversion from summer into my senior year. Josie hadn't communicated any plans for further education, and I speculate she was possibly hesitating until she had an idea as to what colleges interested me. Benefiting from that information, she could send off applications to the same colleges so that we could attend one together. All in all, the two of us expressed mutual optimism that our "attachment" would only flourish despite her being in a void and me preparing to draw my high school years to a close.

Two days before senior year was to commence, I invited Josie to the house without informing my mother. For about two weeks, we indecent teenagers had arranged the date of our…first sexual encounter. And everything had been falling into place easier than anticipated, as the house would surely be empty that Saturday. My father would be at his office in D.C. the entire day, partaking in meetings related to his governmental position. And my mother would be out with friends at the hairdressers, then to lunch, and then to an art museum. The house would be mine for countless hours, and it would be utterly worthwhile in every facet.

Josie arrived at noon, about forty-five minutes after my mother embarked on her leisure activities. We wasted no time in bombing upstairs to my bedroom, *literally* ripping each other's clothes off so that we could explore one another. But, unknowingly, my mother had decided to pass on getting lunch with her friends because she'd developed a mild headache while at the hairdressers. Thus, she returned home and immediately discovered Josie's car in the driveway.

Now, my mother had a rule that she implemented with all her children in which none of us were permitted to have anyone over unless we asked permission beforehand. It didn't matter if it were a friend or a significant other, the rule never wavered. And she almost always declined our requests if neither parent was home. My assumption is that she came inside the house as inobtrusive as possible, so to cause no disturbance. She intended to catch and scold us for a complete violation of her rule, though what she caught was not what she'd almost certainly envisioned. For my mother was sure that she'd open my door to discover Josie and I amid simple yet passionate necking. Without a doubt a scene that'd be embarrassing for all parties. No, what ensued was my mother walking in on her nude son on top of a nude girl that she already had drastically disapproving opinions of.

I can still recall the clarity of my mother's rage-induced screams, demanding that "the hussy leave her house" at once. Josie, her emotions now drowning under choppy waves of humiliation, scuttered from underneath me and snatched up her torn clothes. She screamed "I'm sorry" repeatedly as she sped out of my bedroom, but it did nothing to prevent my mother from chasing her down the stairs.

Unable to fully process the episode, which happened in the flicker of a pan, I hurriedly tossed on my jeans and torn shirt before racing downstairs myself. The crimson fury of my mother's face rivalled that of Satan's pitchfork, so there was no telling what type of severe chastisement she could inflict on Josie. I had to avert any potentially perilous circumstances that could occur, even while under the nozzles of chaotic anguish.

Upon reaching the bottom of the staircase, my mother came back through the door and slammed it shut. She gazed at me for a moment before ambling to the olive-green sofa in the living room. As she plopped down, she buried her face in her hands and said, "I tried so hard to shield you from that road. I thought you knew better. I—Mark, do you understand how horrible it'd be if you impregnated that girl?" Her voice quavered as she spoke, but it wasn't from residual wrath. No, that had transformed into desolate heartache.

My mother then proceeded to break down and bawl, and the sound of her solemn sobbing still haunts me enough to stir goosebumps. I attempted to approach and console her, but she pushed me away and removed herself from the sofa. As she exited the house once more, I peered out the window and observed her place a hand over her face so to absorb the tears.

It's starkly aching to watch a parent sob, especially because they're the ones who tend to demonstrate poise and strength no matter how turbulent some trials may be. But this was an utterly different state of sorrow. It was the first time I'd seen my mother sob since the funeral of her own father a decade earlier. But, in this case, the cause of her tears stemmed from my actions. A death didn't shatter her heart this time around. Instead, it was me…her own child…who executed the deed.

Reeling in a dreary stupor, I aimlessly went down the stairs that led to our basement. There was no conscious rationale for my going into that room, as all my deteriorating capacities were running on a fragile, malfunctioning autopilot. Perhaps wandering inside the basement was like infiltrating the netherworld, the concept of leaving reality behind.

The bleak, monochrome basement was rarely utilized by anyone except my parents. Our washer and dryer dwelled in this room, so my mother would frequently venture here to do chores. As for my father, he'd established the remainder of the room as his personal gym. He had a rather inadequate assortment of equipment at his disposal, though it wasn't surprising as most exercise machines in the 1950s were substandard. Among his equipment were racks of free weights, a few benches, and a multifunctional station that allowed the user to do pullups, dips, and push ups.

I remember staring at the latter blankly for some time before staggering toward the cupboards to the right of the dryer. These cupboards contained bedding apparel, such as extra pillows, blankets, and bedsheets. Retrieving the first bedsheet that made its presence known, which happened to be my old sunflower linens, I placed them to my face and inhaled the recollections of jasmine-scented purity.

Walking to the tri-usage workout station, my hands sluggishly pitched the sheets up and over the pullup bar. Bringing both ends to an even level, I began to construct a ghastly makeshift noose that barely met a beginner's standards. It was wonky in appearance, but the best that could be created by a numb, imprudent novice.

During the noose's creation, the concept of being overly melodramatic never crossed my mind. And, upon reflection, perhaps it was a matter of dangerously exaggerating these circumstances into validation for such a harrowing proposal. But then again, these seeds of woe had possibly been planted much earlier and coveted a reason to emerge. A reason *finally* arose, but it wasn't because of Josie and how our relationship had been, almost certainly, reduced to rubble. No, it was because I'd imposed such dire pain unto my mother…the marvellous woman who nurtured and cherished me. Being the cause of her bereaved sobs was damaging to my heart, my resolve, and my psyche. That was enough for these sombre acts to bow and perform a languid dance of death.

After a brief inspection, the towering pullup bar revealed it was high enough to allow my dangling feet a saucerful of inches to spare above ground. Climbing up to reach the bar, both my feet on the push up handle, I slithered my head through the inept noose and acknowledged the inevitable. Closing my eyes to prime myself for a disturbing thrill, both feet readied themselves to march away and plunge off the arms of refuge.

However, this attempt proved unsuccessful as other coercing reminders of mortality made me hastily reconsider this action. For as much as my indecent behaviours might've shattered my mother's heart…executing this option would've only magnified her grief. It would also devastate my father…my sisters…my nieces…and I couldn't bear to elicit even more misery within my family. Frantically seizing the bedsheets, I withdrew my head from the noose and wildly undid the foolish contraption. Springing off the handles seemed to be the correct choice at first, but the disarray that derived from this attempt nearly being realised was far too intense.

As I connected with the floor, the grief, horror, and hysterics that had expounded due to this rash mess caused my debilitated knees to buckle. The absence of strength caused me to drop and smack against the ground like a pathetic boxer unable to get through the second round. And I stayed there for some minutes, the linens covering my upper face, struggling to comprehend the gravity of what could've been had my adoration for family not triumphed.

In the aftermath of my *improper conduct*, my mother confiscated my car keys for over half a year. Due to this, I was reduced to a meagre bus rider, the lone senior amidst a sea of underclassman. She also held several privileges captive by monitoring my phone calls, refusing to allow any of my chums over, and outright forbidding me from going on dates. My father, though confessing in private that scores of my mother's decisions were excessive, still stood in agreement with her as "you can always learn from a *good* lesson."

Also, it wasn't until I was in college that my father disclosed some background as to why my mother reacted in the manner she did. He told me that my maternal grandmother gave birth to my mother at the age of fifteen. And her pregnancy generated unsympathetic showers of shame unto her, from her own family as well as the community at large. To them, teenage pregnancies were deemed destructive to one's entire livelihood. So, my grandmother had apparently instilled in my mother a strict order that she would never follow that same path, nor would her children. But my mother, not once, expressed those notions with me. It took my father, who had surprisingly taken the news of my ordeal with amusement, to detail my mother's distress in full. Even then, it also took years from him to divulge this information to me.

With regards to Josie, we spoke infrequently during my senior year due to the regulations implemented by my mother. The catch was that I could only ring her up using a payphone, which made chatting maddeningly problematic. Our "attachment" technically terminated that one afternoon, but she continuously expressed a canvas of hope during our phone calls, desperately desiring for our eventual recoupling. That day never turned up as, after graduation, we had a final phone call where Josie exhibited this unforeseen ire over my perceived "lack of effort" in maintaining the fervour of our "attachment." How my inability to break from my mother's commands "offended" her and spurred a will to abandon all hope regarding us.

Though distraught at first, in retrospect I'm honestly grateful that our "relationship" ended when it did. It's gruelling, of course, walking out with someone who's emotionally dependant. I absolutely do not grieve over an "attachment" to someone who'll ring me up excessively in succession after a *single* missed call. The last time I received an update on her whereabouts was in 1973. A mutual friend had informed me that Josie ended up attending Old Dominion University in Norfolk. And that was it. Here's hoping she unearthed some sort of success.

Unsuccessful, however, are yellow bedsheets and their ability to kindle a kindred solace within me whenever I set my eyes on them.

Even a mere mention of my old linens re-establishes nothing more than wounding memories of turmoil. The fact that those innocent bedsheets were hostilely utilized a final time by the one who treasured them most has degraded their splendour. Scorched their memory into nothing short of revulsion. Pure derision even. As far as I can recall, my parents still own those sunflower stained sheets. But they permanently reside in one of the cupboards in the basement, possibly forgotten by most except me.

A robotic trill resonated from nearby, which hauled me out of the daze that'd inadvertently detained me upon awaking. It was erupting from the telephone perched atop the bedside table. Before twisting myself toward the phone, I noticed that my hands were firmly clasping clumps of *these* bedsheets. An involuntary reaction that must've sprouted from the madness that throbbed in my bonce. Thankfully these linens were snowy white, the standard hotel variety, and bore none of the hefty baggage that swirled around my old ones.

Placing the phone to my ear, I said, "hello," in a gruff, grainy voice that came out harsher than I wished.

"Good morning, Mister Courtauld." It was Robin's gentle voice, which immediately subsided any loitering relics of desolation. "I certainly hope you slept well last night. You have a direct call coming in from London, England. Would you like me to transfer them to you?"

"Good morning, Robin. Yes, please transfer the call," I said.

"Perfect. I'll connect you now. Please hold for a moment."

"Captivating" easy listening music mushroomed out of the few seconds of silence that surfaced after Robin placed me on hold. The "brill" tranquillity that drifts among the notes was utterly delightful, even awe-inspiring. Mercifully it abruptly cut off and another exquisite voice replaced those dull melodies.

"From sympathy's turquoise commotion."

"Emerges February's bouquet," I said.

"Marky honey," Francine said, "congratulations on another splendid accomplishment. I'm so proud of you. Yes, I know that I aired all that worry before you left. But in my 'eart, I had full faith that you'd succeed."

I chuckled before saying, "you're far too kind, Francine."

"I mean it. Also, the Lord President has officially confirmed the fulfilment of your assignment. In due time we'll send out a limousine that'll transport you to the airfield. Your trip back to London will be at noon. I, err, *we* can't wait to 'ave you back."

"Good. Thank you very much. I'm quite eager to return."

"Yeah…" Francine's voice trailed off, as though she'd been enveloped by her thoughts. "I—I, um, will inform Lord President Trailsby of your impending arrival. Safe travels, Marky honey."

"Thank you, Francine. Goodbye."

I hung up the phone and sat up on my bed. The first day that follows the completion of an assignment routinely wallops me like a bloody hangover. Exhaustion is colossal, sleep is scarce, and you simply cannot believe that this day is truly occurring. On top of that, it's a chore to round up everything…clothes, personal items, thoughts, shortly after distressing events that transpired less than twenty-four hours ago. But that's how Her Majesty's Church operates. You arrive at your destination, complete your assignment, and depart soon thereafter.

***

Debi decided against returning to Nouveau Rêve with me yesterday. After the remaining members of the "clean-up" crew finished their tasks and lead us to their van, she had asked if they could drop her off at the hospital to visit Abruzzoli. They permitted this, though they required her to change out of her bloodstained garb first. The "clean-up" crew isn't referred to this moniker solely because they cleanse the bodies, blood, and sins from the soulless location of mayhem. They're quite aware of how gory these assignments get, so they'll carry several items of clothing for all allied parties with them in their vans. Lord President Trailsby already supplies the crew with our personal records, and that enables them to bring clothing that'll fit. Sponges and soap are also available, so that we can rid ourselves of any blood that may be visible to the naked eye.

Though the attire is quite bland, as it consists of t-shirts and jeans, it's also nondescript and casual. This sort of apparel is not indicative of who I am, but it's what must be done so to avoid any unwanted attention. However, walking through the front doors of a hotel like Nouveau Rêve in the late afternoon dressed like a drifter certainly was cause for unwelcome stares. After all, a t-shirt and jeans don't exactly mesh well against middle-aged wealth. Fortunately, when I stepped foot in the lobby people were few and far between. Even the front desk area was barren. Due to this, I succeeded in making it back to my room with relative ease.

Despite spending the rest of the evening alone in this room, I never heard anything from Debi. She didn't phone my room, or even venture here when or *if* she returned last night. Now that Her Majesty's Church was preparing to send a limo here, the clock was counting the minutes until my inevitable check out. There was no time like the present to confirm whether Debi was back or not.

And yes, I could've phoned her room but that simply wasn't the logical choice. Visiting her in person was a far more respectable option. Through all our quarrels and quandaries, our partnership officially concludes once one of us has checked out of the hotel. Is that an authentic rule? No, of course not, but it *was* crucial that we chatted before parting ways...as there was plenty we needed to discuss after our innumerable stormy jousts.

Standing before Room 306, I knocked on the door and waited. Unlike our impromptu engagement the previous evening, there were no hints of Eldritch Hawn's saccharine, energized synthpop stretching from beyond the door. Only general silence dragged about.

A gold doorhanger with *do not disturb* printed in black text did present some sign of hope that Debi was here. Then again, it was also likely she had placed it there yesterday before we ventured to the docks.

Suddenly, a dense clicking echoed before the door pushed open to reveal Debi. Her dark auburn hair was devoid of product and down in an unkempt shag that provided her with bangs. Those curtains of hair nearly obscured the entirety of her surprised eyes. Debi wore a bulky, long-sleeved, grape-hued shirt with black geometric lines decorating it. The shirt was buttoned from the waist down, and revealed a white, laced bustier-style bra with a bow in the middle. Trousers were absent from her body, and the length of her shirt was just barely incapable of concealing a pair of hot pink knickers. Finally, her hand was loosely yet confidently holding a toothbrush as though it was a cigarette.

Debi's body, once again, roused my fierce carnal addiction as I observed her. Flecks of concern that had peered from behind dreary drapes yesterday, however, were concurrently resurrected. It still baffled me, how fragile her slight figure was. Especially those arms and wrists. Being that this would be our last encounter before my flight back to England, I dreadfully yearned to express some sort of consternation about this issue with her at last. The key hindrance in doing so was, even now, that trouble of overstepping my boundaries. At the same time, the near reawakening of these concerns found themselves struggling mightily as they were overwhelmed by the memory of Debi's sheer might yesterday afternoon.

Though I failed to witness the unfolding of the scene, the fact that a slight woman possessed significant skill to subdue one of Scobretti's guards, a bulkier adversary, was a titanic feat. Yes, Debi's a CIA officer so it shouldn't knock me for that much of a six. After all, I assume she's been impeccably trained for all sorts of antagonistic conflicts. And, while their concept of training is certainly not as infernal as that of Her Majesty's Church, it must be impressive enough to propel even the daintiest of officers.

"This'll sound surprising," Debi said, "but it's nice to see you, Mark. Come on in."

Debi stepped aside and pushed the door away a touch so that I could enter her room. With my concerns now entirely reduced to insignificant particles, the admiration of my partner's appearance swelled. The sight of her halfway dressed, the absence of makeup or hair product, it only exacerbated the feral magnetism that pounded its rusty nails into my heart. There's nothing more spellbinding than a woman in her natural state, not dolled up in a mask of desecrated faux beauty. Of course, makeup can enhance specific features and create an air of enchanting glamour through its cautious precision. But what's more divine is the wondrous art of a woman's pure facial features.

The mound of clothes that once stood proudly on Debi's mattress now sat atop of an open suitcase at the foot of the bed. The mattress itself, though free of untidy garments, still boasted the form of a mountain range due to the disarray of the sheets. Debi truly must detest the task of bedmaking. A pair of white trousers were positioned on one of the pillows, while a pair of powder blue ankle socks sat on the highest peak of the sheet mountain. The socks signified the triumphant flag of reaching the summit.

I settled in the chair by the desk and said, with a smile, "don't you ever clean up after yourself?"

Debi frowned as she walked into the bathroom, where water was endlessly running from the faucet. "I've got my reasons for the mess, jerkass," she said.

"Is that right?"

A potential response was hindered by the sound of Debi spitting out her toothpaste and clacking the toothbrush against the side of the sink. The faucet then cut off, and that was followed by an excessively drawn-out sniffle that was quite noisy. Upon emerging from the bathroom, Debi groaned as she rubbed a hand towel across her face before saying, "okay, not really. Where do I even begin?" She reclined on her bed, moving her trousers away so that she could lounge against the pillow. "I came back from the hospital around eight and faced judgmental stares from other hotel guests. Probably because I had on jeans and a t-shirt. Anyways, when I got to my room I, well, kind of had a…breakdown."

"A breakdown? Elaborate."

Debi sniffled as she chuckled, though there was a noticeable shudder in her voice. "Yesterday was, no doubt, the most nerve-wracking day I'd ever lived through. The dramatic escalation of the assignment, the *interrogation*, watching Rocco get shot up in front of me, the amount of death that increased by the minute, it was a lot. And everything just seemed to catch up with me once I got back in this room. Residual trauma, I guess. So, I stupidly took the remainder of my packed clothes and tossed them in the air like a basket case."

"You've never witnessed death while on assignment, have you?"

"Never. Targets, they're always arrested and hauled in. They're not…all massacred. It was almost like living through one of those "dead teenager" movies."

"It…*well*, the horror of the episode never truly terminates after you've encountered it. They linger."

"Yeah, they're lingering bad, Mark."

"If you don't mind my returning to the topic of Abruzzoli, when *exactly* were you going to tell me about him?"

Debi, who'd been staring at me with the spirit of a vacant room, finally demonstrated some movement as her eyebrows shifted down. "It was in your files. Rocco was our insider."

"But he was Scobretti's brother-in-law. How the bloody hell did he manage to pull the wool over their eyes?"

"Rocco's been with us for over a decade, so it was easy enough to deceive them. That's one of our key policies: deception. You know, he's married to the Scobretti brothers' sister. And it was her who tipped him off about what her brothers were doing. It's not like Rocco was running around telling everyone that he worked for the CIA. She knew, but she sure wasn't going to tell her brothers."

"I'm guessing Abruzzoli feigned a different profession to avoid unwanted attention?"

"Exactly. Abraham and Sergio, they believed him and were more than willing to bring him into their ranks. Everything looked as if it was going to play out like I imagined it would. Until it didn't."

In Debi's words were some awkwardly packaged insinuations that, almost certainly, faulted me for the turmoil that occurred during the assignment. Such is both accurate and warranted, but only to a certain point. We hail from two intelligence organizations whose procedures couldn't be more dissimilar. They arrest targets. We, err, *I* eliminate them. Despite my disinterest in rationalising the CIA's more *vanilla* procedures, perhaps I should've been more attentive to Debi's role.

Then again, it would've done damn all in convincing me to alter my methods. Also, though she was dazed from the violent drama, what mattered most was that we were victorious in our quest. Right? Isn't that what mattered most? Or was it Debi's mental wellbeing? Surely the latter makes a logical claim, being that the first gash in one's mental wellbeing bolsters successive slashes that'll reduce it to fleshy tatters.

The operatives of Her Majesty's Church face these tribulations right from the first day. They're branded onto our brains with a searing symbol that spurs a vicious resolve to abide by our oath. The brand enables vivid recollections of our worst memories but strive to utilize them as continued education so that we're superior to our past selves. I have it worse than the others by a wide margin, and it doesn't help that they're all numb to their positions because it doesn't always have to end in death. But for Debi and others in the CIA, this isn't commonplace for the masses.

Debi exhibited as much emotion as a disassembled mannequin. Her distant chestnut gems swivelled back and forth between me and one of the walls, unable to fix on a single sight. Allowing her to rot in shambles like me wouldn't be fair, nor would it be an empowering lesson in valour. No, I'm steadfast in my belief that she'd wallow in it for eternity…and it was my responsibility to prevent such a heinous, torturous cycle from ensuing.

"Debi," I began, "you'll unquestionably be exasperated by this. But my organization has no policy that forbids me from disclosing the purpose of my employment."

Debi sighed. "Obviously."

I hesitated, scrambling to round up a truthful definition of my role that was explanatory but not *in depth.* To use graphic phrases or imagery would bring the voices as well as the, mercifully, deceased Phantasms purified joy. Whatever was detailed to Debi also had to elude the clutches of maniacal disorder. It had to sound clear and concise without being indicative of my own mental anguish.

"When I joined Her Majesty's Church in seventy-nine, Prime Minister Harbold decreed a programme within the organization that allowed a sole operative the capacity to operate above the law. To, for lack of a better phrase, rid society of those who soil our streets with their malice. My superiors elected me, at the time their newest recruit, as the one who'd execute said programme. Heads of allied organizations, such as Director Ganderman, heed this decree. It's not special treatment. No, it's for the sake of our society."

Emotion finally surfaced in Debi's gaze, as her gems noticeably widened and gleaned with astonishment. Her eyebrows rose briefly before setting, and she leaned up from the pillow while placing her hands on her thighs.

"I—I—" Debi stammered, the gears in her brain probably revolving at a rapid pace to pull words together from the corners of her mind. They seemed to piece together her realizations decently enough, as she managed to form a sentence. "Ganderman is in on it too? Man, I—I don't really know what to think. I mean, obviously I can see the appeal in keeping more people out of an overcrowded prison system. But you'd hope the answer for that would be *less* violence and crime. Not more." Debi paused; her mouth barely agape as her eyes circled upward. Possible reflection, perhaps? "I guess," she continued, "at the end of the day, I'm glad I'm not on a team like yours. I couldn't live in that kind of darkness every day. That's gotta mess with the mind."

"You haven't a clue, though you've surely got more of an idea now."

Debi rotated her body slightly, so that she could place her legs off the bed. She no longer faced me, her face now gazing at the wall. "Why are you telling me this, Mark? Especially now that it's over with? What does it change? Does it change anything? I'm sorry, but I just wasn't expecting you to unload this on me. I, sort of, expected you'd come by to say hi before you went on your way. But this? You dropping all that on me? It's a lot."

"Remember when you found me seated by the tank yesterday? Too much reflection transpired before you came around. The concept of mortality, sanity, disillusionment…they were potent. And now, with you setting the table full of confusion and torment of your own. Sealing the truth from you was wrong, Debi. It accelerated discontent between us, and all notions of what I believed was covertness instead came off as deceitful. Does it change anything? Not entirely. But, I don't know, perhaps you'd be the first and last uninformed partner of mine to be thrust into the bloody madness that is my profession." I rose from my seat, not desiring to swipe much more of Debi's time. Approaching her, I stuffed my hands in the pockets of my slacks and said, "you don't deserve to drown with me in my impure wine."

Without delay, Debi got up from the bed and placed her gentle hands on both my forearms. She swooped her shaggy bangs from in front of her eyes by way of a fleeting flick of her head. The expression she bestowed unto me was one of sensitivity, her eyes now soft and nurturing as they examined me.

"Mark, more than anything else I appreciate your willingness to be this vulnerable with me. It seemed doubtful up till now, but you spilled your heart. That's not easy for most, and I never thought you would. Your honesty goes a long way."

"You're a good one. You can't bathe in in these muddy trenches. And I should've informed you sooner."

"Hey." Debi pulled me closer to her. "It's okay."

Our bodies were now fastened together, tighter than the impassioned bond between rope and a mistress. My fingers coasted her lower back in smooth, cautious fashion. They drifted deviously close to the top of her tailbone. The unbridled animalism of my most potent vice bellowed a damning repudiation of my most sacred yet *ultimately* unofficial rule, that of shunning heated liaisons with colleagues. Though I'd successfully resisted the magnetic lure of Debi's being yesterday, it was a reluctant decision chosen solely to maintain focus on our *then*-assignment. Now, as we stood in this dangerously intimate position, that chaotic fever fuelled harshly to the point of jittery agitation.

Debi's fingers attempted to compete with mine, as her right hand ventured up to caress my chin. Her left slipped between the fastenings of my shirt, her index finger and thumb making hasty work to push a button out of its hole. This left her with absolute access to my chest. She then used the tip of one of her manicured fingernails to carve a downward path toward my belt.

Her breathing built up, and the fluttering of her heart sloshed against my chest. The velocity of these flutters kept pace with the glittered wings of Crescencia, the arcane enchantress of eroticism. Debi's hips, magnificently designed with curves, swayed like a melodic countryside river complete with symphonic harps. Finally, her face inched ever closer to mine, those mind-altering lips closing in on me. For a split second, her tongue trailed across her bottom lip. Mother of mercy did that do me in like a bloody nutter unearthing an array of stimulating substances.

The demented magnetism of our libidinous temptation refused to obey the decency of hesitancy a second more. In a lunatic heat, we pressed our lips together and kissed. Debi, at a rate of knots, undid my belt and hauled it from around my waist. She then pushed me onto her bed with the might of a Soviet bear. Despite her excessive training, I truly question how this slight woman can muster the uncanny strength she possesses.

Debi took swift advantage of my vulnerable state, leaping onto me as though she was a raving cheetah. She snatched my collar and kissed my chin, lips tracing down to my neck. The enticing sex appeal she exuded heightened my stimulated senses to paradisiacal, mountainous horizons. Damn that miserable *personal* rule to the smouldering valley of the bloody netherworld. Yes, perhaps the implementation of such a pathetic practice *is* necessary but, evidently, it's bloody inept when confronting these desires head on. Understandable, right? So, *at least for now*, it's been rendered null as it simply cannot wrench me from my wholly indecent yet mystifying drugs. In this shape of saintly euphoria, I am a bestial scoundrel doing the bidding of Carnivera, the wife of Satan. Anxious to serve Debi, to afford her rusted pleasures that've been lamentably supressed without her knowledge.

Her ambrosial bodily scents, a stirring pirouette between coconut and vanilla, spiralled inside my delirious nostrils. I glided my hands under Debi's hot pink knickers and grasped the firm arc of her backside. This appeared to incite an escalation of Debi's fervour, as her kisses converted into bites that were a dot rougher than was pleasurable. But frankly, it didn't matter as I quite relished the exquisite sting of lust. See, pain is an essential component to the debased concept of pleasure. In my opinion, pain is a requirement to wholly augment passion…so long as it doesn't gain control over it.

While delighting in these *wholesome* engagements, my eyes inadvertently caught the clock on Debi's bedside table. It was ten fifty-nine, and though Francine never specified an exact time regarding the arrival of the limousine, it would surely be sooner rather than later. Halting the consumption of a fix would, almost certainly, aggravate my already fervid sensibility. Concurrently, keeping Her Majesty's Church waiting has routinely failed to be the correct move.

The clock wasn't the only object on the bedside table that wrangled my attention. Directly before it were spatters of powder, whiter than either snow or tears from a goddess, as well as a silver tube that rested in the middle of the white sandscape. My ears began to play a collection of accumulated noises that I'd heard throughout my time with Debi. The constant sniffles. Mercy, was this true? Were those sniffles *not* the consequence of a raging sinus issue?

Mark, don't you dare judge Debi. Need I remind you of your vices?

Oh joy. While the Phantasms have, presumably yet hopefully, dissolved and been shunted to the graveyard slot of my bonce, Edith hasn't. However, she makes…a bloody point. It would be dangerously hypocritical of me to question Debi about a potential…addiction. If it even is an addiction to begin with. By all means, perhaps it's a recreational activity? Or is this merely an attempt to justify harmful behaviours as I do mine?

Forget about it. You saw how she handled herself yesterday. She held her own. If cocaine was truly a detriment to her abilities, it would've been more apparent. Besides, you have two options right now. Either you scold her for engaging in leisure activities like you're her square of a father. Or…you stop trying to restrain your incessant longing for Debi. She can handle herself…and she clearly wants you to handle her.

A rather dismal attempt at demonstrating humour on Edith's part. Utilizing those ever-encouraging whispers to exchange my rules for hers. It's a shame, really. How lovely it would've been had the demise of the despicable and commanding Phantasms caused a domino-like collapse of the others. But lo…here's Edith conjuring her faulty sorcery.

You'd miss me if I ceased to exist. But why exasperate yourself in the dregs of despair when you could be undressing Debi? She's already clawed her way onto you. Might as well revel in your mutual greed for one another.

Perhaps. Ultimately, though the presence of the summer's snow caused some shakes of concern, Edith was…right. Debi is capable of making her own choices. If she wishes to partake in vices, that shouldn't be criticized. The sole vices that *I* can criticize are my own but, even then, it'd be foolish to even refrain myself from this ocean of menacing lust. Right? Or maybe…maybe this isn't right.

I began to sputter out "Debi…I—" amid her continued kisses that graced my neck, but rapidly found my words being decapitated by that bloody wretch.

No, you're not leaving. And you're also not going to obey that absurd "rule" of yours. Remember what you just realized. Damn that rule.

"What?" Debi asked, struggling to even release her words through a bevy of harsh breaths.

"I…no…*you* belong with me."

Debi withdrew her lips from my flesh and gazed at me with the depth of a gilded sorceress. She formed a gentle, willowy beam that still somehow expressed a vehement ardour that owed to the flushed quality of her enthralling and utterly resplendent face.

"*I* belong with you," she said.

***

Exiting the lift with my three belongings in tow, the sight of Nouveau Rêve's vibrant lobby showcased an awfully bustling space. An abundance of new faces ornamented the room, almost entirely swamping out the few recognizable guests from my first day. The sole similarity these new guests exhibited was, unsurprisingly, their crisp white tennis garbs and gold jewellery. If my job did not demand extensive examinations so to correctly make out even the most mundane face in a group, I probably would've thought everyone here was the same. They were *that* interchangeable. As these guests carried their wine glasses with a severe lack of grace while chortling through gritted, selenite teeth, I travelled past them so to reach the front desk.

Though mindful that Robin was on the clock this morning off the back of her ring earlier, my approaching the desk was not the product of an asinine attempt to seduce her. No, it was *solely* for the purpose of checking out. Yet, to my utter contentment, she stood behind the desk all by her lonesome. Nothing about the stimulating, shapely receptionist differed from our initial encounter. Everything down to her makeup, violet mascara and bronze rouge, was precisely the same.

"Mister Courtauld," Robin said with a smile, though it rapidly faded once she caught a glimpse of my luggage. "Don't tell me you're checking out today."

"Unfortunately, my dear Robin, today is the day," I said.

"Then how come you didn't tell me when I phoned your room earlier? If I'd known I would've found a way to, you know, *take a break.*"

I smiled. "The idea undoubtedly crossed my mind earlier. But yesterday was a long day. Got wrapped up in a lot of phone calls and paperwork, then went to bed with a headache. Experienced all the most *entertaining* aspects of my profession. I'm dreadfully sorry."

"It's fine." Robin looked down, a disappointed visage developing, and sifted through a reservation book. She stopped a page, took a pen, and began jotting something down. "Your room key?"

I handed the bulky, gaudy key to Robin. She thanked me, set it down on the desk, then grabbed another item that was undistinguishable from my vantage point. Robin used her pen to scribble on whatever it was that she had acquired before handing me what was now revealed to be a Nouveau Rêve business card. And on the back of the card was a phone number, along with her name and three basic yet endearing hearts.

"Just in case you're ever back here on business and want to make up for any lost time. Don't hesitate to give me a call."

"And what if you have a boyfriend?" I asked with the cunning intrigue of a mischievous elf.

"Betcha I won't. Not when you're still out there."

"You're too kind."

Robin had to adhere to proper employee protocol so, as a parting act, she extended her hand out with formal graciousness. As I clasped it, however, she briefly converted the reserved conduct to one of intimacy by using her thumb to tenderly caress my hand.

"Safe travels and take care, Mister Courtauld." Robin smiled though she sighed softly as our hands had to part.

"You take of yourself as well, Robin," I said. If only she could be acquainted with my actual name, instead of that barren pseudonym. Alas, such would set off drastic quandaries that would be irreparable and not worth the potential hassle. Taking that into account, I exited the gaudy yet oddly restful hotel.

The weather, obnoxiously warm and discomforting, was rather chipper as it welcomed me outside. A miracle breeze surely would've been a decent companion to have during this one-sided battle. Its sauna-like environment emphasised remnants of the now-pasted on sweat that I'd neglected to wipe off my body after the perfervidly erotic rendezvous with Debi. Our tempestuous union, like all my other intimate jousts, would be permanently carved in the sizeable X-rated section of my bonce. However, due to the prolonged tangle of our carnal deprivation for one another, it stood out for its unapologetic loss of reason and general mayhem. The vision of Debi's tantalizing exorcism was as pleasurably indecent as it was magnificently unhallowed.

Experiencing those sweat-stung, animalized gems rolling and her frantically gasping mouth as she punctured her claws through my chest was a damnable paradise of unmatched beastly jubilation. A trip of psychotic magnitudes that persistently informs me of the vile splendour that occurs whilst yielding to a fix. Now and again, I'll admit, Edith the Tempest knows what's best for me.

My limousine was nowhere in the vicinity, and its absence was certainly accommodating. For all purposes my liaison with Debi *could've* been hastened but that would've been utterly dishonourable. Never should a passionate union, even if it's a mere one-night stand, be accelerated. Such is inexcusable and discourteous toward your partner. Heeding those beliefs, I followed my…err, "heart", and lo there is sufficient time to spare. How lovely it is when those mad decisions work in my favour.

I walked over to a nearby bench right by the hotel's entrance. It was gold, but the colour seemed to have been applied with a spray can rather than actual paint. Sure enough, after setting my briefcase on my lap, I detected some chipping on the backrest of the bench that exposed steel. The sheer tawdriness of Nouveau Rêve, between its overreliance on gold and the clutters of middle-aged tennis enthusiasts, easily made for one of the most outlandish conglomerates I'd ever lodged in. But melted within those impressions was a genuine appreciation for the hotel's desperate desire to boast this tacky extravagance. It unquestionably stood out among its more lacklustre competitors.

A drunken bat soared above my head, which reminded me of a celebratory lap that could formally conclude my first New Jersey outing. Pulling my pack of herbal cigarettes from the inside of my jacket pocket, I placed one of the rose petal nails in my mouth. While grasping the pack, however, my fingers had also brushed against a cool metallic object. By blissful chance this jacket was the same one I'd donned upon my arrival to the Garden State. That meant my brand-new lighter was still nestled in the inner pocket, anxious to finally be used.

Lighting the herbal cigarette invited a wretched flavour, which wasn't startling considering these *were* grinded up rose petals being burnt. Its inordinately charred barbeque scent wafted up my nostrils within a breeze of laughter. There is nothing about these cigarettes, or regular ones for that matter, that lead to even a modicum of satisfaction. But they're regrettably a necessity if my tobacco dependency ever decides to follow the Phantasms' chain and cease. Notwithstanding the scorched but somehow also *damp* taste, and how they deride my appreciation of flavour, smoking these cigarettes at this moment was a merited reward. Not only was it symbolic of yet another decent personal achievement, but it also contributed to my continued quest to disregard the sinister habit for evermore.

While taking drawn out drags of the cigarette, a necessary but ill-considered action that regrettably furthered its brisk smoulder, the comprehension of returning home soon began mushrooming. Though a smidgen eager to hide away again in my sanctuary, mostly safe from the dregs of civilisation attempting to tug me down with them, it wasn't all flowers and gentle rivers. The concept of a homecoming upon the conclusion of an assignment summons a complicated skirmish that is utterly toxic. On one side, the anguish that derives from constant drudging and the continuous decay of my psyche has momentarily decelerated. But there's also the agony of reliving my deranged deeds every single day.

Being officially deprived of the Phantasms will, hopefully, offer a cloud of serenity over my tormented head. Upon awaking this morning, my mental balance had a flicker of clarity for the first time in years. A considerable quantity of brain fog had dispelled and that enabled a sounder grasp of what I planned on finalizing before voyaging back to London. Of course, Edith the bloody Tempest still existed so it wasn't as though the combustion of the Phantasms produced a magical cure. After all, if my gun had bullets there's nothing that would impede me from putting it to my temple and pulling the trigger. Again, my mental woes haven't been salvaged but there's a dazzling star up and afar that glimmers confidence, even if it's almost defunct.

Meandering along the continuous rotting of my psyche, it's caused me to ponder why I've been so bloody reluctant to uncover the mystery of this constant psychological torment. To seek out support from anyone who might possess the key to eliminating this never-ending war that wages on within this internal battlefield. Talking to a *licensed* therapist could alleviate these wounds and my generally dismal attitude. But perhaps I'm too much a stubborn bastard to learn about myself. Or maybe it's the extent of my woeful mental state, and the frightening idea that they'd react poorly. Sure, a professional shouldn't and wouldn't act in such an improper manner, but who knows? There's always the chance that they'll glare directly into my vacant eyes and say, "you're a bloody hopeless nutcase."

That's precisely why it's easier to, at least for now, journey home and concentrate on my important and appropriate requirements than to travel down this drab trail. And those requirements entail reengaging in copious rendezvous with some random women. Unfortunately, it'll be far too late to ring up Your Sweet Cherry Treats and request June or any other escort. So, I'll have to settle for a sex worker on the street. At least it's quite uncomplicated for me to locate them. Besides, regardless of the apparent sleaze they're a more motivating visual to latch onto versus reflecting on self-hate and self-destruction.

Fortunately, the grave suffering goaded by this warm weather wouldn't be punishing me any longer as a limousine rounded the circular driveway. A man, possibly around my age, stepped out from the driver's side and approached me. He was mostly bald but had light brown hair on the sides of his head and sported both forehead wrinkles as well as a scruffy goatee. The man wore a standard limousine driver's uniform complete with a chauffeur cap and white gloves. But he also possessed a lapel pin of the queen's crown.

"One hundred and nine?" The driver asked with stiff Geordie accent.

"Affirmative," I said.

"Right, pleasure to meet you. Name's Joe and I'll be taking you to Drome Airfield. Go on in the limousine. I'll grab your things."

"Thank you. But I'll keep the briefcase with me in the back. It always needs to stay nearby."

"Right."

I shuffled into the limousine as Joe collected my belongings. He returned to his seat swiftly and we departed the driveway of Nouveau Rêve. As Joe drove, I gazed back at the hotel and watched as that ridiculous structure faded away. It was quite miserable…fully apprehending all that was being left behind. Of course, that referred to both Debi and Robin, who were now thousands of feet away. None of my past interactions with allies or women while on assignment were as invigorating as these were. Frankly, these escapades would be sorely missed. Even the difficulties that routinely transpired.

My river raft of tropics was interrupted by a ringing that emitted from the phone up near Joe. He answered it before passing the receiver back to me.

"It's for you," Joe said.

I thanked him, placed the receiver by my ear, and said, "hello?"

"From sympathy's turquoise commotion," spoke the ever-lovely voice of Francine.

"Emerges February's bouquet."

Francine's voice suddenly became muffled and distant, though I could identify the words *how*, *love*, and *voice*. Not even a second later, Francine's words became more coherent as she said, "I'm pleased to learn that you're on your way back to England, Marky honey. However, I wanted to inform you that there will be…a slight change of plans."

"Hmm? A change of plans? What do you mean?"

"Upon arrival," Francine began, "you will not be returning to your residence. You must come upstairs to meet with Lord President Trailsby, where you will be briefed on your next assignment."

There was a fleeting twinge in my chest, within close range of my heart. It was like an ache, though comparing it to the initial thrust of a rusted dagger would be more accurate. Nevertheless, I nodded to myself so to settle my nerves. Conscious not to leave Francine short of an answer for too long, I spit out the word "right."

"We'll see you soon. Safe travels, Marky honey."

"Thank you."

The line disconnected as the phone drooped in my hands. In this occupation, back-to-back assignments are rare. I've only encountered the phenomenon once, whereas a modest few have found themselves facing the prospect as many as four times throughout their career. Normally these are obligations that inspirit my enthusiasm to such a degree that it's utterly spellbinding. But this time around, there's no fanfare. There's no zest for an additional assignment tacked onto the tail of this mad undertaking, not now at least. No, the lone object of feasible harmony was returning to my boring abode, lolling about, and engaging in my carnal fix. Unfortunately, my job is not partial to personal wishes.

A terse, hoarse chuckle abandoned my mouth by mistake as I questioned the purpose of this *subordinate* assignment. Who would the target be? Would they be as vile as Scobretti or even more depraved than that scumbag? Where on this forsaken planet would this excursion catapult me? Would my partner be like Debi, potentially more on par with my beliefs, or utterly inferior? And why on earth can't my superiors allow me a bloody day to recuperate from the bonds of perdition?

Did those atrocious Phantasms make a fair point when they so despicably claimed my superiors had moulded me into their own personal annihilation machine? Do they regard me as a homicidal loon? Trailsby, Pierce, Minister Esprine, they all could very well see the utter melancholia that I try so bloody hard to conceal. Right? And, in that regard, utilizing that information by taking advantage of a morose nit aids them in lessening the decomposition that has plagued our nations. It allows their hands to remain clean while the blood has coated mine so much that it has left them permanently tinted crimson.

No, I'm probably digging through these compact trenches in a skewed, frenzied attempt to justify a reason behind this new assignment. Perhaps it's a severe overreaction that's been brought about by internal warfare that's devastated me. It's just another assignment that's been bestowed unto me because, at the end of the day, I'm the *one* field operative who can preserve the overall well-being of prosperity for the United Kingdom, and for this putrid society.

In any case, I suppose the consequences of my *heroism* or *roguery* will end up asphyxiating my sullen heart during this next assignment, or some years from now. Such is inescapable. It could very well occur while Prime Minister Harbold presents me with a medal for my violent valour. Or perhaps my adversary executes an utterly brill ambush and that's that. Regardless, I've resigned myself to such grief. It'd be more thrilling to be smothered on a bed by nocturnal mistresses …or by my own hands because that's the bloody magnificence of fate, right?

For now, I've permitted a cool surge of cerebral anaesthesia to bathe and sedate my weary figure, reconstructing me into a flimsy dandelion. The imaginary medication will prompt a momentary disconnection from reality that'll last until a bothersome occurrence snaps me from this lurid spell. Edith the Tempest will paint provocative mental pictures featuring a wodge of salacious women, all eager for me to serve them. And I'll gradually lose lustre and become one with Carnivera while succumbing to my unstable inability to rescue myself from my psychological tribulations. It's not as mesmerizing as a firing squad, but it'll do.

Dex Marick is many things, each equally important as the last: a first-time author, a dedicated father, a loving husband, and an avid connoisseur of the illustrious food court soft pretzel. He toys with the duality of man, exploring the dark undertones and subjects typically seen as taboo, while showing levity and humanity in otherwise grim characters. He loves his family, his dogs, and the life they share on the coast of Washington State.

www.ingramcontent.com/pod-product-compliance
Lightning Source LLC
Chambersburg PA
CBHW030631020726
47493CB00006B/1657
9798218239510